MW01492766

THE
HONG KONG
WIDOW

ALSO BY KRISTEN LOESCH

The Last Russian Doll

THE
HONG KONG
WIDOW

Kristen Loesch

Berkley
New York

BERKLEY
An imprint of Penguin Random House LLC
1745 Broadway, New York, NY 10019
penguinrandomhouse.com

Book design by Alison Cnockaert
Interior art by Jiksun Cheung
The Edgar® name is a registered service mark of the Mystery Writers of America, Inc.

ISBN: 9780593548011

An application to register this book for cataloging has been submitted to
the Library of Congress.

Printed in the United States of America
$PrintCode

The authorized representative in the EU for product safety and compliance is
Penguin Random House Ireland, Morrison Chambers, 32 Nassau Street,
Dublin D02 YH68, Ireland, https://eu-contact.penguin.ie.

For Gong and Po

THE
HONG KONG
WIDOW

Prologue

SUSANNA HAS HER lips pursed, like she is sucking on sweetroot. I am telling her what it is like to be attacked by an unknown assailant in a darkened room. How it feels to wake up half a day later, your head throbbing, one eye swollen shut, lying flat on a tatami, the straw beneath you turned sticky, your arms stiff at your sides, your fingers bent like you're holding a ball. One of those small spleeny organs that nobody knows about until they lose it—you've lost it.

You know it's normal not to be able to recall anything of the attack itself. Normal if you can't picture your attacker; normal if everything is hazy in your head.

The problem is that it isn't.

Imagine that you remember the events of your attack perfectly—but you remember it all the wrong way around. In your memory you see yourself on the ground, bleeding badly; in your memory you go closer, bending over your own form, your own face.

In your memory, you are not the victim. You are the attacker.

"Uh-huh," Susanna says, jotting something down on her hand-held electronic screen.

Susanna Thornton is an award-winning author of narrative nonfiction, known for her interest in murky historical mysteries, particularly crimes. Why else has she sat me down like this, if not for a story such as this one? Her initial request for an interview was shocking; her voice on the phone was clipped and stern and gave nothing away. But she can't just want the usual bland impressions of the decades I have lived through, the Japanese occupation of Shanghai, the Pacific War, the Chinese Communist Revolution.

I want her to want more.

I want to see her innate curiosity piqued. I want to hear her laugh openly at me. I want her to tell me that it's impossible, what I have just said, all while her mind spins with possibilities.

But it seems she has little concern for the darkened rooms of my life.

"THAT HAPPENED BACK in Shanghai?" says Susanna, but it's not quite a question and she doesn't wait for an answer. "I don't want to waste your time—I'm here to ask you about Hong Kong. About Maidenhair House."

For a moment it feels as if I am waking up half a day later, all over again.

"I'm sorry. I must have misheard you," I say.

"Maidenhair House," repeats Susanna, whose voice is very clear, whose voice regularly carries over the heads of hundreds of people. "About the late-summer night in 1953 that's turned into an urban legend. About the alleged massacre. About how, when the police were called to the scene, they couldn't find a trace of it—and later called it a collective hallucination."

"Then what is left to say?" I ask, but perhaps she can hear my heart beating slightly faster, just by my voice.

"It's been confirmed that several young women went up to the house that night and were never seen again," says Susanna. "Women who were refugees of the Revolution. Women with no family or friends. Women that nobody would have missed. I've spoken to some Canadian urban explorers who spent a night at Maidenhair about fifteen years back now," she adds, with a hint of satisfaction, "and I got one of them to admit that there was indeed blood. When they went over it with luminol, they found blood *everywhere*. Walls. Floors. Rugs."

She says this like it is a revelation, blood beneath your feet.

Maybe in this country it is.

But in the place I come from, the dirt is always red, if you dig deep enough.

The balloon-whistle of the espresso maker sounds from another room, but Susanna doesn't budge. She thinks the silence will force me to speak. She sweeps her long mat of hair behind her shoulders. I have thought of other things to talk about by now: Perhaps about the time my mother forced me to sell my own hair to a visitor to our village who was trying to add to his collection of female braids; how much I wanted to refuse; how if I were not so tragically proud, I might have begged. But we needed the money and in the end Ma got her way. She cut it just above the jaw.

"I intend to solve it," says Susanna.

She can get my hair back for me?

Even if by now it is scattered across China like ashes?

"I'm going to uncover the truth about that night," she insists. I am not sure this is an interview so much as it is a sounding board, because clearly the story she wants to tell is already formed in her head. I can see it shining in her eyes. "I'll do it with your help or without it, Mama, but I'm going to find out what happened at Maidenhair House. And I'm going to find out why *you* got away."

PART ONE

1

SEATTLE, WASHINGTON
2015

SUSANNA'S DINING TABLE is long, meant for more people than just me and her. At every place setting there is a plate and enough slim silver cutlery that I could make a traditional Chinese cutting of the tablecloth; it is an eerie scene. Once there were three eating at this table every day, of course: Susanna; Peter, her first husband; and Liana, my granddaughter. Then came the divorce; then there were two. Then Susanna married Dean, and there were three again. Then Liana left for college. Then there were two again. And now Dean is gone.

I am here tonight, but my daughter acts like she is alone.

SUSANNA SITS ACROSS from me, reading on her phone, her eyes moving visibly beneath the lids. All the food on the table has just been taken out of the fridge.

I take a sip of my tea. It is hard and gritty, like licking dirt.

"Something wrong, Ma?" she asks.

"It's so cold in here, that's all. Did you take this whole house out of the fridge?"

A short sigh. "You didn't have to stay for dinner."

How could I go, after the conversation we have had?

I had not thought about Maidenhair House in several decades, but now the memory burns brighter than the light overhead. Susanna, naturally, does not see the effect her reminder has had on me; she thinks Maidenhair is like any other murder mystery she has ever encountered, gone rancid with time. I wonder how she learned that I was there that night, but it surely involves more devices, more squinting, more poorly lit rooms.

I imagine a list of women's names, one after another. I imagine Susanna struggling to make sense of it, and in the end, believing what she sees.

The greatest surprise is not her discovery of my presence, nor her self-proclaimed investigation.

The greatest surprise is that my daughter has gotten out of bed.

She has hardly left the house since Dean died, three months ago.

"Yes, I was at Maidenhair," I say, and her eyes widen. "But I have never spoken of that night to anyone. Not because I have something to hide, but because I have had no desire to turn over the past like the dirt of a grave."

It has the effect on her that I hoped for, and simultaneously dreaded: Susanna sets down her phone and diverts her full attention to me.

"But you're willing to talk about it now?" she says.

I notice that she hasn't picked up anything to eat with; she has become as skinny as a bamboo stake. "If you do something for me in exchange."

"What is it?"

"I want you to find out why I remember being attacked, so many years ago, from the perspective of my attacker."

"The thing you described earlier, you mean?"

"That is my condition."

"Forgive my bluntness, Ma," she says wearily, "but I'd say it was a trick of your imagination. Your brain trying to protect itself from whatever happened. But if you want me to find out who attacked you, I suppose we can try. *When* was it? Not when you were growing up? Because 1930s Shanghai, we're talking Japanese soldiers, gangsters, drug dealers, criminal overlords," she says, like I might not know, like I wasn't there. "It might be difficult to—"

"I didn't say *who*. I said *why*."

"Well, it'll have to wait either way. I've booked a flight to Hong Kong, for research."

Susanna sucks air in through her nose, as if to prepare for my objections. I do have objections. I want to say: On the subject of somebody's brain trying to protect itself from what has happened, why are you suddenly so drawn to a story like Maidenhair? To old deaths; to open-ended deaths? You say you want answers; I think you do not want answers. You want to hunt. You want to chase. You want to run. You want to spend your time on people who cannot die in your arms, because they are already dead.

But at least she has gotten out of bed.

Perhaps this is the start of a new stage of grief. First, she could not move at all. And now she cannot stay still.

FOR THE REST of the meal, Susanna keeps her head turned so that her hair hangs over her face, blocks my view of her. Her hair should be streaked with white, but it is dyed dark. Dollhouse hair. To go with the dollhouse food and the dollhouse house. All she is missing, now, is the dollhouse husband. I should tell her about the day I ran into my own future husband, her future father, in a bustling marketplace in Tsim Sha Tsui: I was idling near the hundred-year-egg stall when a young man approached me. He had to stoop to speak to me. I had missed breakfast that morning, and I was hungry; over the rumbling of my stomach I heard him apologize for disturbing me. He was irresponsibly handsome, handsome enough that I forgot one hunger and remembered another. He held out a hand, turned upward. *I think you've dropped this—*

I grabbed my white peony flower hairpin out of his palm.

This young man asked me if I wanted a hundred-year-egg.

By then I was corroding like iron, from the *wanting* of things.

"You have my condition," I say to my daughter. "Let me know what you decide."

Susanna does not answer.

Hundred-year-egg has a tough, almost impenetrable crust, but on the inside, it is soft. It is weeping.

THE TAPESTRY OF clouds in the distance has lifted, revealing the outline of the Cascades. Susanna has surprisingly agreed to drive me home; bent over the steering wheel, she rubs at a red splotch of skin on her wrist. The car's touch screen display glowers rudely at us. I have no idea why the navigation is turned on; Susanna should not need directions to my home, at least not before nightfall.

I wonder if it is always nightfall now, for my daughter.

A phone call flashes on the screen: Liana. Susanna doesn't pick up.

"Is Liana still having trouble sleeping?" I ask, after the ringing dies. "The insomnia, the nightmares?"

"So Peter says," she replies. "Now apparently she's . . ."

"She's what?"

"*Seeing* things," says Susanna, in a breath.

"What does my granddaughter see?"

"I don't know."

"Perhaps if you took her calls you would know."

"Peter says she isn't liking grad school. He doesn't think we should make a big deal out of it."

"Have you spoken directly to him? To either of them? Or you only communicate through those bubble messages that make my temples ache?"

Susanna is too busy rubbing the red spot raw to respond. Liana came up from LA shortly before Dean's death, and mother and daughter have not seen each other in person since. Liana didn't visit for the funeral because there wasn't one; Susanna arranged a quick cremation before making a permanent burrow of her bedcovers. These past few months she has seen nobody but me, and only because I have a key to her house. Only because I refuse to go unseen.

I have been so gentle with her. I have hovered over her like a cloud.

What good has it done?

Now she is finally leaving her house, but going to Hong Kong instead of LA. Now she will finally raise her head again, but only as high as her touch screen.

"YOU REALLY SHOULDN'T be living alone anymore, you know, Ma," Susanna says, opting to go on the offensive. "Weren't we talking once about getting you a place at—"

"At least I do not live in your house. It is a cube."

She flinches at my tone.

"There are memories like nails sticking out of the walls in that place, Susanna. No wonder you are so pallid and sick-looking. You are bleeding out. You should sell it."

"All this was different for you, alright?" she says, her hands rigid on the wheel. "You didn't love Dad the way I loved—"

She can't finish, but her voice is bitterly triumphant. As if to

11

say: *Admit you didn't love him. Admit that you don't know what it's like for me.*

"It depends on what you mean by *love*," I say. "I cherished him. I miss him. But I did not wring myself out like a cloth for him, and he would have not wanted it. You have to understand that by the time I met your father, I had no desire for something so fragile that it would fall to dust in my hands. I had been swimming, gasping for air, for so long: What I had with Dad was a boat. We built it together, knowing it would carry us however far we needed to go."

"Well, I didn't want a boat. I wanted something else," she says hotly, "and I got it."

"If you had a boat right now, maybe you wouldn't be so stuck in place."

"You and *boats*. Sometimes you can't just—can't just move *forward* like that, Mama! That easily! That quickly! I'm not ready to sell the house. I'm just not. I—"

"Have you decided whether to accept my condition?"

Silence again, but this time it is more like static. It has begun to rain. Susanna turns on the wipers, which creak moodily across the windshield. "I want to take care of Maidenhair first," she says, "and then—yes. I can look into your—attack."

She scratches again at her wrist, and this time she draws blood.

IT WAS SEPTEMBER 1953, the last time I laid eyes on Maidenhair House.

But the real story begins many years before that.

I gaze at my daughter, the sweep of her jaw, the craters of her eyes, the frayed shawl of her hair, the way her sweater is buttoned all the way up the neck, nearly a noose.

"I'm going with you to Hong Kong," I say, and she jolts back in surprise.

"Are you kidding?" she exclaims.

"Why shouldn't I go? I have been acquiring air miles for decades. It would be upsetting to die without having used them. I have achieved special status with the airline by now; I can get excellent upgrades." Susanna is still protesting, but we have reached our destination, the small bungalow I shared with my late husband for almost half a century. I want to tell my daughter: Do not go back to your cube house. Do not live in a box. Boxes are what people are buried in. "There is even an extra-fast line, for going through immigrations," I tell her. "That is the most important thing."

"*That's* the important thing? You're eighty-five years old, Ma! Who cares about extra-fast lines in immigrations? You can't just—"

Someone who is eighty-five, that's who. Someone who could fall down dead at any moment, anywhere, right where she is standing. Someone who lived too long on the line, between one country and another; who refuses to die in the in-between place.

2

KOWLOON, HONG KONG
SEPTEMBER 1953

THE FINAL CUSTOMER of the day is an old lady with flaming white hair and a gold-capped cane, like a scepter. A lavish green cloak strains from her shoulders to her feet, sweeping the aisles clean as she browses. She chatters low, as if to herself, a sly stream of gossip about this shoe-shiner's love affairs and that washwoman's slug of a son-in-law. She does not appear to require any assistance, so Mei begins to redress the window display: The brass Buddhas and Jingdezhen porcelain plates must be swapped out for burnished chicken-blood and field-yellow stone. Away come the small model ships and the mother-of-pearl mahjong sets, and in go the festive Mid-Autumn lanterns.

Mrs. Volkova often says that Mei should hang up some of her traditional paper cuttings. Perhaps Mei's signature design, the unfurled peony flower, because aren't such cuttings meant for windows? Isn't light meant to stream through the slits in the paper; the negative space?

But Mei keeps her designs tacked to the walls in the back. She believes that the sun would only spoil them.

THE EVENING HAS grown stale and silent. Volkov's Curio Shop should be long closed by now, but the visitor will not leave. You need the patience of the goddess Tin Hau not to snap like a pencil tip, putting up with people like this; or else you need to be in customer service. Mei sands her teeth together, swipes the sweat from her forehead. It might still be worth it: She senses that this woman could afford to buy this whole building, squat and derelict and dirty as it is, and the wealthy do not often find their way to this part of Kowloon.

The lady says: "You've heard of George Maidenhair, I presume?"

The red diamond character banners slip right through Mei's hands.

Immediately, she gathers them back up. There is nowhere to faint in a display like this, except face-first on the Buddhas. After speaking so long without a stop, *now* the woman is awaiting a reply, but how can Mei respond? Yes, Auntie, I have heard of George Maidenhair. I have spoken his name; I have screamed it into my hands. Yes, Auntie, and he would have heard of me. But look how I am many years, and hundreds of miles, and one entire country, away from all that.

Look how well I can string these banners, without my hands even shaking—

The old woman repeats the four syllables of George's full name. She says that he ran an infamous business empire back in Shanghai. That he all but owned the Paris of the East. That he married the former silent-film actress Holly Zhang. Surely, Mei knows of him, because even the fish-slingers down at Lei Yue Mun know of George, even the rickshaw drivers so skinny their shirts get sucked into their stomachs, even the addicts in their dens and divans lying as still as effigies, even the Triad thugs who have never left the blackened courtyards of Kowloon Walled City—they all know him.

But everybody says they know everybody, in a city nearly built on top of itself, like Hong Kong.

AS SHE LISTENS, Mei turns the character *fú* upside down, so that luck pours out for the Mid-Autumn Festival. It feels like she might be standing on her head. Heat is rushing to her cheeks; they must be as red as the banners.

For a moment she wants to bring this whole window display crashing down.

For a moment she wants to see everything she has spent so long putting up ripped to shreds.

George Maidenhair: taipan and business mogul. George Maidenhair: American-born; Oxford-educated; hell-bound. George Maidenhair, with a laugh as hearty as Tientsin cabbage soup, without any soul. George Maidenhair, whom they called the Golden Man back in Shanghai, some said for his good-luck, ferry-light, tossed-yolk yellow hair, others said for his money, but Mei would say because he was a false god. George Maidenhair, who cracked Mei's entire life down the middle, the way she could one of these porcelain plates, forever beyond repair.

When it comes to George, Mei has just as much to say as this woman. She could be the one talking without needing answers.

THE WOMAN APPROACHES the display. As she draws near to Mei, her cloak flaps fishlike around her. Up close, it turns out, the old woman is not that old at all. Up close the blazing white hair is a wig. The gold-tipped cane might be a weapon. She says that George Maidenhair bought the old Hall mansion on Victoria Peak a few years back and renamed it Maidenhair House. She says, smiling now, as if it's a joke, that the refugees of the Revolution who are pouring into Hong Kong these days no longer need a family name because there is nobody left to share it with, and then there are people like George, who slather their names onto everything.

Mei herself fled the Revolution.

But that is not all she fled.

When Mei left Shanghai in 1948, at eighteen years old, it was with the absolute certainty that she and George Maidenhair could never again live in the same city. They could not coexist. One of them would have to go, or one of them would have to die. Mei feels suddenly cornered, with the display behind her, this woman in front of her, George all around her. She moves to step away from the window, but does not quite manage. Her composure is slipping. Her tongue is swelling to fill her whole mouth.

The visitor seems not to notice.

"Holly Zhang—George's wife—is fascinated by the occult," says the woman. "You may have heard the stories about the old Hall House?"

Say something, Mei.

Say something so that you do not cry out.

"Never," says Mei tightly. She would not have believed them even if she had. Around every corner of Hong Kong is someone peddling another spooky story, another popular myth; there is just as much gossip about the dead as there is about the living. Mei would explain all this, but something is shifting beneath her feet. This lady has obviously not wandered in here by accident. By accident is how *Mei* ended up in Kowloon, after taking train after train from Shanghai to Macau, after barely gaining a place on an illegal junk that foundered right off the coast, after finding herself pitched into the brackish water of the South China Sea, after swimming for hours, after washing up right onto a stowed-away beach with sand so white it scalded her eyes. She was all cut up on the oysters just off the reef and she left a bloody trail up the shore that the locals say is still there.

She stained everything on her way into this shop.

Mei doesn't know what it is that suddenly gives it away: the naked gleam in the woman's larger eye, with the other oddly empty. The way the woman is watching Mei; the way people once watched *her*.

This not-so-old woman is Holly Zhang herself.

The onetime glamour girl; the shining star of silent cinema. The symbol of a Shanghai that no longer exists. Instantly, without warning, Mei can feel the heat of languid, long-ago summer nights. She can smell a wonton seller's shop, tucked into an alley like a card up a sleeve; she can hear the fickle scratch of a jazz record; she can see billboards on faraway buildings, brighter than the moon.

She can see blood on her hands, her clothes, in a puddle at her feet.

Mei might drop the banners again, but there is nothing left to slip through her fingers.

GEORGE MAIDENHAIR'S WIFE has entered Volkov's Curio Shop. Has entered Mei's existence. Has crossed her path. Everything until this moment was just a façade, a cover, just another sweeping-clean cloak, and now it is lifting. Mei has no idea how Holly has found her here, so deep in Kowloon it often feels like she is underground, but in a way it does not matter. The other woman must know that Mei has a history with George Maidenhair. Why else would Holly have come? Perhaps she discovered the custom-made paper shadow puppets that Mei once created for George. Perhaps she is driven by jealousy, by an erroneous assumption about the nature of Mei and George's relationship—Mei is young and Chinese and pretty and poor, after all, and George is some three decades older, white and rich and powerful. Holly would not be the first to make that mistake.

Mei could easily just tell the truth: It is not like that, between me and your husband. It never was.

But by now there is so much bile in her throat, it pricks her eyes.

"I want your help," says Holly.

Holly Zhang is a better actress than Mei ever knew.

What northerner can speak Cantonese like that, all nine tones, whetted like a knife?

"I know who you really are, child. We've met before, you see," says Holly. "Years and years ago. Though you may not remember me, because you were the star then, and I was only one person in the crowd."

3

JIANGSU PROVINCE, CHINA
AUGUST 1937

USUALLY WHEN MY sisters and I hear the noise of the candy-seller man outside, knocking his blocks of wood together as he passes through the village, we whine like pigs and Ba ignores us. Today I do not whine, and yet Ba buys me a handful of sugar melon candies and gives me a tie-up bag to keep them in. He does not buy any for my sisters.

He does not explain why, so of course they only whine harder.

THE LAST TIME Ba bought me a bag of candies, it was right before the Dragon Boat Festival, at the start of summer. He did it to make me feel better, because my sisters had locked me up in the old ancestral hall of the *sìhéyuàn* compound down the road. They had been telling me stories about skeleton ghosts that haunt the hall, and they thought it would be funny.

Ma was the one who found me that day.

My sisters said they were sorry but they forgot about me. I still don't know how long I was there; you can't really tell day from night inside an ancestral hall.

I could not fall asleep that night.

Ma whispered to me: *Whatever you saw in there, Third Daughter, you should not be afraid.*

The real monsters live among us.

The real monsters look just like us.

But then Ma disappeared. Right after the festival.

I thought she might be locked in the ancestral hall too, but Big Sister says they checked there.

IF BANDITS HAVE kidnapped Ma, maybe I can buy her back with my candies. I can trick the bandits into thinking they are worth good money— But then, in the stories that Ba tells us, bandits are always clever as monkeys; in fact sometimes they *are* monkeys.

Big Sister comes over to see what I am doing.

"Do you want to play knucklebones with me?" I ask hopefully.

"No, because I'm not a baby," she says. "And I don't want to touch your slobbery candy."

"I haven't put them in my mouth yet! Please play?"

Big Sister laughs, but without sounding happy. "You know what I think sometimes? I think Ma left because she couldn't take how annoying you are. The sound of your *voice*, Third Sister, it drives people crazy. I bet that's why she ran off!"

My hands close around my candies.

"If you shut up forever, maybe Ma'll come back," says Big Sister, and she slouches away.

I feel very bad and shaky, like a beetle in a jar.

One day I must remember to ask the candy-seller if I can borrow his blocks of wood to clap them over my sister's mouth, or at least my own ears. Sniffling, I pile my candies into a small shiny mountain and make it erupt, again and again, but in the end the only thing that erupts is my tears. Rickety old Nai Nai always tells me I should learn to eat my tears instead, like a good Chinese girl, and then I wouldn't be so hungry all the time either. Sometimes I worry that's what happened to Ma; that my tears washed her away.

AT NIGHT, LYING on the *kàng* beside a snoring Second Sister, I cannot sleep again. I cannot fall asleep well most nights. The darkness in our home is like the darkness in the ancestral hall, and I worry that it has swallowed me.

Let me out! Please, somebody! Let me out—

I jump off the *kàng* and I light a candle and everything returns to normal.

I know I must put the candle out before I get back into bed.

Hopefully, humans can live without sleep and we just don't know it?

Carrying the candle I go over to the little side table where Ma makes her art. Or used to make her art. Ma is a paper artist: She can create anything so long as it is to do with paper, from simple sketches all the way to huge paintings and fancy shadow puppets. Now her pencils and paints and brushes are sitting here, waiting for her to come back, just like the rest of us.

Ma said she would teach me, one day.

Without thinking about it very much, I tiptoe over to where Ba sleeps, where he keeps a framed photograph of Ma by his head, and I pick up the frame carefully. In the photograph, Ma is bent over a little, looking away from the person taking her picture, and smiling. She is as beautiful as the moon goddess Chang'e. If you look right into the photograph, just the right way, you can hear her laughing. I call this picture-magic.

With the frame in my hot hands, I scramble back over to the

art table and climb onto the stool. Then I grab one of her pencils and start to draw the image of her onto a piece of paper.

Sadly, it doesn't look too much like the photo.

WHEN I'M DONE, I make a tiny, sugar-melon-candy promise to myself: I will not speak again until Ma comes back. Because for all I know, Big Sister is right, and Ma left because her ears hurt, because of me, because I am always talking. Or crying. Ma herself had such a nice voice, a voice like silk was trembling inside her mouth. I would never get tired of hearing *her* talk. Even better was when she sang.

Ba always says that she could have been a singer in a bright-light city theatre, in some other life, but this life was Ma's *fate*.

I guess *fate* means that you have to sing in the darkness.

TODAY A MAN called Uncle and his wife have come to visit from Shanghai, the city on the sea.

Big Sister says they are visiting us for the first time *ever* because Uncle feels sorry about Ma being gone. I don't see why he should feel sorry unless he took her. And I don't blame him for not visiting before, either: Uncle is much too big for our home and has to duck his head so that he doesn't hit the ceiling. He has short gray bean sprout hair and serious eyes and he is wearing a thick belted robe with long sloshing sleeves. His skin is like the morning sky, thin and bright.

Uncle doesn't look a thing like Ma, even though Big Sister swears that he is Ma's long-lost older brother. From her long-lost older family.

We don't have enough chairs, so Uncle and his wife sit down on the *kàng*.

Uncle's wife is called First Wife, even though he hasn't brought any others. First Wife is frowny and plucked-looking. She has stiff wavy hair, like cloud-ear fungus cooking in a pot, and wears a qipao with so many flowers sewn into it that I want to sneeze. She looks down at the *kàng* with her mouth crumpling up, as if she has never seen clay baked into bricks to make a bed. Then she gives me the exact same look.

Next to me, Big Sister mumbles that Uncle is fat with his family's fortune and that our Ma grew up rich in Shanghai, but Ma ran away from home, and one day she happened to overhear Ba play the *èrhú* and then she just *had* to marry him, *had* to, even though he was poor as a raccoon dog, because she couldn't get the sound of it out of her head.

But Big Sister is often fat with nonsense.

"Do any of the children show talent for paper craft?" Uncle asks Ba, who is standing by the stove, unmoving.

"Third Sister makes wonderful cuttings," says Ba, which is a huge lie. Ma has never let me touch her cutting knives. Not even her sharpest pencils.

My face goes tickly because her pencils aren't so sharp anymore, now that I've been using them at night.

Uncle looks at me. "You're how old, Third Sister?"

I clamp my lips together.

"She has the manners of a donkey. Is she mute, or just rude?" asks First Wife.

"She's six," says Ba, even though normally I am seven.

"Come here," Uncle instructs me, and Second Sister shoves me forward. Uncle pulls from one of his scoop-sleeves a small white carved horse, opening his hand flat so I can see it better. His fingers are also white. Also look carved. "A gift for you," he says. "It's hard-paste porcelain. *True* porcelain. Go on now, take it."

I don't want to touch his hand so I take the horse with two fingers.

I look over to Ba, who seems small and stooped.

"Third Sister will not do," says Uncle. "You should be called Little Mei." He stands up and nearly knocks his spindly wife right off the *kàng*. "Well then. That is all for now. Perhaps you and I will see each other again, one day," he says to Ba. "If the Japanese army does not get in the way."

My sisters look confused and maybe I do too, because in our village you only say the word *Japanese* in a weird baby-whisper voice.

I do not know very much about the Japanese except that sometimes we find guerrilla soldiers for the generalissimo Chiang Kai-shek lying dead in the ditches, and we don't really know where they came from, and Nai Nai will say in that blaring baby-whisper,

It was the Japanese, and then I imagine the Japanese like dragons, dropping people from the skies.

The list of things we cannot say aloud is getting longer: The Japanese. Ma.

Soon enough it won't even matter that I've taken a vow not to speak; there will be so little anyone can say!

Uncle is leaving, sleeves splashing, robe lapping, First Wife following. I have seen pictures of people who wear robes like that, in Ba's books. Old pictures. Old people. They have long braids like snakes down their backs. There is even a special name for these people, but I forget what it was.

Now I have a special name too.

"You're so lucky," says Second Sister, gawping at my new porcelain horse, but Big Sister only scoffs.

BEFORE SLEEP-TIME, BA takes out his two-stringed *èrhú*.

He hasn't touched it since the day Ma left.

I feel like lightning bugs are lighting up my insides. Maybe he knows Ma is coming back? Could it be? Why else would he take it out suddenly?

We sit on the floor by his feet as he tunes the *èrhú*.

Everything is just as it was two months ago.

All that is missing in the world right now is Ma.

"You want to try?" Ba asks me, holding out the bow.

Ba was giving me lessons before Ma left. He wouldn't offer like this unless she was coming back. She *must* be coming back. And when she does, I will be able to speak again. To sleep again. I nod eagerly and scramble up and take over Ba's place and press my knees against the bulk of the instrument. I only know a few songs so far. Maybe that is why whenever Ba plays, the sound seems to last for hours, but whenever I draw the bow, it is over too soon.

4

KOWLOON, HONG KONG
SEPTEMBER 1953

MEI HAS SPENT all morning drawing a dragon, and it faces down.

Traditionally, a dragon that faces down cannot fly.

She could still cut it and try to sell it to tourists. The larger problem is that her hands have been working without her head. Maybe all artists know what this feels like; maybe anyone who creates anything knows it. Your hands take over, fervently sketching in the details of a dragon, adding sand-dollar scales, tendrils curled into ringlets, toes like arrowheads, while your head is elsewhere. Your head is full of George Maidenhair.

"MEI! MEI, ARE you up there? Mei!"

Mrs. Volkova should really get a job at the docks. She could replace the foghorns.

Mei keeps working because Mrs. Volkova probably just wants an antique chest moved out of the way, and tomorrow she'll want it moved right back. Mrs. Volkova likes to do things that make no difference; she is scared of making differences. Mei's employer is an ancient and tetchy White Russian with a flimsy first name,

Tatiana, and a tragic history involving a soldier husband who was shot on his knees for supporting the wrong side. But Mei never asks questions about Mrs. Volkova's revolution and Mrs. Volkova never asks questions about hers. That is what their relationship depends on.

"*Mei!* A letter's come for you!"

Something shoots up Mei's spine, down her arms, all the way to where she is holding the rabbit brush.

A *letter?*

It is possible that Mei has misunderstood. Mrs. Volkova's speech is more churned up than Mei's paints, between Russian, some degree of Harbin dialect, and Cantonese without tones. But in any language, how can Mei receive a letter when she does not officially live here? When she does not even officially live? She has no legal status in this city. She is a refugee. She is somewhere between the place she comes from and the place she has arrived in, feeling wholly in neither, belonging nowhere. She is in the in-between place.

"I know you're up there!" hollers Mrs. Volkova.

Mei grips the brush until its shape burns her hand.

A large map-wing butterfly shudders close to the edge of her drawing desk, perching on her dish of dye. Mrs. Volkova likes to pin such butterflies to large wooden boards. Mounted behind glass, they glitter like the surface of the ocean, but Mei hates looking at them, hates how she can see the pin between her own eyes in the glass.

She has not moved from her chair.

The last person ever to send her a letter was George Maidenhair.

The map-wing takes off violently, in a flurry of flapping, knocking over the dish as it swoops away, drenching her desk blue. Paint drops off the edges, sloshes over the floor tiles. There are days when Mei might laugh at something like this; and then there are days when it feels like she is the one who is spilling out.

Mixing that dye, getting it just right, was two weeks' worth of work.

Her life here in Hong Kong is five years' worth of work.

Does she want to see that life tipped over too? Does she want to see it pool on the ground like rain?

DOWNSTAIRS IN THE office, Mrs. Volkova is sitting at her own desk, working on a Japanese netsuke, a miniature ivory sculpture. She likes to sand them down so small only she can tell what the netsuke was ever supposed to be. The walls are covered in Mei's paper cuttings: most strikingly the peony, over and over again, in different shapes and colors, though the holes pricked in the paper are always the same.

It is Mei's best-selling work, but one could not say whether this is only because it is the one she makes most.

Mrs. Volkova's pet finch squawks a greeting at Mei from its bamboo cage, while electric fans, balanced on piles of newspaper, squawk harder. Mei has to wade her way in because the disarray in the room is considerable, piles upon piles of unidentifiable curios, anything that has ever happened to catch Mrs. Volkova's eye.

Mrs. Volkova has a certain affinity for things that nobody else wants. Things that are beyond salvaging. That is how Mei ended up with her.

The finch blows out its throat like a toad. The Russian woman glances up at last, eyes narrowed, pointing with a magnifying glass toward the Yellow Mountain of correspondence at the foot of the desk. Mei does not know what it is about letters; why they always give off a whiff of being life-changing when they almost never are.

Tremulously, she picks up the envelope on top.

It carries a sickly perfumed scent, and at once she knows who has written to her.

But perhaps she already knew.

The envelope comes open easy, with one nail. The paper inside is light and flawless, and would be perfect for making paper-cut clouds. Sunny-day clouds. Not the fibrous dark masses Mei has caught glimpses of out the windows today. She inhales, prepares herself mentally. She must use her fingertip to help the strokes settle into their proper places, as she has an affliction known to her only as *word-blindness*.

It is not an accurate term, because Mei can in fact see words. If anything, she sees too many words.

"Well, who's written to you?" says Mrs. Volkova impatiently.

"Holly Zhang." It is the sort of thing that sounds like a lie no matter how you say it. "She came into the shop a few days ago. She mentioned something about . . . but I did not think she would send a—"

"You can't mean the actress?" Mrs. Volkova is rising from her chair, which Mrs. Volkova rarely does, evidently eager for Mei to read the letter out loud. The Russian woman might already be envisioning everything that lines the shelves of the curio shop lining Holly's walls.

Holly Zhang does strike Mei as somebody who might buy dead butterfly boards.

Dear Miss Chen Mei,

I am pleased to invite you to join me at MAIDENHAIR HOUSE, 1 EMERY ROAD, VICTORIA PEAK, from FRIDAY, SEPTEMBER 18
  For six nights

For six séances

In six different locations within Maidenhair or upon its grounds.

You are one of six spirit mediums whose presence I hope to secure
for this occasion. One of you will be asked to leave Maidenhair after
every séance, until there is only one remaining.

The final session will be an exorcism. . . .

If the exorcism is a success, the sole remaining spirit medium will receive a staggering monetary reward.

Feeling her mouth agape, Mei rereads and rereads the amount, in case it is her word-blindness acting against her.

BEFORE SHE STARTED working at the curio shop, Mei lived in the squatter's villages out by Diamond Hill, chock-full of fellow refugees, all of them sharing their strips of sleeping mats, their lungs charring from paraffin smoke. Mei used to wake up at four every morning to toil in a plastic flower factory, working her fingers down to bone; eventually, she quit because she feared that a few more months of wrapping wire around fake flowers and her hands would get fixed that way, like a bear's, and she'd never be able to cut paper properly again. Hoping to save her hands, she sacrificed her body: She became a white-flower girl in the red-light district of Mong Kok. There her hands did not fumble; they stayed clenched into fists until she lost all feeling in them.

Three years she spent flat on her back, living on next to nothing, until the day she happened upon the curio shop by chance.

Even now, she wakes up every morning and feels the tug of gravity, back toward that life.

Even now, she knows she could slip all the way down, effortlessly, the way those refugee shantytowns slide off the hillsides into the sea during the monsoons; like she was never here at all.

"A competition?" says Mrs. Volkova. Mei's employer is not easily taken by surprise. Mei imagines that comes with witnessing the people you love get shot on their knees; nothing will ever compare to the sound of those shots. "A competition to *see spirits?*"

Mei does not know Holly Zhang's life story except in glints, but she knows that rich people love to believe in the supernatural. Maybe when you can have anything you want, you crave whatever feels impossible. Or maybe once you've achieved everything one ever could in this world, you become desperate to believe that there is some other world, somewhere out there, in which there is still more to achieve. In which you can start from nothing all over again. In which everything still lies ahead of you.

Likely, it is even worse for old rich people.

But that is not a problem that spirit mediums can solve, people feeling like ghosts in their own lives, of their former selves.

MEI CANNOT ACCEPT Holly's offer. She should not accept. She should feed this letter to a fire. Not least of all because Mei would rather return to working for a *mama-san* in Mong Kok, servicing flat-eyed foreign businessmen, than conduct a séance. In some ways, it is about the same thing anyway, selling yourself for the entertainment and distraction of others, opening yourself up so that somebody else can forget their pain, just for a moment. Money never feels so grubby as when it's placed into your hands while you have your eyes closed.

But the truth is that Mei is scared.

Six séances.

Six times she would risk becoming possessed. If she even made it that far.

"I don't understand," says Mrs. Volkova. "Why is she asking *you* to participate in this?"

Mrs. Volkova won't believe Mei's answer. Mrs. Volkova believes in things that are tangible. She believes in netsukes. She will have crass follow-up questions such as: Could Mei do séances in the back room of this curio shop? Could Mrs. Volkova offer special deals for the customers, half off a set of enamel water pipes and a reunion with your dead ancestors?

"You look like you're about to lose your breakfast," says Mrs. Volkova bitingly, "so you may as well let this out too."

"I trained as a ghost-seer in Shanghai, Auntie," says Mei. The electric fans are still seething in her direction and her teeth have begun to chatter. "I was once the apprentice of a Great Master. We occasionally opened sessions to the public—Holly said she was present at one of these."

Mei wouldn't have noticed if so. There was only one person Mei ever saw, back then.

"You're telling me that you can commune with the dead?"

"I don't know. I have not used my Sight in years."

"All's the better, I say," says Mrs. Volkova, with a light scowl. "You will refuse her, of course. An aged has-been with too much money and nothing to do with it; I know the type! She wants a court jester, is all. Now then, the water is out again, so perhaps you could go on and take the tins down to the street pumps, unless you're too good for it now, eh?"

It is not the reaction Mei expected. In fact, if Mei didn't know better, she might think that Mrs. Volkova cared about her and what she does, even though Mrs. Volkova says that she will never waste her care on a human being ever again; on anything that cannot be repaired with tools like tweezers and fiber-tube torchlights. But more likely Mrs. Volkova is already making ends meet well enough here in the earthy depths of Kowloon and doesn't want anything to change. Change means gunshots one way or another, even if they're not directly to the back of your head.

UPSTAIRS IN HER bedroom her desk is dry again. Mei hauls out the Four Treasures of the Study: ink, inkstone, brush, and fine paper. She crafts her rejection with the utmost care. She is not as eloquent as Holly, she is not as educated, she is word-blind, but with good calligraphy, you can mask many things. A salted-plum salesman's voice floats up from the street outside the window, advertising his wares; Mei's mouth feels just like a salted plum. This is the reasonable choice, of course it is: to say no, to forget Holly's face, to forget George's name, to carry on in this cavern of a curio shop, mixing dyes, drawing dragons, dressing window displays, bracing for yet another barn-owl screech from Mrs. Volkova. To go on living alongside her own ghosts.

But Mei's hand has been working without her head again.

Dear Madame Zhang,

I am honored to accept your invitation to

Revenge is the map-wing butterfly; if she grasps it too hard, she will kill it.

5

JIANGSU PROVINCE, CHINA
AUGUST 1937

IN THE MORNING, my sisters and I visit Nai Nai at the *sìhéyuàn*. Nai Nai is grumpily sweeping outside the main entrance, and I am a little relieved. The ancestral hall is all the way across the central courtyard and Nai Nai is better than a tiger at keeping us out.

I show her my porcelain horse and she sneers.

"Piece of garbage," she says. Nai Nai has a face like a hairy crab and no laugh at all. Not like Ma. "What will you do with something like that? Can you cook it? Eat it? Drink it? Wear it? Warm yourself with it? Give it to your father to sell."

I shake my head stubbornly and slip the horse back into my pocket.

"Uncle also gave her a new name," pipes up Second Sister.

"A new name? I never heard of anything so pointless in all my life. What's next? He brought new mud for us to step in?"

"I want a new name too," protests Second Sister.

"Shoo, you naughty girls, Nai Nai is busy!" she barks, waving her broom like she'll beat our backsides with it, though she never has, so we're not scared. She returns to her work, bundling the dust by her sandals. She has tiny feet, like a sandpiper. A fortune teller once told Nai Nai's parents that if they broke her foot bones, Nai Nai would marry a rich man, so they did this, but the fortune teller was wrong. Nai Nai married a poor man.

And now she has to do the sweeping on a rich woman's feet.

I turn around when we reach the gates, to wave goodbye, but Nai Nai is not even looking at me. Her face is gleamy red, like a New Year's envelope, and her eyes are wet. She rubs them with her sleeve, but it doesn't help. I want to tell her that soon everything will be alright. I want to tell her that once Ma is home again, Ma can make new lotus shoes for her, the ones that make stubby feet look very fancy, instead of the ugly clogs that Nai Nai is wearing now. Ma can also help with the sweeping, because Ma's feet are perfect and unbound, though they have a tiny bit of webbing between the second and third toes, just like mine.

I open my mouth again, just for a second—

But then, oh! A frog jumps out in front of me.

A few weeks ago we had the great idea to trap golden frogs from the pond and then release them in the courtyard, to annoy Nai Nai. But she caught most of them quickly, because she's faster on half-feet than most people are on full-feet, and worst of all, she ended up boiling them and eating them.

There are people in the world that it's just not funny to play tricks on, and Nai Nai is one of them.

I wish I were one of them. Then my sisters never would have locked me in an ancestral hall to begin with. Then Ma might not have left in the first place.

MUCH LATER, ON the *kàng*, my eyes are heavy and I think that maybe, just maybe, I will fall asleep fast tonight, but before I can, Big Sister rolls Second Sister out of the way and lies down next to me, which she almost never does because she thinks I stink like a yellow ox.

"Ba's going to take you on a trip tomorrow," she says, very quiet. "Just you and him."

I don't say anything because even though Big Sister is older and smarter than me, she does like to tell lies. I *know* I don't smell like a yellow ox. Oxen are very, very smelly. And Ba has never taken any of us on trips before. Where is there to go? China is mostly fields and fields and fields until you fall off into the sea. That's why they build cities on the coast, I think; to stop people walking right in.

"For goodness' sake, Third Sister, you should just talk again," says Big Sister. I can tell she is rolling her eyeballs all the way up and down, the way she often does. Ma used to say her eyes would get stuck like that, like a flatfish's. "This is ridiculous. Ma is dead. Okay? She's dead."

When I don't answer, Big Sister turns onto her side so we are looking right at each other.

"You don't believe me, huh?" she says. "Ma is dead. Everyone knows it. They just don't want to tell us the truth."

For the first time, I realize that Big Sister looks the most of the three of us like Ma. In the face, at least. She doesn't have the webbed feet. Big Sister is also the smartest of the three of us: She taught herself to read using Ba's collection of books, and she even taught Second Sister. She tried to teach me too, but even if I'm not as stinky as an ox, I am as bad as one with learning characters.

Ma is not very good either. That's why she scribbles a dainty little peony flower onto all of her artwork, to mark it as hers, instead of her name.

"It's because of what Ma was doing in secret, for extra money," Big Sister whispers. "It was a shameful thing, and she must have died of it, in some terrible way, so now they have to keep it even more secret, or there will be too much loss of face. They prefer to pretend that Ma never existed in the first place. *They're* the ones who've taken the real vow of silence, Third Sister. Not you."

This is impossible. This cannot be true.

Ma couldn't have died a secret death without me. She *wouldn't*.

"I shouldn't have said that stuff about your voice. And your talking. I didn't mean it." Big Sister's own voice sounds a little funny. "By the way, I've seen the art you do secretly at night. The sketches? I bet you could get really good, if you keep going. Ma used to say *she'd* never stop making art, no matter what, remember? Even if people took away all her materials; even if she was all alone? That she'd make paintbrushes out of mice tails and paper out of catalpa leaves? Remember?"

Now I can't speak for a very different reason: I am crying again.

Where do tears even come from? Is it like the well in the village that goes down so dark and deep, there's always more to pull out?

"Here, look. I have something for you." Big Sister props herself up and pulls something out from under her head. A dark-colored pouch, like the one I keep my candy in, but bigger and flatter. "It's Ma's, or it used to be. She told me to give it to you if anything ever happened to her. I should have given it to you right away. I was . . . I haven't opened it, though. You shouldn't show it to loads of other people, either. It's yours from Ma and you keep it that way."

I sit up and try to open it but it's tied very hard and I am crying very hard.

"You were actually Ma's favorite," says Big Sister.

We are both crying. I didn't think Big Sister even knew how to cry. I guess super smart people know how to do lots of things they just don't show. Through it all she says, *Please say something to me, Third Sister. Anything. Even just one small thing, before we sleep.*

BIG SISTER WAS telling the truth: The next morning Ba takes me, only me, on a long, lazy trip that involves a bumpy ride on the back of a water buffalo, a wagon that pulls us slower than I could scoot on my stomach, and then a train journey that is exciting for about five minutes. It feels like a whole dynasty has passed by the time we get off, but still Ba will not tell me where we are going or why. He seats himself on a bench and I sink to the ground to play with my last few candies. Every so often another train rumbles by. Back home, my sisters are probably catching grasshoppers, and I am missing the fun just to sit around in a boring old train station—

"Good morning," somebody says, stopping in front of us.

It is Uncle's wife! *First Wife!* First Wife in her sneezy skintight qipao!

Ba gets to his feet.

"Do you remember me?" First Wife asks me. She has powdered her cheeks with so much rice flour that if she tried to smile her face might break in two, but she doesn't try.

I look at Ba for help.

"You must speak now, Little Mei," says Ba. He sounds like he might have swallowed my porcelain horse. "You must answer First Wife."

He is using *Little Mei* like it's the only thing he's ever called me.

I stand up, holding my bag of candies. I can feel my heart in my own body, hard and fast as the train. Why is First Wife here at the same train station as me and Ba? Why is she staring at me like this? First Wife leans over as far as she can, which isn't all that far because of the qipao, and latches on to my arm. I gasp. She must sharpen her nails on a wheel.

"This way," she says, not sounding happy about it.

I try to pull away, but she's not letting go. Her nails only dig in harder, and now somebody new, somebody much larger, emerges from nowhere. This enormous man reaches out and grabs my other arm, pinning it down with his own. My bag of candies drops from my hand. The little sugar melon balls roll out onto the ground before I realize what is happening.

Ba is already walking away.

I hear somebody screaming. I haven't heard my own voice in so long I almost don't know who it is.

"Ba!"

He stops for a second. Then he keeps going. He steps on my candies as he goes and they crunch beneath his feet.

Poor-man's-feet, wide and cracked like soil.

"Ba!" I shriek after him, but Ba doesn't turn. The large man has both my arms now. I claw at him, kick at his shins, but he doesn't seem to notice; I turn around in his grasp as best I can, yelling for my father. "Ba! Baba, wait! Don't leave! Don't leave me!"

Ba does not look back.

"I'll talk again! I promise, Baba! I'll be good! *Don't leave me!*"

A new train is coming and Ba is getting on it and I am still here, screaming as hard as I can, using up all the voice I have being saving for Ma. My face is bursting. My tears are running, my throat is hurting, and I'm shouting for my father, my mother, my sisters, even for Nai Nai, but now that I'm finally speaking, it's too late, nobody can hear me, and I can't even hear myself, the noise in my head is so loud. I am hoisted up like a sack onto the big man's shoulder, and the last thing I know is that the beautiful white true-porcelain horse, the one that Uncle gave me, the only thing anyone has ever given me, falls out of my pocket and shatters in a second, maybe because it was so delicate, so precious. Or else because it was bought so cheap.

6

HONG KONG,
2015

WE ARE WELL into the second leg of the journey, from Taipei to Hong Kong, when Susanna begins to stir in her seat. She shifts, turning away at the very moment that her phone, face up on the tray table, flares to life.

It is an email from Liana.

I can only read the start of the first line: *Mom I'm scared that I*

Susanna pulls herself upright, beginning to blink, and I resist the urge to smooth her eyelids shut again; she needs better, longer, deeper, dreamier sleep. But we will be landing soon enough anyway: Out my window, the sun is setting over a lush stretch of islands, and the hills of Hong Kong spike up dramatically from the sea.

Such a short distance there is, between the mainland and Hong Kong, when you see it from an airplane.

I pinch it to nothing between my fingertips.

Susanna reaches first for her phone, instead of speaking to me. Blearily, she swipes at the screen, reading the message from my granddaughter.

"I'll write to her when we land," Susanna says, mostly to herself.

"Why is she scared?"

"Probably more nightmare stuff." Susanna drops her phone into her purse and fishes out her tablet instead. "I wanted to show you the pictures I got from the Canadians, Ma. The urban explorers. I thought maybe it would spark something, jog your memory, before we talk properly. Can we take a look?"

Before I can respond, an image is blowing up in front of me.

It shows a stately colonial house with a touch of chilly grandeur. This is not how Susanna normally conducts oral interviews for her books, I am sure. This is not how she puts together her stories, by forcing her subjects to face their pasts, by holding their heads to it. Maybe she is taking liberties because I am her mother. To a daughter, how can a mother's life before she became a mother mean all that much, really, compared to the life after?

But that is what I have raised her to think.

That is what I *wanted* her to think.

I nod, and Susanna shoves the image away with her fingers, forcibly bringing up the next: an old windowpane through which a narrow stairwell is visible. Next: ivy snaking up a wall. Next: a bathroom, a cracked washbasin, a ceiling streaked with mold. You can almost feel the drip of decay onto your head. Next. Next. Next.

"This isn't it," I say.

Her screen darkens. Susanna splays her hand to revive it.

"This isn't Maidenhair House," I say, in case she hasn't heard.

Susanna stifles a yawn. "What are you talking about?"

"It's similar. But it isn't Maidenhair House. The Canadians, they have sent you the wrong pictures."

"Why would they do that? And I've seen it from above, you

know. On Google Earth. Here, I can show you—" Susanna pulls her tablet closer, flicking rapidly through image after image, landing at last on a gray-green blur, like military camouflage, with a white speck in the middle. "That's the house from above, see? There's the traditional Chinese garden. Maybe it looks different because of the state it's in. Or maybe you just don't remember."

My memory is a hundred times clearer than those pictures. "It's the wrong house," I say again, in case she hasn't heard again.

"Okay, could you elaborate, please?"

"You want me to write my own book about how it is not the same house?"

Susanna peers closer at the Google Earth, like the answer might be in it. She yawns again, searching for that single pale speck, hunched over her screen the way you would hunch over a shrine. Finally, she mutters something about how she's going to write to the Canadians, just to confirm.

She is in her email almost instantly, using a keyboard that appears like magic.

How odd people are. Susanna is so anxious to write to strangers about pictures of a house she has never lived in, not because it matters, but because it *doesn't* matter.

She cannot bring herself to write to her own daughter, because it *does* matter.

I rap at the window.

"What now?" Susanna says irritably, sitting back, but this, at least, is a sight she cannot look away from, even toward a screen: The glitter of Hong Kong by night. The beehive of lights, the dark shining water, the crystalline skyscrapers. The oppressive sense of heat and humanity.

Every time an airplane lands in Hong Kong, you feel it: How can there ever be room for any more people, in a place like this?

It is a universe away from the subdued gray skies we left behind in Seattle.

"I'm sure it was an innocent mistake," Susanna mumbles, still staring. "Those guys have visited dozens of disintegrating buildings all over the world. And the other pictures online, it's always so *misty*, you can't get a grip on . . . well, it doesn't matter. I'm trying to connect with the LLC that owns the house. Hopefully then I'll be able to take a look for myself—"

"Or else they were afraid."

"Afraid of what?"

"Afraid to send you the real pictures of the house. Afraid of what showed up in them."

"What?" Susanna laughs. It sounds like a blown tire.

But she finally shuts off her screen.

She has stopped yawning.

She is waking up.

The pilot's voice comes over the intercom. We have begun our descent. I wonder how deep we will go.

"I DON'T THINK we can talk in here. You're probably tired anyway. We'll start tomorrow," says Susanna, as the hot pot between us begins to boil. The waiters are bringing over the ingredients I asked for, watercress, lettuce, flower mushroom, slices of beef that look like soapstone, but Susanna seems unmoved by the heavy scents, the pillars of steam, that rise from the other diners' tables. She does not even seem tempted by the mix of dipping sauces, which I have created the way I once made my own dyes, dewdrops of this, delicate doses of that. She is itching to return to the hotel, where it is calm and quiet and frostily air-conditioned. She wanted to order to room service.

"I am not tired," I say. "I would like to talk."

She blinks at me. "I'd have to get out my——"

"Maidenhair House. What do they call the urban legend these days?"

"The Maidenhair Murders."

"Bad name," I say, and Susanna smiles reluctantly, not quite wide enough to fit in a bite of food yet. "You must understand, Susanna, that there are so many such tales in this city. So many unsolved deaths." So much unfinished business. "You come here, looking for answers, you will have to face ghosts. You have to be sure you want to do this. You have to be sure you are ready. Tell me, are you ever going to eat?"

Susanna brandishes her chopsticks, pokes at the hot pot. "I'm ready," she says, but her voice is wary now.

I shake out the strainer. "Then I think we should go up to the Peak and see Maidenhair in the flesh, such as it is. Right now. To-night."

Susanna yanks her hand away; she must have been splashed by the bubbling water. "That's out of the question. I told you, I've been trying to contact the owner to set up an interview, to arrange a visit. Breaking in would be a serious breach of—it would be trespassing."

"And the Canadians, they were not trespassing?"

She flushes. "At least they had some experience. What you're proposing is—ill-advised. It's dangerous. I'm not as young as I used to be and you're . . ." She tactfully fails to finish. "To tell the truth, I'm getting a little worried about your big ideas, Ma," she adds, "first coming here, and now——"

"I know the danger."

My daughter's face fills with frustration. "Okay, but——"

"I didn't know the danger back then, of course. The first time

I went. But if I'd let that stop me, then there wouldn't be a story now, would there? And if other people let it stop *them*, then there might not be any stories at all. In the world."

One of Susanna's chopsticks has fallen into the soup, but she doesn't seem to care. She is clutching its mate, looking pained. She has already broken her usual protocol by bringing me here. By ambushing me with those photos.

Will she break it a little more? How desperate is she, to solve this?

And *why* is she so desperate?

There is something Susanna is not telling me, but then there is so much I have never told her. The restaurant has filled up around us; other would-be diners have planted themselves near our table, nearly peering over our shoulders, wanting to take our places. This never happens in Seattle and it is suffocating. But it also forces my daughter to make a choice. She can't sit here and stall. She can't wait for the morning to make everything clear.

"The house could have been renovated," she says morosely. "It would explain the Canadians' photographs, I mean. If the original structure was razed at some point, and a new one rebuilt . . ."

I slide the contents of my plate onto hers, because she is never going to get enough food otherwise.

I understand why she thinks the original structure would have to be razed for the new one to be rebuilt. I know why she finds it hard to fathom that older layers can withstand the weight of the new. It is my own fault; I thought I was doing right by never showing my daughter all of *my* layers.

But I was not born the same day she was. My life did not start when hers did.

Maybe it is time for her to realize that. Maybe it is long overdue.

Maybe she is the one who has been sending me a message, all this time, and I am the one taking too long to answer.

Mom I'm scared that I

"This is . . . completely . . . I'm going to regret this, but okay. Fine," says Susanna. "Let's go. Let's see it."

NIGHTTIME IN THIS city never feels like the end of the day. The streets are busy and rowdy, people pouring out of their workplaces to blow off steam between Lan Kwai Fong and the Admiralty, their chatter echoing through the low-lit lanes all the way up to the Mid-Levels. The Peak Tram is still running, and Susanna trudges on toward the Terminus. At my insistence, she has just written back to Liana, for whom it is early morning. It seems that Liana did not sleep all night.

Susanna looks now as though she is trying to fold herself in half: Her back is arched, her head down, her hands tucked into her armpits.

She stops beneath the spray of lights at the entrance, waiting for me.

"We will walk," I declare, and Susanna's head jerks up.

"Up the *Peak*?" She sounds scandalized. "It's already nine! And we just flew in today! Aren't you jet-lagged? Don't you want to get back to the hotel, get some sleep? Because unless you plan to spend the night amidst the ruins of a death house—"

"This trip was your idea," I say. Waiting tram passengers split into smaller groups, like fish around rocks, trying to move past us, but I do not draw my daughter aside. I see her eyes flicker, almost in panic, toward the ticket office. People who are stuck in one place always think waiting in a line will be their salvation. "Coming to Hong Kong. Searching out death houses."

"Yes, maybe, but not like this!"

"Like what, then? What if we do have to spend the night? Isn't that the sort of thing you and Dean used to do all the time? You investigated a shipwreck off New England, you slept in a submarine. You looked into that string of deaths at that country manor in Scotland, you slept in a barn. Who is this Susanna who wants to go back to the hotel at nine p.m. and go to sleep? The Susanna whose eyes are already closed, that's who. The Susanna who fears to open them!"

"Yes, Dean and I, and that's exactly it!" Susanna bursts out, loud enough to get the attention of a few stray passersby. "You're not him, Ma! Okay? That's the problem. You're not him. *He* should be here with me, not you! This story, Maidenhair House, it was what *he* wanted to solve, and now he's dead! My husband is dead!"

People are watching us openly now. The old Susanna, the normal Susanna, would have been utterly humiliated by such a public display of feeling. The old Susanna never melted down. Rarely even raised her voice. Part of me wants to surrender, just so she will stop shouting. Part of me wants to say, let's just take the tram. Or go back to the hotel. Or go back all the way across the sea; all the way to your home. To your own death house.

But I think she needs to shout even louder.

I think she needs to split open.

"What do you mean? Why did Dean want to solve it?" I ask. Suddenly, I want to pose so many questions that the answers will have to go off like fireworks. "How did all of this start? It is an unusual case, even for an investigative journalist like him, is it not? Even for a writer like you? And why should you have to solve it just because he didn't? You two always accompanied each other on fieldwork, I know. But your projects did not overlap. Are you trying to honor his memory, by doing this?"

"We should have told you," she says, breathing slower.

"Told me what?"

Susanna's anger is dissipating in the humid night air. I am almost sorry to see it go. "We received an anonymous letter," she says. "About Maidenhair."

I AM THINKING of all the other letters of my life, but Susanna is still talking.

"It felt like nonsense, at the time. I told Dean to forget about it and he said he would. But then . . . I discovered, going through his stuff at the house, very recently . . . that he'd been looking into it. By himself. Frantically. Fanatically. You know how he got with these things sometimes. He'd already done a whole heap of background and he was . . ." She presses her lips together until they turn white. "It's just such a strange coincidence, isn't it? That there was that letter, and then he died? Almost like . . . almost like they're related . . ."

"Susanna," I say to her, "no letter had anything to do with Dean's death. You know that."

"I know," she says, but her voice is hollow.

There is no doubt in my mind now that this is still her grief, in a new shape, locked around her.

"What exactly did this anonymous letter say?" I probe. "About Maidenhair?"

Susanna hesitates again, and then: "That the Maidenhair Murders were real. That those women died there that night, and there was *another* young woman, one who lived, one who is never mentioned in the urban legend, in any of the stories, and this one woman was you, but there's more. The letter said that you killed them, Mama. That you killed them all."

PART TWO

7

HONG KONG
SEPTEMBER 1953

ON FRIDAY MORNING the Hong Kong Conservatory raises a storm warning, but not yet high enough to shut down the Star Ferry. Mei peers out her bedroom window: The day does look likely to tip into a typhoon. Rippling gray clouds and that shivery quality to the air. It would be understandable, in these conditions, if Mei failed to show up; Holly Zhang could hardly hold it against her.

And yet, almost mechanically, Mei ducks back inside and begins to pack a rattan basket with everything she thinks she might need, clothes, paper, pencils, charcoal. She double-checks that her white peony hairpin, which features the same design as her signature cutting, is secure in her twisted bun. Holly Zhang did not offer suggestions on what to bring, but Holly did say that she would send a car to fetch Mei from the ferry landing in Central. Mei should not be made to take the Peak Tram, because ethnic Chinese are compelled to sit in the least desirable section, where golden orb spiders drop from the trees directly into your hair.

There was something magical in this detail, something that almost, but not quite, made Mei want to ask Holly not to send a car at all.

Overhead, the cloth-covered ceiling fan plunk, plunk, plunks. Mrs. Volkova will not come out from her office. Is Mei truly capable of murder? Even if she is, is she capable of murdering George Maidenhair? She looks over the rest of her materials. She hesitates. She feels herself tipping into a typhoon. She packs a cutting knife.

AN ELDERLY MAN limps into the curio shop just as Mei is about to leave: It is Mr. Sim, the owner of the traditional medicinal shop at the end of the road. Mei rarely visits his establishment, abhorring its cold, smoky insides, with its barrels of crab and lobster limbs; dried reptiles stuffed in tea baskets; jars of pickled shark fin; bamboo bowls filled to the brim with dusty insect exoskeletons. Herbal remedies for every condition a person could conceive of having.

Mr. Sim, for his part, is a kempt man in his seventies who acts like he would happily stuff and seal Mei in one of his shark-fin jars if he could. He does not like mainlanders and he does not make a secret of it.

He is carrying a box, the kind you might use for shoes.

"Is *that* what you will wear to the Hong Kong side?" he asks. "Have you not seen the weather reports, *siu jeh*? Do you wish to die of the winds skinning you alive?"

Wincing, Mei looks down at her white belted dress and back up again. "Can I help you, Uncle?"

"I brought something for you," he says, with a grunt, and places the box on the counter between them. But instead of opening it, he launches into another tirade: "When I'd heard you'd be away for a week, I couldn't believe it! You? You never go anywhere! And now you're going where they weren't even allowing Chinese when I was your age! Well, I'll keep an extra eye on the shop while you're gone. Not that it needs it. Nobody would ever steal from a place with such a bad-luck reputation. You know what else I heard? That you are the guest of the actress Holly Zhang! You are going to stay at the old Hall House! I imagine that woman has got glued wires in her head something awful, by the way. Fame, it is very bad for the bloodstream."

Mei imagines Mr. Sim concocting little bird's nests of ingredients to help alleviate your fame.

"What have you brought?" she says, biting the inside of her mouth, so that she keeps sounding friendly.

He leans forward so that their foreheads nearly touch. His breath is musty, dense with his own mixtures.

"A gift for you," he says, lifting the lid.

Inside the box is a book.

It has been placed in a bed of leaves and seeds and spices; almost tenderly. The title is in English. Mei was once fluent in English, which of course Mr. Sim knows, being Mr. Sim. For some reason she does not have word-blindness in English. Only in her native language. It is a phenomenon that she has never understood.

"*The Peak House*," she reads aloud.

"It's a novel," says Mr. Sim with authority, "inspired by the Hall House. I thought you should know what you are getting into."

Mei flicks to the first page; her eyes find the first line.

The house was silent, but silence is not the same thing as peace.

"How did you get this?" she asks.

Mr. Sim goes the flat red shade of someone running a fever. "Well," he says, sniffing a little, "the author himself came into my shop a few weeks ago. He said he was collecting folktales of this area for a new project, and he'd heard that I was as much a proprietor of such tales as I am of traditional medicines! Word had gotten round. I spoke with him at great length, and to express his thanks, he left me a copy of this book, but alas, I cannot read English. I give it to you now. For good. You read it, and when you come home, you tell me everything it says. Yes? *Āiyā*, no gratitude?"

"Thank you, Uncle," says Mei, and if she sounds dubious, she can't help it.

He shuffles away, down the shelves, though they both know he won't by anything. Mei glances at the cover again; the author has a foreign name. A foreigner collecting Chinese folktales sounds like another folktale. Still, she wonders at how the writer might have turned stories of the old Hall House into one story. It makes her think of the golden orb spiders, falling down your shoulders, spinning your hair into silk.

ALONG SALISBURY ROAD, on the way to the wharves, Mei passes street hawkers, bicyclists, rickshaw drivers, mothers with babies strapped to their backs, amahs in black collared shirts and black slacks, coolies swinging their bamboo poles and chicken cages. An elderly woman in a pelt-coat, moving on toothpick-feet. Beggars, stricken by leprosy. Mainland refugees, as recognizable as if they were wearing placards to advertise it, pushing along their loaded trolleys. At the harbor the Star Ferry is arriving in a frenzy of steam whistles, water bellowing through the gaps between the wooden planks, and above it all, across the water, looms Victoria Peak, the rolling green of its trees muted by fog.

The Peak House sits like an anchor in her basket. She already half regrets bringing it along. It is, strangely, the first book Mei has ever owned; all the other books of her life have been borrowed.

Oh, but there was once that she dreamed of having an enormous, extravagant library of books—

A library just like George Maidenhair's.

Her fingers curl around the handles of the basket, and she takes her first step off solid ground.

HOLLY ZHANG'S DRIVER is a surly man dressed from head to toe in khaki. He is smoking a short pipe, a face burner, the kind that makes your chest tingle just to see it. Mei has ridden in countless trams and buses, and occasionally in the rickshaws that scuttle around Hong Kong like ticks, but it has been years since she was in the backseat of a car, and his is unusually small. Even with windows, it feels too cramped. She cradles her basket hard in her arms as the chauffeur swerves his vehicle past important-looking buildings pockmarked with war wounds, speeding away from the larger streets, past the open-air trolleys jingling by on metal tracks, through neighborhoods Mei cannot name, and finally up the mountain.

The streets turn steeper. The chauffeur puffs on his pipe. He remarks that the roads of the Peak weren't made for automobiles, but for sedan chairs; that's why they're so narrow. Along one grisly ridge Mei is treated to a panorama of the city and the harbor below: The buildings look like toy models, the bay a slash of blue. The hills of Kowloon rise blackly in the distance.

Kowloon, *gau lung*, meaning nine dragons.

They are all breathing out today, to judge by the clouds over the water.

"You won't have seen a house like Hall House, missy," he says.

So even Holly's servants do not call it Maidenhair. Mei might laugh but she is close to choking, the air hotter and wetter with every inch the car crawls up the Peak. By now she can smell the impending storm even stronger than the pipe smoke. Her dress is soaked under the sleeves. She wants to wipe her face on the furred leaves of the rubber trees along the road; she wants to take a breath that doesn't feel like she's drinking it; she wants this week to be over; she wants to be on the other side of it. There was once that she swore to herself she would have vengeance. She *vowed* to have vengeance. But Mei has made enough vows in her young life to know that a vow is not quite the same as a promise: A promise is what you make when you have all the power. A vow is something you make to feel a little bit powerful, when you are powerless.

THE JUNGLE IS closing in like walls, tree branches clasping overhead, forming tunnels.

Mei presses her face to the car window, which steams.

The form of a house is coming into view.

At first glance it resembles any other British colonial structure: whitewashed, unremarkable but imposing, with tall pillars and blank façades. But to the sides of the main body of the house are two small wings, and these have been built in a radically different style: They are made from a menacing dark stone, with sharply cut arches and high-pitched pointed roofs, stuck on like rice paddy hats. Traditional Chinese-style lanterns hang from the eaves, snapping in the breeze.

It is as if somebody has sliced a temple in half and placed a government building in between; such is the contrast.

In one of the upper-story windows, a curtain flutters; a face shifts into view.

Mei shrinks back into her seat.

"Don't look up at the windows," advises the driver, and her heart thuds.

The car pulls to a stop. The driver turns around in his seat, his scrawny cheeks still puffing away, even though he's pulled out his pipe. He looks resigned. "Look here, missy," he says, "I could drive you back down. If you want. Just say so."

"I don't understand," says Mei. Her throat is so tight that the words come out like coughs. "Don't you work for Holly Zhang?"

"Work for—*no*," he says. "I don't."

"Why do you say it like that?"

The man that Mei now, horribly, understands to be a taxi driver and not a personal chauffeur, smacks his lips in a laugh. "Not a local, I see. Well, welcome to Hall House. Or what are they calling it now? Maidenhair? This here is the most haunted place on Hong Kong Island. But I reckon you'll discover that for yourself, soon enough."

HOLLY ZHANG GREETS Mei at the door, opening it before Mei even has a chance to knock.

Mei might have had difficulty prying her hands off her rattan basket in any case. With the driver's warning a whisper in her head, she follows her hostess through a small vestibule that swells into a palatial entrance hall. The atmosphere is gloomy and hushed except for the *tick-tack-tick* of Holly's high-heeled shoes on the naked teakwood floors, but Mei notices little about her surroundings except for the large, shadowy double staircase in the center of the hall, the upper landing washed in complete darkness.

"First you must settle in, of course," says Holly, as they begin to ascend the stairs. *Tick-tack.* "A meal will be served at seven o'clock in the Dining Hall. At that time I shall be pleased to explain further the purpose of my competition, and our week together." *Tick-tack.*

Holly stops, as if to check that Mei is following.

Tick-tack-tick-tack-tick-tack.

Mei snaps her head around, but there is nobody coming up the stairs behind them.

It was just an echo. Or perhaps it is her pulse. But she must not let her foreboding show. She hurries closer to Holly, and they are on their way again; Mei resists the temptation to take the stairs two at a time. Nonetheless, she is breathing fast by the time they reach the landing.

"After dinner, we will assemble in the Red Library," says Holly, "where the First Séance will be held."

Here the floor is thickly carpeted, and every step goes deeper than it should. Every step feels like drowning.

The hallway ahead is lit by pale orbs of electric light. Mei fixes her gaze upon them.

"Maidenhair is divided into three parts," continues Holly. "All of you will be staying here, in the central part of the house. You are not to venture into the North and South Wings alone." A full-throated laugh. "The layout of this house is so confusing, my husband believes it was designed that way on purpose."

"Will Mr. Maidenhair be joining us for dinner?" Mei asks, hating the suddenly hoarse quality of her voice, a door being forced off its hinges. "You did say so much about him, Auntie," she continues, in this new, hoarse, worse voice. "At the curio shop."

"George is presently away. Traveling."

An inner voice from the dark dragon pit inside of Mei says: *Perhaps it's better this way.*

George Maidenhair never even has to know you were here.

Nothing has to change.

Now you can just go home.

But where is home?

Is it Shanghai, the city that turned Red behind her?

Is it Kowloon, the beach that turned red behind her?

Mei realizes, with dismay, almost with horror, that she has come here because she *needs* something to change. The life she currently leads is no life at all: It is the in-between place. It is purgatory. She has come here to be liberated, to be able to breathe again, and she remembers too well the war of her childhood; she knows too well that you can only be liberated by blood. There is no other way. Holly says that George will be home in time to meet the winner. *Tick-tack.* George likes winners.

8

SHANGHAI
AUGUST 1937

WHEN I WAKE up, it is daytime and we are next to a tall bamboo fence. The air smells like ripe fruit in a bad way. The large man shrugs me off his shoulder; First Wife steps forward and takes my hand. My legs are wobbling. I am being held up by her dragon-nails. The large man opens the fence and we enter a cobbly court-yard, a lot like the one that Nai Nai sweeps every day, but much cleaner.

Past this courtyard is a red rectangle house, with square win-dows and a yellow roof.

The door opens and my heart lifts—maybe it's Ba, maybe he took another train here, maybe he's been waiting for me this whole time! But it's not Ba; it's a lady with bug-bitten red lips and big fawn eyes. She wears jewelry everywhere, around her wrists, her neck, dangling from her ears. I don't understand the language she is speaking. Have we left China? Is this the moon? Can you take a train to the moon? Where is Ba? *When can I go home?*

~~~~

FIRST WIFE SAYS to the lady in the doorway: "My new foster daughter speaks no Shanghainese, Third Wife. Little Mei scarcely speaks Mandarin as it is. Her education is sorely lacking."

"Little Mei?" says Third Wife, wrinkling her nose.

"His choice, not mine," mutters First Wife, wrinkling her words.

I begin to cry.

First Wife releases my hand and I crumple, but Third Wife quickly gathers me up and pulls me through the door. First Wife says she must rest from the journey and asks Third Wife where the housekeeper is. Third Wife says the housekeeper is busy with the babies, as the nanny has run off today to join her family in Nanking, because everyone is running off right now. In her qipao, First Wife can only take shuffling steps, smaller than Nai Nai's, but she is still able to walk away, and suddenly I am alone with the one called Third Wife, who is even more of a stranger than First Wife, because at least First Wife I had seen once before today, and so I cry harder. Third Wife offers me a rock caramel candy if I'll just be quiet, but I can't, I *can't*. No candy can make up for the candy I lost at the train station, and anyway the air is already so sugary in this house that it would only make my teeth hurt.

"Turning down candy?" Third Wife says knowingly. "But it's alright. You must be tired. Perhaps it would be better for you to meet everyone else tomorrow."

"Everyone?" I bleat. "There's nobody here but us!"

"To the contrary, *xiǎo bǎo*! Besides First Wife and me, there is also Second Wife, though you'll have to meet her a few times before she'll remember you. And let us not forget the children—my own two little ones, and Second Wife's daughter, Aiyi—as well as the servants, at least the ones who haven't abandoned us. Oh, but you are a lucky, lucky thing, because all this . . ." Third Wife sweeps her arm wide. "This is *your* home now! You can go anywhere you wish in it." She pauses. "Except the attic."

"Why not the attic?" I ask, curious but still crying.

"Oh, the wood is rotting. But at your age, I imagine you'll have better fun exploring outside anyway. So long as you don't go near the well in the back."

"Why? Is it rotting too?"

"Second Wife's other daughter drowned in it many years ago. Trust me, if First Wife catches you near it, she'll cane you raw."

I sniffle, but I'm not afraid. Nai Nai often makes similar threats, and she never acts on them. Besides, if I wanted to soft-shoe out to the courtyard and sneak a look into the well, First Wife would never catch me. I can be *very* quiet. I have always been the best of my sisters at hunting frogs—

Relief pours over me like hot bean soup.

It is so obvious what I must do: I will *run away*!

All the way back home! They have no way to keep me in this house, do they, now that the big man who carried me on the train has gone? Look at how First Wife moves around, slower with a bound-body than she would be on bound feet! And Third Wife is probably the type of person who is easily carried off by the wind, or else she wouldn't need to wear so much jewelry.

Uncle can't chase people. He would trip over his own sleeves.

"Are you hungry?" asks Third Wife. "There is pickled melon skin left over from lunch. . . ."

I will run away first thing tomorrow.

As I drag myself down the hall behind Third Wife, I make new vows to myself: I will never again be fooled by uncles with scroll-sleeves and false-porcelain horses, and I will use my newfound experience riding trains to help catch the bandits who might've made off with Ma. I give a small hopeful prayer to the ancestors that nothing bad happens just because I broke my nonspeaking vow. I *could* try to stop speaking again, but it would be much harder. Now that I have used my voice, it's like a pet cricket that doesn't want to go back in its cage.

FIRST WIFE'S BIG bedroom is divided in two by a tall golden screen with dark edges and swans at the bottom. Her bed is on one side of the screen. My bed is on this side. I have never had my own bed before. First Wife comes over, sits down on the end of it, and stares woodenly at me. She looks different at night. She has wiped the powder off her face, but that's not all; maybe that qipao was the only thing holding her together and now that she's in a long, shaggy nightgown, she is coming apart.

I stretch out on the sheets like a starfish.

"Do you like it here, Little Mei?" asks First Wife stiffly.

"Your house is nice, First Wife. But—"

"You will call me Mother. All the children in this household do."

Mother?

I'm never, ever, ever going to call anyone Mother except Ma! But I don't want to upset First Wife right now by saying that. I'll call her nothing instead, and I doubt she'll notice. "I think I should go home tomorrow," I say, louder now. "I am worried about my sisters. They must be getting bored without me. I am much better at knucklebones than them. You have to have fast hands for knucklebones, because you have to turn over as many—"

"I know this game," says First Wife, with a sigh.

"Oh, great! We can play against each other tomorrow when we take the train back!"

Another long sigh.

She probably has to breathe extra hard at night, while the qipao is off.

"Listen to me," says First Wife, and my heart sinks. *Listen to me* is what grown-ups say when they're not listening to *you*. "Your family in Jiangsu is—occupied, and you are now a citizen of Shanghai. Isn't that exciting? Shanghai is—" She stops for some reason. She makes a swallowing sound. She must have gotten too excited herself. She starts again: "Shanghai is a city where dreams come true. That is what my own parents told me, long ago, and you must have dreams. All children do."

I dream of getting my Ma back.

I dream of having a bicycle to ride away on, to make running away easier.

"You will have a much better life now that you are here," she continues, "and you will bring luck to my life, in return. Everyone knows that fostering a child is the surest path to pregnancy, but I have certainty even beyond that. The fortune teller has seen it." First Wife picks at the bedspread. "She has told me that after you, because of you, I would bear a son. The only male child in this house."

What is she talking about?

And doesn't she know what the fortune teller told Nai Nai's parents?

Has she *seen* Nai Nai's feet?

"Life?" I say, in case I've got it wrong. "You mean that you want to keep me . . . forever?" Life? *Life?* Until I am *dead*? Lives are so long! Nai Nai is as old as a dragon! First Wife gives another gluey sigh, and that's it. That's *it*. I will have to start running away from this house as soon as she turns her back. As soon as this room goes dark. As soon as my heart stops beating so hard. There is no time to waste.

⌒

THE NIGHT AIR feels warm and fatty, but it is still easier to breathe outside than inside the house. I am back in my scruffy dress, the one that I arrived here in; I am back in my broken-sole shoes; I am back in my two braids, although I'm not very good at braiding myself. I smell like train tracks and Big Sister will make fun of me for it when I get home, but I won't even mind, in fact I will hug her for hours, even if she is bony and pokey and painful.

And speaking of smells, what *was* that sweet smell inside Uncle's house?

It reminds me of the one time after the plum rains when Ma put a blanket out under the cherry blossom trees and shook out the tree branches until the blossoms fell to the blanket. Before Ma could gather them up for cooking, I stuck my head into the pile and sucked the scent right up my nose. I couldn't smell anything else for days. Everything I ate tasted like paper.

I stop at the bamboo fence for one last look around, and up.

The sky has so few stars.

Where did they all go?

What *is* this place?

Somebody grabs my shoulder.

"Hey!" I yell. "Let me go!"

It's First Wife. Her physical weakness was only pretend! She is *very* strong!

Now she has me by the hand but she's not holding it, she's bending it further and further backward and it hurts so much I almost wish she'd go ahead and break it, and she's pulling me back into the house. Not just in the house. *Up* the house.

Up all the stairs, round and round and round.

As she yanks me along, she snaps that she's taking me to the *attic*.

The one that Third Wife said was *rotting*.

She drags me up more stairs, darker, twisty stairs, until finally we have reached a wooden, unpainted room with nothing in it but an enormous ugly wardrobe. There are windows cut into the ceiling but they're too high to climb out of. Is this what an *attic* is? An ancestral hall, only smaller? An ancestral hall, only *darker*? First Wife can't leave me on my own, can she? She wouldn't abandon me here, would she? I start to scream and I cling to her, still screaming, but she kicks me down to the floor.

My head spins and my screams sound far away.

She is not like Nai Nai after all.

Some adults will hurt you.

She is leaving. She is locking the door behind her.

I know what being locked in sounds like.

Let me out, please, let me out, I try to say, but I am still screaming too hard.

Her footsteps fade.

Everything will be okay as long as I don't look. Yes. I just won't look. *Looking* is what happened last time I was locked up. *Looking* was my first mistake. I close my mouth and my eyes too. Funnily enough, I am not crying. I've noticed that my tears fall easier when people are watching, but when I'm by myself, they often just sit and soak in me. They become part of me.

I think this is what the word *rotting* means.

I hug myself tight, still closed up everywhere, until I feel something pinch in the pocket of my dress.

There's something *in* it.

The last time this happened, it was a bamboo rat that my sisters had caught by the creek, and it bit into my finger so hard I thought I'd never get it off.

I dare to look a little, but only down.

A pouch?

Ma's pouch!

Big Sister must have planted it in this pocket before I left with Ba, without my even realizing!

I guess the bamboo rat was good practice.

Oh, and if I hadn't tried to run away, if I hadn't put this dress back on, First Wife would have thrown it out with this piece of Ma still inside! Oh, thank the ancestors! I draw the pouch from my pocket and try to open the tied string but it won't come undone, and so I roll up the pouch like a scroll instead and then the string just slides off.

I reach in and pull out a folded-up square of paper.

I unfold it so fast it almost squirts away.

It is a painting. Ma was often painting, of course.

It is *what* she has painted that makes my chest feel sticky.

The picture is of *this* attic, with the same large wardrobe, from the very spot I am sitting in right now. But if Ma is Uncle's little sister, then I guess she used to live in this house, so that isn't the problem.

The problem is—

I look at the wardrobe in front of me, and then I look back at Ma's painting, and then back at the wardrobe, and then again at the painting.

I can't tell if my mouth is still closed or if I am screaming again.

Ma has painted a white hand coming out of the wardrobe.

9

HONG KONG
SEPTEMBER 1953

MEI HAS WAITED what feels like an eternity for dinner, but maybe what she has really been waiting for, since the moment she first opened Holly's invitation, is an explanation.

There are six spirit mediums indeed, or at least six strangers in Holly's Dining Hall, plus Holly herself.

Did Holly get the guests she wanted?

Is she going to tell them why they must do *six* séances? Will they be asked to contact six different spirits? Will they all attempt it at once?

Or will it be one person doing one séance, every night, while the others watch?

THE DÉCOR OF Holly Zhang's Dining Hall is obscenely grand, a blur of gold leaf and marble and mirrored walls. Mei shields her eyes from the mirrors. She realizes, with a flush of self-consciousness, that she is underdressed for this meal; the others are wearing enough layers to preserve a corpse. Holly Zhang, at the head of the table, has stepped straight out of the era of her own films, all palm fronds and slim cigarettes, her lips leaky red, her teeth a blinding baking-soda white, her wig garishly dark, a dress hanging off her shoulders without any shape, curtains off a rod.

Servants begin to scurry past, carrying platters of goodies: Pan-fried pork pastries, curled like fists. Black sesame balls. Inside-out coconut buns. Washed-yellow egg tarts, the crusts already crumbling.

Mei nibbles at a pastry served in paper that is higher quality than most of her painting paper. She has to scoop out every bite with a spoon the size of a thrush egg. When Holly asks if the food is to her liking, Mei plasters on a smile, wide enough that it throbs.

Holly has not said anything yet about what they are really doing here, and the more Mei eats, the more it pushes her questions to the tip of her tongue.

TO MEI'S LEFT sits a young woman who undeniably looks the part of a professional spirit medium, her face painted opera white, her eyes so smoked with kohl she can hardly open them all the way. She goes by Mistress Lau and says that she will not answer to anything else; that she is originally from Guangzhou; that she needs money to bring her family to join her in Hong Kong; and that she expects to win. Directly across from Mistress Lau sits Peng, a girl with nondescript features who goes ruddy red every time she is addressed by the young man beside her.

This young man wears a well-cut western-style suit, and Mei cannot quite tell if he is Chinese or white. His hair is a few shades shy of black, and his eyes are a strange, sooty blue. He has not given any name, at least not to her.

Seated to his left, and to Mei's right, respectively, are identical female twins, Delia and Cecelia. They appear younger than Mei's twenty-three years by half a decade if not more, and they speak mostly to each other, in a language that might be their own.

Tell us about the competition, Mei wants to shriek at Holly by now, but instead she chews and swallows and sips.

The trays of treats continue to arrive. The methylated spirit lamps make shadows on the table linens.

To Mei, this beautiful food is overcooked; the drinks go down dry. All she can taste strongly is her own unease. So far she has seen scant evidence that this is the most haunted house in Hong Kong, but in a way, that only makes it worse. There are ghosts like Hungry Ghosts, who have long lost their memories, little left of them but their own immense mouths, or Wrongful-Death Ghosts, murder victims, desperate for justice; ghosts that do not try to hide their presence.

And then there are the others.

The ones that are nowhere to be found; until you turn around.

The young man has been staring at Mei long enough that she feels like one of her own paper-cut puppets, stuck on sticks.

"My name is Jamie," he says at last, in Cantonese, in the accent of somebody who has studied it too hard. "James Nakamura, but friends call me Jamie. And you are?"

Mei recoils at the sound of his family name. So he is Japanese, or of Japanese descent. Nonetheless, she is about to answer, but then she realizes: There is something about him, his well-tailored expression, to go with his well-tailored clothes, that is *familiar.*

How? Why?

Could he have been an Important Customer, from Mei's days and nights in Mong Kok? Did he ever give her that same smile, as starched as card stock, far down the mountain, as far down as Mei has ever been?

"Do you not speak?" he asks.

"My name is Chen Mei," she answers, in Mandarin, without meaning to, but she is rattled.

There is a stilted pause.

"Your accent. You are from Shanghai," he says, matching her Mandarin.

As is he. Mei hears the telltale notes in his voice; the way he might even slip into Shanghainese if she asked nicely. Perhaps he, like Holly, was once in one of her crowds, though she can't decide whether this would be better or worse than his being one of her Important Customers. Normal Customers just wanted a good time with a Chinese girl in a qipao with an eyelash-slit up the leg; they liked shy glances and sweet smiles and demure tones. Important Customers, on the other hand, did not buy. They *commissioned*. They were looking for things that did not quite exist. Their desires were not flesh-and-blood; any kind of touch, any reminder of physical reality, would ruin it.

They often liked watching her let down her hair. Fifty years ago, they might have liked watching her unbind her feet.

Jamie Nakamura would have been Important, she is sure of it. He has that self-assured, assertive aura, that faraway look in his eye.

"When did you leave Shanghai, then?" he asks.

"Right before it fell to the Reds," she says tersely. "And you, Mr.—"

"Please, just call me Jamie."

Again, silence.

"But if Mr. Nakamura is what you prefer," he adds, his voice level.

Mrs. Volkova scoffs at Mei's antipathy toward the Japanese, but then, Mrs. Volkova's husband and family were killed by their own people. Their own government. There is something different about being killed by your own people; not better, just different. For one, it is harder to know whom to blame. Harder to picture the face of your enemy. Mei could fill all these silences between her and James Nakamura easily, if she wanted: She could tell him she was not always a refugee. She was not always alone. She was not even always Shanghainese; her name was not even always Mei. She was another person once, with a home and a history, a mother and father and sisters. She used to put on shadow puppet shows for them, with puppets made by her mother, drawn in even more detail than people have in real life.

Have you ever seen puppets cut from their strings, *Jamie?*

Have you ever seen the way they fall?

"YOUR ATTENTION PLEASE," says Holly, rising from her chair, and all heads turn to her.

Mei feels everything she has just eaten turning over in her stomach.

"I am honored to have the six of you in my home," says Holly. "I know you are all wondering why I have asked you to gather here, and now you will have your answer."

A servant enters, and then leaves, just as abruptly, before Holly goes on.

"I'm sure some of you, if not all, have heard the stories about this place, dating back from its construction. I am fond of such stories, I must admit. They were part of the appeal, when my husband and I were searching for a residence here in Hong Kong. Who doesn't want to live in a haunted house?" asks Holly, with a bell-like tinkle of laughter. "Or so I thought."

Even when Holly stops laughing, Mei can still hear the sound of it, bouncing around the Dining Hall.

Ha-ha-ha-ha-ha.

Tick-tack-tick-tack.

She is not the only one. They are all hearing it. Glances are being exchanged.

Mei grinds her teeth to keep her nausea down.

"I have seen things in six different locations in or around this house," says Holly. "These are where the six séances will be held."

"Things?" ventures one of the twins, Delia or Cecelia, Mei has no idea.

"I have witnessed what I believe to be paranormal activity," Holly says, slightly testy now, "in six different locations. I have been told by multiple people that what I have seen is all simply the product of my own . . . shall we say . . . overactive imagination. A house like this can play tricks on your head. Even my husband, bless him, does not believe that any of it is real. Perhaps he is right, but either way, the six of you, over the course of these six nights, will find out."

"How?" pipes up the other twin.

Annoyed, Mei tells herself that they are too young to know better. To keep silent until Holly is done talking.

But perhaps she simply envies them.

They are not afraid.

"We will visit each location as a group," says Holly, "and you will take turns, one after another, to try to speak to whatever . . . entity . . . exists in each location. Ideally, at least one of you will be successful in making contact, and in discovering what these ghosts want. How I can appease them, so that they stop . . . *showing* themselves to me." Her voice loses a degree of confidence, but she recovers: "I am hoping that it will soon become evident to me which of you is the most powerful, because the sixth location . . . is haunted by . . . an entity I do not think it is possible to speak to, as such, or to reason with. This entity must simply be banished. I cannot live in this house alongside it."

AS SOON AS Holly has left to prepare the Red Library for the First Séance, the talk at the table turns immediately to the notorious history of the house.

It was built by a Lord Timothy Hall, explains Mistress Lau, in the year 1889. His wife hanged herself in it a few years later, but that was only the beginning. There was a dinner party at the turn of the century, hosted by the original Lord Hall's son, which ended with the discovery, the following morning, by a local deliveryman, of the mangled dead bodies of all the invitees as well as the host. There was the episode ten years ago, during the war: With the Halls interned at Stanley Camp, Japanese gendarmes, *Kempeitai*, occupied the house, intending to use it as a site for the planned mass executions of Chinese prisoners. Before they had the chance, however, they turned on one another. They were found in the Great Hall; the stair railings were burnished with blood.

This house seeps into your head like wastewater, says Mistress Lau. You will see things.

We will all see things.

The mood in the Dining Hall has changed; everyone's voices are creeping quiet.

"Look!" shouts one of the twins, pointing somewhere behind Mei, and Mei twists around by instinct, looking to see, like everyone else, remembering too late that the walls of this dining hall are marked with mirrors.

It was just a joke; to break the rising tension. The one twin begins laughing and the other one does too and their reflections do too.

Mei's reflection is also laughing.

Mei lifts a hand to her lips, which are sealed shut.

10

SHANGHAI
AUGUST 1937

I THROW THE painting, and the pouch, across the attic, straight at the wardrobe, and I put my hands over my face because it's too much, it's just too much, because here I am, kidnapped by *kidnappers*, brought to a house that stinks like it was cooked in sweet potato soup, so thirsty that I would drink from a fishpond, so hungry I will start gnawing my own elbows soon, locked in an attic that is not so different from an ancestral hall except emptier, or maybe it's not empty at all, because maybe there's somebody hiding in the wardrobe, maybe that's what that hand in the painting is, and it is too much, it is just all *too*—

Something rustles behind me.

First Wife?

Oh please, oh please, I won't run away tonight, just let me out of here—

I peek through my fingers, with more sobs ready to go.

It is not First Wife.

It is not anybody I have met in the house so far.

Standing by the hole in the floor where the stairs go down is a girl with hair piled on top of her head, and there is a long pearly stick stuck through the hair, like an axe in wood. She moves toward me gracefully, more like gliding, on feet even smaller than Nai Nai's, wrapped in bandages. She has the gray skin of a river dolphin. Ma would say this is because of bad liver-blood in the body. I hope it is just the bad light, as there is only a small spoonful of moonlight on the floor and none of it is anywhere near her.

She looks at me and raises her hand, with the thumb curled in.

It's bad luck to hold up four fingers like that, because the word *four* sounds like the word for *dead*, but I don't dare to say this. Her lips are moving, mouthing something, her cheeks huffing in and out, and then she takes her four-finger hand and brings it to her body, pressing it against her heart, as if pointing.

I think she's trying to tell me her name.

Four?

Wait a minute.

Fourth Wife?

I can't remember how many wives Third Wife said there were. This girl really doesn't look old enough to be married to Uncle, but Ma always did say that it's the sun that steams people like bread buns. Maybe spending time in an attic slows your aging. Why is she still mouthing stuff at me? Doesn't she talk out loud? Did her Ma go missing too? Did she make her own vow? The girl gives me a smile—no, she is not smiling. She is just opening her mouth as far as it will go.

She has only half a tongue! Not even half!

"Did you chew it off in your sleep?" I blurt out.

The girl holds up one finger now and moves it across her mouth slowly and I understand, even though I really wish I didn't understand, that somebody cut off her tongue. She notices Ma's painting on the floor, and before I can stop her, she is bending over, a really strange kind of bending, like her back can't curve, and she picks it up.

Then she looks up at me.

There is something coming out the corner of her eyes. I can't tell what it is.

"My Ma painted that," I say, trying to sound braver than I feel. "It's got her pretty peony flower signature in the corner, do you see it?"

I'm not sure she sees. She is still staring at me.

"Do you see that . . . that hand coming out of there?" I point to the painting, and then to the wardrobe against the wall. "I don't know why she would draw that. Do *you* know?"

The girl nods.

First Wife should have been more careful, dragging me up here, because my hands, my knees, my heart are full of splinters, and now I can sense every single one of them.

"Wait. My Ma used to live in this house. Did you . . . *know* her?" My mouth feels crinkly.

Nod, nod.

"But it's been a long time since you saw her, huh?"

She shakes her head.

"What? Have you seen her recently?"

A new nod.

"This year?"

Another.

"Did you see her . . . *this summer?*"

More nods, even bigger ones.

"You mean . . . she was here? After the Dragon Boat Festival? After the planting season?"

A few blinks this time. Fourth Wife must not know what the planting season is. By the look of her I would say she might not know what the sun is. But that doesn't matter. I don't even care about being hungry or lonely or locked up anymore.

Ma was here in Shanghai!

79

Ma left Ba and my sisters and me and came here to Uncle's house, and she never went back!

What if she didn't go willingly? What if that large bulky man brought her here, the same way he brought me, right over his shoulder? What if she was kidnapped too?

I am on Ma's trail. I have my first clue.

If she cannot come to me, then I will go to find *her*.

I AM MOSTLY asleep when First Wife hauls me out in the morning. Stumbling down the stairs, I try to tell her that Fourth Wife is still up there, but First Wife doesn't pay any attention. She takes me to a room with a big table covered with towers of food. Everyone is helping themselves to it. She shoves me into a chair and one of the servants slaps a plate down in front of me.

But I am not scared of First Wife, or anyone else, anymore.

I know the truth now. They're just stealers. They stole Ma. They stole me.

They'll be sorry if they steal Big Sister, because of how mean she is!

I plink at the plate with my chopsticks. I would be stuffing my face already but I don't want to show how hungry I am. Besides, it's hard to eat when you're sitting across from a woman with a face like a lemon.

First Wife, who is greeting everyone formally, calls this lemon-woman Second Wife.

Now I remember. The one with the daughter who drowned in the well. Second Wife looks like she might be drowning too only nobody has noticed.

Next to Second Wife is a girl around Big Sister's age. She is addressed by First Wife as Aiyi. Second Wife's still-living daughter. Aiyi has her mouth full of her own greasy hair and is chewing on it. Maybe I will ask her to play later; since I am not leaving this house quite yet.

I am not leaving Shanghai without Ma.

Third Wife sits at the end of the table, taking bird bites of food. "So, did you have a good first night with us?" she asks me.

She must not see the splinters sticking out of my skin.

"Don't distract my foster daughter, please," says First Wife severely. "She is skinny as a root and needs to eat."

"Little Mei, why don't you come with me tomorrow?" Third Wife says, like she hasn't even heard. "We could take tea at the Cathay, do some shopping at the Sassoon Arcade, some sightseeing on the Bund? It'd be a chance to see the *real* Shanghai."

"Aren't we in the real Shanghai already?" I ask doubtfully, as First Wife grabs the chopsticks out of my left hand and presses them into my right.

Now I have even more splinters.

"Oh please. This is Amherst Avenue," says Third Wife, breaking into a laugh.

First Wife has her own chopsticks poised in midair, like she might use them to pinch Third Wife's mouth shut, but I think we should just let Third Wife laugh. She looks like she might boil over with it otherwise. Like a pot of rice.

"Little Mei has no time for your nonsense," snaps First Wife.

"We can't keep her in a kennel! You're up for my nonsense, aren't you, Little Mei?" Third Wife looks over at me and winks. "There are some fun shops by the water. I think we should get your ears pierced! Or should we go to a spoken storybook performance?"

I think Third Wife would be good at spoken storybook performance.

"You would be foolish to venture too far into the International Settlement," warns First Wife, and she starts speaking in a bristly mix of my Chinese and hers, so that I can only understand some of what she is saying. Checkpoints. Blocked roads. Warships. Fighting on the rail lines. "I have read that the generalissimo and the Japanese have struck a deal," she says, "and everything north of the Yangtze will belong to them, and everything south of it to us. But things are changing quickly, even by the day. Even someone as spoiled and silly as you, Third Wife, must sense the impending danger."

Japanese.

A tasty shiver goes through me.

"There have been typhoons off the coast all month," says Third Wife, even though nobody said anything about typhoons. "They never blow in."

"You're a child, with your ridiculous optimism," says First Wife harshly.

Where is Fourth Wife, I wonder? Why does she not take breakfast with us?

Even if she is the lowest-ranked wife, does she really have to eat in the attic?

Oh well. I'll try to find her later, to ask her more questions. I won't mention it to First Wife, though. There could be even smaller, darker places in this house than the attic, and I don't want to be locked up again. At home if I say something saucy, like *pig gas*, I have to spend the day tearing up ginkgo leaves or scrubbing spoons, but that is back home. That was as bad as punishments ever got.

I am in bandit territory now. Stealers' territory.

"Fine. You may take her tomorrow. But only if she finishes all her chores today," says First Wife.

"Thank you, First Wife. You know I have to enjoy myself while

I still can," chirps Third Wife, and she pats her lower belly like she's way past full, even though she's barely eaten a thing.

First Wife lowers her eyes to her own plate.

I switch the chopsticks back to my left hand while she's not looking.

"If you don't start eating right now, you'll be washing your mouth out with soap instead, Little Mei!" First Wife blusters, but she's still not looking.

I hold my chopsticks high and then bring them swooping down like falcons toward the rice rolls, the dough sticks, the firm-fried pancakes. I will do whatever it takes to find Ma and bring her home. This must be *my* fate; this must be why I have been brought here. It is true that I do not actually know if people get to choose their fates or not, but I imagine it is a lot like choosing what to eat from the enormous breakfast feast in front of you.

AFTER BREAKFAST FIRST Wife tells me to help the servants prepare lunch; and after lunch I must help prepare dinner. There is a rolling wheel of meal after meal in this house! There is no time at all to look for Fourth Wife, and when I ask the servants where she might be, they go white as flour and don't answer. They put me to work stirring soup, and as I stir, my head fills with quivery little thoughts.

I need to get a message to Ba and my sisters explaining why I can't run away yet, but who can write this message for me?

I can't ask the wives for help or they'll tell Uncle, and the servants will likely just look sick again.

Stirring like this reminds me of sketching. Of the blunt pencils and sloshy brushes I left on Ma's art table back home. I need to keep practicing; I need to make progress. If I get good, then maybe when Ma comes back she'll never want to leave.

THE WHOLE DAY goes by, and the night, with no sign of Fourth Wife, and I am starting to think that she *lives* in the attic because there is no other explanation.

In the morning, after breakfast, First Wife puts me in a brown buttoned dress and says that if I come home with my ears pierced, she will make me seal the holes with lard. Then, at last, I am off to the real Shanghai with Third Wife. I thought we would be walking but we are going in a shiny box on wheels that she calls a car. There is a man who controls it and tells it where to go and Third Wife tells him where to go. She says he is the family driver. I must look nervous, because Third Wife asks if I'm alright, and I say that I don't like being in shut-up places without any air.

She has the driver crank down our windows and the wind smells like salt.

"I've brought my camera," Third Wife says, showing me a heavy black object that folds in on itself, like a fan. "It takes pictures. You know what pictures are?"

"Of course I know what pictures are," I say, shocked by this question.

"You know why I've brought it?"

"Because you want to take pictures?" And they call *me* dumb as a duck egg!

"Because," she says, "shelling has started in the north of the city, and from the roof of the Cathay, we will see the bombs landing on Chapei. The Japanese are taking Shanghai, Little Mei. They are already here. But don't worry. They won't come into the International Settlement or the French Concession; they wouldn't dare. No matter what happens, we are safe." She raps on the window. "Let us out here. We'll walk to the Bund, little one, and you can see the Whangpoo in all its glory! And smell it too." She laughs. She holds the camera tightly, like it's worth more to her than all the jewelry she's wearing, her necklaces and pendants and peacock bracelets.

The day is hot but rainy. Rainy hot days are truly the worst kind of days. But Third Wife still does not look worried about typhoons.

Outside, there are people everywhere on the streets, stuck in long lines, holding bottles, looking sleepy; others sitting on the sidewalks, sweating into puddles, their hands cupped, held out to us. Whole villages' worth of people, all on the same street. Third Wife labels everything we see: *trolley cars* rattling by; *buses* that smell like pig gas from behind. There are kids on bicycles— bicycles!—and skinny men pulling carts and wagons and rickshaws; and more and more cars—

I am gawking. I close my mouth so that a bird does not make a nest in it.

THIRD WIFE STOPS at the river to take pictures with her camera. "Gunboats," she says, but the river is so packed with boats that I cannot tell which ones she means. "Those large dark forms are battleships, way over there. Those little flat-bottomed ones are sampans; you must know those. Beyond that, you see, that is a Japanese liner, bound for America, full of people too scared to stay in Shanghai. It will stop at Kobe and then it will go east, across the whole of the Pacific. Can you imagine that, Little Mei? Going over half the earth?"

Her voice sounds small. Like it is already going over half the earth.

Steam rises up out of the ships. My breath rises up out of me.

I do not think we are supposed to be here. Not like this. Not today. And don't people usually take pictures so that you can remember good times later? Like Ma in that photograph at home, smiling at something no one can see? Why would anyone want pictures of *gunboats*?

We squeeze our way down the street. Third Wife holds my hand. Hers is soft and cool even though mine is swelling like a wound in this horrible heat.

The sky is turning from gray to orange.

The rumble in the distance, I do not think it is thunder.

There is a blasting sound overhead; around us people are looking and pointing upward. I do not look upward because I am too afraid; I am grateful for her hand. In the distance there is a bridge bulging with even more people, all of them headed directly toward us.

There is nowhere to turn.

"I want to go inside," I say, tugging on her, but Third Wife doesn't hear me, because of the crowds and the boats and the blasting.

"I've brought you along today," she says, "because it's my fault that you're in Shanghai."

Huh?

"Now you're here; now you belong to First Wife; now there's nothing I can do about any of it. All I can do is show you that the world is so much bigger than that house, Little Mei; so much bigger than First Wife and her fortune tellers. You know, I always wanted to be a photographer," she says. "From when I was your age, in fact. I thought I would work for the *Shanghai Evening Post*. Or even for one of the American papers . . . all I lacked was the courage. I have never quite had the courage I needed, you see, to expose things, even people, for what they truly are. But perhaps I can make up for it now." A squeeze of my hand; a squeezed-sounding laugh. "Look, there it is, Little Mei! The Cathay. Come. The rooftop will be busy, I am sure; it will be a proper spectacle!

Do you see what I mean about the wide, wide world? Can you feel the charge in the air? How can anyone even feel alive in a fancy, frilly house surrounded by leafy trees and silence and servants and superstition?"

What is she *talking* about?

What is *happening*?

Third Wife smiles at me. "You mustn't tell First Wife about everything we see today, Little Mei. She wouldn't understand. She wants *that* life; she will do anything to protect it. But I think that the Japanese coming may be a blessing. Yes, some roads will close, but others will open. You and I can have our adventures out here, I will take you under my wing, but you can't say a word to anyone back there. You have to trust me, alright? You can keep secrets, can't you?"

"Was my Ma here?" I blurt out.

Now she stops, with people pushing by on both sides. "What?"

"I'll trust you if you tell me the truth about Ma! Was she here? In Shanghai? At the start of summer?"

Third Wife isn't smiling anymore. "Who told you that?"

"Fourth Wife. In the attic. I mean, she couldn't really talk, she had only half a tongue, and bandaged feet . . . not that the feet were what stopped her talking." It doesn't seem like anything is going to stop *me* talking. I feel the words running out of me like soy sauce out of the raw-egg-and-rice dish that was Ma's favorite, where you bury the open egg in the well-steamed rice and then you pour the soy sauce right over—

"Fourth Wife?" repeats Third Wife.

"I think she wanted to help me. She said she knew Ma. She said she saw Ma. And I'm looking for Ma!"

We are under an archway. There is shouting from somewhere. I hear howling sounds from the river, on the other side of the road. But I am less afraid now. I think that every time I say out loud that

I want to find Ma, I feel less afraid. I feel less lost. I know where I want to go. I know why I've come.

"Fourth Wife," says Third Wife again, slowly.

"She was wearing a hair stick with pearls on it," I say.

How many wives does Uncle *have*, that people can't keep track of how many there are?

"A hair stick. Yes. Now I remember. I think I know the story," says Third Wife. "A girl who supposedly lived in the house sometime last century who screamed so much at night that her husband removed her tongue. She then cut her own throat with her hair stick. If you see her ghost, and the ghost removes the hair stick from its hair, then the wound reopens and she bleeds down the front of her. Right? Is that what you've been told? But I would like to know who is trying to scare you with this. The servants? Aiyi?"

I shake my head vigorously. "I *saw* her!"

Third Wife tries to smile again. "Alright, but I'm afraid there is some confusion, Little Mei," she says softly. "I don't know what you saw, but it was not Fourth Wife. Your Ma was Fourth Wife."

11

HONG KONG
2015

IT BEGINS TO rain, light and feathery, as we trundle up the Peak path. Our going is slow, and I wonder if Susanna will complain again, try to talk me down again, but it seems she has shouted herself silent. I watch as she zips her jacket as far as it goes, even though the temperature is higher here than at sea level, if anything.

My daughter was keeping it to herself all this time, that she and Dean received an anonymous letter claiming her mother was a murderer.

Because it was unthinkable? Or because she was thinking about it? Because she didn't want to ask; because she was scared it might be true?

Susanna must have been curious. She must have been *dying* of it. And yet she said nothing.

That is how well I have shut her out.

That is how well I have kept her from knowing me.

"I don't think you killed them," Susanna says. "I *know* you didn't kill them. I know you're not capable of murder, Ma."

Look at how well I have shut her out.

Look at how well I have kept her from knowing me.

THE RAIN FALLS flatter, if you are moving at an angle. We are able to brush it away just enough to see where we're headed; the jungle is changing shape all around us. We have passed the point, on the way to the Upper Terminus, after which it is not worthwhile to turn around.

I nudge her to the edge of the walkway and wordlessly she takes in the view: the mural of pure black sky; the jeweled skyline of Central below; the thick swaths of trees; the step paths so steep they could be ladders, disappearing between apartment buildings.

It is the last glimpse she will have of civilization until daylight.

"You don't seem scared," she observes, her voice watery. "To go back to Maidenhair."

"I know what to expect there." I reach for her hand. In it, I feel her heart. *She* is scared. I doubt she even knows why. You just feel it, when you reach this point on the mountain. You feel the promise of the house, waiting for you. "That's why I am going with you. You can't ever go to Maidenhair House without me, Susanna."

"Why not?" She looks at me, with the rain bright in both eyes.

"You cannot enter Maidenhair without me. Say it."

"I'm not—"

"This night is it."

"But I might have to," she says. "I might need to. I have to get to the bottom of this, Ma. I have to do it for Dean—"

"It won't bring him back, Susy."

"You don't understand," she says, clearly clawing for the words to try to make me understand. "I told him to disregard the letter. I refused even to entertain the idea of it! If I hadn't, if I'd been

90

more open, he wouldn't have needed to research Maidenhair in secret. If I hadn't, he might still be alive!"

"Susanna," I say, drawing out the syllables of her name this time, in hopes that I can bring her back from wherever she is, at this moment, whatever unspeakable memory, "I told you, and I'll keep telling you, that your husband's death was a tragic—"

"The house is cursed," she says. "That's what I read."

I look at her, anguished.

"That's what you're talking about, isn't it? *You* believe in the curse." She stands straighter, like she thinks she has me cornered now. "That's why you don't want me to go back by myself."

"You think Dean died because of a—"

"I don't know what to think, Ma! I don't. I don't know. Except that he should be here. He should be doing this. And since he's not, I'm doing it. That's all."

She sounds delirious.

She sounds like she *wants* him to have died because of a curse.

Susanna is the last person in the world I would ever expect to believe in curses.

For all the times I have shocked her, over the past twenty-four hours, she has now done the same to me, twice over.

"This was the last house the Canadians ever visited, you know," she says, almost idly. "They haven't stepped foot in the ruins of another abandoned space since they left Maidenhair."

AS WE PEEL off the main path, Susanna pulls her hood full over her head. Her jacket is black and her pants are black; her face seems to sit above it all like a moon. We reach the Bridal Bridge, not a true bridge but a skinny stretch of road so named because it is often sheathed in white fog. Tonight the way is clear; tonight the house is beckoning us closer.

We carry on, across the Bridge, beneath the tree-tunnels, and back out into the open. Rainwater fills the potholes along the path. Only a bit farther now.

There is a slow gasp beside me, as Susanna glimpses the house.

It is gleaming wetly, almost glowing.

Maybe I do know what to expect, but I am not immune to the sight of Maidenhair.

I tell myself that it is only because it is nighttime, that Maidenhair House looks exactly as it was. If we came here by day, surely it would be changed. More like the mansion in the Canadians' photos. The cracked façades. The foxed windows. The grand decay. At this moment, Maidenhair looks as though it is being lived in. It looks as if it was just built.

"There's someone *there*," says Susanna. "In the window—"

And so it begins.

THE UPPER STORY windows of the main house are flickering with light.

"Nobody lives here," says Susanna, a tad shrilly, "it's abandoned," and I can see the possibilities racing through her mind: Squatters. Intruders. Criminals. Campers. Canadians. She reaches for the light as if she hopes to hold it, but she is too far away. Do not touch it, my daughter. Do not reach for the very first light you see, just because of the darkness you live in.

A soft strain of music emanates from the house, as if someone has wound it up like a toy, but not hard enough.

"You'll see him," I say.

"What? Who?"

"Your husband," I say. "Your dead husband. You will see him."

12

HONG KONG
SEPTEMBER 1953

The First Séance

MEI IS GIVEN half an hour after dinner to spend alone in her room, freshening up, before the First Séance is set to begin.

The room is small and modestly furnished, containing only a stump of a nightstand, a lamp with a slanted shade, a wooden chest, and an iron bedstead, low to the ground. There is a squinty clock on the wall, tick-tick-tocking away, reminiscent of Holly Zhang's high-heeled shoes grinding down the floor tiles. Slowly turning them to sawdust.

To Mei's mind this room was likely never intended as a bedroom at all, not in a house like this one.

Perhaps all the real guest bedrooms are located in the two forbidden wings.

She had not planned to unpack entirely, as she had not planned to stay all six nights. George's absence until the final night has changed this. Now Mei has to survive all six séances. Now she has to *win*. How can she possibly win?

The last séance she ever conducted was during the war.

Think of how many ghosts have been created, since then; how many new kinds now exist.

Think of how it is one thing to be a spirit medium before a war; and how it is another, to be a spirit medium after.

MEI OPENS HER rattan basket wide on the bed. She removes her clothes, Mr. Sim's gift of *The Peak House*, a bundle of paper, and a carved cigar box. She peels away a few sheets of paper, carefully, like slices of lotus root. She digs out a kneaded eraser and then a charcoal stick from the cigar box, testing it against the pads of her fingers until it stains.

In séances, she does not speak to spirits, and they do not speak to her. Nor do they speak through her. Not exactly.

They *sketch* through her.

The clock tells her she still has time, so Mei peeks into the gauzy pages of *The Peak House*. She scans the chapter list; she has not read a novel in years but vividly remembers the sucked-in whirlpool sensation of it, and she half wishes Mr. Sim had given her nonfiction instead, a handbook, an encyclopedia, a tourist guide, even though it feels blasphemous to think such a thing. As if she could ever look at one of her drawings and wish she were holding a photograph.

Just a page. Just one or two. No more than that. She won't let herself be drawn in too deep.

She turns once more to the beginning. The font is tilted just so, like wind has blown the words across the page.

The house was silent, but silence is not the same thing as peace.

Her room is silent.

Mei's neck prickles with the feeling of it. As if silence can be a feeling! She claps the book shut and resolves to read it in the morning, in a different room. She has the Sight, the yin yang eyes, as they call it here in Hong Kong; she should be less afraid of ghosts than anyone. But that is just not how it works. She has the Sight. The yin yang eyes. And so she is the most afraid.

HOLLY ZHANG MEETS her six guests in the Great Hall. She explains that the Red Library is in the South Wing of the house, on the ground floor. They will walk in single file. They are not to look behind them. They are not to look into the rooms they pass. They are not to speak.

If they hear somebody speaking, they should assume it is not one of them.

If they hear somebody calling for help, they should not answer.

Mei could not answer even if she wanted. Her throat is as dry as incense.

Holly leads them out of the Great Hall through a set of heavy double doors, down a hallway lit only by palace lanterns, airy spun silk wrapped around a curved wooden frame. Each one is decorated with a unique pattern, but the light they give is yellow and foul. A turn, and then another turn, and then another.

Mei is second to last in this procession.

She can't say when it is that she starts hearing too many footsteps behind her.

Don't look back, Holly said.

Don't look don't look don't—

But it is a reflex, and she looks; she turns her head just far enough.

One of the twins is there, eyes large and unblinking. Delia, Mei thinks—

But past Delia, at the end of the hall, is someone else.

Mei whips her head back around, her breath boiling in her cheeks, and she dares not look again, no matter how many footsteps she hears.

⌒

THE RED LIBRARY is not Red at all. The walls are a stained gray and the ceiling is crisscrossed by dark wooden beams. A single glass display case of books stands against one side, books that look like they are not meant be breathed on, much less read. In the center of the room are six blackwood chairs without cushions, arranged in an uncanny circle, as if there were once a table between them, now vanished into air, and the spirit mediums are invited to choose any chair they wish.

Mei chooses the chair that faces the display case. She had thought there would be a table, but luckily she has brought *The Peak House* as a surface for drawing on.

She flattens her stack of paper with her palm, again and again, over and over.

She watches as Delia takes the seat across from her, next to Cecelia. Delia offers Mei a sunny, toothy smile.

A thought goes up like a flame.

What if that's not Delia?

What if that's the one who was following?

It is a ludicrous notion. Mei doesn't even know why she would think such a thing. That Delia has been replaced. That the real Delia was snatched away, right behind Mei, right while they were making their way here. Jamie Nakamura catches Mei's eye; his expression is skeptical. But if he has something to say, he never gets the chance, because Holly has stepped into the circle and reveals what she has been hiding in her hands.

A handful of *qiú qiān* sticks?

Yes, fortune-telling sticks, flat and fragile and painted red at the tips. Holly holds them out, the ends still stuck in her fist.

Holly is about to make them draw lots.

"It's only fair," says Holly. "Someone has to go first."

HOLLY ZHANG HAS placed a candle in a sleek brass holder in the center of their circle. Mei notices now that Holly has swapped wigs since dinner; this one is a glory of corkscrew curls. She has also changed gowns; this one is long and loose and forms a lake on the floor. It will catch fire if the older woman moves too close to the candle. Holly Zhang must have played many roles, empresses, courtesans, servant girls; Mei wonders how many times Holly has played hostess.

"If there are any questions, ask them now," says Holly, lightly crowing. She seems to change voices, too, as easily as the rest. "I will not entertain them later, once we have started."

A stark silence follows.

"Nothing?" asks Holly, like she doesn't believe in the silence.

"There should be offerings of food and drink," says Mistress Lau, with defiance. "The spirit is less likely to feel cooperative, without offerings."

Mei thinks abstractly of their rich, heavy dinner, of the ducks cooked bronze, dotted with slices of taro; the bowls of rice, letting off steam like a locomotive; the silver-thread buns; the hot candied apples; the gleaming goblets of rice wine. Mistress Lau is right. Holly should have saved her best for the dead, not spent it on the living.

"Is that so?" says Holly. "But I'm afraid I can't trouble my staff at this hour."

In the candlelight, Mistress Lau's painted face looks a nearly translucent white, the shade Mei would use for insect wings. "That would be a mistake," says Mistress Lau, "in my experience."

"Perhaps tomorrow. Anyone else?"

The twins raise their hands, as one.

"Do you know the name of the spirit you believe haunts this room, Auntie?" asks Cecelia. "It would help us make contact."

The girls lower their hands, still woven in each other's.

Holly's mouth closes like a drawbridge; opens again. "This Library is where Lady Elinor Hall, first wife of Timothy Hall, was found dead by hanging," she says. "Right over our heads."

Mei's mind goes black with fear.

"If that is all, we will now go in the order determined by the bamboo sticks, longest to shortest," says Holly. "Mr. Nakamura, we will begin with you."

DURING THE SÉANCE, Mei will go into a trance; later she will have no memory of it. She will create sketches of things she has never seen; she will have no memory of sketching either. There will be rips in the paper where she has shaded too hard. Her hand will burn from clenching her utensil; her mouth will burn from clenching her jaw. Her eyelashes will feel matted with ash. She will wonder for a long time after if the spirit has left her completely, or if there are traces of it still on her, all over her, inside of her, the dark charcoal dust.

THEY HOLD HANDS, forming a circle, as Holly leads a guttural chant that Mei only understands slivers of. When the chant is finished, the séance is meant to begin; Jamie Nakamura attempts to call for the spirit of Lady Elinor Hall, but the candles stay lit and his entreaties go unanswered. Either Jamie Nakamura is not powerful enough, or it is not the spirit of Lady Elinor Hall that haunts this room, even if Holly has seen the figure of her on a rope.

Mei's thoughts are growing misshapen from being turned over too much, like dough. Her gaze flits from one person to the next: from Holly Zhang to Mistress Lau to the twins to Jamie, whose blue eyes have darkened with frustration, to the one called Peng, who has her shoulders hunched, like she hopes to shine their shoes with her forehead.

"Mistress Lau?" says Holly.

Mei is so tense she does not know how she will last till the end without breaking in two.

They hold hands again. The chant begins again.

When the formalities are over, Mistress Lau withdraws a shiny thin blade; a straight razor.

Somehow Mei can feel the pinch of each candle flame as it dies. One by one.

Mei has never drawn in the perfect molten darkness. She has never been possessed in it. There was always a shard of light; there was always a window; there was always a way out—

There was always her Great Master.

She had not entirely realized: She has never conducted a séance without her Great Master. Not even once.

Now she is alone.

MISTRESS LAU IS rolling up her long, slack sleeves, revealing a forearm as white as bone.

Mei cannot watch. She *cannot*. She knows that this is the preferred method by many mediums; self-mutilation, an offering of flesh; she must look past the people, to the glass display case. She ignores the hiss of breath from Mistress Lau, in the damp second that the blade slips under. She ignores the sickening rush that goes through her. She can hear the knife beginning to carve characters into the skin; or can she? Does she only imagine it, because she knows it is happening?

Think of something else, Mei, think— How can *this* be George Maidenhair's library? for example—a room built like the galley of a ship, with a few meager bookshelves, a few glossy spines—

Where is the gothic library of his boyhood fantasies, that George once swore to Mei he would someday build? It would have sliding ladders and spiral staircases, he said. It would have shelves within the shelves. It would have hidden doors, unseen handles, underground passageways. George was a *book person*, and book people like it when there are secret worlds in the walls, the same way there are secret worlds between the covers of a book—

The books behind glass remind Mei of dead butterflies.

It is over. Mistress Lau is finished.

There is blood dripping off her elbow, into her sleeves.

"Leave this house," says Mistress Lau, in a monotone, reading off her arm. *"Leave this house while you still can."*

MEI WAS ONCE a *book person* too. She once lived for stories. She once would have read *The Peak House* from cover to cover, right there on her bed, missing this séance, missing her chance, missing chunks of her own life. She once would have finished in the dead of night, closing the novel, closing her eyes, breathing in, refilling her lungs, nearly gasping for air, reeling from the knowledge that she would never read that particular book for the first time ever again.

Let go . . . close your eyes . . . let them in. . . .

Mei has to remember why she is doing this. She has to hold on to her hatred, tighter than she holds the charcoal between her calloused fingers. It must not slip from her grasp for a second. The bitter truth is that she once loved George Maidenhair, and somewhere in the roiling depths of her, she still loves him. But that love is what makes the hatred possible. That love is what will make this revenge, instead of repayment. That love is what will make it murder, instead of an execution.

13

SHANGHAI
AUGUST 1937

THIRD WIFE DECIDES that we shouldn't go up to the roof right away, since I have gone as green as jade. She says we can stop into the Sassoon Arcade first, where the glass-shard sounds from outside cannot be heard; how about we have a peek into the Lantern and Treasure curio shops and pick me up something pretty? I guess Third Wife believes pretty things always make people feel better. I guess that is how Third Wife ended up with so much jewelry.

Third Wife says she thought I *knew* that my Ma was Fourth Wife.

How could I not know?

She pulls me along and I follow blindly.

Wherever we are, it is still heaving with people, same as outside. I thought the Lantern shop would sell lanterns but it actually sells all sorts of things: Peking glass, brass statues, ballerina music boxes, enough silk to fill rivers.

Weirdly enough, Third Wife's distractions are working: My heart still feels horrible, but my head is clearer.

Ma seemed so *findable*, after my night in the attic. She seemed closer. Now she seems farther away than ever. Now it's like I never even had her at all, because she wasn't who I thought she was. The Lantern shop has lanterns for sale after all: There they are, shoved together on a single shelf, looking like wasp nests, papery and plump, dark and unlit, not showing the way.

THE ROOFTOP OF the Cathay does not feel like a rooftop because there are so many grown-ups around, you can't even see how far off from the ground you are. All you can see is the grown-ups, and above them, the dreary gray sky.

Third Wife has let go of my hand because she needs both hands for her camera. She has such a strange, satisfied smile on her face, it *almost* makes me forget about Ma being Uncle's wife instead of his sister and how everything I have ever been told might be a lie. Third Wife points the camera upward gleefully, as if today is a day we will all want to remember, even though I already wish it had never happened.

Somebody shouts something but I do not understand.

Then the grown-ups go quiet.

There are airplanes flying over our heads.

Third Wife gasps, a scratchy chicken-feet sound.

"Chinese Air Force. They're hoping to hit the Japanese *Izumo*," remarks the white man next to us. His Chinese is very, very good; maybe even better than mine. "Those planes were given to Chiang Kai-shek his last birthday. See those markings?"

Third Wife might not have heard him; she is too busy with her camera.

"What are those dots below the planes?" I ask the man.

"They're bombs, they're—" He stops.

Suddenly, there is chaos.

"They've missed the—" comes a yell.

"They've *missed*!"

"They've hit the Bund!"

"Get inside!"

"Get inside!"

But Third Wife is still taking pictures. I try to grab her arm but there are so many people pushing past me that I keep slipping off. The white man says to Third Wife, "Ma'am, you need to get your child out of here," and he's sounding rather upset, and people are screaming in all directions, and at last Third Wife turns. Her eyes look like the lanterns finally come to life and her camera is in her hand like she was born holding it. She looks at the man and the man looks at her and both their faces change, and I would say, I would *swear*, in that moment, that they know each other, and she opens her mouth to speak, but something happens to the building we are standing on, something happens to the ground beneath my feet, and I am caught in the tide and I cannot fight it anymore and I am flowing away from her forever.

SMOKY SMOKE. SMOKE in my eyes, smoke in my mouth, smoke inside my head. I hear something, but there is smoke in my ears, too, of course. I touch around my ears and then I look at my fingers and they're licked bright red and for a second I think: Am I painting a picture with Ma? Is that what I am doing? Am I home?

Time is passing, I think.

I am looking up at the sky, the one that Third Wife hopefully got good pictures of, before it fell down on us.

MY LEGS ARE dirty. My head is bleeding. My ears are singing. The cars that were so shiny on our way here are blazing fire. The buildings are missing all their doors. I stand up and I feel very large because I am the only one standing. It is interesting that I can cry at almost anything in the world but right now my eyes are dry. Maybe they are too full of smoke. Maybe I am so full of smoke that I will have to go live with dragons.

I WALK SLOWLY down the Bund, past the river, over the tram-lines. I see a lot of things without exactly seeing them, without knowing what they mean.

Geysers of water shooting straight up from the street; the opposite of a waterfall.

Bodies without heads or arms or legs, looking like a rag doll after a dog gets ahold of it.

Babies face down, even though babies should never be face down.

Big, big cars rush by, in the opposite direction I am going. A runny-eyed grandmother stops me and tells me I should go to the hospital and that there are ambulances and British Army armored vehicles waiting to treat the wounded if I go back up Nanking Road, and I don't really understand any of it so I say, "Amherst Avenue," and she points with her shaky fingers, and I keep walking. Ma used to say it is a very special talent to be able to keep walking.

That was before I knew she was really saying it was a very special talent to be able to run away.

Ma was Uncle's Fourth Wife before she became Ba's only wife. Before she became my Ma.

I might have a soybean-brain, but I can figure this much out: My mother left Shanghai and started a whole new life, and she probably never planned to go back.

But then she *did*.

Why?

And will it be easier or harder to find her, if the bombs turn this city inside out?

AT UNCLE'S HOUSE the servants wipe me down and put me in a basin-bath and then I am asleep and then I am awake again, just like that, and everything hurts, *everything*, even the singed tips of my toes. Second Wife's daughter, Aiyi, is in the room with me, sitting in a chair at the foot of the bed, reading a book. When she sees that I am awake, she closes her book.

"So you're alive," says Aiyi. She has to say it through her hair, which she is still chewing. How does she read through hair like that? How does she *live*? Has she made a hole for breathing? "You had so much glass in your skin, we had to pull it out of you like hedgehog quills, you know."

I crane my head to look at her better.

Aiyi sniffs. "They wanted me to stay with you in case you died in your sleep," she says. "You've slept for two days straight."

"Where is Third Wife?"

"What do you care? Didn't you leave her behind? I'll go now and tell Mother you're awake."

"Wait," I say croakily, "please."

She waits, with another cranky sniff.

I think she might get along well with Big Sister.

"Will you write a letter for me?" My head is a little dizzy. "I can't write but I need to send a message to my Ba and my sisters. I need to tell them that I can't run away yet because Ma came here to Shanghai before she disappeared—that's what the girl in the attic told me—and I need to find Ma. And tell them not to worry, just not to . . . worry . . ."

My left hand is in *bandages*. I can't move it.

I hadn't even seen it until now.

"Girl in the attic?" says Aiyi, snickering.

"The one with half a tongue. I have so many questions to ask . . . but she can't . . . talk . . ."

"Oh, that one, sure," says Aiyi. "But hey, you know what? If you want to know more about your Ma, the ones you should really be asking are the servants. Me, I've heard that your Ma *saw* things. Bad things. Things nobody else could see. She wasn't right in the head. But I guess you aren't either, huh? Or else you could go to school. Yeah, I heard the servants talking about it, how you're too dumb for school. Such a shame, because then you wouldn't need other people to write your letters for you."

I feel pins in my cheeks, sharp and painful.

"If you're wondering what happened to your Ma," says Aiyi, "the answer is most likely: She had to be sent away. You know where they send people like that? People with lots of loose thread ends inside their heads? There's this secret place run by the Christian missionaries up in the Purple Mountain, that's where. Way, way up high so that nobody can hear the screaming, because they have to suck the patients' brains out with straws. Better hope it never happens to *you*, since you don't have much brain to begin with." Aiyi breathes out and her hair dances. "But if that's where your Ma's gone to, then you're better off if she never comes back. People don't come back from those places the way they were."

I will not cry again. I will *not*.

To my surprise, the tears behind my eyes dry up, and the pin feeling fades.

I think I am stronger now that I've survived the real Shanghai.

I am made of more than just bandages.

"Fine," I say, lifting my chin. *Ow.* "Go tell First Wife I'm awake."

IN THE AFTERNOON I am summoned to Uncle's special study room, better known as the Magnolia Room.

I haven't seen Uncle even one time since arriving in Shanghai.

The housekeeper is the one who brings me to see him. The housekeeper is a leathery old lady with enough hair on her face to sew a sweater. She tells me that Uncle is a scholar and spends so much time holed up in his study he has to rip himself out by the roots each time he leaves. The Magnolia is bright and open and has doors onto the garden; there are framed paintings all over the walls, all of mountaintops. Uncle sits at a large table, painting on a drapey piece of paper.

"You have been in bed awhile, Little Mei," he says, drawing his brush back and forth. "Though that is not always a bad thing. Sometimes we all need to feel that we could be floating anywhere in the universe, for all that we can see of our lives down below."

Now he looks up, to make sure I am listening.

I nod knowledgeably. The way he speaks, it's like he's swallowed the Five Classics of Confucius. Ba used to read the works of Confucius to me and my sisters at night to help us go to sleep, because Confucius will make you fall asleep faster than a handful of red dates, and without the tummy troubles afterward— But now I wish I hadn't thought of this, because now my chest feels wobbly, remembering Ba and his ratty volumes of Confucian teachings, and how Ma barely knew how to read or write, even though she was supposed to be from fancy-pants Shanghai and he came from a village where people used spit as their signatures.

"I know you're not happy here. I understand how you feel, Little Mei, a lot better than you think," says Uncle. "We are all of us bricked into the lives we lead."

The way he is looking at me makes me wonder if this is my chance.

"Was Ma here?" I ask.

"I beg your pardon?"

"Was Ma here in Shanghai? Before she disappeared? 'Cause I know you've been keeping things from me. I know she was your Fourth Wife. Not your sister at all."

"I have no idea whether your mother ever returned to Shanghai," he says, in that same Confucius-style voice. "All I know is that you are here now, she is not, and that is that."

If I say anything more, I'll be love-smacked on the eyeballs. I can already tell.

"You can tell me she's dead all you want, but I won't believe you." My voice is too loud. "I won't believe it until I see her dead body just like I saw all those dead bodies in the *real* Shanghai. I know what a dead body looks like now; you can't fool me. Where is Ma? Do you know? Did you kidnap her because she ran away from you many years ago?"

Uncle takes a shallow breath. "I had hoped to assess your artistic proficiency, at some point," he says. "I thought you might have inherited your mother's—"

"I can't do art!" I lift my bandaged hand like I might throw it at him. "I am left-handed! Just like Ma was!"

"You are dismissed, Little Mei, until you are done acting like a demon," he says coldly, "and I am not to hear of you mentioning your mother again."

I want to throw one of his curtain sleeves over his head. Maybe it's because I almost went up in smoke, maybe's it because I slept so long they thought I'd never wake up, but I am done pretending. I am *done*.

"I know about the girl living in the attic too!" I shout at him.

"She should be down here, with us! It doesn't matter if she doesn't have a tongue! It doesn't matter if she isn't speaking! Even if a person is quiet, they're still *there*! Why do you have to keep everyone away from their own family? You can't just—you *can't*!"

How good it feels, fanning the fire inside of me!

Uncle makes a sound through his teeth.

"I hate you!" I scream. "I hate this house! I hate everyone in it! I don't want to do art with you! Only with Ma! I just want my Ma and she was here and nobody will tell me *where she went*!"

First Wife is entering the room.

Over the sound of my own shouting I can hear Uncle instructing her to remove me from his sight. But she doesn't have surprise on her side this time, not like at the train station; not like out by the bamboo fence in the middle of the night. Glaring hotly at her, I plant myself in a chair. If Uncle thinks he can hang me up like one of his mountaintop paintings, he can go right ahead and try.

First Wife's face looks tight enough to burst its seams. Tighter even than her qipao.

I don't care! I am prepared to be love-smacked! To be hate-smacked, even better!

A handful of servants come in and they drag me out and pull me into the garden, where First Wife gives me fifteen strikes with the bamboo cane. I scream and I am still screaming as the servants lug me back inside afterward. Back in bed, I howl and howl and howl, lying on my belly as my bottom burns, as everything inside of me burns, until I fall asleep.

When I wake up, Ma's pouch is on my pillow.

The pouch I left in the attic; I almost forgot about it!

So Fourth Wife comes downstairs sometimes. It must be just a matter of catching her. . . .

⌐⟋

I MUST HAVE fallen asleep again, because when I wake up it is very dark and there is a movement by my bed.

"Shh," says Third Wife, putting a finger by her lips, nodding toward the golden screen, toward First Wife's half of the room. "Shh, Little Mei, it's just me. It's late. Everyone else is asleep."

"Oh!" I say, and everything hurts a little less.

Third Wife lies down next to me in the bed and leans her head against mine.

"I'm sorry I left you in the real Shanghai," I say miserably. "I *was* worried about you. Just not right away. I'm sorry about that too."

She laughs. "You didn't leave me. We lost each other, as one might expect, in such a scene! How do you feel, *xiǎo bǎo*?"

"Not good. First Wife beat me like a rug."

"Is that what troubles you?"

"There's also this thing that Aiyi said, about Ma . . ." but I can't say it.

"You must understand that Aiyi still blames herself for her sister's death," says Third Wife. "Guilt like this, it can hang over you like a veil."

I think that's just her hair, but I don't say so.

Third Wife sits up and pulls off her earrings, cupping them carefully. They are super fancy bird-feather earrings, and they look like they could take flight, right out of her hands.

"Did you ever watch your mother knead dough?" she asks.

"Many times," I say, unsure.

"You must have seen her flatten it out. Mold it. Make it smooth."

"Yes, of course."

"That is what First Wife is trying to do to you, Little Mei. In a way, she means well by it: You are the raw dumpling dough, and she will mold you with the hard rolling pins, with the bamboo canes, if she has to, but it would be so much better, so much nicer, so much easier, to do it with the hands. If only you stop resisting; if only you let her. Be respectful. Bow to your Uncle. Eat more at meals. And above all, about your Ma—"

"I don't care if First Wife canes me until my backside comes off, I will not stop looking for Ma!"

"If you act like you have forgotten her, then you will have an easier time in everything you do here."

"You mean I should *lie?*"

"I only mean that so much of life is a spoken storybook performance."

"Do you think Ma ran away from us?" I ask, even though it hurts to say it. Maybe my throat got seared by the smoke. "Because she ran away once, didn't she? From this house?"

"She had her reasons, back then," is Third Wife's mysterious answer.

"Was Uncle not nice to her?"

Third Wife shrugs. "I wouldn't say so. Certainly, he appreciated her artistic talent. He just didn't care much otherwise; he has much dearer pursuits. One wife, two wives, three wives . . . they come and go easy, if there is no male child." Another laugh, but it has a hard edge, and she closes her hand around her own earrings. I can almost feel the bird-bones breaking. "Your Ma and I, you see, we were close in age, and became friends. For a few years after she left I heard nothing from her, but then she began to write to me. That is how we came to know of your family's existence, and over years and years, she and I kept up our friendship this way. But then we heard that your Ma had disappeared, and, well, First Wife went to the fortune teller's. And then she felt like it was fate. That she should adopt one of you."

Fate again.

My heart feels like it's dropping. Right into my belly.

"I must go to my babies now," she says, sliding off the bed, taking her earrings with her. "Get some rest, *xiǎo bǎo*, your skin feels hot to me."

"But . . ."

Third Wife looks down at me. Her eyes are very light, like there is snow falling inside of them.

Remember, Little Mei: You cannot live just for your Ma, she is saying. *You must find your own path.*

If you do nothing but follow in your mother's footsteps, then in the end, you will fit into her grave the way you once fit into her womb.

She turns away, and because she is so bright, I can see that the back of her head is nothing but blood.

14

HONG KONG
SEPTEMBER 1953

WHEN MEI BLINKS her eyes open again, the electric lamps are on.

"Miss Chen, there you are," says Holly, with some faint dusting of concern.

It takes Mei a moment to realize that Holly is addressing *her*. She had forgotten the faraway fantasy feeling that comes after; the way she has to slip deliberately back into herself.

That is the worst part of a séance: Mei herself becomes the in-between place.

She releases her stick of charcoal, rubs at the pebbly imprint of it against her fingers. The fuzziness is being replaced by relief. She did it. She got through it. One session down. Five to go. And she drew something; even if her eyes are still unfocused, they can make out the sheeny dark strokes on the page in front of her. In Shanghai, Mei would typically create several sketches during séances, depending on how many questions the customer chose to ask the spirit.

Tonight there is only one.

Holly Zhang must have asked only one question.

"Miss Chen?" Holly again, her voice striking like a mallet.

Mei lifts her gaze from her lap. The chair across from her is empty.

Delia is gone.

Delia is gone.

That can't be. The order of séances was: Jamie, Mistress Lau, Mei, Peng, and then the twins. How could Delia have been eliminated already? The leftover twin, Cecelia, is twisting her hands together like she doesn't know what to do with them, without her sister. Mei vaguely remembers overhearing at dinner that the twins only had each other, in the whole world; that they lived in an apartment like a coffin; that they planned to use the prize money to start a new life in America; that they did everything together. They had reminded Mei of a pair of shoes.

The chair stays empty, no matter how long Mei looks at it.

"Can we see what you've done, please, Miss Chen?" asks Holly.

Mei hands over the sketch. "Where's . . . ?" she asks, but something blocks out the name in her head, just for a second, a solar eclipse.

There is something conspiratorial about the silence that ensues.

Holly holds up Mei's sheet of paper, so they can all see it.

What did Holly ask?

Why was *this* the spirit's answer?

The sketch shows a large mirror.

Inside the mirror, someone is trapped, hands spread against the surface.

"Delia has left the competition," says Holly. "Come; we will return to the Great Hall the way we came, and then you will be dismissed to your quarters."

JAMIE NAKAMURA CATCHES up to Mei outside her room, and wearily she faces him. His eyebrows furrow, presumably at the state of her. Mei knows she is badly spent, all her qi leached out of her; there are few emotions as exhausting as pure slick fear.

Tomorrow she may need twice the feast she had tonight, if she is to do this all over again.

In Shanghai, at least, the séances were better spaced out.

"Shame about Delia," he says, sounding like he means it.

Mei manages a nod.

"I thought you might want to know," he says. "While you were . . . drawing, out of nowhere, Delia started screaming. Screaming like I've never heard. And then she just clean ran out of the room. Cecelia tried to follow, but Holly said that anyone who left the room would be disqualified. That's how it happened. I suppose in a way it's a day's stay of execution for the rest of us, if somebody leaves of their own accord, but it's weird, don't you think?"

At this moment, Mei finds it about as compelling as washing her feet.

She wipes something wet from her eyes and says, "Can I help you with something, Mr. Nakamura?"

He gives her his usual skin-deep smile. "That sketch you made," he says.

She feels her own expression flattening. "What about it?"

"The mirror. What's it mean?"

"I don't know," she says, her patience snapping like fishing line. "It is the spirit's response to whatever question was asked; it has nothing to do with me. For example, if a customer says, *Who murdered you, dear aunt?* then I might draw the face of the murderer. Did you not hear what Holly asked? You were all there."

"When Holly realized that you were being possessed, that it was working," he says, "she suddenly went very close to you, and none of us could overhear the exchange."

"Then I suppose we shall have to be content with the sketch. Good night to you—"

116

"Did you know who the spirit was? That made you draw the mirror?"

"No one knows unless the spirit chooses to reveal it," she says curtly. "I would have thought *you'd* know that. What are you really, a newspaperman? Why are you asking me so many questions?"

"I am," he says, "in fact, a writer."

Mei draws back, unnerved by this. He doesn't look like a writer. Mei met several writer-friends of George's, back in Shanghai, and they mostly had thick middles and smiles like brick walls, at least until they'd had a few drinks. Some of them had fought in wars on faraway continents, with just enough fingers left to use typewriters, and every single story they wrote was actually their own. Some of them were journalists, and sometimes, in the middle of sharing stories, they'd get a gleam in their eye like they were telling the Four Great Folktales of China all at once. Others wrote novels. Those ones rarely met Mei's eye long enough for her to tell if there was a gleam or not.

Jamie Nakamura does not have the speckles of ink all over his clothes that would give away if he worked for a paper, and he is much too young to have fought in the same wars as George Maidenhair's friends.

"The thing is, that mirror," says Jamie. "I've seen it before. It's in this house. In Maidenhair House."

CURIOSITY REARS UP within her but Mei squashes it like a hornet. It is one night into this competition and she can already tell something is skewed. That Holly is being purposefully reticent; that Holly desires something unshared and unspoken; that it is not by ability alone that the winner will win. But maybe that is good news: Mei has never been the most capable of mediums. She learned this early, in Shanghai; within minutes of meeting her Great Master.

He could see more than just ghosts.

He could see more than just the past.

"NO, THANK YOU. I have to sleep now," Mei says brusquely.

"Are you serious?" Jamie asks. "You don't want to hear what I have to say?"

She feels a touch of queasiness in her cheeks. "Why?"

"Why tell you about the mirror?"

"Why are you helping me? Aren't we opponents?"

Now it is his turn to look surprised. "I didn't think of it like that. I just thought that if you saw it, it might shed light on why you drew it. I'd love to know." His gaze shifts to the bundle she is carrying, of paper and charcoal and *The Peak House*, and his blue eyes turn bland. "The mirror is in the North Wing," he says. "In a room called the Portrait Gallery. But we'd have to go right now. The servants will be up and about by morning, and we can't chance it during the day—Holly will have our heads if she catches us anywhere near the wings."

"I don't think so. I don't know. Perhaps tomorrow night," says Mei, her lips cracking.

"Are you sure there will be a tomorrow?" He amends it quickly: "I only mean that either of us could be the next one asked to leave. But it's up to you, Miss Chen. The North Wing isn't for everyone."

AND HOW DOES Jamie himself know about the mirror?

Who is James Nakamura really, beneath the easy good looks and the shop-mannequin smiles?

But she won't ask, because if she asks, he might tell her. He might tell her everything about him, his whole life story, and for all she knows he grew up deathly poor in Shanghai's Little Tokyo, in a lane house that stank of opium tar and open sores, begging, taking beatings from Chinese gangsters for being Japanese and beatings from Japanese soldiers for not being Japanese enough. Mei doesn't like hearing life stories. The truth is that half the appeal of living with Mrs. Volkova has always been that the old Russian woman is happy to stay strangers.

Mrs. Volkova is temperamental and grouchy and spiky as a buckthorn bush, yes; prone to talking about herself, no.

Mrs. Volkova came of age during the Bolshevik Red Terror. That will cure it in anyone.

If Mei asks Jamie, then Jamie might ask *her*.

Mei can't stand it when people feel sorry for her. She prefers cruelty to pity. Actually, she thinks there is not a whole lot of difference. It is all about power.

"VERY WELL, THEN, Miss Chen," says Jamie, with a light bow of the head. "See you in the morning."

He walks away, down the darkened hall.

Mei has another flash of recognition, without any memory to go with it. She's *seen* him before; she has; she must have. It is an electrifying feeling, slippery, saltwater; the sensation of an eel swimming around her ankles. But how could they have encountered each other? In what possible context? Look at him: wealthy, or at least wealthy enough to give the impression of it; white, or at least white enough to give the impression of it. Look at her, only nominally above the dead in the hierarchy of Hong Kong society.

And yet by now she is sure that he was never a customer, of any kind. That he has never come this close to her before.

It is bizarre, but Mei wishes Jamie were not a writer. It makes her like him better, it simply does, and she does not want to like him. Just like she would not want to learn anything about George that might make her forgive him.

MEI IS JOSTLING the handle of her bedroom door, trying to open it, trying to balance all the materials in her arms, when she hears a noise behind her.

It is not quite a voice.

It is not quite human.

She blows out a breath and is shocked to see it in the air; as if the temperature has plummeted. She couldn't have gone with Jamie to the North Wing. She *can't* go. Look at her; look at how skittish she is; she isn't made for sneaking around at night. And even if she saw the mirror, she would not be able to make sense of her sketch. Mei cuts things. She does not join them together.

There is a noise behind her again, but it'll just be Jamie with more questions. Or it'll be Holly, come to say a sly good night. Shifting her things in her arms, not wanting to breathe for fear of seeing it turn solid, Mei turns around.

Her heart rises in her throat.

Somebody is standing right in front of her.

Somebody she knows. Worse yet, somebody who knows her, knew her, down to the bare broken core of her. That is what betrayal means, after all. Being known. You cannot be betrayed by strangers.

It is George Maidenhair.

15

SHANGHAI
SEPTEMBER 1937

I AM ILL. I have been ill for so long it might be forever, and the bed that felt so big the first time I laid out on it now feels tiny. And greasy. And gross. My fever has been so high that the servants say they can steam rice off my ears. Because I am ill, I have missed the period of mourning in the household. The housekeeper says that Third Wife's body was found near the Sassoon Arcade, in the middle of everything that spilled out of the shops; just another one of the pretty things damaged that day.

"But Third Wife didn't die," I say. "She can't have died at the Cathay. She came to talk to me. During the night . . ."

The housekeeper says that the doctor will give me something stronger for my fever.

AIYI COMES IN daily and reads passages from her schoolbooks out loud because First Wife has told her to. They are so dull and dry that even she has to stop sometimes and shake herself back awake.

"So, why are you telling everyone that Third Wife is still

alive?" she asks me. When I tell her, she hoots and says, "It sounds like you were visited by Third Wife's ghost!"

Aiyi is still not very nice, but Third Wife's comment about the guilt and dead sister must have worked, because I feel bad for her now instead of mad.

"This is boring," Aiyi declares. "I am bored. But not so bored that I want to write your dumb letter to your father and sisters," she adds.

"You would get along well with my oldest sister," I say wisely. "I think you two could be best friends."

She grimaces. "I'm too busy for friends. I have to study for my exams. I'm going to university in a few years."

"I don't have any friends either. Wait, I know!" I sit up even though my head is still pounding, and reach under my pillow. "You can help me with this instead. I bet you will find it more interesting." I swallow a little because every time I look at Ma's paintings my mouth fills with saliva. "My Ma left me paintings in this pouch," I say bravely, dumping out the folded-up pieces of paper, peeking to make sure I've got the one I want. "One painting is of the attic upstairs, and another is of a house. I want to show you the house. Maybe you've seen it somewhere?"

I flatten out the painting of the house.

Aiyi gives a horrified little gasp.

"I'm sorry about the girl," I say nervously.

"Girl?" she stutters. "Is that a girl? Is that what that is? Holding on to the gates?"

"I don't . . . I don't know. I think so."

"I mean, is that even a *person*?" Her voice is rising. "Why would anyone—"

"This was made by my Ma," I say defensively, "and unless you think you could do a better job you really shouldn't insult other peoples' art. Actually, she worked hard on her paintings, so you shouldn't insult it even if you *could* do a better—"

"Alright, alright," says Aiyi, all gruff and grumpy. "But I . . . I have. I mean, I do. I know this house," she says, and she makes a gulping noise herself.

"That's great," I say encouragingly. "Where is it?"

"It's in this neighborhood. But why?"

"Do you want to come with me and see who lives there? Once I'm better?"

"No way," says Aiyi, turning up her nose like a suckling pig. "I'm thirteen years old, Little Mei, not five like you."

"I'm *seven*!" Or was it six?

"I bet that's one of the things your Ma *saw*," Aiyi says sourly. "A ghost. Just like you saw Third Wife's ghost. And the girl in the attic."

"Third Wife and the girl in the attic didn't look like that," I say. "They looked normal. Mostly."

"Okay. Whatever."

How could they be *ghosts*? Ghosts only show up during the Tomb Sweeping Festival. Nai Nai used to say they get upset if you haven't done a good enough job sweeping, but then Nai Nai was always looking for things to sweep. I suppose there are other Ancestor Ghosts, the ones who eat at altars covered in feast-food; but

First Wife keeps such an altar in this bedroom and I've not seen any ghosts anywhere near it.

It is very tempting to steal at least a lychee off the offering plates.

Then there are the funny ghosts you read about in books, like the legendary corpse-hoppers, but Ba said those weren't real.

I think I should be the one telling Aiyi stories, instead!

Aiyi sighs and shuts the book she was reading from. She's not going to be able to find her place later. Once I am better, I will make her a bookmark out of paper and then she'll never lose her place again.

FIRST WIFE SAID I could get out of bed today if I wanted, but she didn't say I could sneak into Third Wife's room to check if Third Wife was actually dead.

If she finds me in here, I'll be spanked up a flagpole.

I stand in the middle of the room, looking around. Third Wife's bed is so high up she must have had to step on the heads of her servants to climb into it. The room is very quiet and smells like nothing.

Third Wife is actually dead.

I don't know why this makes me so sad. I only knew Third Wife for a few days. I should be saving my sadness for people like Ma.

But still, it goes through me, in a weird cresting wave.

Did I only dream that I saw her, that night?

I wander over to the mirror table. The table looks like one of the ancestral altars, just with different offerings: half-open ointments and oils and powders and curly dried-up seahorses in tins with no lids. I pull open the top drawer and find more dead dried stuff and a few pictures cut out of newspapers. I open the bottom drawer; it is full of what look like letters.

Didn't Third Wife—or Third Wife's ghost—unless I did dream her—say that Ma wrote letters to her?

It's super strange, since Ma couldn't read or write. She couldn't even write her own *name.*

I don't know what to believe anymore.

I look in the middle drawer.

Photographs!

Maybe they were taken by Third Wife herself!

I take out a stack of photos, sit cross-legged on the floor, and look at one after the other. Not that I know anything about photography, but my opinion is that Third Wife was very, very talented! There are pictures of buildings covered in banners; people with their arms slung around each other's shoulders and their heads thrown back happy; babies on their mothers' backs, fists up by their mouths; horses with manes like water—

Near the bottom of the stack is a photo that makes me gasp.

It's of *Ma!*

She is smiling, just like in the photo we have back home, but looking away again.

I guess she never liked to look straight at cameras.

I know it's her. I can hear her laughter. Picture-magic, just like always. But this version of Ma is younger, with a thinner face, full of angles. This must have been taken a long time ago. I am looking at my mother from before she had me. From before she had *Big Sister.* From when she *wasn't even Ma.*

But what is *that?*

Way past Ma, in the distance, is a shadowy shape. There is no lamp on here in Third Wife's bedroom, so it's hard to tell, but I think the shape is . . . *watching* her.

I think of her paintings; of the hand coming out the wardrobe door.

Of the girl-thing at the gates of that house.

My neck goes icy cold.

I turn around fast. There's nothing there. Only Third Wife's furniture.

I put all the photos back where I found them. I am almost fully recovered and I am back on track now. I am going to fulfill my chosen fate of finding Ma, and that's not all; I have decided that I am going to become a great paper artist. The best cutter ever. I tell myself this is my way of honoring her. I tell myself that it would make her happy. But really I just want the hurting to stop and I hope that I can cut it right out of me.

WHEN AIYI COMES by in the afternoon, I tell her to read to Third Wife's babies, too, because nobody does, probably, now that their mama's gone.

She looks annoyed. "They're babies. They wouldn't understand."

"I don't understand what you're reading either," I say honestly, "but I still like it when you read to me."

"I'll look in on them," Aiyi says shortly. "But I won't read to them because that would be stupid."

THE DAY FINALLY comes when First Wife throws off my blankets and tells me to get out of bed, because I need to go for a walk or else my legs will turn to grass jelly. Sleepily, without exactly knowing what is happening, I follow her out. It is early but the air is already heavy and swampy. First Wife says that the seasons are changing.

127

First Wife says that an outing like this will get my blood pumping so that I can feel it, but I do not want to feel my blood. I want to go back to bed.

"Even the servants are not awake yet," I whine as she pulls me through the courtyard.

"The servants! Listen to you, the Empress of China!"

Grown-ups are so bad-tempered in the early morning.

"The later it gets in the day," First Wife says firmly, steering me through the fence and down the street, "the likelier we will run into neighbors, and all the neighbors know you were at the Cathay on that horrible Saturday in August. Lots of people died that day, but you survived. That looks bad. *Why did* you *live? How did you get out in time? How did you find your way back here?* People say terrible things about others because it makes them feel better about their own stinky-stray-dog lives. Well, I won't have it!"

"When are the Japanese leaving Shanghai?" I ask. "Has Chiang Kai-shek stopped them bombing Chapei?"

I am proud of how smart I sound. As if I even know where Chapei is!

Anyway, I am only asking because I have this sudden sense that First Wife wishes she had somebody to talk to, about the Japanese. About what is happening in China. Maybe about what is happening in the whole world. Uncle doesn't care about the world, and Third Wife's dead and Second Wife's barely there and Aiyi is too buried in books and the servants are too scared, so there's nobody to discuss it with her.

But instead of answering, First Wife only makes an exasperated noise. I take it to mean that Chiang Kai-shek is not doing what he should. If it were up to her, the generalissimo would be out here with us, walking early enough to avoid his neighbors, feeling his blood in his body, while she instructed him on how to run the country.

We turn a corner.

I stop and she nearly falls over me.

That is the house.

The one from Ma's painting.

There are the gates, only there is no girl attached to them, thankfully.

I run right across the street; First Wife lets out a yelp. I go right up to the gates and I peer through them, but before I can try to open them and get through, First Wife grabs my arm. She lets loose a stream of irritated jumbling words that I now know to be Shanghainese.

"Who lives in this house?" I ask her, but she isn't looking at me anymore.

The door to the house is opening and a man appears.

Is that—is that the man from the Cathay rooftop?

The last person who ever spoke to Third Wife—while she was alive, at least?

This is too many surprises all at once and I don't know which one to be surprised by most. The man has spotted us; he's coming up to the gates. First Wife is still not saying anything. The closer he gets, the more certain I am that it is indeed him, but now he has a scar on his jaw that looks only half-healed.

He stops in front of the gate.

"Suyin?" he says.

Suyin? What is *Suyin?*

It is one of those white-flame words, like *Japanese.*

"Suyin?" he says again. "Gracious, how long has it been?"

First Wife looks like all the blood in her body was pumped straight to her face. We might have walked too far.

"Fifteen years," she says finally. "My husband thought you'd sold the house."

"Ah, no," he says. "I thought about it. But I always knew I'd be back eventually. What a time I chose, huh?" The stranger looks down at me next. "I know you," he says, with astonishment. "I saw you with Jing, didn't I, at the Cathay? Just the other day, right before . . ."

Jing?

Why is his Chinese so good, his accent so perfect, and yet nothing he says is understandable?

"Is this your daughter, Suyin?" he asks.

At this, First Wife goes silent again. She looks like she may have swallowed her tongue. I think she may be choking on it. I will have to speak up.

"*I* am her foster daughter," I say, with more boldness than I feel. "And you shouldn't ask people who other people are, if those other people are standing right in front of you, you know!" I have said the word *people* too many times. I don't think he knows what I'm talking about. I don't either. I'm just trying to cover up my confusion. "Who are *you*? Why were you at the rooftop and now you're here? Are you everywhere? Are you *magical*? Who are you?"

Even though I'm the one who asked the question, suddenly I know. I just know.

This man is going to be the one to write my letter for me.

The stranger's smile is kind. "George," he says. "My name is George Maidenhair."

PART THREE

16

HONG KONG
2015

MY DAUGHTER LOOKS between me and Maidenhair House, the dazedness in her face almost unseemly, like she can already picture it, her dead husband staggering toward her, his skin turned silver, his features bloated, his footsteps trailing the black water of the underground cave in which he died. Dean and Susanna were highly trained technical divers. They'd first picked it up for one of Susanna's projects, years ago, and quickly got addicted. It suited them, their personalities—an endless darkness full of possibilities, the feeling that nobody else had gotten there first. That fateful dive went well until the end; they were decompressing when it happened. It turned out later to be a heart attack.

But they had been at depth too long for Susanna to do anything but finish decompressing, with her husband's vacant eyes staring straight at her.

Susanna swam back up alone and crawled onto the surface alone but no matter how high she goes, even all the way up a mountain, she cannot leave him behind.

⌐⌐⌐

BEFORE EITHER OF us speaks again, the door of Maidenhair opens.

The person standing there regards us with deep suspicion.

Time has ground him down: His hair is thin, his shoulders set too far forward, and he has to hold himself upright by the door-frame, his fingers grasping for it. I always thought perhaps the unusual gray of his eyes might fade over the years, but it hasn't; his eyes remain the brightest, boldest thing about Detective Chief Inspector Ryan Li, so many lifetimes since I last looked into them.

Former DCI, that is.

I heard he left the police force not long after he was called to Maidenhair House on the eve of Mid-Autumn in 1953.

As far as I know, he never went back to it. The police. Or the house.

"Who are you?" He sounds like he's suffocating.

"Hello," I say regally, as if this is an entirely uneventful chance meeting, at close to midnight on a random weekday in the middle of summer, sixty-two years on, in a place I am sure we both planned never to set foot in again. "What a coincidence, to see you here, Mr. Li. You may not remember me, but my name is Chen Mei. We met once . . . right here . . ."

I am unsure of how strongly I should remind him of how we met.

I know the effect that this house, and that night, had on this man.

I know that Ryan Li spent a full year in psychiatric confine-ment at the new asylum at Tuen Mun, after it opened in the six-ties. I even wrote to him a few times; his wife wrote back with updates. She hoped they would leave Hong Kong eventually, for her native Taiwan. She thought it would help him. Susanna is bristling beside me, not able to understand our exchange in Cantonese—not that she would understand Mandarin all that well, either, because I never taught it to her. I desperately didn't want her to feel torn between two cultures. Between two worlds. I wanted her to be whole; to come from one single place. To be one single person.

How can I expect her to understand, now, how many people I have ever been?

"This is my daughter, Susanna," I say, trying again, "and she's interested in seeing the house. We didn't think anyone would be here; we were just going to take a quick look around."

"Miss Chen," says Ryan Li, and his tense shoulders fall. "Yes. Miss Chen. Yes, I do remember you."

Susanna lets out a tiny puff of air, tortured by her incomprehension.

"Why are you here?" I ask plainly.

"I live in Taipei," says Ryan. "My wife, my grown children, they all think I'm on a medical holiday in Singapore right now. You must forgive my astonishment, Miss Chen. I wasn't sure if I was seeing things." His mouth twists, not quite a smile. "As for what I'm doing here, well, I received a letter. An anonymous letter."

RYAN USHERS US into the house. Here I am in the Great Hall again, after all this time, and it is as dark and forbidding as any liminal space abandoned for decades would be. He hands us flashlights; Maidenhair no longer gets power. I flick my flashlight on and off experimentally, and every time it goes on, I feel a bite of unease that I will see something in the darkness. A face. A figure. A memory. But I see nothing.

Susanna aims her flashlight all around, at the doors to the wings.

Nothing.

I explain to Susanna that it seems there is a second letter.

"English is better?" says Ryan, switching readily.

"My daughter also received a letter," I say. "It made some . . . interesting accusations. Perhaps yours did the same?"

"No," he says, and then, taking care with his answer: "My letter did not accuse anyone. The opposite, in fact. It instructed me to come here, to Maidenhair, and not to tell anyone. Not that I would—I knew what my family would say, so I lied. But this deception is nothing compared to how I have already been living a double life, all this time: content on the surface, convulsing in misery below; haunted, so many years later, by one single night. And that's why I'm here. To have some relief. Some closure. I just want to know what happened. I just want to *know*."

Here Ryan pauses.

Susanna's face is going slack with incredulity. I don't even have to swing the flashlight her way to see it. But if she has studied the Maidenhair story the way she says she has, she must know about Ryan Li; his name would have come up long before the names of the women who died.

"What did you mean by *opposite*?" Susanna asks.

"My letter was a confession. The person who wrote it claimed to be the murderer." Ryan Li turns to me. "If there's any coincidence to all this, Miss Chen, it's that the letter asked me to come to Maidenhair tonight. To meet. And here we all are."

SUSANNA DOES NOT speak up for me this time. She does not say it is unfathomable, her mother as a murderer. Anything seems possible, I suppose, at this hour, in this place. There is a sudden crashing noise from above, startling us all, and Ryan Li shines the flashlight toward the stairs; I see the pale gleam of something that almost looks like teeth. The glow of his flashlight bobs madly, following the balustrade, the hallway that leads to the bedroom where I once slept, here at Maidenhair.

Where I might have slept for six nights, if not for *that* one.

"You know I didn't do it," I say. My heart is pounding faintly. "You know it wasn't me."

He sighs. "I don't know anything anymore."

"So you have just been sitting here? Waiting for the murderer to show up?"

"As it happens, I was looking for a way to the basement."

"You are planning to go down to the basement?"

"I was told to go down to the basement. By the letter."

Susanna exhales; we all hear it.

"Anyway, I've *found* a way, Miss Chen." He laughs, a brittle sound. "Behind the stairs. I just can't seem to . . . open it."

THERE IS SMALL, empty, airless space set beneath the main stairwell, with a slanted ceiling, exactly the kind of space I once dreaded most.

Ryan Li pulls aside the mat on the floor, and beneath it is a trapdoor.

I bend creakily, trying out the edges.

My fingers close around the ring pull.

"Hold on," says Susanna, now sounding *much* more like the Susanna who writes best-selling books and gives talks in universities and goes home to a husband. "I think we need to slow down and think a minute. First of all: these anonymous letters. The one left for my late husband and me. The one to you, Mr. Li—Mama, are you even listening?"

I give a tug, and the trapdoor seems to suck the whole floor up with it.

I did not know I possessed such strength. The ring pull has scalded my hand; my legs are quaking; but a way into the bottom half of Maidenhair House is open. I straighten gingerly. In the yawning space below, I see the shapes of steps.

"We should compare the letters," Susanna insists. "It's got to be the same writer. How many letter-writers can there be?"

But Ryan has turned away. His shoulders move a little, like he is trying to hold something in. Or maybe he is just laughing. Maybe he thinks it's funny that Susanna does not understand how this city, this country, was once full of letter-writers. There was even a letter-writer in my home village; his job was to take dictation from all the illiterate village residents so that they could correspond with their loved ones in the cities. After he died, I wondered how the loved ones in the cities would ever find out.

"I'm sorry," Ryan says, facing the wall. "I just need a moment to—I can't—"

"I agree. This is irresponsible in the extreme. We need to prep, we need proper equipment," says Susanna, heatedly now. I know she's thinking about Dean. About never taking chances like that, ever again. About never descending, ever again. "Or, better still, to send someone who knows about such structures all the way down, to check it's safe—"

What kind of life must you lead, to believe that something— anything—can be safe all the way down?

The kind of life I wanted to give my daughter.

The life that I hoped she would have in America. The life where there are no trapdoors and there are also no ceilings. I did not give her a Chinese name; I worried that if I did, it might be replaced by a number. I did not cook her Chinese food; I thought it might burn a hole through her American tongue. I did not show her how to play *èrhú*. Piano is good, I said. Or violin. Music is just supposed to fill the silence. It is not supposed to tell a story.

Ryan Li is turning back around, rubbing the side of his head.

The house is silent, and then there is a sound: a muffled slam.

"What was that?" says Susanna, her eyes like scalpels.

Another noise.

Closer now.

Ryan lets out a loud breath.

"What's *in* this house, Mama?" Susanna whispers.

Maybe not just the past.

Maybe also the future. My daughter's future.

17

HONG KONG
SEPTEMBER 1953

The Second Séance

GEORGE MAIDENHAIR IS turning. Walking away. But how can it be George? Holly said he wasn't here—and Holly has no reason to lie about it—and George would never hide from his houseguests—

Most of all, George would never turn away from Mei.

"Wait," she says, startled by the agony in her own voice. The hallway swims in her vision. "Wait."

The figure keeps going.

Mei breaks into a run.

It's me! It's me, Little Mei!

The figure has faded. Mei turns in circles, forgetting where she is, where she started. But if she had caught up with him, what would she have done, anyway? Killed him the moment he was within reach? The sharp end of her white peony hairpin would be enough if you went for the jugular. He would spray blood like a fire hose. But that is not exactly what she wants, somehow; she wants them to *face* each other. She wants to see every emotion in the world pass over his face as he realizes he cannot escape his fate. Oh, and how sure *is* she, that that was George? Can she trust her own judgment, after such a long day, in such darkness? What if it was just the house, making her see things? The way Mistress Lau said they all would?

Mei has never heard of houses creating figures. Houses cutting their own shadow puppets. Houses putting on shows.

MEI HAS NO idea where she is. She ran too far; she doesn't know where this hallway started; she can't seem to find her room again. She'll try again in a moment. She leans against a window, trying to think over the crashing tides in her head. There are tiny paw prints of rain on the glass.

The nearest door opens, shocking Mei upright.

Mistress Lau steps out. It is some ungodly hour of the night and yet she is still in full face paint. "Miss Chen," she says archly. "Jamie Nakamura was just asking everyone where your room was. Did he find you?"

"We spoke briefly, yes," Mei says guardedly.

"What about?"

"This and that. Nothing important. Would you be able to—"

"I can tell when somebody has the Sight, you know."

Rain splatters hard against the glass.

Mistress Lau clearly has something to say.

"It is part of my own gift," says Mistress Lau. "For example, I can see the Sight all over you, right now, like grains."

"And so?"

"Jamie Nakamura doesn't have it. He doesn't have the Sight."

A sudden silence, marked only by rain.

"He can't see ghosts," says Mistress Lau. "He's not like us."

"So he's a fraud," says Mei, feeling unexpectedly defensive. "Is that so surprising? That out of six spirit mediums—"

"It's not that."

"Then what *is* it?"

Mistress Lau says, "I think he is dead."

Mei's blood chills in her veins.

"I think even Holly doesn't realize."

"That's ridiculous," says Mei, her mouth running dry.

"When you two were talking, what did Jamie say? Anything strange? Anything you can't quite wrap your head around?"

The way Mistress Lau asks, Mei can tell that she overheard Jamie telling Mei about the mirror.

"He knows things he shouldn't, doesn't he?" Mistress Lau says, in a serpent's silky hiss. "If you ask me what happened to Delia in the Red Library, it's that she *saw* him. The *real* him, I mean. He may look human, but it's a mask. It's no different to how I wear this white paint. He is one of the entities that haunts Maidenhair; that cannot leave it. And that's what sent Delia off screaming."

"I don't want to hear this anymore," says Mei fitfully.

"Cover your ears and eyes if you like. I don't think it'll help you, in this house," says Mistress Lau, and she turns on her heel and slams the door shut behind her.

MEI WAKES EARLY. She has slept terribly, but at least the night is over. She opens her window, letting in a sheet of mosquitoes. The outside air is wet and sweaty; the sky is darkly marbled overhead, but it is enough daylight that she dips into the first chapter of *The Peak House*.

The story is about a troubled young man, plagued by his memories of the war, drinking too much to keep these demons away, who unexpectedly inherits an estate on Victoria Peak. The estate is said to be cursed. His neighbors tell him about the Lotus Lady, the malevolent spirit of a young woman who drowned herself years ago in the lotus pond in the garden.

Nobody knew her name, where she had come from, what she

was doing at the house, or why she had waded into the water and breathed it in until her lungs curdled.

If she had not become a ghost, the people who lived in the house never would have known she died.

If she had not become a ghost, they never would have known she had ever been alive.

It takes willpower Mei doesn't altogether possess to stop reading. She tells herself she will have plenty of time to read later today, but she has to physically strain to shut *The Peak House*. On her way down to breakfast her mind hums and cackles with theories about the Lotus Lady's death. In the Dining Hall everyone greets her and she can hardly return their greetings, because she has left her brain inside her book.

HOLLY SAYS THEY can spend the morning as they wish, so long as they remain indoors and do not venture into the wings. Every time Holly says they cannot go into the wings, Mei is struck both by the inexplicable desire to do exactly that, and an equally powerful urge to flee the house entirely; she gives in to neither. There is a Music Room and a Cinema Room for entertainment, as well as plenty of diverting games in the salons.

Mei has already decided to disappear back into the pages of *The Peak House*.

"We will assemble in the Great Hall shortly before lunch," says Holly. "Unfortunately, the weather makes it so that we cannot wait until tonight to hold the Second Séance. The ground will have gone to tar by then."

"You mean the Second Séance is going to be outside?" asks Mistress Lau, with open skepticism. Mei agrees with her: The storm is already here, and these seasonal typhoons can turn furious quickly, tree branches falling, power lines snapping, debris flying, wind that could strip the hide off an animal. "Could you not switch the order of the séances? Perhaps in a day or two it would be—"

"The Second Séance will take place in the five-point pavilion in the garden," says Holly. "By the pond."

The garden. The pond.

The Lotus Lady.

Mei feels a flutter in her throat, like a songbird.

Mei settles on a sofa in the atrium at the back of the house, which has large glass windows overlooking a large veranda being beaten by rain. Storms are good for something: reading.

George Maidenhair once said that all *book people* love to read in bad weather.

She resolves to read until she has forgotten where she is, and what she has to do this afternoon, but no sooner has she cracked open *The Peak House* than the French doors are flung apart.

It is Peng; she stands in the doorway without entering.

Peng strikes Mei as somebody who has worked as a domestic. She is young but looks crushingly tired. She goes easily red in the face, and the way she speaks sounds like someone failing to light a match. During the First Séance last night, she went into a trance that looked exactly like sleep, except that her eyes were open; she did not speak or react. Mei did not think it was a normal spirit that possessed her, one with something to say to the living. It looked like something *preying* on her. Draining her. But nobody else seemed perturbed by this, and now Mei wonders if perhaps that is simply how Peng appears in trances.

If that is why she appears to be half in a trance all other times too.

Right now she keeps looking steadily and slowly around the room, at the furniture, at the looming glass windows, until Mei wants to shake her.

"Where did he go?" Peng asks, her voice high and woodwind sweet.

"Where did who go?" asks Mei warily, her hand already parting the pages.

"The child."

"What child?"

"I saw him run in here," says Peng, almost dreamily. "Oh, there he is."

Mei dares to look Peng in the eye. "There isn't anyone else in here."

"He's right behind you."

"Stop it."

"I can see him, though. Right over your head."

Mei feels a whistly breath through her hair and her arms explode in goose bumps.

"Stop it," she says again, sharply, but Peng isn't listening.

"Come, little one," Peng coos. Her smile is friendly and fearless. Her eyes are fixed on the empty space beside Mei on the sofa. Mei wants to edge away from it but she feels frozen. "Come. I'll help you back to your room. Oh. Oh, I see." Her face shutters. "He says you live in his room. He says he couldn't sleep, because of you. He says he had to stand at the foot of the bed, all night, because of you."

"What are you talking about?" Mei demands. "What's wrong with you? Why are you acting this way?"

Peng tilts her head at her. "Who are you?" she asks.

Mei opens her mouth and finds she has no reply at all.

Peng drifts out the way she came, as if she is dancing.

AFTER HER RECENT interactions with Jamie, Mistress Lau, and Peng, Mei is loath to have any further contact with any of her fellow competitors, and she moves to her bedroom to read. In time, at last, her other cares diminish, and the world of the book envelops her. She begins to feel bad for the Lotus Lady character, even though you're probably not supposed to feel bad. If Mei died, who would know? Who would care? Who would mourn? What is one more refugee in a city that shakes with them? Mei's death would make no difference. Mrs. Volkova would replace Mei the way she replaces her netsukes.

ON ANY OTHER day, in any other weather, the garden of Maidenhair House might be beautiful. There are luminous gilt screens and pale stone paths and traces of artificial streams, cutting through ornamental rock beds, and after one last gravelly stretch, there is a large clearing, surrounded on all sides by bamboo.

In the center of this space is a body of water large enough to be called a lake.

The surface is laced with lotus, but Mei can hardly see it through the rain; the only source of light is water glistening off the white-painted pavilion on the far side of the pond.

Holly is already leading them that way.

Here is some respite, at least; the roof does not let any rain through. Mei and the others sit upon the built-in benches, with Holly still standing, haranguing them about the original construction of the garden. Mistress Lau has painted herself festively today but the rain has washed the paint down her cheeks, like sidewalk art draining into gutters. Cecelia is clutching some kind of good-luck talisman; her hand bulges with it. Peng keeps looking toward the lotus pond. Jamie Nakamura looks the most relaxed of any of them, but Mei does not want to think about Jamie.

Mei withdraws her paper and pencil from the pocket of her dress. She will not use charcoal for the remaining séances; she prefers charcoal generally, but she is hoping for finer detail tonight. For starker lines. For a more vivid image. For less ambiguity. For clues, even if she can't quite admit it to herself yet, as to what Holly might have asked. Her materials have stayed dry, but as she did not want to risk damaging *The Peak House* in this down-pour, she has nothing to draw on other than her knee, which is soaked. Better to use the bench she is sitting on.

She only hopes that she has replenished her qi enough since yesterday that she can drive the spirit out when the trance is over.

She would rather die than become possessed.

"A few times, when I have come out here by myself," says Holly, "I have seen what looks like muddy prints going in and out of the water."

Your gardener, Mei thinks fervently. *One of your servants. Your husband. It could be anyone—*

"Handprints," says Holly. "I believe that someone crawls, every night, on their hands and knees, from the pond to this pavilion."

UNNERVED BY HOLLY'S words as she is, Mei feels a twinge of sympathy, odd and misplaced, much like her sympathy for the Lotus Lady.

Imagine what it would be like, trapped in the lotus pond.

Imagine looking up, seeing those slivers of sun overhead, cutting through the leaves.

Imagine every time you opened your mouth to cry for help, it filled with water.

Mistress Lau speaks up: "We cannot hold the séance like this, Auntie, respectfully." She does not sound especially respectful. "You are not able to light candles in this weather. No candles, no offerings, no protection. We should go inside."

"Anyone who wants to leave is welcome to leave," says Holly.

No one opts to leave.

They each must drop whatever they are holding, to clasp hands.

Who will be eliminated from the competition tonight?

Or will somebody run out screaming again?

18

SHANGHAI
SEPTEMBER 1937

GEORGE MAIDENHAIR ASKS if we would like to come inside for tea. He seems to have forgotten that he was headed someplace before we showed up.

I really hope First Wife will accept. Not only because I am hungry from all the walking and blood-pumping and standing up to strangers, but because I desperately want to know why Ma left me a painting of George's house, and I feel like my best chance to find out is to go in.

I beg First Wife with my eyes to say yes.

"Very well," she says. She is pink in the face. Maybe the sun has risen too high and now she is melting. "For a few minutes."

George opens the gate and shows us up the path to his house. On the way, First Wife apologies for how sleepy I look even though she's the one who dragged me out of bed. Then she apologizes for how I'm not standing up straight enough, and I worry that she's going to start forcing me to wear qipaos like hers. But before First Wife can apologize a third time, probably just for the fact that I am breathing, George takes us into a room with beautiful whispery curtains and shelves with so many books that I actually might not be breathing anymore.

He rings a bell for his housekeeper and we all sit down.

"Do you own all the books in the entire world?" I ask him, open-mouthed.

"I plan to one day," he says seriously.

"You could open your own shop!"

He laughs at that. "Before I inherited my father's business," he says, "I trained to become a teacher. That's where all these books come from. They're the ones I once hoped to share with my students. You like to read?"

"My foster daughter is illiterate," scoffs First Wife, and I feel heat creeping up my neck.

George Maidenhair politely pretends not to notice.

"She's Limei's youngest," says First Wife. "You remember Limei? She skipped town on us around the time you left for America, if I remember correctly. Well, she took up with somebody new fast as you please and ended up with three daughters."

Limei?

Ma's name was *Limei*?

I am in such awe of this discovery that I almost don't catch how George has lurched a little off his chair.

"Ah," he says, sitting back again. "Limei. Yes. Of course."

He knew Ma.

But of course they knew each other. She wouldn't have painted a picture of his house for nothing.

"I spoke to Little Mei's birth father at length, before we adopted her," First Wife continues. "He tried so hard to educate her, but it was all to no avail. Limei could not be taught to read either. Some people are just unteachable."

"I don't believe anyone is unteachable," says George, but

mildly, like he doesn't want First Wife to realize that he is dis-agreeing with her.

"Me neither," I say. I don't really know what he means, but I want to support him.

I wonder if George has kids. If he does, they're lucky. I would love to live in a house made out of books instead of bricks.

"Well, if Little Mei's father couldn't, it's unlikely anyone can," First Wife says crisply. "For a farmer, he was educated, bright, and played the *èrhú* beautifully. Some people are just innately talented, don't you find? *Tiān fèn*, a gift sent from the heavens. It makes you think, if only that person had been born to another life!"

"It was his fate," I say.

They both turn to look at me.

"My Ba. It was his fate. To be a farmer. Even though he could play the *èrhú* well enough to make an emperor cry. What is your fate, Mr. Maidenhair? Do you like it?"

First Wife turns red as a welt.

George Maidenhair laughs again, a nice soft sound. I think his laughter gets caught in his beard. "Not always," he says. "I never thought I would have to fill my father's shoes. But I have a lot to be grateful for." He sets down his tea and something sad fills his face but it's gone quickly, a cloud passing over the sun. "You know, I believe I could teach you to read, Little Mei. If you wanted. With your permission, of course, Suyin."

"Oh," says First Wife, and her mouth makes a circle, like a fish's. "I . . . that is, I would need to . . . to check with my hus-band." Then, before anyone can say anything else about it, First Wife asks George Maidenhair about his business, which soon turns to talk of the war, and to the 'Bloody Saturday' that he and I survived at the Cathay. They talk on and on, and First Wife doesn't even sound like First Wife anymore. She doesn't use her usual sword-words, and when she reaches over to swat my hand away from the plate of biscuits left by the housekeeper, I don't feel her sword-nails.

She almost looks . . . *happy.*

I think she likes talking to George Maidenhair.

I think she likes George Maidenhair.

I think maybe she has liked him for a long, long time.

But eventually their conversation becomes boring, so I rifle through his books even though I can't read them.

"That's *Jane Eyre.* Perhaps my favorite book," says George.

"Oh," I say, impressed, trying to imagine what it's like, to have a favorite book. To have read so many that you can *pick* one. "What's it about?"

"It's about a young woman who goes to live in a great big house that holds a great big terrible secret. Are you intrigued?" asks George, smiling, because he already knows that I am.

ON OUR WAY home, First Wife says that George Maidenhair was just being nice, offering to teach me. I don't understand what she means. I don't think it's nice to offer to teach somebody if you don't mean it.

"It's out of the question, anyway. You should forget you ever heard his name," says First Wife.

How can you forget somebody called *George Maidenhair?* Especially when everyone else around you is numbered?

First Wife says we need to hurry home now because the others will be wondering where we've gone. They will worry because the streets of Shanghai are crawling with Japanese soldiers. Even worse, our neighborhood is crawling with nosy neighbors. First Wife's ears are still smoking red, but the rest of her face is back to normal. She is turning back into the First Wife from earlier this morning. But it's too late. It's too late because now I know there is somebody else in there, underneath all the rice powder and rouge, a somebody whose name is Suyin, who once wanted something besides a baby, and I wonder how much she's had to cane herself, to stop herself wanting it.

THE NEXT DAY, I return to the Magnolia Room.

I apologize to Uncle and ask if I can study paper art with him. If he is pleased by this, he does not show it. He frowns and asks me to cut something out of paper, and afterward he says it doesn't even count as art, because it is so bad.

In the afternoon, Aiyi comes in from school and I give her the bookmark that I made. I drew a girl reading a book on the front.

"Is this supposed to be me?" she asks.

"It can be me, if you prefer. I'm going to learn how to read very soon," I say, and I tell her all about George Maidenhair and the photograph and the house and the book about a great big secret.

"How are you going to convince First Wife to let you?" asks Aiyi, sticking the bookmark into one of her books.

"I'm going to be very well-behaved from now on and show her that I—"

"You *could* do that," says Aiyi, "or . . . you could do something else."

"Like what?" I say, trying not to sound too excited, because I think we are becoming friends.

"First Wife is superstitious, you know. Worse than the servants. And I've just had an idea."

"What idea?"

Aiyi finally tucks all her hair behind her ears. She never looks this eager when she studies. She doesn't seem to love books the way George Maidenhair does, and I'm not so sure she should be going to university to read *more* books. But you can't just *say* this to people, can you? You can't just tell them that maybe they're on the wrong roads. That's the funniest thing about fate, I guess: All the mistakes you make trying to find your fate are also your fate.

"Listen up," she says. "The first thing you need to do is . . ."

NOW THAT I am entirely well again, First Wife insists that I join her every night for bedtime leg-slapping. This is a ritual that involves rolling your stockings to the ankles and hitting your bare legs with an open palm to increase blood flow. It seems like nearly everything First Wife does is for the sake of her blood.

First Wife says it's a good way to make sure your limbs are still alive; I didn't know that parts of you could die and you don't even realize it.

First Wife and I start to leg-slap in silence, right there on the floor, slap-slap-slap-slap.

Right now I do feel like the dumpling dough, the way Third Wife said I would.

"I want Mr. Maidenhair to teach me to read," I say.

"We're not going to bother him again," says First Wife.

"The girl in the attic says you should let him teach me."

First Wife stops leg-slapping.

I have to be careful, but by now I understand: The things that people don't want to talk about? Those are the things that have the most power. The things that people are most afraid of. *The Japanese.* But if you're willing to say those things out loud, then some of that power gets smeared on you. Some of that power starts to belong, a little bit, to you.

"What are you talking about?" snaps First Wife.

First Wife is always so *angry*. The servants say that long, long ago, First Wife was engaged to Uncle's older brother, but then he died of a slow-crawling illness. Then her in-laws forced her to marry Uncle, even though neither she nor Uncle wanted it. She hoped for a baby, at least, but she couldn't have one, and now she's almost forty years old and stuck with an ungrateful scrawny shrimplike foster daughter and likely never will have a child of her own, no matter how much she kowtows to the ancestors, no matter how many times she slams her head into the floor until it bleeds.

They say that First Wife does not like her life.

People who do not like their lives—

They are the sort of people who turn to fortune tellers.

They are the sort of people who will believe anything.

"The girl missing most of her tongue," I say. "She wears a hair stick with pearls in it."

"Who told you about her?" First Wife sounds like she has leg-slapped her own voice. "Was it Cook?"

"I *met* her, when you locked me in the attic on my first night," I say stubbornly. "I didn't know who she was. She has bound feet. You know, feet like the ends of table legs?"

I am starting to think that grown-ups are like paper cuttings. They look whole from a distance, but they're actually made up of *loads* of holes and you have to find the right hole to run your string through. First Wife might have more than most people; that's why she has to wear a qipao like a bandage. I wonder if she is in love with George Maidenhair, and that's why she looked like somebody took a torch to her bare bottom when he smiled at her. I wonder if George could ever convince her to leave Uncle and marry him instead and maybe to wear looser clothing. I wonder if I could go live with them in his nice white house and have all those books to myself.

She would stop being First Wife. She could just be Suyin.

But somehow I do not think it is going to happen that way.

"Because her tongue's been lopped off like a fish head, we can't talk so good to each other, the girl in the attic and me," I explain.

"So she wants me to learn to read from George Maidenhair. He was a teacher and knows a special method for teaching, and once I learn, she and I will be able to talk by writing. She has *lots* to tell me. As a ghost, she knows lots of things that living people do not know," I add, and slap my knees extra hard.

My limbs do feel alive. Super alive. What I've said to First Wife is not *so* far off from the truth, but my whole body is buzzing, as if I've handed her a whole sack of lies.

Maybe this was my first *spoken storybook performance.*

ON OUR WAY to his house, First Wife says that Mr. Maidenhair is a busy and important man, because he runs a whole *empire* all by himself, like how the emperor ruled all of China or the tsar ruled all the Russias. It sounds like there's usually someone who sits on a throne. George Maidenhair will have to get a haircut if he wants to wear a crown. And he should trim his beard while he's at it. It is long enough that flying squirrels could nest in it.

And yet, despite how busy and important he is, George Maidenhair has found three afternoons a week to teach a child with a wrong-way-round head how to read.

First Wife sits across the table from us, watching intently, as George stacks books into an anthill in front of me.

First Wife will be attending all our sessions. She said it's because George is still a stranger, but I think it's because she doesn't want George to be a stranger.

"Your mother had difficulty reading and writing because she was word-blind, Little Mei," is the first thing George says. "And I wonder if—"

"What disease is this?" First Wife interrupts.

"It is not a sickness, Suyin." His voice is very patient. His voice says: *Do not interrupt us.* First Wife retreats into silence. George continues: "You see, Little Mei, your mother and I were good friends for several years, before I had to return to America. At that time, I had no idea how to help someone with word-blindness. But if I'd had, I would have offered to teach her, too. And I would have started by saying this: There is no shame in it. There is nothing to be embarrassed of. In fact, you should be proud, because it will be difficult, it will be hard work, but you are about to do it anyway."

I feel a wiry tightness in my chest and I don't know why.

George Maidenhair places a plain brown book in front of me.

I had been really hoping we would start with the woman-going-to-the-big-house-with-a-big-secret book.

"Go on," he says, "open it."

I open it, with deep suspicion.

I stare at the up-and-down lines of spider leg strokes that I know to be Han characters, even if don't know how reading works.

"Nothing is happening," I say, my suspicion growing.

"Nothing has happened yet," he says, "but trust me, things *will* happen. Things beyond your wildest imagination."

"This book is so ugly. Can't we use a prettier one?"

"I agree it is plain to look at," he says gravely, "but that is what will make the transformation all the more astounding. It is best to begin one's reading journey by looking at such books. You do not expect—right now you do not even believe—that something in-credible will rise out of these pages, but it will. That's why books are magic, Little Mei. The only magic in the world."

"WHEN DID YOU know my Ma?" I ask, when First Wife leaves to use the flush-toilet.

"It was a long time ago," George says.

"How long?"

"Alright, well, she would have been eighteen or so, when we

met, and I was about twenty. And now I'm thirty-eight, so it's been a—"

"You're *old*," I say, and he laughs again. I think he likes to laugh.

"I know you must miss her," he says. "Suyin told me that your parents felt you would be safer in Shanghai. But the Japanese *will* be driven out of China one day, Little Mei, and when they are—"

"Ma's missing," I say.

"Missing?" He looks confused.

"Since the Dragon Boat Festival."

"The Dragon Boat Festival?"

He's like a myna bird, repeating everything I say! "Ma is *missing*," I say, slow and loud. Maybe he's better at reading than he is at listening. "Ma has been missing for months. Nobody knows where she is. She came here to Shanghai for a little bit, I think, but nobody talks about it, and anyway, she disappeared. My sister thinks she died doing something shameful, and that's why nobody talks about it. I am looking for her, but one person is not easy to find, you know, in a city like this!"

George's face has gone so pale beneath the beard, he looks sick.

I wish I already knew how to read. Then at least I'd have something to do while I wait for him to answer.

"Suyin did not . . . mention this to me," he says at last.

"I *told* you, we're not supposed to talk about it. That's why I had to wait for her to go to the flush-toilet."

"The countryside . . . as well as Shanghai itself . . . is in chaos," he says. He sounds like he's trying to convince himself, more than me. "With all the people moving about, the roads closing, the soldiers pouring in, the conflicts— A lot of people are unaccounted for. It's possible that your mother just couldn't get home somehow. Or—"

"Could you help me write a letter to my Ba and sisters? To explain that I am here in Shanghai looking for her?"

Now George looks worried as well as confused. "You mean they don't know that you're in Shanghai?"

"No, they do, but— Wait. You could help me *find* her!" I say urgently. "Since you have an empire, and all! I think she missed you, after you left for America. She even painted your house!"

"My house?"

He's back to repeating. I reach into my dress pocket and take out Ma's pouch. I take it with me everywhere now; I don't want to risk someone stealing it. "There are three paintings total," I say, taking care not to press the pouch too flat. "I thought there were only two, at first, but that's because the first two were folded up and fell out easily, while the third one was sticking to the inside of the pouch. Here, see this one? She painted your house."

"But what is this?"

He's pointing to the girl-thing, holding on to his gates.

"I don't know," I admit. "But you can see her a bit better in the third painting."

I show him the last one.

You can't really see her better.

It's just that she's coming closer.

19

HONG KONG
SEPTEMBER 1953

MEI JOLTS AWAKE to the sound of a scream. She is alone now in the white pavilion: Everyone else is down by the lotus pond. They are crouched over the ground. Mei senses a layer of liquid all over her, sweat or rain, she can't tell, and she gets to her feet, makes it down the steps. *What's going on?* She yells, but it is lost to the storm. She need not have asked anyway, as it is soon obvious: Peng has just been pulled out of the water.

The girl is murmuring incoherently, dribbling pond silt, but she is alive.

Mei feels her stomach unclench.

Holly is brushing Peng's matted burnt-straw hair off her face.

"She ran in," says Mistress Lau. "She started babbling that there was a woman right there in the pavilion with us, and before any of us could tell her otherwise, she took off. Went straight for the water. Tripped and fell. Mr. Nakamura got her out."

"Had she—was she in a trance?" asks Mei numbly.

Mistress Lau stands up straight, hikes up her skirts to the ankles, sodden with mud. "No," is the direct, disdainful answer. "It started during *yours.*"

Again, is what goes unsaid.

Jamie Nakamura mutters something in Shanghainese, and Holly answers. Mei doesn't try to follow along. She never quite got the knack for Shanghainese, and even when spoken between friends, it will never fail to sound like a threat. She watches as Jamie lifts Peng into his arms, to take her back into the house. Mistress Lau and Holly trail behind, arguing in low tones, followed by Cecelia, who is squeezing out her blouse, like she means to dry it, in the middle of a deluge.

Soon enough they have all gone inside, and only Mei remains at the pond.

She has not yet shaken off the cobwebs of her own trance; she does not yet feel like she lives in her own body.

There is a shock of gold between the lotus pads. A koi.

Anything that dies in that pond will be eaten down to the bone.

Mei turns her face into the storm. Her hair, her skin, her eyes are full of rain, as thick as oil. All around her, the bamboo rises, blends into the blackboard sky. In Confucian tradition, making use of the natural landscape to enhance a garden is called *jièjǐng*. Borrowed scenery. All of this feels like *borrowed scenery*. A borrowed moment in time, separate from her real life, in which Mei is staying in a mansion on a mountain, surviving séance after séance, battling a storm within and without, reading the first novel she has read in years, all while planning to kill the man who taught her to read, the man who did not only destroy her life, but changed it. Saved it.

HER SECOND SÉANCE-SKETCH. She left it in the pavilion.

Peng might have thought she saw someone, but it's no different from what happened earlier in the atrium. Mistress Lau was right: This house plays tricks on your head. There is nothing to be frightened of, except whatever is already inside you.

Is that why you are so afraid, Mei?

Mei stalks back to the pavilion, dragging mud with every step, and finds her sketch on the bench, her pencil lined up neatly beside it.

What does Holly Zhang keep asking?

Mei has drawn stairs going down.
But even without thinking too hard, she knows—
These stairs exist somewhere in Maidenhair.
Just like the mirror.

⌒

THE RAIN IS still falling like arrows and it is dark enough to pass for night by the time she slips into the house, via the veranda.

Jamie Nakamura is in the atrium, reading on the sofa she was reading on earlier, his feet up on it, like he owns it. When he sees her he says, "If I'd known you were still out there, Miss Chen, I'd have gone out to get you. Good grief."

"I had to rescue my sketch," Mei says, teeth clattering with cold, "to give to Holly."

"Come on. Let's get you warmed up in the kitchen."

Mei has the bleakly amusing thought that if he is a ghost, a longtime inhabitant of the house, then at least he is a decent host.

IN THE KITCHEN, as Jamie boils hot water to drink, Mei rummages through random cupboards and comes up with a tin of cheap imitation duck, the kind you have to scrape out with force and eat in chunks. She is suddenly famished; she slides onto a chair and begins to eat with her fingers until Jamie hands her a pair of chopsticks, without comment.

"Is Peng alright?" she asks, through her mouthfuls.

"She'll be fine. Once the storm lets up we'll get someone here to check her out. I went to the North Wing last night, by the way, after we spoke," Jamie says casually, taking the seat across from hers. "Maybe I shouldn't have, but I couldn't sleep, wondering about the mirror you drew. If it was actually the same one. But the door to the Portrait Gallery was locked. Holly must have locked it after yesterday's séance," he muses. "If you ask me, I'd say she wanted to be absolutely sure you wouldn't look into that mirror."

Mei has already eaten far too much salted duck. Her tongue

feels like she's shaved it. "Holly has six strangers in her home. She might have locked all the rooms beforehand."

"She never locks them. Until now," he says ruefully.

"But how do you know?"

"Let's just say this isn't my first time in Maidenhair."

This penetrates her haze at last. "You've been here before."

"A few times, yes."

"In what capacity?"

"What are you, a newspaperwoman?" he asks, but his tone stays affable. "I was doing some interviews, for one. It was for a book. The very one you're reading, in fact."

She nearly spits out her sip of hot water.

The Peak House?

He is the author of *The Peak House?*

Mei cannot, she simply cannot, reconcile the blithe, almost indifferent man in front of her with the writer of that novel. Of those words. Of a story that already has her well in its grasp. The knowledge is stupefying and she couldn't even say why. Perhaps it is like the life stories, the ones she hates to hear, because it is so much easier when you see only the top layer of people. It is so much cleaner.

Silence is not the same thing as peace.

Perhaps not just in houses, but in people too.

"But it's—it's not your name on the cover," she protests.

Jamie gives a half-hearted chuckle. "It's a pseudonym. Tell me, if you had my name, would you use it on your paper cuttings?"

"How do you know I cut paper?"

They stare at each other in the vague darkness.

"Mistress Lau thinks you might be a ghost, you know," Mei hears herself say.

Now he laughs out loud. "Can't you people tell?"

"It's not always that easy. Are you saying you're not?"

"Sorry to disappoint you, but I'm alive as you are, Miss Chen.

That woman's just trying to get into your head. She's got children on the mainland, you know. She'd do anything to win this. I'd take it as a compliment—she must see you as the primary competition."

"Why did you just say *you people*?"

A long silence; and then a sigh. "Fine," he says.

"Fine *what*?"

"I'm not really a spirit medium, alright? I'm Holly Zhang's stepson."

"You're—"

"I'm George Maidenhair's biological son. I'm Holly's stepson."

"But George Maidenhair doesn't have a son," Mei says, sputtering. "He has no children."

It might be easier to believe that Jamie was dead, after all. He is George's son? She has been conversing with George's son? No, it can't be. There is the Jamie Nakamura she met yesterday at dinner, the one who made wild claims about the mirror, the one who has just warmed her up. And then there is Jamie Nakamura, George's son. These have to be two different people.

But then Jamie *is* two different people, isn't he? Shanghainese, Japanese? White, American, heir to a house perched poorly on a hill?

What does *he* see when he looks in a mirror?

"I'm illegitimate, by his onetime Japanese mistress," says Jamie. "In short, I'm not a ghost and I'm no threat to win. Holly hired me to track all of you down, and asked me to participate, to pretend to be one of you, because she thought it would look more balanced." He offers her an apologetic smile. "But in the spirit of honesty, I'll add that your name was already familiar to me. You don't just draw and paint and whatnot. You make paper puppets. More to the point, you made my father's entire collection of shadow puppets; the ones he keeps in his Puppet Room. I've seen your name on all of them. Maybe you should have used a pseudonym too, huh?"

GEORGE LUGGED THE shadow puppets Mei made for him all the way from Shanghai to Hong Kong?

He keeps them in a room called the *Puppet Room*?

Mei imagines puppets hung on every inch of every wall, all of them staring into nothing forever.

Mei wishes you could set fire to only one room in a house and not have the fire touch any of the others.

Mei wishes you could erase only one memory in your mind and not harm any of the others.

MEI MANAGES TO swallow one last grainy bite of false meat. "I was told that *The Peak House* was inspired by Maidenhair," she says. "That's why I was recommended to read it."

"It is," says Jamie. "I drew on the history of the house."

"Is the Lotus Lady a myth?"

"Have you seen her walking around?"

"No, I mean—did someone tell you the story, or did you make it up?"

"In a way, I barely made up anything in that book," he says baldly. "What I didn't base on Maidenhair, I based on myself. My own experiences. First novel, you know." He shrugs, a gesture that is surprisingly genuine; the effect is disarming. "As for the Lotus Lady, yes, I was told. That's a popular one. Nobody seems to know who the real-life woman who drowned might have been, except that since then the house has repeatedly been the site of . . . I guess *carnage* is the most accurate term. All largely swept under the rug because the Halls were a prominent family. Close to the governor, and so on. And the Peak's always been a little bit above the law anyway. In every sense."

"I've heard about the Japanese officers," says Mei.

She is still reeling from his other revelations; she is amazed to be able to keep up her end of their conversation.

"Yup, 1943. The Halls tried to live in the house again after they got out of Stanley, but it was just too much. That's why they sold it to my father. He loved this house the moment he laid eyes on it. If you knew him, you'd know this is his kind of place. Gothic and sinister and full of nooks and crannies. But in any case, Maidenhair's got a reputation, among the native Hong Kongers at least. They say you shouldn't attend parties here or gather as part of any group. Because when you do, everyone ends up dead."

"We're part of a group right now," she says, setting down her chopsticks.

"Hey, don't look like that. It's just a story," he says. "Cooked up like pig liver at a streetside *dai pai dong*. You know how it is."

THEY END UP talking until long after her water has cooled, and the more they talk, the more she understands that her initial, instinctive distaste for Jamie was not for *him*, himself. How could it be, when she does not know him; not really?

It was for what he represented: his people; their brutality; the bloodshed. The war. The losses. The lives.

Not just the ones on the battlefield.

He was only a symbol; a stand-in; a paper-cut puppet.

Is that how Mei perceives *everyone* she meets? As shadows?

Is *Mei* an Important Customer?

Pining for something that is out of reach, and determined to stay pining? Knowing that everything she wants can never be, and if it can never be, then she may as well rot like a log, she may as well wall herself into a curio shop, she might as well be sleepwalking?

Not letting anyone else too close, because nobody, nothing, can live up to her memories?

Who could ever be as Great as her Great Master?

The problem is that memories twist over time. They become fantasies. Ideals.

They become perfect.

But the only thing that is ever perfect is the uncut piece of paper. The life unlived.

LATER, AS MEI tosses and turns in bed, it comes to her, spontaneously, as all such ideas do, although this one is truly terrible. Do other people have such thoughts? Evil and small and curling slightly? Mei compares these thoughts to cuts in paper: Once you have them, you can't un-have them, the way you can't un-cut. And the more you try not to have them, the more they multiply, until you have nothing but confetti in your hands.

George Maidenhair has a *son*.

He always wanted a child. He would have been a wonderful father; Mei has no doubt of that.

There is one revenge Mei could seek, that would ensure he suffer for eternity, instead of a few seconds.

There is one way to take away his whole future, the same way he took away hers.

There is one slice Mei could make, deeper than across his neck.

Through his heart.

Through his son.

Of course she will not do it. She will not hurt Jamie Nakamura to hurt his father. But just thinking it, just conceiving of it, makes her feel inhuman. As if Jamie is two people and she is not even one. Mei moves onto her side and she feels a single tear slide from her eye to her mouth and it stings like seawater and she wishes, for the first time since she left Shanghai, that she did not want revenge. That all the stars had not turned dark inside of her.

20

SHANGHAI
NOVEMBER 1937

I AM STARTING to realize that Ma didn't just have a whole different life before she had me, one that I had no idea about. Now I am not just trying to find her; I am trying to find that other person too. To know her. To understand her. *Limei*.

A CLANG FROM the front door, and I scurry to be the first to answer. This isn't hard because almost all the servants have now fled our household to return to their families, which has put the housekeeper into a permanently bad mood, but anyway, when I pull open the door I see none other on our doorstep than Big Sister.

Big Sister!

I barrel into her for a hug and she shimmies out of it, as if I still smell oxlike, even though I've taken more baths over the past two months than I did over the past two years at home. She holds up a crumpled ball of paper and I recognize it instantly.

"You got my letter!" I squeal. I lead her inside, yelling for the housekeeper. "I didn't write it by myself. George Maidenhair wrote it for me. He sent it off too. He's very kind. Oh, you don't know who George is. But I'll tell you all about—"

"I'm not supposed to be here," Big Sister says, as the housekeeper comes stomping in.

The housekeeper has floral blooms of redness all over her face. She works too hard now and often overheats. She glowers at the two of us.

"Can you go ask Uncle if my sister can stay with us awhile?" I ask hopefully.

A bit more glowering, but then she gives in. Her hair is up high and tight in a turnip-bun and it bounces comically as she marches off.

"Why shouldn't you be here?" I ask Big Sister.

"Because Ba doesn't know I've come," she says, "and he wouldn't have let me, if he'd gotten wind of it."

"The trains *are* dangerous," I say, parroting First Wife. "How did you get past the Japanese?"

Big Sister says, "By being smarter than *you*," which reminds me to introduce her later to Aiyi.

I ask if she's hungry, and she is, so we skip to the kitchen and she eats soup dumplings while telling me all the news from home. The village is obviously worried about the Japanese invasion. She asks if I have had any brushes with the Japanese and I tell her about the bloodshed and destruction of my first weekend in Shanghai, how I ended up on a rooftop hotel that no longer exists, and how there were Chinese fighter planes flying right over my head and how my left hand no longer bends well at the wrist.

"The Japanese military has promised their emperor that all of China will be under Japanese rule by the end of the year," says Big Sister. "With Shanghai fallen, we are the only pocket in this part of the country left to fall. I keep telling Ba we should leave; half of

Nanking has already left! But you know how stubborn he is. He thinks playing the *èrhú* will save him."

I am still so confused as to why the Japanese want to rule China at all.

Even now they're here in Shanghai they don't seem all that happy about it.

"Will we all have to learn Japanese?" I ask. "Because I am only starting to learn good Chinese. That's what First Wife says."

Big Sister snorts at this.

I think Big Sister would get along better with First Wife than I do. I think when you're the first of anything, you think you're the best one and everyone else is a bit worse. You can't really help it.

I change the subject to Ma.

I explain everything I've discovered so far. I tell Big Sister how I am studying with George and soon I will be good enough at reading and writing to talk to the girl in the attic, although some days I forget about the girl in the attic and just want to learn to read for the sake of it. There is no particular hurry these days because Ma is here, I know she is, and she's not going anywhere: Nobody can leave Shanghai now that the railways belong to the Japanese. In fact, Big Sister may have to stay with us a very long while, but that's okay. I have missed my sisters more than I expected. When you miss people in that soft quiet way, sometimes it's hard to realize how much you *do* miss them.

"George Maidenhair is helping too. He has been looking all over, asking people about Ma. There is nothing yet but we will keep trying," I say confidently. "So you see? You were wrong about Ma dying a shameful death. Just like you were wrong about Ma and Uncle being brother and sister. She was one of his con-kew . . . con-koo . . . one of his *extra wives!*"

"I was wrong about a lot of things," says Big Sister.

It isn't like her to admit such a thing. She must have missed me too.

"About Ma's pouch," I say. "I know you said not to show people but I've showed lots of people by now. Sorry."

She just nods, her mouth moving with soup dumpling.

"You want to see what was inside?"

Another swishy nod.

"Now, first of all, don't be scared," I warn her, taking out the pouch, but she won't be scared. Big Sister is so brave. Not scared of the Japanese, and not scared of girl-things that look like they could crawl right out of the page and into your lap. "*This* painting shows the attic of this very house," I say grandly, hoping she doesn't ask about the hand. "*This* painting is George Maidenhair's house. It's in the neighborhood nearby. And *this*, this third painting . . . George says this tower with the characters on it is called the Great World. I've never been there but George has. He says he's been there loads and loads of times and it was always super exciting. Doesn't it look exciting?"

If you can look past the girl-thing.

"Ma must have drawn it for a reason," I say, as Big Sister chews. "I want to go there, but First Wife forbids it. None of us are allowed to leave the French Concession. She said she'd cane us so hard we'll be sleeping on our bellies until the New Year! And she really does do the things she says she'll do!"

Big Sister slurps down another dumpling.

"Please don't eat *all* the dumplings," I tell her.

"Let's go there," she says. "You and me. To the Great World. Today. Right now."

"Just because the Japanese didn't catch you coming into Shanghai doesn't mean you've turned into an immortal all-powerful goddess, you know," I say indignantly. "I almost *died* last time I went into the International Settlement. I just *told* you the story!"

"What you just told me is that the Japanese aren't doing much here, and that it's your new mama we actually have to be afraid of, if anything."

"Aiyi would love this plan," I say, "but that doesn't make it a good one."

"Who's Aiyi?"

"My new *you*!"

To my surprise, Big Sister laughs. She takes two more dumplings and puts them in her mouth at the same time. I do the same and soon we are both laughing. It turns out that laughing with your sister is the one thing in the world that fills you up even better than soup dumplings.

WE ARE STILL giggling and sneaking out the door when I hear the housekeeper calling my name. *Little Mei! Little Mei, where are you? I asked Master about your sister and he wants to talk to you . . . Little Mei!* I hesitate, but Big Sister grabs me and we scamper quickly across the courtyard. Uncle won't mind Big Sister staying with us. Uncle doesn't really mind anything so long as no one bothers him. We have so many empty rooms now. And besides, I've been doing really well with my drawing exercises lately and he's allowing me to use his pencils for free sketching. He told me to start with cranes. He said that's how he started when he was young, on big flying birds, on their widespread wings. Nowadays he only draws mountains.

BIG SISTER SEEMS to know where to go better than I do, in the center of town. We see Japanese women tottering along in their high sandals, traveling in packs, and even soldiers, but they don't pay us much attention. The streets are busy and lively and not very different from how they were that day with Third Wife. Still, I feel uneasy that we are doing this, and it's not until we reach the Great World that my doubts are drowned out by wonder: In Ma's painting, the view of the Great World is partially blocked by the girl-thing; in real life, this building is impossibly wonderful.

I look up and up and up the tower in the middle, lit like a float in a festival, while Big Sister tries to herd me toward the doors.

It is not easy because as many people are trying to leave as are trying to get in and you can't tell which way any of them are going. It is like trying to swim between schools of fish. Big Sister is gripping my upper arm hard. She says I need to stay close, because if she loses me in here, she's lost me for good.

Inside, the sights and sounds are even more magnificent: magicians and musicians and dancers; birdcages and balloons; tables with people squeezed in so close together that I am breathless just watching them. But Big Sister is pulling me along, not letting me look, and when I protest, she says: "We have to hurry."

"Hurry?" I holler back, but she doesn't answer. "Shouldn't we be looking around? Or asking for Ma? Maybe somebody here knew her. . . ."

We keep going up and up and round and round. How many floors *is* this building?

"Big Sister," I say, thudding to a halt, "I'm thirsty! I can't go up anymore!"

"I'll get you a drink when we get there."

"I'm thirsty," I whine.

"I'll carry you," she offers.

This is tempting because then I will be high enough to see over everyone's heads. I'm always the smallest person around, everywhere I go. "Okay, but how do I know you're strong enough?" I say, crossing my arms. "I'm much bigger than I was in summer, you know. How do I know your ankles won't snap like twi . . ."

Jing!

I spin around.

Jing, come say hello!

"What's wrong now?" asks Big Sister impatiently.

"Just . . . somebody just said the name Jing," I say, as Big Sister sighs. "It was . . . Third Wife's name . . ."

Suddenly, I see a woman dressed all sparkly and shimmery coming toward me. She is laughing too loud; a laugh that hurts my ears. It is an extremely young Third Wife, but it *is* Third Wife, I know her; I always know people by their laughter. But how can it be? How can it be, when they scooped Third Wife's mangled dead body off a pile of mangled dead bodies only a few streets away from here and they laid it out for a weeklong wake at the house and then they buried it with her favorite full-bloomed flowers?

Third Wife is headed straight at me and she is holding a drink that frosts at the top, and seeing me, she smiles, but it's not a smile like she knows me. It's a smile like she pinned the two ends of her mouth to her upper cheeks.

"Third Wife," I yell, "Third Wife, it's me! Little Mei! Big Sister, we have to stop—I see one of Uncle's wives!"

"Uncle took a singsong girl for a wife?" says Big Sister dubiously.

"She's not a singsong girl! She's a photographer!"

"Come on, we're wasting time," says Big Sister.

Then it wasn't a ghost, was it, when Third Wife visited me late that night, after First Wife caned me raw, right before I got sick? Third Wife must be alive after all. She must have . . . must have somehow *faked* her death and . . . and come here to work at the Great World instead, and . . .

And abandoned her babies?

And shed twenty years right off her face?

And never bothered to retrieve the photographs she took at the Cathay?

Third Wife comes close enough for me to see the two dangly bird-feather earrings in her ears.

That's not Third Wife.

I turn to Big Sister. I let out a small panicky pant.

"No," commands Big Sister, "no. Stop it. No. Don't worry about her. Come on, Third Sister, follow me and—"

"Something's wrong here," I say shakily. "This isn't right. Third Wife is dead."

"You want to find Ma, don't you? We can find Ma easier together. You and me! The two of us!"

Something comes over me that feels like another illness.

I'm backing away from my sister.

"The Great World was bombed," I say blankly. "It was destroyed on the day Third Wife died, three months ago. George told me so. Where am I? Where am I, *jiě jie*? Where have you brought me? What's going on?"

We are interrupted by another gaggle of sparkly-dressed women, all of them laughing the way Third Wife always did.

I wish I hadn't asked.

I don't want to hear what Big Sister is about to tell me, but she's going to tell me anyway.

And this, this moment, is when I finally, after all this time, begin to understand what *fate* is.

It is not any of the things I ever thought it was. It is not a path. It is not a journey. It is not a place you end up. It is not your mistakes. It is not your choices.

Fate is the thing you cannot stop from happening, even though you would do anything to stop it.

That is all.

"HI THERE," SAYS an unfamiliar voice.

When I try to open my eyes, the light feels like a splash of hot frying oil.

They're dead, they're all dead.

"It's going to be okay," says the voice, "you can stay lying down as long as you like."

The voice is young and so thickly accented it sounds almost furry.

Ba and Second Sister and Nai Nai are lying burned and half-buried in the smoking ruins of our village.

And me too, Third Sister.

I am dead too.

We are all dead, back home.

"You are in my humble little abode," says the voice cheerfully. "My shop!"

The Japanese swords still sticking out of us.

"I put the CLOSED sign on the door," adds the voice. "Since I thought you might be out awhile."

No one came to save us, and there is no one coming to save you. That's why this is the best way. This way you and I can be together. This way I don't have to be alone. No, don't be frightened of me! Yes, I am a ghost, but I am still your Big Sister. . . .

"They're all dead," I whisper, and I open my eyes.

A boy is peering down at me. He looks about ten or eleven years old. He has scruffy light brown hair that sticks up a little at the ends and large glasses, which he pushes up his nose. "Huh," he says, sounding relieved. "I was a little worried that you'd never come out of it. I've never seen anyone stay in a trance that long. I spotted you just standing out where the Great World used to be, see? Just staring at the wreckage. And I *knew* that look, so I thought I'd wait for you, but then you started climbing *into* the rubble and there were some soldiers hanging around so I thought it would be safer to get you out of there. Oh, sorry, I've always got lousy manners! My name is Max. Max Friedman. I'm from Munich. And you are?"

Ba. My two sisters. Nai Nai. Our neighbors. The whole village. Burned. Butchered. Gone.

All at the hands of the Japanese.

Wŏmen zhēn dǎoméi. . . .

I open my mouth, but I cannot find my tongue.

"You're probably wondering how I knew you were in a trance," says the boy. "Or maybe you're wondering how I can run a shop, when I'm, you know, a kid." He smiles. He has a wide, sincere smile. "It's because I'm just like you!" He reaches over for something and places it on his face. It's a mask; a full-face black mask, with black ribbons over the eyes. "I can see ghosts," he says, making his voice boom, larger and lower than before. "People pay *big* money for it. Seriously, they do. Especially if you wear a mask and a cloak and stuff." He takes off the mask and smiles again. "I know, it's not all that impressive, but one day I'm going to have more than a ramshackle little room in a back alley, just you wait! One day I'm going to be a Great Master."

PART FOUR

21

HONG KONG
2015

SUSANNA IS LOOKING past me, as is Ryan.

My back is to the door, I can't see what they see, but with my other senses I know who it is.

It has been many decades now since the mysterious disappearance of Holly Zhang from Maidenhair House. Most people assume that she returned to the mainland and died there.

By now, of course, she *ought* to be dead.

I turn around, bracing for the sight, but when I see her, I do not feel repulsion. Look at how her face is flaking at the ears. Look at how the skin stretched over her cheeks has a marked translucency to it, like ice over a pond. Look at how she is scarcely passable as the same person, other than the eyes and the perfume that she wore all those years ago, that same syrupy scent.

Look at how none of us can defeat time, not even her.

Holly's head swivels between the three of us, just slightly too far.

"Hello, Auntie," I say, and when I do, Ryan finally recognizes her.

"But . . . this isn't possible," Ryan Li blusters. "Holly Zhang, she was born in—I don't know when she was born—but her first film came out *more than ninety years ago.* She was in the movies when *I was a kid.*" He has gone from whispering to shrieking in a few seconds: "She should be dead! She has to be dead! Do you see what I mean, both of you? Do you understand now, what this house does to people? I tried to explain, back then—I tried to tell everyone— You see things that aren't real, that can't be real, and yet they're right in front of you and they . . ."

He is hyperventilating too hard to continue.

Holly, unmoved by his raving, shifts her filmy gaze to me.

"Miss Chen?" she rasps, in that familiar rubbery voice of hers. "But you look so different. We are both of us old women now, eh?" She turns her attention to Susanna next, whose face remains blanched. "And who's this? Not your daughter? Do you have your mother's gifts, I wonder? No, I can already see that you don't. What a shame."

Susanna has been rendered speechless; a rare occurrence.

Ryan Li leans against the wall, still heaving.

"Did you write anonymous letters, Auntie?" I ask Holly, because no one else seems able to. "To Dean Thornton, Susanna's husband, accusing me of murder? Or to Mr. Li here, asking him to come to Maidenhair?"

"Letters?" Holly wheezes a laugh. "You think I want people here? You think I want to have to explain this, explain myself? But now that you *are* here . . ." She gestures with one limp hand to the trapdoor. "You may as well stay awhile, have a cup of tea. I rarely get company."

Holly Zhang, forever the hostess.

"We were planning to go down anyway," I say. "Mr. Li? Susanna?"

Ryan Li makes a guttural sound that might pass for a yes.

Holly turns expectantly to Susanna, who is now holding both hands over her face.

Susanna surely knows that Holly Zhang was born in the 1890s. And now it is the year 2015. She must realize that Holly is not normal. But it takes much more to believe in ghosts than it does to believe in curses. A curse feels like a kind of fate, and everyone wants to believe in fate, deep down. Of course, I could have taught Susanna as much, but I did not want my daughter to have any knowledge of the supernatural. I did not want her to know my suffering. All this time, all these years, I have reassured myself with the old proverb: *Yǎn bù jiàn wéi jìng.*

What you do not see with your eyes stays clean. What you cannot see does not exist.

It is a fallacy. But it is such a comforting one. It is why, sometimes, a whole new world opens up right in front of you and you hide behind your hands, just to avoid looking right at it.

HOLLY GOES DOWN the trapdoor first, balanced precariously on her ice-pick high heels, but she has the benefit of knowing where she is headed. I go next, with Susanna close behind, and Ryan Li last of all, his breaths louder than our footfalls. I hold my flashlight as best I can, the light wobbling against the barren walls, the soft wooden steps. We are dropping further into darkness. The stairwell curves round and round again; there is no handrail. My knees shriek at the strain. This is the latest I could have come here and done this. Another five years and I might have to be carried; another ten and I'd never make it back up again.

Though I have never seen the entirety of Maidenhair's basement, I know the rooms are connected by tunnels like capillaries. A house within a house. A house possessed by a house.

WE FIND OURSELVES in a heavily furnished chamber, the out-
lines of furniture still spotty without adequate lighting. Holly flicks
on a big-beam flashlight, the kind you hold like a watering can,
and the scene in front of us springs to life: The walls are drenched
in art deco, imported wood and animal furs and stretched skins.
A row of carved antique cabinets stands off to one side, probably
dating back to the dynasties, clashing with the brassily polished
table in the center.

Susanna makes a dry, breathy noise. To my daughter, a room
like this is not a memory. It is a museum. A mummy's tomb.

"Please, come, sit down," says Holly graciously, gesturing toward the black-veneered chairs around the table.

"Dean would have loved this décor," says Susanna.

"He was interested in prewar Shanghai style?" I say, because I
didn't know this about him. It occurs to me now that I could have
gotten to know Susanna's second husband a lot better than I did.
Maybe it made me uncomfortable, the way he always wanted to
get to the bottom of everything. Susanna does too, but as a scholar.
Dean did it as a detective. The former believes there are no simple
answers underlying the past. There are no single causes. Everything is a slipshod mix of various factors and forces. The latter
thinks that you can find the past contained in a neat little box, like
pirate's treasure, and everything you destroy to get at it, all the
collateral damage, well, none of it matters, compared to what
you're unearthing.

"It was one of many eras that captured his imagination," says
Susanna, sounding wistful. "People can get attached to specific
moments in time, in history, you know, Mama? And end up wanting to know everything about them. And even end up daydream-

ing that they could somehow go back and *live* them, even though rationally those times were often tragic and terrible."

I feel that way about many moments in my own history. In my own time.

I will be gone one day soon, and then I will get my wish: Susanna will never understand who I was before I had her. She will never be burdened by my secrets. And why would I want her to be? It's different, so different, isn't it, if you hear about massacres and atrocities, about exile and emptiness, from afar, in school, from strangers? You might feel sad and sorry, or even aghast and angry, but only in your mind. Not in your body.

You are not *soiled* by it. You are not *contaminated*.

It feels worse and worse, the closer to the history you come.

I think that is why you cry when you read novels sometimes but you never cry when you read textbooks.

But I have been wrong. So very wrong.

All this time I thought I was staying silent for her sake, when I was really doing it for mine.

RYAN LI SHUFFLES over to the table and barely makes it. He drops the flashlight at his feet; light rolls over the room. His pallor is anemic; his nostrils are flaring fast.

"Can I offer anyone some melon-seed tea?" asks Holly.

"Forgive me for asking this, but isn't it a hassle to go up and down those steps, Ms. Zhang?" says Susanna. "Why not live on the main floor?"

I can tell by my daughter's tone that she is now determined to believe there is an entirely logical and reasonable explanation for Holly, and that she is going to arrive at it, if we just sit here long enough. Perhaps she has even begun thinking of the sensational story she can pen when she gets home: The Return of Shanghai's Long-Lost Silent-Film sweetheart! A story of murder, mediums, decades gone by, trapdoors, basements, shiny underground salon rooms, of your own mother!

"I don't like how lonely it is," says Holly.

"Is it not lonelier down here?"

It is then that we all hear it—

A noise coming from inside the antique cabinets.

All of them.

Even Ryan Li lifts his head.

"Oh dear," says Holly. "We've woken the others."

22

HONG KONG
SEPTEMBER 1953

THE STORM, LOUD and angry, keeps Mei awake through the night, until she returns to reading, and just as she passes the half-way point of *The Peak House*, she puts it down and gets out of bed.

She dresses quickly and leaves her room and goes down the hall to Jamie's, where they parted yesterday evening. When he answers, still more asleep than awake, she says that she wants to see the mirror. No one else is up yet. Just *see* it. She doesn't know what's come over her.

This is just the feeling she gets, halfway through a book.

Maybe her willpower slid off yesterday with the rain.

"It's locked, remember?" says Jamie, rubbing his eyes.

"I can pick the lock," says Mei.

She pulls the white peony pin out of her hair.

Her braided bun immediately falls apart, into sulky waves. The pin sits flat on her palm. Jamie seems hardly to notice, but of course it is not momentous to him, only to her, because Mei never removes this peony pin. She bathes with the pin in her hair and sleeps with the pin in her hair. She never stops feeling its gleaming point digging into her scalp. Often she wishes it would hurt more than it does. Wishes she could remember more than she does. Often she fears no longer feeling the pain. Fears getting over it. Fears recovering. Fears wanting to feel something else. Fears moving on.

THE NORTH WING seems to slope upward, into the mountain. Mei watches for furtive shapes, for anything emerging out of nothing, but there are no sights or sounds except for the house being thrashed by the storm. The South Wing was glittery and luxurious, with its lanterns and large hanging landscapes and carpets like ankle-deep water, but the North Wing is the opposite. Gray and grim and barren. The lights consist of naked bulbs on a wire. The walls are uncovered. Not even papered.

"The servants live here," says Jamie, as explanation.

They reach a hallway so dingy Mei feels the dust riding up her stockings.

It does not feel like anyone lives here.

"Right. There you are," says Jamie. "Feel free."

A quick try of the handle confirms that it is still locked. The pin goes in smooth and silent. Though she has done it only rarely, lock-picking is a much simpler craft than her others. Jamie exhales, either impressed or disturbed by her talents, she can't tell.

"A word of warning, about the Portrait Gallery—" he begins, but the door winces open and Mei is through.

There are indeed portraits on the walls, dozens of them, covering nearly every inch of the room that is not the windows, but you would not know at first glance that these were portraits. That these were human faces.

The eyes have been blacked out in every single one, as if by Mei's charcoal.

Against one wall stands a mirror, reflecting all these grotesque, desecrated images. It is unmistakably the mirror from Mei's sketch, larger even than it looked, nearly twice the size that she is. And that means that whoever was speaking through her during the First Séance wanted her to find this, to stand here. It wanted her to feel as she does, as though she is falling.

Mei rocks slightly back on her heels.

"Ancestral portraits, belonging to the Halls," says Jamie. "A friend of the family felt that the portraits were watching her, and so she . . . she did this to them. Or so the story goes."

But Mei is no longer listening.

At once she knows where the stairs are. The stairs from her second sketch.

"I CAN'T LOOK into mirrors," Mei says, turning away and closing her eyes. "Tell me when you have taken it off, and face it away from me."

Jamie is touching it, trying it out. She can feel the dancing of his fingers on the frame; all her other senses are heightened when she has her eyes shut.

"Why can't you look in mirrors?" he asks, with a light huff; he must be hoisting the mirror off the wall.

"The last séance I ever did in Shanghai," she says, the most explanation she can give, "it went wrong."

MEI AND JAMIE are staring into a straight downward stairwell that extends distressingly deep. Her sketch did not prepare her for the sight, and yet she feels a stab of triumph: She was right. A mirror that was actually a door, with a hidden staircase behind it. *Now* Mei can believe that this is George's house, and for a short, surreal moment, she wishes that George himself were the one showing it to her. That they could have every conversation they ever had, all over again. *Every book is an unknown set of stairs, Little Mei. Some go up and some go down.* What do you mean, Teacher? Books are always flat. They are flat as deserts. *Tell me: Have you ever encountered a set of stairs that you didn't feel like climbing?* I always feel like climbing if I don't know where it ends up, Teacher!

Exactly.

"Mei?" says Jamie.

"Yes?" she says abruptly, noting a little late that he has used her first name for the first time. That some distance has been crossed that is greater than the length of the Portrait Gallery.

"Do you smell that?"

"NO," SHE SAYS, "I can't . . . I have to stay up here."

"We have to. There's something down there," he says.

"I can't. I can't. I have a fear of—a phobia," Mei says. Her ears are ringing. Her chest is filling with that horrible soaring smell. Her thoughts are tightening into knots. "Of enclosed spaces. I always have. When I was a child—but never mind. I suppose I had this moment of courage, this morning, going to you, coming here, but maybe it was just that I've barely slept for two nights! I've used myself up in the séances, Mr. Nakamura, and now I'm done. I can't go down there, I just can't. It'll be some—crawl space—with a ceiling that—will touch your head like hands—and—"

"Okay. Okay," says Jamie, as her breaths turn ragged. "I'll go. You wait here."

Wait here with *them.*

The faces with no eyes.

But the *smell.*

Mei knows, even from the top of the stairs, that there will be no saving whatever is down there.

❧

JAMIE REEMERGES WITHIN minutes. Mei has not moved. The smell is thicker than honey now. *It's Delia,* he says. He keeps saying it, over and over. Mei has to dredge her memory for a moment, for the name: Delia, one half of Delia and Cecelia, the teenage twins; the one who ran off during the First Séance; the other is sleeping somewhere in this house.

I think she's been stabbed. There's blood everywhere. On everything. The wounds, they've gushed down to nothing. . . .

Mei is alarmed to discover that she feels no sadness, no horror, no urge to cry. She has felt sympathy in all the wrong places, for all the wrong people, recently, and at the same time she has grown insensitive to death. She is one of the wounds that gushed too long. All she can think of, in this surreal moment, is how she will extricate herself from this situation, because they will have to alert the authorities. The competition will be over. A house that was once full of spirit mediums will be equally full of police. And the others *saw* Mei's sketch of the mirror; the mirror that opens onto those stairs; the stairs that lead down to a dead body; the dead body of one of her competitors in a competition whose prize is life-changing.

It doesn't matter if Delia was eliminated before she was murdered.

No one is going to believe that Mei had nothing to do with it.

IT ISN'T PRISON Mei necessarily minds; it's the idea of serving time for *this* murder, instead of the one she came for. She will never gain access to George now. She will not have her revenge. She will have to return to the real prison, that of her own life, without any walls or floors or ceilings or bars, only windows into a past that will never again be hers.

NONE OF IT makes any sense to Mei. Delia was last seen alive in the Red Library, during the First Séance, before something sent her screaming. Everybody then saw Mei's mirror sketch.

Why would the killer leave the body anywhere near that mirror?

Unless the killer didn't see the sketch? Unless the killer is someone else? Why would it have to be one of her fellow spirit mediums, after all? Just because they are strangers?

Or did the spirit possessing Mei, during that trance, somehow *know* where Delia would end up?

And wanted her to find the body?

Mei's whole head is pulsing with too many questions.

But at least she knows this: The killer has to be human. Mei has seen firsthand how vengeful spirits harm people, and it is nothing like this. It is not messy and bloody and disgusting and dirty and visceral. They keep their hands clean. Afterward, they go on like it never happened. They go on the way George Maidenhair went on.

"MEI," SAYS JAMIE, saying her name like the downward slicing of a sword, "Mei, there's something else. It's about your hairpin."

For a moment Mei thinks he means that the girl was stabbed to death with Mei's pin, which isn't possible, because until an hour or so ago that pin had been in Mei's hair for six years.

But he explains: Delia has been mutilated, and yet *mutilated* is not the word he would use. Etched deeply and deliberately into the girl's back were the long, shapely curves of *petals*. Jamie says her blouse was shredded and she was turned onto her stomach, so he could glimpse it through the flaps: the whole of a peony flower disappearing down Delia's body. Even without examining closely, he could see the craftsmanship in the act; the intricacy; the boldness. The murderer is more than a murderer, and the victim has not merely been murdered.

Delia has been turned into a work of art.

"Someone carved the design of your hairpin into her skin," Jamie says again, slower.

But it is not just a design.

It is also a signature.

Ma's signature.

Mei is literate, of course. She does not use the design the way Ma did. But it is, nonetheless, Mei's *signature design*. The one she is known for, in her pitiful corner of Kowloon; the one she reproduces almost manically, at a rate that would her put her time at the plastic flower factory to shame. Some days, in fact, she feels like she is working on the same single cutting, forever, even though by now she has made hundreds, because it never seems to be enough, it will never be good enough. Because you cannot fill old holes by making new ones.

MEI WOULD BELIEVE that Jamie Nakamura is a writer now, the way he is looking at her. Like he is more intrigued by the design than by the death, like he no longer cares about returning to his normal everyday life, because he just has to understand what is happening. There is simply no other option.

"I didn't do it," she says.

"Then someone wants you to take the fall for this," says Jamie.

"Or someone's sending you a message. Where'd you get your hairpin?"

"It was originally my mother's design," says Mei, knowing this is not what he has asked.

There is a pause in which the whole room seems to slant.

"I see," says Jamie. "And where is your mother now?"

23

SHANGHAI
AUGUST 1942

I FIND MAX stacking tarot cards at his fortune-telling table.

He looks beyond bored and if not for his hands moving you might think he'd fallen asleep with his eyes open. Max Friedman has no interest in tarot and only bought a stack to please the customers. He is not thrilled by séances either, even if he does them all the time.

His true passion is for using the scrying mirror, a glossy pane of black obsidian in which he can see the future.

I do not have that gift. I can see nothing in the scrying mirror, except maybe the night sky.

"CAN I HELP you?" I offer, and Max smiles, gestures for me to join him. His spanking-new spectacles sit unbalanced on his nose. I often wonder if the customers know how young he is. How young we both are. I am twelve now. He is fifteen. As we work, he wipes away the sweat already fermenting on his face; it is an overripe, half-rotted summer day. I notice for the umpteenth time that Max's hands have little indents on the pads. I have only ever known one other person with that many calluses: Ba, my father, from working the fields. And yet it's not possible that Max came from a farming family, is it? How many farmers are there in Munich?

But of course I'm mostly wondering all this because we rarely talk about it.

The before-Shanghai-time.

His, and mine.

I don't seem to be able to say it out loud, that I left my family behind only for someone to come along and smudge them out, to stack their bodies like these cards.

"WHAT ARE YOU reading with George Maidenhair these days?" asks Max.

"*Jane Eyre*," I answer, "by Charlotte Brontë. In the original."

"You like it?" he says, a little sheepish, because he's curious about my lessons with George but he won't agree to come along to one. He claims it's because his English is no good, even if he managed to pick up Chinese without any problem, young as he was when he arrived here. I suspect that Max is embarrassed by the fact that he has nothing and nobody and fends for himself, but I don't think it's embarrassing at all. I think it's extraordinary. I think *he* is extraordinary. But whenever I think about *that*, I get that same shifty feeling I get looking into the black obsidian mirror, like there's some real chance that I might trip and topple into it.

"Very much." I keep my voice very casual: "Can I ask you something?"

"Sure," he says. His throat bobs. "What?"

"I want to try doing a séance by myself."

Max bunches up his face like he really needs to sneeze.

We don't do much talking about the past, and we do even less talking about my future.

About what I am still doing here, five years after he found me by the Great World.

After Uncle confirmed what Big Sister's ghost had told me about my family, about the attack on our village, I started seeing ghosts everywhere. Not just Big Sister's ghost, but ghosts of complete strangers. I couldn't keep them at bay. Max explained that when you're sad, lonely, always looking back, and your qi is imbalanced, ghosts can smell you like sharks and will hound you relentlessly. He helped me learn how to control my Sight better so that I didn't drip qi all over the streets of Shanghai. He also gave me small tasks to do around his little shop and I've started saving up money in the hopes that one day I can return to Jiangsu and rebuild my village.

After five years, I am not haunted by spirits, I am not haunted by the deaths of my family, and I am not haunted by the mystery of Ma's disappearance.

I suppose we could just keep on going the way we have, me helping out, Max working on becoming a Great Master. I have been spending more and more time here, of late, since Uncle doesn't care where I go and First Wife can't speak against anyone hanging out in a spirit-medium shop, not when she spends all day kowtowing to her own dead people. Nothing has to change. But the fact that the war just keeps on going and the Japanese keep on staying and the world keeps on spinning has made me realize that a lot of things don't change unless you work really, really hard to make them change.

Why do I want things to change?

I don't even know.

I just do.

Maybe it's because I'm reading *Jane Eyre* and I want things to change for her too and I am sick of waiting.

"The truth is," I say hesitantly, "that I don't think I'm ever going to be the greatest paper artist in all China. I . . . I've tried very hard and Uncle's taught me so much and I'll never stop, never, ever, but I'm not actually all that good. Maybe *this* is my real destiny. Ghost-seeing. Why else would I have the Sight?"

"Yeah, okay," he says. "If you want. We can try it."

"Who taught *you* to do séances?" I challenge him.

He smiles. "My grandmother," he says. "She raised me."

He's never mentioned his family like this before.

But then, when have I asked?

"Tell me about her," I encourage him. "Your grandmother."

"Back in Germany, she was teaching me the Four Steps, four stages, for seeing the future," he says. "Step One is: *You see the future and you try to change it*. Step Two is: *You see the future, but you no longer try to change it*. Then she got an exit visa for Shanghai for me. Couldn't get one for herself. My grandmother said the last two steps could wait; that we would see each other again. I was actually supposed to meet my aunt and uncle here, but they'd already left, and I haven't heard from my grandmother in a long time. So now I am stuck on Step Two. My hope, my dream, is to be able to discover those last two steps on my own, and work through them. That is when I will have truly become a Great Master, like she wanted."

Neither of us says anything for a long minute. His upper lip is lightly fuzzed. I had not noticed this before. Maybe I will be needing spectacles soon.

"You think your grandma's okay?" I ask.

"She was really old," says Max, and there is just a single drop of pain in his voice.

IN *JANE EYRE*, it turns out, Rochester's wife has been living secretly in the attic, and this reminds me of the girl in Uncle's attic, the one with only half a tongue and bound feet. Before this I had not thought of her in years. I have not seen her since I was seven. I know the servants say she killed herself, but who knows, maybe she was once locked in there the way I was and everyone forgot to let her out again.

ONE DAY WHILE I am finishing a sketch of a tiger—I have recently advanced to tiger after many long years of birds, rivers, trees, landscapes, fish, oh so many fish, and more fish—Aiyi whisks her way into the Magnolia Room. She looks around to make sure Uncle isn't there, which he isn't, and then she takes a seat across from me and folds her hands over her lap. Aiyi is studying in university now. She often laments that the Japanese will probably be defeated just as she graduates and that someone else will take over and her degree will end up being worthless. She says degrees are a bit like money that way.

I always keep my mouth shut so I don't accidentally give her life advice she hasn't asked for: *Stop studying, because you hate studying, and you hate being a student!*

I think Aiyi would be happier as a criminal mastermind.

"What are you drawing?" she asks. "Is that the American flag?"

"It's a *tiger*," I say in dismay.

"If you say so."

I continue shading the tiger.

"Yuchang has asked me to marry him," she says.

We all knew this was going to happen. Yuchang is her class-mate and longtime sweetheart and he follows her around obses-sively and even wrote a hilarious poem about how every time he sees her face he feels like a starving man being served a plate of moon cakes. I think he wrote it to be funny, because he wanted to win me over, because Aiyi once told him that he would need to win my approval, not just Uncle's, in order to join the family.

Aiyi doesn't know that I overheard that particular conver-sation.

"There's going to be a big party in a few months' time. To cel-ebrate the engagement. I've already spoken to Muma about it," Aiyi goes on, referring to her own mother, Second Wife, though speaking to Second Wife is a lot like speaking to a rock. "And Mother, of course," she adds, meaning First Wife. "Mother thinks it'll be good for our friends, the ones that are still in Shanghai, anyway. And guess who said he doesn't mind, so long as he doesn't have to attend? Diedie," she says, meaning Uncle.

"But are you inviting *me*?" I say, and she rolls her eyes.

"I was thinking," says Aiyi, "that we could use some enter-tainment."

"Ooh! I'll put on a puppet show! I've just learned a new tech-nique for—"

"Absolutely not. I will *never* understand your interest in shadow puppets, I promise you that. More like . . . your friend."

"My friend?"

"Max Friedman."

"What about him?"

"I want to hire him, that's all. For the night of the party. He could speak to spirits, tell our futures, that sort of thing. Everyone'll love it. Could you ask him to do it?"

"I don't think you should hire Max," I say. "Besides, you don't even believe in ghosts."

"Want him all to yourself, eh?" says Aiyi tartly.

"It's not that," I protest, putting down my pencils, because I've gone and overshaded the tiger's eyes and now they look like pits. "I just don't think it's a good idea."

Aiyi smiles at me, ever serene. "Just ask him, *mèi mei*," she says, meaning *Little Sister*. Meaning me.

MAX SAYS I shouldn't do my first séance in the presence of a customer. It should be just me and him in the back room of the two-room fortune-telling shop. We won't use any fancy tools or materials either; nothing but a few sheets of paper and a thumb-like piece of charcoal so that he can scribble down whatever the spirit says through me, if I am successful. I am terrified and electrified in identical amounts to find out more about my own power.

Not all spirit mediums can do the same things.

Some see ghosts but they cannot conduct séances.

Others can start séances but they cannot end them.

Max can do pretty much everything. If it turns out I cannot get rid of the spirit at the end, then he will be able to do it.

"If you close your eyes," he says solemnly, "it'll help a lot. Either way, you should soon try to send the qi flowing out, down your arms, through your fingers."

Max never seems to close his eyes.

"I'll help you this time," he says, "because sometimes the spirits are shy. There are other tricks mediums use, to make contact, but I don't need them, and we'll find out how much help you need as we go along. It'll be like falling asleep, Little Mei. You'll wake up and you won't even know it happened."

Sometimes I wonder how he sleeps. How he can bear it, everything he knows, past and future, yesterday and tomorrow, life and death, yin and yang. Whenever he looks hard into the obsidian mirror, there's always a trickle of blood from his mouth afterward, and I can't help thinking that it's because he has to bite himself to keep from screaming, from crying out, from stopping his Sight. I'm not sure about any qi flowing, because all I feel is beads of sweat popping up on my forehead like sugar peas, but Max takes my hand and says it's going to be okay.

"CAN YOU HEAR me?"

Light penetrates in sharp points, a constellation.

"Mei?"

"I'm here," I say, and my eyes are open now, but I'm still not totally sure where *here* is.

"You drew something," he exclaims.

"I . . . what?"

"I don't know," he says. "It's pretty cool. You picked up the charcoal and you just started to . . . I've never seen anyone draw during a séance. I've seen plenty of other stuff. Talking, writing, even doing dances. But not drawing!"

I grab the piece of paper from him, and my sense of exhilaration disappears in an instant.

It takes me a moment to recognize what I am looking at, but luckily—or unluckily—it still stands out in my memory. The question is *why*? Why would I sketch *this*? What does it mean? I have not entered Third Wife's bedroom in five years. Not since that day I finally understood that she was dead. I never planned to enter it, ever again, and besides, everything in there is draped in white sheets now, looking more ghostly than her actual ghost ever did.

So why have I just made a drawing of her vanity table?

24

HONG KONG
SEPTEMBER 1953

The Third Séance

"I HAVEN'T SEEN my mother since I was seven years old," Mei answers bluntly.

"So there's no chance that *she* did it, then?" says Jamie, not looking like he is kidding.

Of course Ma has nothing to do with this. Obviously, the killer desired to implicate Mei in this murder—to embroil Mei in this even more than she already would be, given the mirror sketch—and cutting her peony-pin design into the victim is an effective if high-effort way to go about it. Jamie says the reason he asked is because, having seen Mei's hairpin, he thinks the design was replicated with rather shocking accuracy. Such confident lines, and on such a rippling surface as human skin. The killer made it look easy. Effortless. Natural. Instinctive.

That is not how Mei learned the design. Mei did it by sheer brutal repetition.

But then how?

If the artist wasn't Ma, and wasn't Mei, then who? How can any murderer be that skilled?

It is disheartening to realize that of the many emotions coursing through her, the most vivid, the one that makes Mei feel like she has pricked her finger on a thorn, is envy.

ON THEIR WAY back through the North Wing, the weak spitted light of the bare bulbs begins to flicker. Mei stops at a window, where the glass panes are twitching loudly in their frames. She pulls apart the curtains and jumps back at the hiss of the rain. Recovering, she looks through the glass, streaked with water, toward the garden below. The bamboo is breaking; the grass is being flayed by the wind.

Usually, Mei adores the monsoon season; the way the weather makes you feel like the world is ending right over your head.

But usually she is not in Maidenhair House.

"We're going to lose power. I better telephone the police while I still can," says Jamie grimly.

"How can they send anyone out in this?"

"I still have to call. And then we should tell the others."

"Shall we not wait for the authorities to arrive? It will not make much difference, except to create panic. Delia is dead."

"The murderer might still be in the house, Mei."

He is right. They could all be in danger.

Mei has grappled so long with the idea of becoming a murderer herself, she nearly forgot there were others in the world. And, after all, just because you feel like you have nothing to live for, it does not make you invincible. Just because you are obsessed with vengeance, it does not make you a god. Mei feels herself sway a little, with sleeplessness, and as they reenter the main house. Jamie suggests that she rest in her bedroom; he'll fetch her once he's talked to the police. Mei accepts this plan gratefully and it is only once she is alone, lowering herself into bed, that she thinks: Can she trust Jamie? *Will* he call the police?

What if he only *pretended* to find the body, because he was the one who placed it there?

She thinks of her peony design set into Delia's back, the way he described, like cuts in clay. And it does not quite seem to fit, the haphazard, heavy-handed manner of a murder by stabbing, and the icy postmortem precision of the peony. As if they were done by different people.

Everything will make better sense in the morning. No, but it *is* morning. Everything will make better sense by tonight.

PEOPLE HAVE VERY strange thoughts right before they fall asleep, on the cusp between sleep and wake. It is, after all, another in-between place. Thoughts like: And what if they *were* different people? The killer and the carver? Which one would be the worse person? Who would be the more evil? The one who causes the destruction and death of a fellow human? Or the one who casually disregards it?

Mei does not know anyone who might be able to answer such a question, except her Great Master.

She knows that he would disapprove of her quest for vengeance. He disliked all violence. He disliked all bloodshed. He sincerely believed that you could fight evil with good. If it were up to him, Mei thinks bitterly, then the war might still be going on.

WHEN MEI WAKES up, everything is wrong.

It is even darker outside her window than it was before.

She sits up in bed and her eyes are starched dry. How long has it been? How long has she slept?

What if she leaves her room and discovers that everyone else is dead? Or gone?

That she is alone in Maidenhair House?

She used to have a dream like that: In it, she is trapped in the ancestral hall of that long-ago compound, and when she finally manages to escape, her family is gone. Everyone is gone. Mei wanders her village looking for anyone, just one person, but finds nobody, and eventually ends up back in the ancestral hall.

And then the door shuts behind her yet again.

Don't be silly, Mei.

IT TURNS OUT the others are easy enough to find because they are in the Great Hall, standing in a group at the bottom of the stairs, and arguing at high volume: Holly, Jamie, Mistress Lau, Cecelia, and even Peng, whom Jamie said was eliminated from the competition last night, following the incident in the garden.

The storm must have prevented her from leaving Maidenhair.

Peng has a giddy look in her eye.

She is the only one watching as Mei comes down the stairs.

"Mei," says Jamie, noticing at last, and everyone else turns, rather tersely, to look at her.

"What time is it?" she asks, still disoriented.

"Late afternoon. Four?"

"I slept . . . the whole day?"

"You seemed to need it."

"Excuse me," says Holly. Holly is dressed in a swanlike nightgown with pointed tips at the shoulders. Her voice rings out, reverberates loudly. "As I was saying, nobody can go out in this. It is impossible. But we also cannot sit around blinking at one another until the police arrive. Nor will I needlessly distress my staff with this news. They are busy with dinner preparations. We will act as normal."

"We need to stay together," says Jamie. "Safety in numbers—"

"That strikes me as entirely unnecessary, Mr. Nakamura."

"Unnecessary?" says Mistress Lau spitefully. "We're in a house with a dead body!"

Holly's nostrils flare. "I can assure you, the North Wing is far away enough that—"

"Far away enough?" Mistress Lau gives a bark of laughter. "Your argument is that your house is big enough to feel like two houses, Auntie? And so we needn't concern ourselves with things like being murdered?"

"Please," says Jamie, "let's not—" He stops short.

Mei knows what he was going to say. *Let's not turn on one another.*

Cecelia is saying nothing. Her eyes are bloodshot, a rangy red.

"Where do *you* stand on this, Miss Chen?" demands Mistress Lau, whose eyes are also red, but with paint.

"I think," says Mei, and she tries the words out before she speaks them. "I think we should do the rest of the séances. All of them. Tonight."

JAMIE'S FACE CLOSES, but Holly's is ablaze with interest.

"Go on," says Holly.

"Once the police show up," says Mei evenly, "Maidenhair will become a crime scene. All we have is tonight, Auntie, if you still want to crown a winner."

Holly clucks her tongue. "You must have gotten plenty of sleep indeed, if you have enough energy for four séances in a row, Miss Chen."

Yes, it is difficult, dangerous even, to conduct séances back to back. The chances of losing too much qi are higher. The chances of becoming possessed are thus higher; of having to be shaken out afterward by somebody else, like a purse. But Mei has other things to lose now. She doesn't know whether Jamie has told the others about the peony design, but there will be no hiding it from the police, and the police are not going to want to investigate the death of a teenage girl on Victoria Peak very thoroughly. They will want the easiest, quickest suspect, one whose own removal from the fabric of society will be seamless. The spirit who showed her the mirror and the stairs is Mei's best chance, if not her only one, to understand why and how her design was carved into Delia's skin. That spirit is trying to tell her something, and she will simply have to make sense of the sketches she produces. But even as her resolve hardens, Mei knows the truth: She is not motivated solely by the desire to clear her own name. She wants to know what Holly really wants from this competition.

What Holly has been asking.

Mei's curiosity is not dying down; it is surging. The more she feeds it, the stronger it gets. The more she learns, the more she wants to learn.

Just as George Maidenhair, the best teacher she ever had, once promised her.

"Of course she's sad," says Peng.

A tick of silence.

Mei had nearly forgotten Peng was present.

"What are you . . . who are you talking to?" asks Mistress Lau, with force.

"To Delia."

Cecelia lets out a gurgled cry.

Peng is still staring at the stairs.

Mei remembers the unseen child Peng spoke to in the atrium and she thinks, for one savage half a second, that she could kill Peng herself, just to make this *stop*, and then of course she is bathed in shame for thinking it.

"Delia isn't here," says Mistress Lau flatly. "There's nobody there."

Even Holly has gone the cold pale shade of her own nightgown.

"Delia wants to know why you're not crying, Cecelia," says Peng. "She wants to know if it's because you're not sad."

THE THIRD SÉANCE is to take place in the Music Room, again in the South Wing. Cecelia has refused to participate, but does not want to be left on her own. Peng has come along too, but of course Peng has been removed from the competition, and is not fit for it anyway. It is Mistress Lau against Mei against Jamie, so really it is Mistress Lau against Mei, but Mei no longer cares about winning. By far the greater threat is the police.

If she can avoid arrest, by now she is sure she can stay hidden in this house until George's return.

So many vast areas of Maidenhair seem deserted, undisturbed even by the staff.

That level of dust, in the North Wing alone—

"I haven't been completely honest with you," Jamie murmurs to Mei, as they reach another indistinguishably dark hallway, en route to the Music Room. Holly has not said anything about not speaking, this time. There are no more instructions. There are no more rules. "About the reason I began researching the history of Maidenhair. It wasn't arbitrary, my interest in this place. I definitely didn't know it was going to become a book; not when I started out."

"No?" she says, her throat closing.

"No," he says. "I got a letter."

He received a *letter*? A letter that inspired him to write a novel?

Do words make people want to write more words? Like war leading to more war? Like death leading to more death?

BUT BEFORE JAMIE can explain, they have reached the Music Room. The collective mood remains sullen, even though the room itself is fantastical; it has string instruments on display on every wall, gleaming like hammered gold, and elegant European-style fresco ceilings. A grand piano stands in the corner; behind the piano is an *èrhú* propped against a blackwood stand.

"Do you play the spike fiddle, Miss Chen?" asks Mistress Lau, grumpily, evidently noticing where Mei's gaze has landed.

Mei played but she did not have Ba's hands. Look at it, the python skin pulled tight, the bow laid flat between the strings. She remembers how his fingers would shake, up high on the neck of it, the vibration stirring the air. *The* èrhú *is the ancient sound of rain,* Ba used to say. *That is why people cry when they hear it. They are raining.*

"From other rooms in the house, I often hear someone playing the piano in here," says Holly. "And I hear singing."

"And then you come in here," says Mistress Lau, "and it stops? And there's nobody sitting at the bench?"

"I come in here," says Holly, "and the room is full of people. It is a party. It is the start of the dinner party. The one that ended with all of them dead by morning."

THE WHOLE HOUSE remains caught in the grip of the storm, yet the atmosphere is peaceful. A melody plays distantly, in soft, isolated notes; Mei will chalk it up to her imagination.

It is Mistress Lau's turn first, and when Mei sees the other woman's arm, she feels seasick.

The character-cuts from Mistress Lau's straight razor have not yet begun to heal.

Mei assumed that Mistress Lau would cut into herself in a

different place, during every séance. But she doesn't. She cuts into the same skin. The same wounds. Over and over and over.

Mei watches, in abject horror, as Mistress Lau prepares to do it again.

The difference today, unlike yesterday in the garden, unlike the first night in the Red Library, is that Mistress Lau's arm is now so butchered, she cannot read what she has written. She has done it all for nothing. Mistress Lau lets out a curse, and even though Mei has not even begun her own séance, she realizes, all of a sudden, that this prize may be hers for the taking. Maybe she should have known from the start, after the life she has lived. Victory is not about power. Victory is about survival.

THE QI IS just beginning to leave her, *just*, when she has the idea.

Oh, these ideas of hers—

But now that she has had it, she cannot forget it.

Holly is drawing nearer.

Mei knows what it looks like from the outside, watching somebody go into a trance.

She stiffens her arms and legs. She lifts her pencil level with her chin, as if she will write in the air if she has to. She closes her eyes and then opens them wider than they were.

She is going to *pretend*. Just for a few minutes. Just long enough for Holly to believe it.

She begins to let the qi go; but not enough that she can slip under.

Will Holly be able to tell?

But Holly herself must not have the Sight. If she did, she wouldn't need them, after all—

Holly is standing right in front of her now. All Mei sees is that buttery white nightgown.

All she hears is those single plucking notes.

Holly asks if she is still Mei, and Mei shakes her head.

Holly asks if she is the same spirit that took Mei over last time, and the time before that.

Slowly, Mei nods.

This is it.

Mei is about to learn what question it is that Holly asks her, during these séances, to which the mirror and then the stairs were the answer.

She holds her breath hard.

"Well then, George, my darling," says Holly. "Hello again."

25

SHANGHAI
SEPTEMBER 1942

IT'S BEEN DIFFERENT between me and Max lately, though I can't exactly say how. One warm September night we go up to the steeply curved roof of the lane house next door and we let our legs hang over the edge, in a way that feels tingly dangerous. Max says that when he first arrived in Shanghai he worked as a dope runner in the Badlands. He was only nine and a half, but the big bosses were recruiting boys as young as six off the streets, and you didn't need to know any Chinese to boot. It was going well enough until the day he took a few too many blows to the stomach in defense of a suitcase full of *poppy juice*, and one went near all the way through. He lost his glasses on the street that same day and had to get them replaced.

Funny how without glasses, he says, everything can seem a lot clearer.

Funny how in the darkness, everything can seem a lot brighter.

"I went into Third Wife's bedroom to look at the vanity table," I begin, and Max relaxes as well as anyone can on a roof, to listen.

THERE I WAS, standing in the center of her shrouded furniture, memories playing like film reel in my head: Third Wife laughing, eyes gleaming; Third Wife pulling at her earrings like they were pinning her down; Third Wife that day on the rooftop of the Cathay. I had the distinct thought that if Third Wife hadn't died, well, she'd be throwing Aiyi the biggest engagement party Shanghai had ever seen! She'd be able to make everyone forget, if only for one night, about the armored cars and the barbed-wire fences and the flag of the Rising Sun!

Or maybe she wouldn't be throwing parties, if she were alive now.

Maybe she'd have long stashed her babies under both arms and moved out of Uncle's house for good. She'd have begun her *real* life. She'd be going out every day, climbing more and more rooftops, always headed higher, the smile on her face as blinding as the flash of her camera.

ANYWAY, THE SHEET came off the vanity table easily and some of Third Wife's countless perfume bottles teetered, but nothing got knocked over. I don't know who the spirit was during the séance I did, and of course I have no idea why I drew that vanity table. I don't know what that spirit was trying to tell me. But right then, narrowing my eyes, looking at the sketch and then looking at the table, it dawned on me: the *letters*.

The letters in that bottom drawer.

The letters Ma supposedly wrote to Third Wife—

The letters I wouldn't have been able to read, five years ago, but now I can.

"Unless the spirit's message was really that I should wear more perfume," I say, making a face, and Max smirks. "Unless the spirit was Big Sister all over again, informing me from the afterlife that I still smell like a yellow ox."

Weirdly, I almost miss them now, her insults.

I had no idea people could miss the things that once made them miserable.

"I don't think anyone has an idea of that, do they?" says Max, sounding a little bit far away even though we've never been closer than this. "Until they leave home."

The nighttime has turned black but I can still see. It is like we are sitting inside the obsidian mirror.

THIRD WIFE'S LETTERS were still in there, filling the drawer of her vanity to the brim. Most of them were from names I didn't recognize, but Third Wife did seem like the type of person with a huge gulping circle of adoring friends and acquaintances. I started to read. I began to get that feeling I often do after reading too long, like someone has just thrown a bucket of water over me: My vision was charring. The characters blurred. I knew that George Maidenhair would tell me to stop, because you can't make *word-blindness* better by force, because it's not a kneecap popped out of place. . . . but *then* . . .

I found some letters from my Ma.

"ALRIGHT, I'M SO curious now I can literally taste it," says Max, though that's probably just his taste buds malfunctioning because no food in Shanghai tastes like it used to. Shanghai does not have as many blinking-neon billboards and sweat-soaked dance halls and painted-palm-tree hotels and steamed-up skewered-chicken stands as it used to, either. The Japanese have turned this whole city into *pàofàn*: yesterday's rice. No color, no texture, bland as a boiled sock. "What did your mom's letters say?"

The paper was the special stationary of the village letter-writer; thus solving the mystery of how Ma was able to write anything.

The penmanship was blessedly large. The tone of the letters was awkward and didn't really sound like Ma at all, but my strong suspicion is that Ma couldn't say everything she wanted to say outright, since it was all going through the letter-writer.

Letter-writers and spirit mediums have more in common than I ever knew.

"Weren't you afraid someone would catch you at this?" asks Max.

The only one who might have caught me was Aiyi.

First Wife is *pregnant*, by some miracle, after all this time, and is so nervous about it that she will not leave her bedroom. Uncle hardly ever ventures upstairs anymore, and our remaining servants would never, ever enter Third Wife's bedroom without being ordered to do so. They are convinced that Third Wife's soul will not rest until the Nationalist army avenges her death and drives the Japanese out of Shanghai. They don't seem to realize that it was the Nationalist army itself that killed her, that missed their targets, that dropped the bombs that hit the Bund, but I don't think it would matter, once people have made up their minds about such things.

This is what Ma's letters said:

OCTOBER 1936

Dear Jing,

After a year in Nanking, our new village is painfully small. Compared to Shanghai, it is a speck on somebody's shoe!

    Hopefully, we can live here longer than any of our previous places.

    We are making ends meet. A woman down the road appeared to be sick. I knew what it really was, of course. Afterward, her husband was beside himself with gratitude for my help, and paid in fruit.

DECEMBER 1936

Dear Jing,

The girls are each dealing with our move in their own way. Big Sister is angry that we pulled her out of school to come here, demanding constantly to know why. Second Sister remains withdrawn. Third Sister has attached herself to me. She does not seem to recall our life in Nanking, for which I am more than a little grateful.

JANUARY 1937

Dear Jing,

You remember what I did for my neighbor?
    Today she came by, thanked me . . . and asked me to contact somebody for her. She offered to pay.
    She offered good money.
    An old woman in the village has taken a shine to my daughters and tells them to call her "Nai Nai"; she keeps an eye on them while I am busy.

MARCH 1937

Dear Jing,

She has found me again.
    Now I cannot even enjoy the abundant cherries this season . . . not when she could be around any corner.

When will it stop?
When will I ever be free?

APRIL 1937

Dear Jing,

I understand now that there is nowhere I can hide that she will not find me.
  I have run for long enough.
  I must act.
  I must fight.
  She must go back to where she belongs.

JUNE 1937

Dear Jing,

Dragon Boat Festival coming up soon.
  I am going to Shanghai.
  Hopefully, I will not be away from my children for long.

"WHOA," SAYS MAX, in a tone like he's already slid right off the roof. "Who is . . . *she?*"

"Frankly, I was more shocked about the fact that my family ever lived in Nanking," I say. Max chuckles and so do I, even though none of this is funny; it's just that sometimes you have to let air out at moments like these, to relieve the pressure. "I never

219

knew or noticed that we *moved*! Our home always looked about the same from the inside, and there were always the same people, and nobody said anything, so I guess I just didn't realize."

"I understand," he says. "It's as if . . . the people you're always with are the real walls of your house."

"Yes, it's true," I say, and we smile at each other, and my mouth feels full of sand.

"So, to read between the lines, your Ma was conducting séances for tea money?" he says.

"Well, to be fair, she probably couldn't sell as many shadow puppets in our village as she could in Nanking."

"She started conjuring ghosts? And exorcising them? That's how I'd interpret the part about *the woman down the road* who was sick. And then she started being followed by a vengeful spirit who had followed her before. And she concocted a scheme to stuff the vengeful spirit back wherever it . . . *she* . . . came from, in Shanghai?"

"Yes," I say, "and I think *she* came from the wardrobe in my Uncle's attic."

I PULL OUT Ma's pouch of paintings, which I have brought up here specifically to show Max. I haven't looked at them in years, but I used to look at them so often I have them more or less memorized. I hand the pouch over. The moon has risen big and brilliant, more than enough light for paintings like these. He looks over each one closely: The skinny hand popping out of the wardrobe door. The girl-thing holding on to George's gates. The girl-thing blocking the Great World.

"My theory now is that Ma returned to Shanghai but failed in her quest to put this creepy girl-thing back in the wardrobe, and instead the ghost *got* her," I say simply. "And that's why Ma disappeared. And that's why nobody knew what happened to her. Though Third Wife must have suspected."

I think Third Wife wanted me to find out, in her way. Third Wife wanted to be a photojournalist. She believed in exposing things.

"Why is there a flower on all of these?" asks Max.

"It's a peony," I explain. "Ma was basically illiterate and couldn't sign her work, so she created this design to use instead. I think it's the most beautiful peony in the world."

He must agree, because he spends longer looking at the signature than at the actual pictures.

"You think there were even more?" muses Max. "It's such a small collection. Three paintings. Maybe some fell out on the road from Nanking to your village."

"WHY DO SOME ghosts show themselves to me, and can look like normal people, like Third Wife and Big Sister," I ask, "but other ghosts can only be contacted through séances, and I never see them at all?"

"I think it's to do with qi," says Max. "To appear human to you like that, it takes a great deal of energy. Most spirits have very little left, especially if a lot of time has passed since they died. And taking a form you would perceive as human uses up what little they *do* have. It's different during a seance— They're borrowing your qi, they're using your body to communicate, and that's easier for them. Once they have no qi left at all, if they haven't managed to move on, then they fade completely. Some people call this the second death; the real death."

"You don't think that Third Wife used up all her remaining qi just to talk to me that one night, do you?"

"Could be she did."

"Big Sister must have been full of qi; to be able to lead me all the way to the Great World . . ."

Max says: "Vengeful ghosts have much more qi than all other kinds."

"You think my sister was a vengeful ghost?"

"Vengeful ghosts aren't evil. They're just in pain that won't end."

"But they try to destroy things. And hurt people."

Max breaths out low and long. "Yeah. They do."

"I could never, ever, my whole life long, forgive the girl-thing if she hurt my Ma."

"Then you know," he says, "exactly how a vengeful spirit feels."

THE NIGHT AIR has cooled, but we don't move. I wonder how long two people can actually sit, just looking at the sky. When it starts to feel a bit strange, I ask Max what the addicts in the Badlands are like; the infamous *opium ghosts*. Drenched, dirty, defeated-looking, Max answers. They often look like they've just crawled out of the Whangpoo by their bare hands. Their teeth unscrewing from their mouths. Gums gone to pulp. Eyes like cracked eggs. He says he'll never touch the stuff or even anything laced with it, like those Golden Bat cigarettes.

The subject runs out and the silence takes over again.

I ask Max if he is willing to do a séance at Aiyi's engagement party and say that she'll pay. He says yeah, sure, but I can have the payment, if I want, since she's my family and I'm trying to save up money.

But that dream, of rebuilding my home village, has somehow lost its appeal.

That dream has become *pàofàn*.

It was never my home village anyway, as it turns out.

"Aiyi said . . ." I say tentatively.

Max looks over again.

"Aiyi said that she and Yuchang are planning to run away, after the party. To escape Shanghai for America. And she's asked me to go with them."

His eyebrows rise well over the rim of his spectacles.

"I don't . . . I don't know whether I should go. You can't tell anyone, by the way. She said Uncle and First Wife would try and stop her if they found out. I wondered if . . . if maybe you could look into the scrying mirror," I say in a rush, "and foresee what will happen. So that I can know what to do. Because on the one hand, to live in a place like America, I think I might like that. But on the other hand . . . it would be very hard to leave Shanghai now. Now that I am so used to it."

"I don't have to look in the mirror," Max says quietly, "to know that you should go, if you want to go."

"But I want to know my future. The way you do."

"I almost never look into my own future."

"Never? Really?" I say, trying to get us both to smile again, but it's not working.

It feels like we are on a much higher rooftop, all of a sudden. It feels like we are much closer to the edge.

"Very rarely," he says. "I can't change it anyway. Because of Step Two, remember? That my grandma taught me. *You see the future, but you no longer try to change it.* So there's no point in looking. And sometimes I think . . . sometimes I think there are only two options, really. Looking or living. Which am I going to do?"

He sounds so young that I almost want to cry.

"I would miss you," I say. "In America."

"I would miss you too," Max says, "but we could write letters, you know, until you have a whole drawer of them, just like

Third Wife," and then we're both smiling finally, smiling until it aches.

I CAN SEE why people like going to Max for their fortunes. He isn't afraid of saying the bad things. It is comforting to be around people who are willing to say bad, sad, real things; in an odd way, this gives you more hope. Max suddenly reaches out and catches something between both hands. I can see glints of light through his fingers, like he has trapped fireworks, or lightning, or a ray of the sun. But actually it is just a firefly and he opens his hands and the firefly flits away and he watches it go and there is an expression of wonder on his face, and in this moment I think how amazing it is, that he is somebody who can see everything there is to see, and he can still experience wonder, he can still feel awe.

26

HONG KONG
2015

THE ANTIQUE CABINETS each have oval latches right in the middle of their two doors, and rhythmically the latches have begun to pop.

A whomping sound; Ryan Li has fainted.

"Who are the *others*?" asks Susanna, transfixed by the nearest cabinet.

"The ones that died the last time your mama was here," says Holly. "Did you want tea after all?"

"You shouldn't keep them in there," I say. "Nobody should be locked up in the dark."

"Oh, now you care, Miss Chen?" says Holly. Her voice sounds like it could break skin, but her smile stays put. "How many years has it been? And lest we forget, it all happened the way it did because of you, did it not?"

"I don't do that anymore, Auntie."

"What, speak to the dead?"

"Blame myself for that night."

IT IS ALMOST chilling, to see that Susanna is no longer scared.

"So where are they? The *ghosts*?" Susanna says.

"You won't be able to see them," says Holly. "They're too weak." Holly's gaze flicks back to me. "I'm shocked you let your daughter come here, Miss Chen. Does she not realize how much a person can ruin, by running one finger down the tapestry of her mother's past?" A shifty smile. "I know her *look*, too. The look of someone who thinks she can click every little piece of someone else's life together and then hang it on her wall like a trophy. Let me guess," she says, addressing Susanna again. "You hope to find out what happened that night. And now that you know who I am, you want to hear my version of it."

Susanna is still hypnotized by the cabinets, but she can't deny it anyway.

"So let's begin," says Holly.

This seems to bring Susanna back to reality. She rifles in her shoulder bag until she comes up with her trusty tablet, her screen-stylus. "That would be great. I—"

"What is *this* thing?" Holly indicates the tablet.

"It's a—"

"You plan to write my story on a spirit slate?" Holly smiles even wider. Tiny saliva bubbles foam at the corners of her mouth. "I'm afraid I cannot permit that. There is bad luck, and then there is just stupidity!"

"I don't have to use this," says Susanna. "I can record you on my phone—"

"You think I want this voice of mine on record?" cackles Holly. "Please, child. I was a silent film star for a reason."

Susanna scrounges in her purse and pulls out a pen and a pack of tissues.

The cabinets are closing again.

Click-click-click-click.

I don't know why this is a worse sound than when they opened.

"WELL THEN," SAYS Holly, "let me be frank. You must be able to tell: I am disintegrating. I can't go on much longer. And I don't *want* to go on. Not like this." A hacking laugh. "Truth be told, I am grateful to whomever wrote those letters! Grateful that you're here. Grateful that you've come. Because for a while I've been thinking . . . that perhaps now, after all this time, there would be a chance for me at redemption still." Holly looks at me squarely. "I lied, Mei. That night. I lied to all of you."

27

HONG KONG
SEPTEMBER 1953

WELL THEN, GEORGE, *my darling, hello again,* Holly said, as if she is talking to her husband through Mei. But George Maidenhair cannot be the spirit that took Mei over during the first two séances, because that would mean that George is dead, and George cannot be dead. George is alive, because he has to be alive. Because there is no other way for Mei to kill him.

MEI KEEPS HER gaze fixed on the shoulder of Holly's nightgown. Her eyes strain so hard she is seeing red at the sides. She allows herself to take one short breath. It is like drinking Holly's perfume.

"Let's try again, shall we, George darling?" says Holly.

"Where's Peng? Where'd she go?"

It is Mistress Lau's voice.

"Where is Peng?"

There is a blast of blustery air. The door to the Music Room is opening. Mei can hear it on its hinges.

Holly gasps, close to a cry.

Another shout, and this is enough pretense for Mei to burst out of her fake trance, and she whips around, even though she wanted Holly to finish. Even though she is desperate for Holly to finish. Peng is there, standing in front of them; she is barely upright, her hands cupping her wounds, but alas, she has too many wounds and not enough hands, too much blood and not quite enough breath to say, *Help me, help* . . . before she swoons to the ground.

For a moment nobody moves. For a moment Mei wonders if she is in a trance after all.

It feels like a waste for Peng to die like this, when she was saved from the pond only yesterday. Or else it feels inevitable.

CECELIA IS SOBBING like a child. Mistress Lau chants to herself, the beaten-rug chant of monks. Mei feels that if she stands up she will sink to the ground and never be able to get up again.

Holly and Jamie are bent over the body, but of course it is hopeless, Peng is dead; you can't lose that amount of blood and not be dead.

Cecelia finally stops crying.

"Who's doing this?" says Mistress Lau, in a calm voice that somehow sounds worse than the crying.

The Music Room is icily silent.

Mistress Lau stands up. Her words fly like spittle. "Who's doing this? *Who's doing this?* Which one of you is behind this?"

Jamie stands up too. His face is thunder. "Who says it's one of us?"

"Who else would it be?"

"I don't know! But we were all here, weren't we? We were all—"

"Miss Chen was in a trance. I was trying to stop my own bleeding. I have no idea what you and Holly and Cecelia were doing. *You* don't even have the Sight. *You*—"

"Stop it!" screams Cecelia. "Stop it, all of you! Just stop! Stop!"

"Stop?" shouts Mistress Lau. "We're being killed off. One by one. And you want me to *stop*?"

Cecelia dissolves into crying again.

Mei thinks she must be in a state of shock. She still hasn't budged. She's the only one without any blood on her, by now. She just heard Holly address her as *George*. She just learned that George Maidenhair might be dead. And now Peng *is* dead. For some reason she hates to think of what people will say, if all of them die tonight. That they turned on one another. That the house did it to them. The murderer will get away with it because this is Maidenhair.

"LET'S THINK. LET'S just *think*," says Jamie, holding his head between his hands, like he can empty it of thoughts, like coins. "Delia was the first to be eliminated. From the competition. The first night. Then Peng, last night. What if it means something? Their deaths, in that order?"

"That's the most brainless thing you've said all day," snarls Mistress Lau.

Mei does not think their deaths mean anything. Most deaths do not mean anything. At this particular moment, in which she feels like she is watching all of this unfold from a great distance, she recognizes that even George Maidenhair's death might not mean anything. Maybe she never even thought it would; never truly believed that his blood would wash away her grief; never even wanted to lose her grief, but rather lose herself in it. How can she know, when a great gaping gash was ripped through her before she left Shanghai? How can you know yourself all that well when you're walking around like that? How can you ever be sure you want what you think you want?

If George is truly dead, if he has taken her revenge away from her, then he has taken everything. Without his blood on her hands, she is empty-handed.

"The killer *is* one of us," says Holly. "There's no one else here."

Even Cecelia looks up, with the way Holly's said it.

Mei finds her voice at last: "What about your servants, Auntie?"

"I didn't want to tell you the truth. There are no servants in this house," says Holly. "No maids, no cooks, no one. Nobody would work here. Nobody ever has."

JAMIE SHAKES HIS head. The lack of sleep shows in his eyes. "What do you mean, no servants?"

"There are no servants in this house," repeats Holly.

"But I've seen them. I've *spoken* to them."

"Me too," says Cecelia, her voice thick with tears.

"I've seen the servants too," says Mei unsteadily.

"I haven't," says Mistress Lau. "I haven't seen any servants. I haven't seen anyone since I arrived but the seven of us."

Mei licks her lips, dry as paper.

"They've been serving us our meals," says Jamie, wretchedly now. "They live in the North Wing. I've seen them go in there at night!" He begins to laugh. "This is a joke, right," he says. "Fess up. You're pulling our leg. Peng and Delia are actors, aren't they? This is stage blood!" He wipes his hand on his jaw. "Get up, Peng, the fun's over! Am I right? I've got to be right. This is all one huge disgusting jo—"

"The house makes people see things," says Holly.

"I haven't seen anything," says Mistress Lau again, "and I have more power than all of you put together."

Mistress Lau sounds more scared than she did when they were talking about the killer.

231

THE AIR IN the Music Room has turned copper. They have let Peng stay bleeding because there is no way to stop it. Mei hears herself suggest aloud that they should do the next séance. They should keep going. Is that really her voice? Does she sound that placid? Why is she not afraid, to go into a trance, to wake up, to discover that someone new has died? There was only one other time in her life when she was as single-minded as this: back when she wanted to discover the truth about her mother.

She *has* to know what Holly was going to say before Peng burst in. She *has* to know what has happened to George.

"I don't care about this competition anymore," Cecelia says. Her eyes are puffy as a carp's. "How could I? How can *you?*"

"I would understand if no one wished to participate further," says Holly, her voice flat with fatigue, "given the circumstances."

"No, wait," says Mistress Lau, brushstroke eyebrows rising. "No, I never said that."

MEI WAS AWAKE the whole time in the Music Room. It's true that she was focused first on Mistress Lau and then on Holly and never noticed Peng leaving. But Peng was murdered *out there* and Mei is absolutely certain that nobody came in after her, through the door, which means the killer has to be *out there* too. The killer *can't* be one of them. She ventures to say: Holly might not have servants, but what about an intruder? Someone who broke into the house and hasn't left?

The Fourth Séance was supposed to take place in the ballroom.

"The ballroom has no windows, and only one entrance," says Holly, as if she has come around to Mei's thinking, even if her tone is doubtful. "In theory, at least, we would not be taken by surprise in there."

It sounds like the kind of room that makes Mei want to scurry into her own head to hide.

On their way, Mei falls back with Jamie.

"The letter," she says, soft. "You said a letter made you write your novel?"

Jamie answers just as softly: About five years ago, not long after George had purchased Maidenhair, Jamie moved in temporarily with George and Holly. He was drinking too much, wasting his time, bemoaning his whole life—and then an anonymous letter arrived. It was slipped under his door. It was maddeningly incoherent, and it took him weeks to fully decipher it, which perhaps created an artificial sense of urgency, but decipher it he did.

"What did it *say*?" Mei presses.

"I can tell you," says Jamie, "if you promise not to panic."

Her pulse flares with anxiety at these words, but she nods.

"Okay," he says, "Holly Zhang quit the Shanghai film industry in the late 1920s and seemingly disappeared, right? The '30s were tumultuous, of course, both in China and in the world—not to mention, talkies became all the rage. So for better or worse, nobody thought much about Holly until she showed up again during the war, in 1943, and reentered Shanghai society. She met my father and married him and the rest of the story, everyone knows. Or thinks they know."

They have stopped.

Holly is saying something at the head of the group.

"If I interpreted it correctly, according to the letter, that woman," says Jamie, almost inaudibly, "the one who appeared out of nowhere, who married George, who is in front of us right now, is not actually Holly Zhang. She is somebody else. And the letter would not say who. For me, you see, that was the beginning of an obsession."

28

SHANGHAI
OCTOBER 1942

TODAY GEORGE MAIDENHAIR is reading more *Jane Eyre*. We sit in opposite armchairs by the fireplace in his family room. The sentences in *Jane Eyre* are as matted as wool, and sometimes George has to repeat himself for me to understand, but his patience is boundless.

I interrupt to ask: "So that's it, then. There aren't any real ghosts in this story?"

"Depends what you mean by real ghost," says George, still patient.

"I mean it quite literally, Teacher."

George considers this. "You know, I remember, years ago, when you told me about seeing Jing—Third Wife," he corrects himself. "Another time, you saw a girl in the attic, on your first night in Shanghai, one who couldn't talk because she didn't have a tongue, isn't that right? I know you believe you have a gift for seeing beyond our world, Little Mei. And *I* believe that you saw those people. But that doesn't mean they're ghosts."

He loves to do this: State things that make no sense, and then explain them, and then somehow stitch it all together so it makes perfect sense.

I think this is *his* gift.

It would have been put to excellent use if he'd ended up becoming a teacher like he planned.

"There are other explanations," George says, "besides the supernatural."

"Like what?"

"Hmm." His voice is thoughtful. "Well, for example, if the woman in the attic couldn't talk, then she would have made a good listener. Maybe that was what you needed at the time. Sometimes our brains give us what we need in unexpected forms, and when we don't require that help anymore, it goes away."

People who live and die inside your head?

Honestly, this sounds even more frightening than anything supernatural.

"Anyone in your position, Little Mei—alone, in a new house, in a new city, taken from everything that she has ever known, and being punished on top of it all—might be lonely. Might be scared. Might do anything for some quiet company." George's voice is gentle as ever. "There is a phenomenon that is not uncommon with children, especially at the age that you were when you first arrived in Shanghai: the emergence of an Imaginary Friend."

The woman in the attic did not seem like a friend. Not exactly.

I wonder if there are Imaginary Non-Friends?

"I disagree. That woman is a ghost, stuck in that attic for eternity," I say candidly. "And I think I could help her. Set her free."

Now George Maidenhair closes *Jane Eyre* and looks at me straight.

He breathes in deep like he's going to speak without stopping for another five chapters.

"I haven't said anything, because it is not my place," he says. "But your mother meant a lot to me, and you do too. So I'll say it now: You have been spending too much time with that—with that teenage *charlatan.* Max Friedman. You have such tremendous potential, as all children do, and all you need is light to grow to meet it. But that kid, that—that self-styled *Master*—is keeping you in the darkness. Filling your bright, keen mind with all manner of balderdash, all the while not seeing, or worse yet, seeing perfectly, that you take it as gospel." George clears his throat loudly; he must have been keeping this speech stuffed in there a long time. "I am aware that it is part of your culture, to believe in ghosts, in an afterlife, and as you know, I too am drawn to these ideas. But there is a difference between cultivating an interest in the things you do not understand, and letting yourself be consumed by them. One's beliefs, whatever they might be, must always be balanced with a fully formed life in the here and now."

"Max is my friend," I say, and I know I sound annoyed.

"He's a confidence trickster. He knows what he's doing."

"He's not *doing* anything! He's the only one who's always been honest with me. Everyone else lied. About Ma! About my family! Uncle *knew* they'd all been slaughtered by the Japanese, and wouldn't even admit it to me until *I* confronted *him* about it!"

"Sometimes people withhold the truth from those they care about, because they believe it will cause needless pain. What your Uncle did, he did to protect you. His intent was decent—"

"Then that was his mistake, because I don't need to be protected! I'm almost thirteen, you know!" I'm nearly shouting. "I think that *that's* the only darkness, Teacher: when people try to keep you from your fate, and say it's for your own good. You say I need light? I don't think there is any light, except the truth!"

George falls silent, but he doesn't look angry.

He never gets angry.

His patience *is* boundless and I don't know what it says about me, that more and more, every day, I am tempted to see where his limit lies.

I could reassure him by telling him that I have now decided to join Aiyi and her fiancé to America; that I am indeed abandoning Max, even if every time I think about it my stomach clenches up cold.

What I *won't* tell George is what I have decided to do beforehand.

I am going to scrape together the courage to go back up to the attic, to talk to the spooky half-tongue ghost, to the only person— if you can call her a person—who might have witnessed whatever ultimately happened to Ma.

Who might know for certain if Ma tried to put that girl-thing back into the wardrobe, and failed in the worst way.

I can't *not* do this, before I go to America. And shouldn't George be able to understand that? It's just like how Jane Eyre had to leave Thornfield Hall, isn't it? Because you can't just go off and play Rochester's wife on a beach in France and act like everything is fine, can you? Not even if you love him dearly. Not even if you can see that blissful alternate life in your mind like a scene in a snow globe. Not when you know that high up in an attic, directly over your head, is somebody who might change everything, waiting there, stuck there, right where you left her.

MAX IS NOT a fraud, but he *is* a good showman, and I can see how someone might get confused. His enthusiasm is infectious. His earnestness is lovely. Now that I can do séances too, he has spread the word that he has taken on an apprentice, a master-in-training, one whose abilities differ slightly from his own, and suddenly we have small crowds in the fortune-telling shop. Sometimes I lie awake at night and I think about the puppet shows I put on for my family years ago, and how somebody always ended up snoring. There was always one element missing. One crucial quality I lacked.

Max has it, whatever it is.

He has it and it lights up his eyes when he grins at the customers and he has it and it lights up something inside of me, like I am the firefly that breathed in his hand.

IT TAKES NEARLY an hour for me and Aiyi to break into the attic. Neither of us have ever picked a lock before. I had to beg Aiyi to come with me, because I don't want to be in the attic alone, and she relented saying, *Just in case there really is some weird lady up there.* I hope that one day she will become a criminal mastermind after all, and picking locks and exploring mysterious places are both things that future criminal masterminds should get good at.

We trudge up the dusty stairs and Aiyi is panting by the time we hit the landing. *You never get out of breath like this studying,* she complains. I don't mention that I often get breathless reading books.

The attic is filthy dark. The windows are grayed over and the ceiling is full of spiders.

The half-tongue girl is crouched next to the wardrobe; almost on all fours. Cowering.

"So, is your friend here?" asks Aiyi.

The girl's hair is messier than it was five years ago, still piled like a cake on the top of her head, still staked through with her pearly hair stick, but there are wayward ringlets falling out everywhere. Her dress is dirtier, too, as dirty as the rest of the attic.

She stands up when she sees me.

Aiyi goes over to the wardrobe and tries to open it.

The wardrobe spews dust but stays shut.

"Do you remember me?" I ask the ghost. My voice is thin, needly. "I was here five years ago and we tried to talk to each other, but we couldn't. I've brought paper—I've brought it so that you and I can talk to each other by writing. Back then I didn't know how to read and write. But now I do."

The girl only watches me.

There is something dark coming out the corners of her eyes, too muddy to be tears. She had that last time, too; I'd forgotten. She has it worse now.

"Wait, what?" says Aiyi, turning around. "You see her? There's somebody here?"

"I want to talk about my Ma," I say, determined. "You remember her?"

At last, a slow, frigid nod.

"Did you see what happened to her? *Did* something happen, while she was up here, maybe? Trying to . . . um . . . to force somebody . . . or something . . . into that wardrobe?"

Aiyi turns again, to look at the wardrobe.

The attic is very still.

If I hear a sound from inside the wardrobe, I might scream.

Nothing.

Then there is another nod from the ghost. She does not wipe away the dark streaks that now run down her cheeks.

I asked too many questions; I don't know which one she's agreeing with.

"Oh. Okay. That's great. Can you write down what happened?" I ask, my heart pummeling my rib cage. "I thought that maybe—in exchange for your help—I could help you, too. I could help you move on . . . I mean, I've never done it before myself, but I've watched somebody do it. And I would promise to try my best. I'm sorry I didn't come up here earlier, by the way. You must have been really lonely. I know I was—and that was only one night!"

But the ghost does not take the paper I am offering her.

I begin to offer qi with it.

The energy is pouring out of me, which is a little risky, but my hope is that she can use it to write.

She doesn't. The stuff from her eyes flows thicker, in globs. She takes one half step closer to me because she can only move in half steps, with bound baby-feet, and instinctively I take a step back, but I don't turn away. This is my last chance. People never come back from America. If I don't succeed now, I will never, ever learn what became of my mother. It's not that I think about Ma all the time, the way I used to; it's not like I can't live with myself unless I find out what happened. It's not that I plan to devote my whole being to solving her disappearance; not again.

It's just that it would be tragic, to come *this close*, and not make it.

All the greatest tragedies in the world are about coming this close, and not making it.

That is what I have learned best from books.

"Please," I start to beg, even though the ghost might only soak the paper through, with that inky substance still rolling off her. There is qi still rolling off me, and she is taking it, but she still doesn't write. "Please, tell me what you saw!"

Our eyes meet. The girl's eyes do not look quite the way I remember.

Nothing in this attic looks right.

Run, the girl mouths at me. *Run.*

AFTER DINNER I prepare to go to Max's.

The way I am feeling, having lost so much qi in the attic, I don't know if I can stand to face the clusters of people who now flock to watch our séances. I could fail to show up, or ask Max to cancel any customers we have scheduled, but that would only make me feel even worse than I already do, that I am soon to leave Shanghai forever.

As I am reaching for a new pair of stockings, First Wife calls out from behind our shared golden screen: "Little Mei?"

"I'm on my way to Max's," I yell out tiredly. She doesn't usually ask where I'm headed anymore. Especially not since she got pregnant. Everything is about the baby.

I felt so caged, when she first adopted me.

Now I have so much freedom.

Sometimes all this freedom doesn't feel as good as I thought it would.

"Come in here," First Wife commands.

I peek around the screen.

In bed, with blankets up to her elbows, First Wife looks more like a broken child's toy and less like a full-grown woman. She no longer sets her hair but lets it snarl down to her shoulders. She no longer wears qipaos because the doctor says they might suffocate her unborn baby. She no longer looks at me, I'm sure, without hearing the fortune teller's prediction ringing in her ears: that by taking me in, she was assured a healthy male child.

Curse that fortune teller, I want to say to her. Curse that fortune teller, who should have just told you that you would love your adopted child as if it were your own!

But she didn't, and I can't say it either, because First Wife is still terrifying, even when she's lying down and definitely has not bathed in a long time.

Even when she herself is terrified.

Looking at her, my heart fills up with pity and I *hate* that, I *hate* pitying her, because I want to hate her. I want to resent her. She brought me here to Shanghai against my will and she has done nothing but cane me and criticize me ever since—except when she's in bed like this, about to bark orders that she expects me to drop everything for and obey. Fetch my newspapers, Little Mei! Water my potted orchids! Clean my slippers! Get the laundry off the bamboo poles! Stop *looking* at me like that!

At least First Wife does not make me thread her eyebrows

with cotton anymore because she no longer cares about her appearance.

"I want you to stay in tonight," she says.

"Why?"

She can't possibly be worried that I'll be nabbed by the Japanese. The other day she sent me to the early-morning market all the way at the mouth of the French Concession just to buy *good luck red thread* that can supposedly save a fetus's life if you sleep over it.

And George Maidenhair thinks ghosts are an absurd idea.

"I want you to decorate the ancestral altar," says First Wife, blinking in that way that makes people look even less like they're actually awake. "I had a dream this afternoon that it looked as it used to. I want you to restore it."

We both give sliding looks to the unadorned ancestral altar, which has lain neglected for months now, if not years.

"I can't," I say. My mouth feels like it's been sewn up by her good luck red thread.

"That was not a request. *Kuài gěi wǒ zuò wán.*"

"I'm sorry. I'm busy. I'll do it tomorrow morning."

"I am your mother and you will do as I say."

"You're *not* my mother," I bite back, "and I won't have to do as you say much longer!"

Oops.

"What does that mean?" First Wife demands, lifting an inch or so off the pillows.

"I mean that I'm not your servant, that's all, and I said I'll do it in the morning."

"You will do it right now," she orders, impressively harsh for how wilted she looks, "or I—"

"Or you'll *what*?"

First Wife glares at me. I can almost see her nostrils smoldering, like a dragon's. "You are an ungrateful louse of a child, you know," she says. "I saw you just the other day, after you sold a drawing to Mrs. Liu. So proud! But just wait until you have sold everything, Little Mei. Just wait until you have sold everything."

She falls back against the pillow again.

"Third Wife warned me about you," I say.

I shouldn't. I shouldn't say a word. I know it. I should either shut up and do the ancestral altar, or shut up and go to Max's.

Her eyelids flutter. "Third Wife?"

"Third Wife said that you were content in this life and would do anything to keep it. But I'm not. I'm not going to marry someone like Uncle, and be named after a number, and spend all my time trying to have his children until I am sick with it, and be cruel to the children that I do have! I'm not, I'm not, I'm not, so I'm not going to do as you say anymore, because I would do anything *not to become you!*"

First Wife sits up again, slower this time.

Stop, Mei, *stop talking!*

But there are trains you cannot stop even by flinging yourself in front of them.

"I bet I know who the father of your baby is," I hear myself say. "It's George Maidenhair, isn't it? I've seen the way you look at him. I've seen the two of you talking together, under the golden rain trees outside his house! If you mistreat me, I will *tell* Mr. Maidenhair that this baby might be his, and once Mr. Maidenhair learns *that,* he's not going to just let you and Uncle raise his baby! You know he won't! Because *he's* not Chinese, and *he* doesn't have to spend his whole life pretending he's happy even when he's not, just so that his family doesn't stink of shame, the way Uncle has to, the way Aiyi has to, the way Third Wife did, the way Ma did before she ran away, *the way I will never do, not as long as I live!*"

First Wife opens her mouth, only a slit.

We both know I have said too much.

"It is remarkable," says First Wife, her voice like sleet, "how a child as smart as you could be so wrong about everything."

"Smart?" I retort. "Did you just call me smart? Because you've just spent the last five years telling me I am as dumb as moss."

As I leave the house my heart is still pounding and my body is cackly all over, like I have just swallowed a radio.

By the time I reach the fortune-telling shop I am fully energized by our fight, by the horrible thrill of going too far, but this only makes me feel guilty, as if I have stolen First Wife's qi, punctured her and pulled it out of her. I resolve to make the ancestral altar as grand as it ever was once I get home, even if we have only half the food we did back then; maybe to surprise her with it when she wakes up.

Because, sadly, deep inside me, deeper than you could reach with a soup ladle, I still want to please First Wife.

I want to please her, and I want to anger her, and I want to hate her, and I want her to love me, all at the same time.

Maybe she is a little bit of a mother to me, after all.

In the morning, I discover I have accidentally slept over at the fortune-telling shop. Yesterday was so long and so awful; I am thankful for a new day. Max and I never see each other in the morning so we are both a little shy.

"I was thinking that you should be the one doing all the séances from now on," says Max. "The sketches you make . . . people really love that, as they should. I'll keep doing the mirror; the fortune-telling. It's what I prefer anyway. And that includes the séance at your cousin's engagement party; you should do it."

"Aiyi wants to talk to ghosts *and* get some fortunes told," I say.

"Greedy," he says.

We smile at each other.

"Could we do it together?" I ask.

"Okay," he says. "Together."

29

HONG KONG
SEPTEMBER 1953

The Fourth Séance

THE ELECTRICITY IS still off but there are a few paper lanterns on the floor and Holly lights them, one by one, until the room comes to life.

All the walls of the ballroom are mirrored.

In every direction, Mei sees her reflection.

Most of Mei's reflections move with her, as she shuffles after Holly and the others, but there is one reflection that does not. There is one that stands still as Mei makes her way to the center of the ballroom. There is one that stands still as Holly instructs Mei and Mistress Lau to lie on their backs, right there on the varnished floor, and to look up at the ceiling.

There is one reflection that remains standing as Mei lies on her back, looking up at the ceiling, as instructed.

There is one reflection that is not actually her.

This is why Mei cannot look in mirrors.

"I have seen a . . . figure . . . creeping across this ceiling at night," says Holly.

The way she says it is chilling.

Like she has never thought this *figure* was human, not even once. The bigger problem is that the ceiling is mirrored too.

HOLLY LOCKS THE ballroom door behind them. They are safe. Or else they are trapped. Mei stares at herself and Mistress Lau in the mirror above.

Mei can't look in mirrors.

Someone touches her hand and she jerks from it, but it is only Jamie, lying down next to her. She exhales and surrenders to a fresh wave of weariness. She'll rest her eyes while Mistress Lau is undertaking her usual procedure, that's all. Then, once she's got a bit of energy back, she will sit up stockily as if possessed once more; she will take hold of her pencil like her fingers are claws; she will wait for Holly to sidle over and ask the question Holly was about to ask in the Music Room. The question Holly wants to ask *George.* Mei will keep her gaze off the mirrors at all times, no matter what she sees moving in the periphery of her vision, no matter if she hears a murmur from within saying: *Mei, release me. Release me, Mei—*

"Delia!" somebody cries.

Cecelia?

Mei's eyes feel clipped shut.

"Delia! My sister is out there! Can you hear her? Can you hear her asking for me? *You have to open the door!*"

Mei forces her eyes back open. She sits up to see Cecelia hurling herself at the locked ballroom doors, face aflame with pain, fists pounding. *Open the door, we have to let her in!* Mistress Lau is already holding the straight razor over her arm, the blade hovering, while Holly looks uncharacteristically helpless, unspeakably old, asking Jamie, *Should I open the door? Should I?* Cecelia is going to break the mirror on the back of the door, if she keeps this up.

This whole room might shatter. Mei's reflection could come crashing down on her. Maybe that is what makes Mei stand up at last and go over to Cecelia and put a hand on the girl's shoulder and let a touch of qi go, even though she should be hoarding it, not giving it away, until Cecelia stops screaming.

IF GEORGE IS dead, could it have been his ghost that Mei saw fleetingly outside her room on Friday night, that first night? But it is now Sunday night. If George's ghost could appear to her like that, he wouldn't be waiting around. He would speak *to* her, directly, openly, as he always did. At the very least he would have offered to read aloud to her, in their old tradition, because that way it'd go much faster, and *The Peak House* is one of those books where you wish you were already at the end when you begin, because you want to know it, and then you wish you were back at the beginning when you end, because you want to experience it all over again.

This is a phenomenon that only *book people* can understand.

There is so much that only George Maidenhair ever understood.

He would probably sympathize with her; that Mei wanted to kill him. He would say that in her shoes, anyone would have wanted that.

MEI MUST HAVE fallen asleep. She has no recollection of lying down again, or of any trance, pretend or otherwise; of Holly asking her anything. The lanterns are burning low, festering. She blinks up at the ceiling and they are all lying down now, sleeping, spread out across the floor of the ballroom, even Holly.

Mei's reflection, in the ceiling, is still asleep.

Mei's reflection opens its eyes suddenly; stares straight down at Mei.

"Do you know who killed them?" Mei asks; a shaken whisper. "Do you know what's happening?"

I do, says her reflection, *and I'll tell you who it was, if you release me.*

MEI TASTES IRON on her tongue. She tries to wake the others, but with that taste, her tongue doesn't work right. Jamie sits up with a groan. Holly is already stirring, and then Mistress Lau, but Cecelia does not awaken. Her skin looks like slate.

Cecelia is dead, just like Peng is dead, just like Delia is dead.

They have all been sleeping on a blanket of blood.

Jamie starts shouting, asking, *How did this happen?* And, *How could this have happened right under our noses?*

Jamie keeps shouting but Mei can tell he isn't angry at any of them.

He isn't even angry at the killer.

He is angry at himself, for falling asleep when he probably didn't mean to. He had probably intended to stand guard all night. But his shouting is futile and his self-loathing changes nothing, except that it makes everything worse. Maybe it always does. Maybe if you blame yourself for the bad things that happen, for the blood you're standing in even if you didn't spill it, it's like you're doing the killer's job for him, stabbing yourself, over and over and over.

Mei feels an unexpected weight lift from her own shoulders, ever so barely, the way you'd shrug off a scarf.

MISTRESS LAU HAS been trying to revive Cecelia, or at least to examine her better than they did the others, perhaps because the urgency is greater, because the killer is running out of people to kill. As if the murderer has been hosting his own competition. One by one by one. But as Mistress Lau moves the girl's hair away from the nape of her neck, the hair so coarse with blood it looks like seaweed, the ripped fabric of the shirt seems to give way on its own, revealing Cecelia's back.

And there it is.

Mei's signature design; Ma's signature.

Just as Jamie described he found on Delia.

Maybe it is on Peng too.

"What in the world?" breathes Mistress Lau.

Mei can't believe it, and even if she could, she can't understand it. All this was done while the rest of them were sleeping? And how can the cuts be so *flawless*? Look at how they shine from the skin; the same way they hang in windows; like there is sunlight coming out of Cecelia. Look at how the peony is both beautiful and monstrous. Look at how there is not a stroke that Mei herself could do better. But she cannot look as long as she'd like, because Holly's eyes are on her now.

On her hair.

"Your hairpin," says Holly.

Now everyone is looking at Mei.

"Did you do this?" asks Mistress Lau, voice rising dangerously.

"I saw your cuttings in the curio shop, Miss Chen. This design is yours," says Holly. "And how could a random intruder have done something like this? You're the only one of us with the skill."

Holly's scorn is worse than Mistress Lau's anger. And Jamie's silence is worse than the women's accusations.

They think she did it. They think she killed Cecelia.

"If I killed her, why would I add my own design?" Mei asks sharply. "Why would I do something that points at me, that casts such heavy suspicion upon me?"

"I have heard of such killers. Leaving their . . . leaving a *brand* on their victims," says Mistress Lau, whose fury is now tinged with hysteria.

"I was in the Music Room when Peng came in! You *know* I was there!"

"You could have killed her before that," is Mistress Lau's wild-eyed reply. "It would have only taken a few seconds to stab her, while the rest of us weren't looking, and stash her somewhere. Only she wasn't fully dead, and found us in the Music Room, before succumbing to her injuries!"

"Does that sound plausible?" Mei says, her throat hot with the injustice of it. She *didn't* kill Peng. Or Cecelia and Delia. She hasn't killed anyone. She *hasn't*. The only way she could have killed someone without knowing it is—

If she did it while in a trance.

Mei doesn't know what she does, while in her trances, except sketch.

What if she does other things too?

Other kinds of art?

Cutting?

Carving?

Killing?

But the others were all awake, while she was under—

"Look at the past two days and tell me what's *plausible!*" Mistress Lau screams, the sweat finally showing beneath her layers of paint.

If the others gang up on Mei, they can do whatever they want with her. There is nobody here to prevent them. Except the murderer, most ironically. For a short moment, Mei is so sleep-deprived, her head so murky, her reflections so many, that she almost doesn't mind either way. George might be dead. *George Maidenhair might already be dead.*

What if that was the real purpose of this competition, from the start?

What if George is dead but Holly still wanted something from him, so she hired a bunch of spirit mediums to try to contact him, to see which of them he would be willing to speak through? And then, once she got what she wanted, she was going to have his spirit exorcised from the house?

Or at least that was the plan.

Somebody else, it seems, has other plans.

"The door's open," says Jamie.

It's the first he has spoken since he stopped shouting.

The door of the ballroom is indeed ajar. The sliver of space between door and frame seems to be letting in a windy coolness and Mei welcomes it, for how heavy with blood the air has become. The murderer *is* an intruder. The murderer came in and killed Cecelia and left. Mei feels the relief trickle through her. Maybe now they will stop accusing her. Maybe now they may even speak up for her, when the police come.

But Mei can pick locks from the inside too.

"I SAY WE tie up Miss Chen," says Mistress Lau, breathing erratically. "I say we—"

"She was in a trance," says Jamie, just as Mei notices that she is holding on to her pencil, now tipped with blood. "Look."

He points to a piece of paper that lies several feet away, far enough from the body to be safe, and Holly all but leaps to it.

See?

She wants an answer from George—

Seeing the sketch, Holly's smile pulls tight with frustration.

Mei takes the sheet of paper from the older woman and looks down at what she's done.

251

It's a drawing of a shadow puppet show.

It is unsettling, showing shadows cupping a circle of light; with the figures on rods, drawn in dark, dashed lines. Mei thinks back to the mirror, the mirror that turned out to be a door. To the wall that turned out to be a staircase. Everything was always something else, in George's favorite stories. And if he is in fact dead, then her first emotion might be disappointment, then satisfaction, below that despair and horror and regret and perhaps below that, a longing for how things might have been, how differently it all could have turned out, but what she feels right now is: *alive*.

That telltale buzz beneath her skin, that lets her know she is human. She is here.

Just like the very first day she showed up as his student.

Just like the very first time she started to read a book.

She has not felt it in five long years.

Do you know what the best feeling in the world is, Little Mei?

Is it happiness, Teacher?

It's the feeling of wondering: What is going to happen next?

That can't be right. That's not even a feeling!

It is a feeling. And it's the best because inside that feeling is the desire to live. The determination to keep going. The knowledge that there is still something worthwhile ahead of you.

"The Puppet Room," says Mei.

Holly's mouth snaps open, but she says nothing.

"Auntie," asks Mei, "where did your husband keep the shadow puppets I made for him?"

30

SHANGHAI
DECEMBER 1942

EVERY DAY THE newspapers spout new headlines about the different invasions and battles and bombings and sinkings, all the way from Russia to Egypt to Guadalcanal. But tonight we can forget about all that: It is the night of Aiyi and Yuchang's engagement celebration. Aiyi's girlfriends from school glide along the Peking carpets, clad in butterfly dresses, their hair curled at their chins like seashells. The men are dressed dapper in suits, slick and stylish. There are ice buckets and rattan fans, as though the summer's not over, but it is. There are pastries and candies and sweet nuts, as though Shanghai does not eat bitterness every day.

It is a party but it feels more like a theatre play of a party.

The guests are directed into the Orchid Room for the séance. Aiyi and Yuchang seat themselves at the long table. The room is full of clanking glasses and frothy laughter and drunk young people, red-faced as corpse flowers.

I take my own seat at the table.

Max is lighting five candles, one for each traditional Chinese element; a pleased murmur is already going through the guests. He pulls out the black scrying mirror next and I look away because something, the mirror or Max, is making my heart beat a little bit too fast.

First Wife has poked to the front of the crowd. Uncle has excused himself to his study but First Wife no doubt hopes one of her ancestors will show up.

One of her ancestors ought to show up, after the effort I have put into the altar!

Look at that belly on her; she looks more pregnant every day; healthy and plump and cherry-cheeked. Apparently, she has now passed the dangerous time, when babies can slide right out of you like soap.

Will the fortune teller's prediction finally come true?

It is shocking, how much I hope so.

How much I want First Wife to have her heart's desire, even if it wasn't a daughter like me.

Max says something witty and draws a splash of laughter from the audience, although in their current state, that isn't too hard. Then he says, dropping his voice dramatically, that there is no way of predicting what will happen once I slip into the trance. He shows them the scroll he has brought—it looks positively ancient; he must have steeped it in vinegar—and the set of charcoals. He explains how the séance will proceed.

Afterward, he says, when it is over, he will tell anyone's fortune who wants it, using the mirror.

The candles flicker nicely.

"First," says Max, "we will see if there is anybody here."

He doesn't usually do this. It's only for effect. He takes the chair adjacent to mine and he lets his gaze move around the room and his glasses fog up. There is not a sound around us. Everyone is rapt.

"Is there somebody here?" he asks.

It is almost comical to ask this, in a room full of people.

Nothing, and then—a knock. A tap, more like.

In the center of the table.

A gasp from our audience. Max gestures for silence.

"Do you have something to say to us?" he asks. "Tap once for yes, twice for no."

Another tap.

I cannot see the audience very well, but I can see that some-body new has come up beside First Wife, and is standing behind Aiyi's husband-to-be.

My pulse begins to drill through both my wrists.

What is the girl from the attic doing down here?

Did she mistake the paper I was holding out to her for an invi-tation?

"Alright," says Max, "then let's begin."

I would close my eyes, but now the ghost is looking into them and I can't.

Max nods at me. "Mei?"

The audience thinks this is part of our act; nobody moves.

"What is it?" he asks.

"She's there—she's—"

The ghost rolls her eyes backward, and when they roll to the front again, they are plain white, without irises. Her hair tumbles down violently from the top of her head, covering half her face. Max rises quickly from his chair. He holds out his arm and I know he is trying to draw qi off her, away from her, to get her to crum-ble, to force her into fading, but something is *happening* to her. Her face is going flat and blank and empty and her hands lift and I see that one of them is holding the pearly hair stick, right by Yuchang's neck, without quite touching.

Yuchang begins to struggle for breath, his own hands clawing at his throat.

"Yuchang?" says Aiyi, bewildered, reaching for him.

The guests finally seem to sense that something has gone amiss but nobody is stopping it. Maybe they *want* to witness something bigger than themselves. Something unbelievable. Even if it is bad.

The candles are going out.

I am frozen solid from my own revelation: The half-tongue ghost is a vengeful spirit. She always has been.

"Yuchang!" Aiyi yells. "Something's wrong! Something's—"

There is an explosion of noise. The guests spin in all directions. The vengeful spirit does not move. I jerk back to life and start to scramble across the table, knocking aside my paper and the dead candles and I hear Max shouting at me to get out of the way but I can't let Yuchang die like this, I *won't*, and I know that the qi is streaming fast out of me because I am scared and I know that the more I lose the more the spirit will lap it up but I don't care, I must, I must try, and I reach Yuchang and I push Aiyi off and I try to wrench the ghost's hands away from him, though they are not actually *on him*, and then I try to seize the hair stick, but I cannot get a grip on it, and by now Yuchang is not making any sound at all. Tears are pouring down my face or maybe it is sweat and I am using all the strength I have, but it's not working, *it's not working*, just like it didn't work when I tried to get free of a large man at a long-ago train station, because sometimes you're just not strong enough, you're just not good enough, you're just not enough.

Yuchang's lips are bruised-looking and his eyes look like the dead candles and he falls forward, almost onto my lap.

Aiyi begins to scream.

Max is behind me, grabbing me, asking me if I'm alright, but before I can answer, the vengeful spirit takes hold of him by the shoulder and shoves him to the floor.

The spirit is heading toward First Wife, the hair stick held high.

The white pearls have turned red.

First Wife is fixed in place, her hands clutching her belly, bewildered.

"No!" I scream. *"No!"*

Aiyi is crying, collapsed over Yuchang, while her friends are shouting for help, and I hear Uncle's voice in the distance, and then the last candle goes out.

I cannot see anything.

I cannot see anything except the black obsidian mirror, glistening from its place on the table.

I do not understand how a black mirror could be a source of light. But I do not care. I go toward it while shouting for First Wife to run, *run, Mother, run*, but she doesn't answer, and then I see her. Her hands have dropped from her belly. She is unblinking. But she is still alive. The vengeful spirit is beside her, already lifting its hands. I know I cannot stop it killing her. I am not Max. I am not a Great Master. I am not even Little Mei, underneath it all. I am Third Sister; the child my parents hoped would be a son; the one who couldn't even read; the one who never stopped talking. The one who couldn't save Ma.

I do the only thing I can think of doing.

I pick up the black stone mirror and I raise it high over my head and I bring it crashing down on the vengeful spirit, and in an instant, as perhaps is to be expected if you go around slamming black mirrors over things, everything goes dark.

HERE IT IS, the truth that I always wanted.

The truth is this: I didn't really know what to live for, if I wasn't looking for Ma.

You need *something*, you know? When your family's gone and your country's being occupied and you can see the dead and you don't know why. You need a reason to scoot your bottom out of bed in the morning. For a long time, I thought Ma was all I had, but right now I'm realizing that I had many other things. Other things that now lie scattered like fish heads in the gutter; and I may never be able to collect them back again.

A WEEK LATER I knock on George Maidenhair's door in the late afternoon and he opens it, his eyebrows shooting high up his head.

He is careful not to sound surprised when he says: "You've been missing for several days now, Little Mei. Your family has been here looking for you."

"I was just hiding in their backyard," I say, in a toad-croak.

He glances askance at my clothes, which I've been wearing for that whole week, and which tore while I was climbing over his gate. "Come inside," is all he says.

In his dining room, I sit where I always sit for our lessons.

"I wanted to disappear forever," I say, with a sob that turns into a hiccup, "but it didn't work."

"I'm glad it didn't."

"Is First Wife okay?"

George hesitates. Maybe he is remembering the conversation we had some time ago about light and truth and good intentions. "First Wife is fine," he says, "but the baby, unfortunately, is gone."

"Oh," I say vacantly.

George's housekeeper brings us a tray of tea and digestives.

"It seems Aiyi left a note," says George, "and hasn't been seen since."

I hope she went to America after all. I hope I haven't crushed every single one of her dreams.

"Aiyi must think I killed Yuchang," I say, as the steam from the tea burns my eyes. "She doesn't believe in ghosts. And from the outside it must have looked like I murdered him. She'll never believe that I didn't. She'll never forgive me."

"She might," he says, "if you give it a little bit of time."

"But then I did kill him."

"I wasn't there, but I know you didn't, Little Mei."

"I did, Teacher. I'm the reason the vengeful spirit was able to kill anyone. I *gave* her all that qi. Up in the attic, when I visited her with Aiyi! I gave that energy to the ghost because I wanted her to be able to write down on paper what happened to Ma. Which she didn't, so it was all for nothing anyway. And then, worse of all, during the séance, you see, I got in the way when Max was trying to defeat her. I got in the way because I couldn't bear that it was all my doing. All my own fault."

"You reacted by instinct," says George. "That's what good people do when others appear to be in danger."

He will always think the best of me.

It's nice when people do that, but at the same time it is awful. Because *you* know the underlying essence about yourself, and now you feel like you can't show it to them.

George says, "Your friend Max came by here too, while you were gone. Looking for you."

"I broke his mirror."

"He mentioned that. I offered to pay for a replacement. He said that he was done with the whole business, however. He plans to pursue a different line of work."

"What?" I draw back. "Because of . . . because of this? Because of what happened? Because of *me*? No, he can't do that! If it had been Max, alone, by himself, everything would have been fine! I should be the one who never does it again."

It can't be just because of me, can it?

I remember that conversation we once had, about how he

never used the scrying mirror for his own benefit, the way he said *looking or living.*

Maybe he's choosing living.

But then how will he become a Great Master? How will he learn all Four Steps of seeing the future?

George sips his tea so I take a sip too and it hasn't cooled down one bit, but I'm glad it hurts.

"Can I stay with you for a little while?" I whisper. "Here? Please?"

"I don't think that's a good idea," he says.

"Did it look to you like *First Wife* is going to forgive me anytime soon?"

"You're scared to face her," he says, "and fear is never a good reason to—"

"Well? Did it?" I say, higher-pitched.

George sighs.

"*Did it?* Don't lie to me, don't you dare!"

"No," he says. "No, it didn't."

I start to cry.

"Alright," he says. I hear the extreme reluctance in his voice, but I know he can't stand to see me cry. "Alright, alright. I'll talk to First Wife and your Uncle. But if you do stay, this will only be for a short while, mind."

I keep crying, and eventually George holds out his hand. I take it. His hand is warm. I feel as icy as the inside of a vase. The tea has not helped at all, but his hand does a little. I should say thank you, Teacher. Thank you for teaching me to read the right way up. Thank you for talking to me for hours about ghosts even though you don't believe in them. Thank you for being here three afternoons a week, every week, for the past five years, even though you run a busy business empire. Thank you for never not being patient, even when I tried really hard to make you mad.

I know George loved my Ma. He hasn't tried to keep it secret. I know that he would have done anything for her.

For a long time I thought that spending time with her daughter was just another thing he could do for her, but I don't think that anymore. I think he spends time with me for *me*.

The truth is that I'm as much *his* daughter, by now, as I was ever hers.

I swallow a few tears and try to smile.

"I enjoyed meeting your friend Max at last," says George. "He should have come around much sooner, to introduce himself. I know he's worried about you. If you like, Little Mei, you have two hours—two hours exactly, from now—to go to him and let him know that you're alive and okay, before you are due back here, to do some reading before dinner."

I FIND MAX in the fortune-telling shop, stacking tarot cards again. Again and again and again. He looks up swiftly and his eyes go so big behind his glasses that I nearly want to laugh. He knocks over the stacks, standing up, and then he comes over and he is squeezing me in a tight hug. Afterward, I cannot quite get my breath back. I don't know if I'll ever get my breath back, around him. We do not clean up the cards; we let them fall where they will. We go up to his neighbor's roof, but we end up not talking, just sitting there in the good kind of silence. The sky is milky with clouds.

I wonder if this war will last forever.

I wonder what happened to the ghost of the attic, because the last thing I remember is breaking the mirror, and how the vengeful spirit felt solid beneath it, how she made a sound almost like speaking, how all the glittery glass pieces fell to earth like shooting stars.

PART FIVE

31

HONG KONG
2015

HOLDING HER PEN over the tissue, ready to write, Susanna has that frost-glazed look in her eye that people do, in the throes of anticipation. It is similar to the look she had when she first started dating Dean. They were lucky to find each other, Susanna and Dean; to have that second spring of love, in that stage of life with preexisting children and full-fledged careers and eyes that crack at the corners. They were both divorced, both embittered, both lonely.

After their first date Susanna called me and said: *I'm too old for this.*

That was a moment I wished I had raised her more Chinese. I wish I had shown her that the older, the wiser, the stronger, the more deserving.

I made a joke. I said, *But he likes old things, look at all his documentaries,* and she laughed—half a groan—for the first time since the divorce. It never occurred to me that maybe I was right. Maybe, on their date, Dean showed so much interest in Susanna's existence before she knew him that she began to reevaluate that existence. To see it as more than worthless and wasted, even though it was past.

RYAN LI HAS come to. He sits up, looking the way I feel after long airplane rides and longer layovers, after the trek up a mountain that wants to send you rolling right down, after those staggering stairs.

"What's going on?" asks Ryan dimly. "What . . . where are we?"

"Maidenhair," says Susanna. "Underground level. You fainted, Mr. Li. Do you need something to eat or drink?"

This is what she says, but her eyes say, *I'd much rather you just faint again, please, so that Holly Zhang can take over the talking.*

"I think I'm . . . alright," Ryan mumbles, and he digs in his pocket and comes up with a candy bar.

He also comes up with a ball of crinkly-crushed paper.

The letter.

His letter.

Susanna spots it too. "We have to compare them," she says immediately. "You don't get up, Mr. Li, I'll come to you. But we have to compare them." Susanna moves like a whirlwind, grasping the envelope away from Ryan, who looks like he may not have realized what he was holding. She reads in a flash, as fast as she does everything else. She does not have dyslexia. She does not have the Sight. She has her own gifts.

"Same writer," she declares.

Susanna reaches into her bag, pulls out a small binder with elastic bands, flips to one of the colored tabs, and shows us her own letter, pressed flat in a transparent sheet protector. She's right: The two letters were written in black felt-tip pen, in the same penmanship. In traditional Chinese characters, no less; not simplified ones. The kind I grew up with, that they still use in Hong Kong and Taiwan, but not on the mainland.

Not the type most people would be taught nowadays.

"You don't read Chinese," I say, "and neither did Dean, did he?"

"We got it translated, Ma." *Obviously*, is what she doesn't add. Translated.

It makes me think of another letter, delivered long ago to another unsuspecting recipient, that had to be painstakingly deciphered.

Jamie's letter.

"Did your letter have postage, Mr. Li?" asks Susanna. "Because mine had none. Someone came directly to my house to deliver it."

She keeps her face straight, but I know we're both thinking of her cube house, the minimal security, the curtains that are more or less like her sheet protectors. Somebody peering into the window, going round the back, rousing the cats but not enough that they'd make a fuss, not that they ever did. Somebody knowing where she and Dean lived. Somebody stalking them, waiting for a good moment to slip a letter like this one right into the middle of those lives.

I draw both letters closer. I wish the letter-writer had used English. I wish I had my reading glasses with me.

But even so, I think I know who wrote these.

"ALRIGHT, ENOUGH OF this," says Holly, losing patience. "I was about to tell my story and I should like to get on with it. If you'd sat as long as I have down here, without anyone to talk to but *them*, you might be more sympathetic!"

My daughter switches modes, picking her pen back up, looking poised. She knows she can talk to Ryan Li later. The letters are hard evidence. They're not going anywhere. Holly Zhang, on the other hand? If Susanna doesn't interview her now, there may well be no further chances.

"You lied," I say, and Susanna's mouth turns down.

Maybe she thinks I am talking to her.

"You were saying you lied? That night?" I prompt again, and Holly nods.

"I'm not who you think I am," she says. "I am not Holly Zhang."

32

HONG KONG
SEPTEMBER 1953

HOLLY ZHANG PULLS out one of those pasty pink Hong Kong tissues that feel like tree bark, that can take off a layer of skin alongside your sweat, and begins wiping her face. The ballroom has turned humid with the scent of blood and Mei would do anything to leave it. But no matter how many times she asks where the Puppet Room is, nobody answers.

THE PUPPET ROOM. George did always encourage a younger Mei's artistic endeavors, but she remembers that he was stunned to hear how many hours she spent each day, working with the wrong hand, trying to get better, to be better. He didn't know that she secretly believed, had always believed, even though she had never really been given a reason to think this, that Ma left and never came back because of *Mei.*

Because she was no good at art; or because she was just no good.

It's easy to think such things, when you're Little, when the world and everyone in it still revolves around you, and Little Mei wanted so badly to be worthy of Ma's love.

Mei understands, now that it's far too late to go back and change anything: Love is not *earned*, anyway. There is never a need to work for it. Yes, Mei became skilled at her craft, but that's not the same as being meant for an artist's life. She didn't have the passion you need in order to become a great master at anything. All she had was pain.

Mei does not enjoy making art.

She never has.

And if she had had the courage to do something about it earlier, if she had just stopped trying to create all the paper art in the world that Ma couldn't, because Ma disappeared, then maybe none of this would have happened. Maybe Mei's whole world would not have turned to scraps.

"NOBODY KNOWS WHERE the Puppet Room is," says Jamie at last.

Even Mistress Lau has gone quiet, and is looking rightfully bewildered.

"You said you'd seen the puppets," says Mei.

"I said that I'd seen the *puppets*. I've seen the puppets, and I saw your name on them. But that was back in Shanghai. George made a Puppet Room here in Maidenhair, and he refused to tell anyone where—"

"I'm sorry. Her name? On puppets?" interrupts Mistress Lau. "And why are you talking like this? Do you *know* George Maidenhair?" Now that the face paint is coming off, Mistress Lau is looking more and more like any other tired woman in the middle of the night. Maybe Mistress Lau doesn't like looking at herself in the mirror any more than Mei does, and seeing her own dried bean curd skin and lips like shaky lines and eyes full of old wounds; maybe that's why she started painting her face. Sometimes you start painting and you don't know when to stop. You start painting and you end up with customers with whole rooms full of your shadow puppets.

When nobody hurries to answer these questions either, Holly finally deigns to speak again.

"The Puppet Room was going to be the location of the final séance," says Holly. "The last session."

"How were you going to hold a séance there without knowing where it was?" Jamie points out.

"I was going to learn where it was through one of you," says Holly. "During the séances. It's the only question I've been asking."

"WHY WOULD YOU want the final session to be held in the Puppet Room, of all places?" Jamie asks Holly. He sounds downright belligerent. "You said you chose the six séance locations because you'd seen something in those rooms. If you don't even know where the Puppet Room *is*—"

"Because," says Holly, her tone turned hostile too, "my belief is that we'll find your father's dead body in it."

Jamie's face looks like it was wiped clean by the pink tissues.

Mei remembers how she felt when Holly said, *Well then, George, my darling*, the way it slinked down her spine.

"Your father is haunting this house," says Holly. "George is haunting it and he can't move on because I can't find his body. The séances were to help me find his body. And then the winner was going to help him move on. Are you satisfied now, James? Is that good enough for you?"

271

⌒

THE MIRROR IN the Portrait Gallery led to the stairs. The stairs must lead to the Puppet Room.

Jamie would have mentioned if there were shadow puppets down there, surely. Even if he was distracted by Delia's dead body— But it has to be. There *has* to be something he didn't spot. Right now, in this moment, Mei is so determined to understand everything that if she had the choice between surviving tonight but never finding out what is happening here at Maidenhair, and finding out but being killed, she might choose to find out and die.

But is she determined enough to go down those stairs?

Mei has faced her phobia many times over the years. She just spent a night in a room without any windows, after all. But this is a ballroom at ground level. That would be a basement chamber that she might not even be able to stand up in. It all started with the ancestral hall, when she was seven years old; of course she knows that. She knows that her fear is unfounded. She's just never admitted to anyone, what she saw in there.

Not even to herself.

"MY FATHER'S . . . NOT dead," says Jamie. "You said he was traveling. You said—"

Mistress Lau breaks in: "Wait. George Maidenhair is your—"

"I had to tell people *something*," says Holly. "George hasn't been seen in weeks. You know how he'd sometimes say he was going into the Puppet Room and then take ages to come out again. Well, he hasn't come out again."

Mei has a fleeting sense of secrets being spit out like melon seeds.

"And now I know for sure he's gone," says Holly. "Because I've spoken to his ghost. Through Miss Chen. At least during the first two séances—"

"His ghost. His *ghost*. I don't believe this. Why didn't you tell me when he first went missing?" Jamie says. His voice leaks anger. "Why didn't you tell *someone*? Why didn't you just hire a search team to go through the whole bloody house for him?"

"In case he was perfectly fine, that's why! You want people talking? You want people up here asking questions? I have to find his body first, before we involve outsiders."

"You think he's dead and you're worried that people will *ask questions*?"

"You could have checked in on him earlier," says Holly, steely-eyed. "You could have come here. You were too busy getting drunk with your degenerate friends and your cheap women to spend time with your father. You have been more than happy to leave it to me. *Hǎo de*, and this is how I choose to go about it—"

"Yeah? Letting him wander around this house by himself? Letting him go missing for weeks? I can't—this is incredible. This is beyond the pale."

Mistress Lau tries again: "So George Maidenhair really is your—"

"The Puppet Room is somehow connected to the Portrait Gallery, in the North Wing," says Mei, and this has the gratifying effect of silencing all of them. "That is what the spirit has said. And that is where we must go."

MEI LIKES THINGS that *other* people have made. Earrings. Hairpins. Lanterns. Brocade scarves. Embroidered slippers and umbrella hats. Cloisonné metalworks and Siamese silver and ivory. Paper cuttings by better artists than she could ever be, prettying the walls and windows. She particularly likes objects with histories, with stories, with dark, intricately woven provenances, that imbue the objects with something like a soul. The first time Mei ever really knew what she wanted to do with her life, it turns out, was the moment Third Wife first walked her into that famous curio shop in Shanghai, on the morning of Bloody Saturday in August 1937, right before the bombs fell. Some people are born to create things. To take nothing and mold it into something.

Others are born to collect things.

Just one more thing that Mei and George had in common.

"THE PORTRAIT GALLERY," mutters Holly, as they enter the North Wing and it becomes dark in all directions. "The Portrait Gallery. Of all the rooms in this place, it had to be the Portrait Gallery."

"This way," says Jamie.

"How I hate this house," Holly grouses. "After I bury George, I'll sell it. Or do you want it, James? To write another book?"

"Another book?" says Mistress Lau. Mei glances at her, surprised by the lack of fire in her voice.

"I've written a novel inspired by Maidenhair," says Jamie. "That's all."

"By the myth of the Lotus Lady," says Holly, with a light sneer.

"Really? What happens in the story?" asks Mistress Lau.

But they are already approaching the Portrait Gallery. Holly hauls out her keys again, but they aren't necessary. Mei and Jamie left the door unlocked. The door swings open. Holly goes first, then Jamie, then Mistress Lau, then Mei last of all. The mirror is still off the wall and the open stairwell is like a gaping mouth and Holly lets out a groan as if she has done nothing but come across secret stairwells recently. She and Jamie head straight for it, but Mei notices that Mistress Lau is preoccupied by the portraits.

She seems struck by one portrait in particular, which has been hung at about her height, of a young woman with bobbing curls of hair.

Whether this young woman might have been beautiful in real life, one will never know, because of the damage to the painting.

Mei is about to tell Mistress Lau what Jamie told her, about the eyes that followed one of the Hall family friends, but suddenly Mistress Lau turns around and yanks down the high collar of her frog-buttoned shirt.

"I'm wearing the same choker as *she* is," says Mistress Lau. "In the painting. See?"

Mei stammers in reply.

"You see it, Miss Chen? You see it on me?"

"I see your necklace, yes," Mei says. There is a roar in her head. "But—"

"She's dead, isn't she? The girl in this painting. All these people are long dead?"

Mistress Lau makes a sound like the choker has tightened around her.

"Mistress Lau," says Mei, but she doesn't have a chance to continue.

"That's me. That's a painting of *me*. I'm *her*," whispers Mistress Lau. "I'm her, aren't I? I am this girl. I'm her." She releases her collar. She looks down at her hands. "That's why I couldn't see the servants. The things everyone else saw. Even though I have such power. That's why: because *I'm a ghost*. But how did I die? Why can't I remember? Why can't I remember, Mei?"

Mistress Lau is wearing a choker indeed. But the woman in the painting is not.

Mei looks into Mistress Lau's eyes and does not see Mistress Lau in them anywhere.

She sees the house.

GEORGE MAIDENHAIR WOULD have liked the curio shop in Kowloon, all the way down the sorry end of Nathan Road. He might chuckle at the idea that Mei's become little more than a rag-and-bone man. He might enjoy hearing how the shop had long gone unoccupied because of its bloody, unlucky history, and how Mei was able to take advantage of that. But she knows what he'd say about Mrs. Volkova: *There is a phenomenon that is not uncommon with children, Mei.* Mei would defend herself: She got the idea from the old name of the place, Volkov's, formerly a bakery-café. Served piroshki and cream puffs to expatriate White Russians, until the proprietor was murdered by a Soviet agent. George would say, *Anyone in your situation, in a city you can't accept as your home, in a life you can't accept as your own, might want someone to talk to. Better yet, someone who doesn't talk back all that much, except to tell you what to do.* Mei would defend herself further: Yes, it happens to children, and she isn't a child anymore; she's twenty-three already, was twenty-one when she'd saved enough to make rent on the shop. George would say, *Then why did you need an Imaginary Mother?*

33

SHANGHAI
FEBRUARY 1943

AT BREAKFAST EVERY morning I read the papers. Everything is going through the censors, so naturally what I read is that the Japanese are doing extremely well in the war. Afterward, I exercise briskly in the courtyard; followed by two hours of lessons on my own; followed by silent reading; then lunch. The afternoon is for my art, with tea at five; it is often the only time of day I see George. Friends of his will join us at times, most of them grumpy but entertaining. After tea, George usually leaves again and I am permitted to do as I wish, but I have an early curfew and George's housekeeper is adamant that she will squeal on me if I miss it even by a few minutes.

She says this because she knows I'm going to Max's.

Max has a new apartment and a new delivery job and sees way more of Shanghai than I do. Max being Max, he doesn't shy from describing any of it, from the skulls that wash up the river to people being bayoneted at the hassled checkpoints. Tonight, as we sit on his roof, he tells me about the severe gasoline shortage and how nobody is driving anymore.

Tonight there is another bombing raid but it's all the way across the river. We can see tiny dots of light, of fire.

"This won't go on forever," says Max quietly. "Nothing goes on forever. Not this war, nothing."

I look over at him and feel the clap of my heart and I think, even though I don't say, that he's wrong. This fire will burn forever.

WHEN GEORGE TELLS me it is time for me to go live with Uncle and First Wife again, I am shocked. Shocked and frankly devastated. There is something nice about the dullness of staying with George. It is dependable. It is reliable. There is a structure to my day, to my life, like the back of a chair, like the skeleton frame of a lantern.

"Suyin misses you," says George.

That's got to be a lie, and George has *never* lied to me. At least not that I know of.

"I can't keep you here against her will, Little Mei."

"I'm not going."

"She's not going to punish you for what happened."

"I'm not going. I'm happy here. I want to stay with you."

A lengthy pause. It is so silent between us that I can hear the clattering sound of a rickshaw going by in the street.

George says: "I was in love with your mother, you know."

Of course I know.

I watched Ma break the neck of a poisonous snake once. I wonder if that's how she turned him down.

"Was it unrequited? Like in *Wuthering Heights*?" I ask, with sarcasm, and I dislike myself for it.

"I'm sure it was. She was married to your Uncle, at any rate. So I never told her," he says. "And then, of course, it was too late. It did teach me something, though. You shouldn't leave it too late, when you care about people. So I'm not going to leave it now; I'm going to tell you that if I could adopt you as my own child, Little Mei, I would. And I want you to know that you'll always have a home here. But at the same time, you should be with your family. A family that is, if imperfect, good at heart."

"Uncle doesn't care whether I'm dead or alive," I say. "And First Wife—"

There are too many broken dreams between me and First Wife.

An almost-mother and her almost-daughter.

"Little Mei—" he begins.

"If you cared about me, you'd let me live with you."

"When you're older, you'll understand that—"

"Ba left me at a train station, and now you're abandoning me too!"

"That's not the same—"

"Then why does it feel the same?"

It turns out that there are some questions even George Maidenhair does not have the answer to.

I always thought it would be a moment of triumph, posing such a question, but the victory is bittersweet. I think secretly I had been hoping that he knew everything there was to know in the world, because that is what we hope of all our teachers. It is disappointing to see that they're human too. They're just stumbling around too, looking for footholds, loving people they wish they didn't love, probably missing their own teachers, wondering in their deepest souls if they actually know anything at all.

MAX LISTENS TO my rant from start to finish and gives me a half smile.

"Wait," I say, slowing down, "why are you looking like that? What's going on?"

I am still full of fizzy energy and try to sit but can't.

"They're relocating all of Shanghai's *stateless refugees* to a special restricted area," he says. "It's in Hong Kew."

"What does that mean?"

"A ghetto. For Jews. I won't be allowed to leave it. Not 'til the war's over, I reckon."

Now I sit, but mostly because my legs have gone watery. "What?"

But I've heard him perfectly well and he knows that.

Max takes off his glasses and rubs his eyes. He looks like an entirely different person without his glasses on. If he wanted, he could try to use his Sight to foresee the end of the war. But he won't. He won't even say *why* he won't; why since that séance at Uncle's house, he hasn't used his power at all. It seems like now would be the time to use it. Now that the whole earth is cracking open around us.

"Can I come with you?" I ask, surprising both of us.

"To the restricted zone?"

"I'd go anywhere with you," I say, "and I'd rather that, anyway, than back to Uncle's house. Unless you'd prefer not. Then say so. And I won't."

"I can't ask you to come with me," says Max, fumbling a little for the words.

"You didn't ask. I asked."

"You'd need new papers. . . ."

If he tells me to stay behind, I won't shout at him the way I shouted at Mr. Maidenhair. I'm all shouted out for today. Mostly, I am just tired. Mostly, I want to stop wondering where my real home is. Max and I are still very good friends but we are also three years apart in age at a time when every year is starting to feel like ten years. And we have spent comparably little time together since I moved in with George; Max definitely has new, better, older friends by now. In fact, sometimes it even seems, when it's just the two of us and there's a sensation in my chest like a bird is opening its wings, that we are strangers.

"I've seen a lot of evil," he says.

He sounds much older than sixteen, all of a sudden. Like every year is *actually* ten years.

"In governments. In armies. In individual people. I've kept my head down so long, trying to survive in this city, that sometimes I forget it's even possible to look up." He hesitates. "But whenever I do look up, I'm really glad to see you there."

He makes me sound like the sky and I feel, for a second, like the sky.

"The war will seem a lot closer," he warns. "If you come with me."

I don't remember a world without any war. All my life, there has just been more and more of it, like shading the same sketch, over and over, darker and darker: the Japanese building more and more guard posts and barricades; more and more young children lining the sidewalks, offering themselves to strangers as servants; more and more bodies piling on the riverbanks. In books people always lose their normal everyday lives in one fell swoop, like your legs being cut out from underneath you. But it turns out you can lose it one mahjong tile at a time. You can lose it while you're not even looking.

I LEAVE A long letter of explanation for George and, to tie up loose ends, I decide to leave one for Uncle and First Wife too, explaining my decision. But just as I am placing it discreetly at their front door, the door opens and Uncle himself steps out.

This is my chance to speak aloud everything I've written down, all the apologies and the angst and the awkward good wishes, but Uncle and I do not have that kind of relationship. For years we only talked of art, and only in technical terms. Uncle had his own teaching style; it felt a bit like being snapped into a cattle yoke. He once said it wasn't my fault that I'd never be as good at painting as my Ma was. That was as close to praise as he ever got.

Tell me to stay, I silently urge him.

Tell me to stay and maybe I'll stay.

But he doesn't. He grunts and closes the door in my face.

This is as close to goodbye as we'll ever get.

I thought Ma ran away from him, years ago, but probably she just walked, because I don't think he would have gone after her. Whatever Uncle really cares about, whoever he really is, he's painted right over it.

ACCORDING TO MY new papers, Max and I are second cousins, not that anybody's paying attention to anyone who might want *in* instead of *out.* Hong Kew was already buckling beneath the vast number of resident Chinese and Japanese and Russian nationals, long before the arrival of any *stateless refugees,* and now the lines of laundry are hung so densely over my head as I walk its narrow lanes that the days feel like nights. Some people have jobs outside the zone, but my life has shrunk down to these few roads.

After five years in the grand houses of the French Concession, I had forgotten what it felt like, too many people and too little space.

Max and I live in a lane house with several other European families. He and I share a room, each sleeping on straw mats and shivering beneath ghostly cotton *xiàn tǎn* blankets. There are no toilets, no electricity, and only a public bathhouse down the road with shower rooms. We use buckets for night soil; the only privacy to be had is thanks to a grimy plywood partition that the couple upstairs donated to us, probably feeling sorry. We cook our food on hot plates, what food there is; the rice and lentil from the corner shop is mostly a mix of small stones and birdseed. Fleets of cockroaches live happily alongside us, often scooting over my feet while I sit in the communal kitchen and sketch.

One night I think Max is asleep but then he says, "Do you miss your old life, Mei?"

I don't know which old life he means. The one I started out with, the one with Ma and Ba and my sisters? The one at Uncle's? Or the one at George Maidenhair's, that often feels more like a dream, for how short it was? Or maybe he just means everything. Everything up until this very moment.

I have now written several letters to George, but he hasn't written back. Or else he has but the Japanese administrators are reading the letters and ripping them up.

"If missing means wanting, then no." I turn on my side, toward him, but Max is looking up at the ceiling. I ask the question that has pickled inside of me by now: "Do you miss seeing the future, Max? Other people's futures, I mean, not your own."

"I'm better off without it," he says. "I'm happier."

But what about your grandmother? What about being a Great Master?

Then Max turns too. His eyes meet mine. His gaze is soft and bright.

"Sometimes I get scared, though," he says. "Sometimes I get so scared."

34

HONG KONG
SEPTEMBER 1953

The Fifth Séance

MISTRESS LAU IS hallucinating. The same way Peng and Cecelia and perhaps Delia did before they died. But before Mei can
shake the other woman back to her senses, Mistress Lau has
swooped around and is running for the opening to the stairwell.
She is soon pattering down the stairs; but her morbid words seem
to stay up here. *I'm her, aren't I? I'm a ghost.* . . . Holly and Jamie
barely seem to have noticed. They are still standing by the mirror,
now arguing about George. About when and where he was last
seen. About how confused, how weak, how helpless, how close to
death he already was. About whether Holly should have hired a
nurse, a full-time caregiver. About whether a good son, an Asian
son, would have become his father's full-time caregiver. This is a
fight that could go on for years, with everything they have both
held back, that is only coming out now because George is not here
to prevent it.

Mei's thoughts are rolling every which way, like marbles.

"Mistress Lau," she says, as loudly as she can, and the pair
of them look up. "I think Mistress Lau is going to be the next
to die."

HOLLY GOES DOWN the stairs with hesitation, her candle aloft, calling for Mistress Lau, but Mei grips the edges of the walls. *You are not seven anymore. You can face darkness. You can face evil.* This isn't working. She tries to think of something else. Such as: Could she have found it in herself to kill someone who was *confused*? If George didn't know who she was, would that count as revenge? If he didn't know who *he* was, if he couldn't remember anything he'd done, would it even be the right person that she was killing?

These stairs do not go straight down. There is a sharp turn, right where you run out of light.

"Go on," says Jamie. "I'm behind you."

Mei could have applied to be George's caregiver herself. How easy it would be to commit murder in such a situation, and yet when she imagines it, she pictures long days spent reading aloud to him, hours and hours, of their roles reversed at last. Of him asking for one more chapter; of her granting it. Of him wanting to know the end; of her sadness, knowing the end was near. *Yes, you're doing it, Mei, you're doing it—* Mei has reached the bottom of the stairs, the lowest step, the deepest layer, and here, at this level, this part of herself, Mei knows, she knows at last, that it was never George that she blamed, never George she actually wanted to punish.

Look at the way she's lived, the past five years.

She has been punishing herself.

It's alright that you loved him.

It's okay.

You have been locked in an ancestral hall long enough, Mei.

"WHERE'S JAMES?" SAYS Holly, all acid, when Mei steps off the bottom of the stairs and into an empty room that stinks of old death. There is Delia's corpse in the corner, as Jamie first described, and there is Mistress Lau, kneeling in the other corner, trying to get her choker off, looking like a rabid animal, still rambling to herself, *I'm a ghost, I'm a ghost.*

"Jamie? He's right—"

Mei turns and stares straight up. She sees only blackness.

Where is he?

"Where is he?" demands Holly.

"I don't—"

A hammering noise now; a shout. Something about a door. There's a *door*? What door? There was no door behind the mirror. Only the opening to the stairs. Or at least Mei had not noticed a door. But she had purposely not looked very hard. Holly elbows Mei out of the way and pounds back up the steps.

"There's some kind of hatch, that closes up this stairwell," Holly yells back down to Mei. "James? James, are you out there? What happened?"

I don't know! I can't get in! Jamie's voice.

Mei's thoughts go white.

A door has closed behind her.

A door that will not open.

She is standing in an underground room with one dead woman and one woman who thinks she is dead but isn't.

To Mei's growing horror, one of them is starting to stand up.

It is not Mistress Lau.

Delia is smiling. Blood drips off her dress.

Mei has to gasp for breath.

"You want to know what I think?" says Delia.

She is speaking with a young child's singsong voice.

Mei thinks she might vomit; she dares not open her mouth.

"I think he's just faking it. I think he's just pretending he can't get it open. He's herded us all in here and now he's going to kill us." Delia's eyes widen. "Don't let him kill us, Mei. Please don't let him kill us."

HOLLY HAS COME back down. "James was saying he'd fetch help," she says, but her face is raked with worry. "But then he went quiet and I . . . Miss Chen? Are you alright?"

"He went quiet and you thought the killer might have got him?" says Mistress Lau, who has adjusted her clothes and risen from her kneel, seemingly recovered, like none of it ever happened.

Delia stands there, still smiling, still bleeding.

Do they not see her?

Mei shudders so hard she has to grab at the wall to stay standing.

But she grabs too much of it.

The wall is not a wall.

It is a screen. It is a sheaf of paper, wrapped painfully over a wooden frame, and the paper rips, coming off like it was barely on in the first place, revealing uneven, hacked-in shelves.

On these shelves, standing tilted on their rods, are shadow puppets.

Mei has found the Puppet Room.

When Jamie Nakamura first uttered the words *Puppet Room*, Mei imagined hundreds of puppets, upon dozens of shelves, an audience of them. She imagined that George would have hired other artists to make more; he wanted more. But all of these are hers, and only a handful. Mei can't remember how many she made for him, only that each one took months. She would count, but she is having an attack of word-blindness. Puppet-blindness. They are all moving out of order and washing sloppily together and her eyes cannot tell them apart anymore.

She hears Holly calling for her, but she is already sliding away.

35

SHANGHAI
JUNE 1945

THE GHETTO IS full of young people, and Max and some of his friends have organized weekly *Kulturabende*, discussion groups on subjects like politics and history and economy, that take place in an abandoned courtyard. I often go along to listen. I don't speak much German and can't understand what is being discussed, but it's almost nicer that way. You can feel the words pouring over you like you're standing beneath a waterfall.

I have never actually stood beneath a waterfall.

One day I will.

I have gone back to my goal of becoming a paper artist, since I don't know what else I could be. I work on my craft, laboriously drying out the pamphlets and flyers that I find trampled on the streets, nothing like the nice soft paper I had at Uncle's house, but I've heard it said that using worse materials makes you better. I decorate the windows of our home and offer good-luck cuttings for people to hang over their makeshift bomb shelters; sometimes I put on puppet shows for the local youngsters. Max says that when the war's over I could try to open my own gallery, my own shop, and I do like the idea of my own shop.

The future seems unearthly bright, considering our whole lives are contained in one single square mile, surrounded by a city under siege.

And then a letter from George Maidenhair arrives.

It says that he got married, but doesn't say to whom. It says that he's moved into a local Shanghai mansion infamously known as the "House of 100 Rooms," but doesn't say why. It says that he wishes he'd kept better in touch, but doesn't explain why he didn't.

It is the first I have heard from him in over two years.

MAX COMES HOME and says he's secured a job teaching violin, of all things, to one of the Japanese administrators. Before this I had no idea that he could even play violin. Apparently, in Germany, he was fairly decent and there was even some talk of him playing in a youth orchestra. I ask if he might attend music school now, here in Shanghai, after the war. No, he says, he can't; or rather he won't. He hasn't played in nearly a decade and he'd never be able to make up the difference.

The Japanese administrator must be awfully bad at violin if he can't tell that someone hasn't played in nearly a decade.

Max shows me the violin that the administrator has given him. I inspect it with great interest. I pluck at one of the strings.

It stings the pad of my finger, sparking memories.

"My father was a great musician," I say.

I am sad as I say this, but suddenly I am angry, too, angry even though I rarely ever think about it anymore, angry because I don't think I will ever stop feeling sad. I think of that cottage in Jiangsu made of mud and the bed made of mud and the bowls made of mud, and I wish that the people had been made of mud too, instead of flesh and blood. I think of that one photograph we had of Ma, in black and white, turning red in Ba's hands as he tries to hold on. I imagine Nai Nai trying to outrun the soldiers on her bound feet, the wrappings catching on the rocks of the courtyard because she hasn't swept it well enough.

It is 1945. The Japanese destroyed my village in 1937.

Eight years, and I still cannot stem my sadness.

Eight years, and Shanghai is still at war.

Since the Allied invasion of Europe last year, optimism has abounded in this city. Everyone believes that the end has to be nigh. But a part of me can't help thinking that it wouldn't be good enough for the Imperial Japanese Army just to turn around and go home. Not after everything they've done. There has to be something more. There has to be something equal. There has to be something that *makes them feel the way I feel.*

My fury is frightening.

Max lifts the violin to his shoulder and begins to draw the bow. The piece he chooses is slow, the high notes like the breaking of glass.

I SHOW GEORGE'S next letter to Max in case it's my word-blindness acting up in a way it never has before, and Max confirms what I've read: George wants me to make a series of shadow puppets for him. There is a large puppet theatre in his new house and he wants to put it to use. Each puppet must meet a set of rigid specifications, which he has outlined on a separate sheet. He is willing to pay, and then some.

Even if he weren't my beloved Teacher, for whom I would do any favor in my power, I couldn't possibly turn this job down, no matter if I get a small squelchy feeling in my gut at the thought of it.

"He just wants to help me out financially," I tell Max. "Why would he want a dozen paper puppets, really?"

"Is that what's bothering you?" asks Max.

"I don't know. Maybe I'm thinking about it too hard. Maybe he's just always liked puppets. I think my Ma even made a few for him, back when they were friends."

"It's not the puppets that bother me," says Max, in an amused voice, but I know he's serious. "It's the idea of a puppet theatre in *that house.*"

"What? The House of 100 Rooms, you mean?"

"You don't know it? Or the stories people tell about it? There have been calls to tear the whole place down to planks."

"But George *loves* stories," I point out. "He also loves houses. He loves stories about houses! Houses with horrible dark wonderful amazing secrets. He inherited his previous house from his father, you know, but he told me that he always planned to buy another one, once he could figure out where he wanted to live forever. Once he didn't have to travel so much. A house with trick doors and . . ."

I miss George so much that it cuts off my voice for a second, so I go back to the letter.

THE AIR RAIDS over Shanghai grow worse until finally, in July, the Americans begin to drop bombs directly on the ghetto. Yet this does not deter Max and the others from running the *Kulturabende*. The bombs continue to land and everyone continues to meet.

I continue to attend.

One heady night, explosions ring out in the distance. As the smoke rises, however far away, the air-raid alarms groan to life. Max stands up and goes to the front of the crowd and unexpectedly starts to reminisce about his childhood in Munich. I am spellbound, because here are the answers to all the questions I had

when he and I first met, back when all he ever spoke of was becoming a Great Master. He is changing. He is changing, he is
growing up, we both are, everything is going to be different, and
at this realization my heart skips, and I remember where I am
again.

The louder the sirens blare, the louder Max speaks, until he is
shouting.

Japanese antiaircraft guns begin to whir. The bombs are still
falling.

When the tracer bullets go off in the sky, they look like skipping
stones. Max is screaming now, but nobody can hear a word of it.
All I can see is the cascade of light falling to earth behind him. I
shout: *Max! Max, get down!* Other friends are urging him down too,
as the people around us scatter, but Max only screams and screams
until tears stream down his face.

What is he doing? What is he *thinking*? What is he trying to
prove?

At long last he is coerced off the platform and I pull him home
along the streets. It is utter pandemonium. We stumble into the
house, where the elderly couple who live upstairs are stoically pre-
paring supper, the husband seated at the kitchen table while the
wife is cooking a broth that will taste like wet hay, and right there,
at the doorway, Max stops and he says, "Mei, wait," but I almost
can't hear him because of the commotion just before, and even if
I could, I don't want to wait. My throat is scorched from screaming his name. I am so mad at him that I could throw my shoe at
him and hope it would hit him right in his adorable head!

"You could have died!" I scream at him, and our neighbors'
mouths drop open. Max and I have never fought before. "You
want to die? Do you want to die?"

"I wasn't going to die," he says.

"Tell that to the Japanese kamikaze!" The kamikaze only hit

warships, don't they? But right now I will fling anything I have at him and there isn't much.

"I wasn't going to die," he repeats.

The couple is observing us intently but their Chinese is about as good as my German. The woman has stopped stirring, her husband has looked up from fixing a shoe, and both look worried. I suspect Max has spoken much louder than normal not because he means to shout, the way I'm shouting, but because we both still hear the bombs going off in our ears.

He sounds very sure, that he wasn't going to die.

So sure that it almost, but not quite, makes me wonder how he knows.

"IF YOU DON'T like making them," says Max one evening, just after he has finished giving a violin lesson next door, "then shouldn't you stop?"

Max sets down his violin case and gives a mock shiver at the sight of a puppet whose hair will not stay put. George wanted this one dressed in the ceremonial kimono of a geisha, long enough at the back that it looks like a leash, with a sash tied in a bow. He wanted me to paint the face in tinted white.

Geisha hair is annoyingly elaborate and now that I've made it high enough, it won't stick.

"I know I look like a pig at a trough with all this ink on me, but I really don't mind making them," I reply, gritting my teeth as the makeshift wig falls forward yet again. "In fact, I relish the—the challenge of—*rotten tea eggs*! Why is this not working? Why? I swear, this puppet is laughing at me. Look at her! Do you want to have a head like a fallow rice field? Do you? Do you?"

"I don't," says Max soberly.

"I was asking *her*!" I turn the puppet face down even though it may damage some of the other intricately placed pieces, just because I'm sick of her smile. "As I say, it's not that I dislike making them," I say again, with a melodramatic sniff, as Max laughs. "It's that . . . I don't know. Why, *why* does he want all of these puppets?"

"Puppet tea parties?" suggests Max.

"Stop it," I say, and swat at him. "I'll touch you with these paint-covered hands, Max Friedman, if you keep making fun, and so you know, I mixed blood into this paint."

"You *what?*"

"It's just from my toes. George read something about how there is animal blood in all this old Chinese paint or some such. And so he wanted blood in the puppet paint— Yes, I know. I don't even mind experimental techniques, but I told you—something is strange!"

Max looks flabbergasted.

"I mean, he is very eccentric . . ." I hedge.

"Blood on a puppet, that's practically a voodoo doll," says Max. He grins again to let me know he's joking; or at least I hope he is. "Just don't make one of yourself, and you should be alright."

THE FINISHED PUPPETS are slid into envelopes and are sent across Shanghai to George. He sends back corrections or instructions or money. For month after month we communicate like this, in writing, as if we are back in his house as student and teacher, passing a slate back and forth. George used to smell of book covers and cotton wool and dry crackling logs, but that's not what his letters smell like. Long, long ago, in my fairy-tale childhood, Ma would make her own soybean paste, and to make your own paste, you have to let the soybeans go to mold— *That* is what his letters smell like. Death in slow tiny steps.

Sometimes I have the unbearable thought that maybe I am not writing to George Maidenhair at all.

IT TAKES ME a long while to believe the war is over. Funny how the things you want most are the things you refuse to hope for.

Allied planes circle overhead, dropping leaflets that spell out the Japanese defeat, but all this does is feed the rumor mill; rumors are followed by weeks of riots, followed by an influx of bedraggled Nationalist soldiers, followed at last by the Americans. Then American and British ships are churning up the Whangpoo, coming into port; then the Stars and Stripes are raised on the flagpoles; then one day Max reaches into his pocket without any warning and he pulls out a slender box and he opens the box and inside is a decorative hairpin, and he lifts it from the velvet lining and that is when I see that it is not just any hairpin.

Ma's peony flower.

"I had it made bespoke," Max says, blushing, his glasses dipping down his nose, "from one of your cuttings. I know how much that design means to you."

The detail is so fine, I'd almost believe that Ma is still alive, looking at it.

"I love you," he says. "I'm in love with you, Mei. I don't even know when it started, but I think . . ." He raises his head, looks into my eyes. "It's never going to end."

I loop my long hair into a bun, sticking the pin in deep, until it scrapes. It would be easier, and look better, if I used a mirror, but I cannot use mirrors. I have not told anyone about the way my reflection no longer reflects me, not the way it should; Max would probably want me to investigate further but I don't want to investigate further. I don't want to look deeper. I would rather look at him. I would rather look toward our life together. Cautiously, Max reaches out his hand, taking mine by the fingers, the way you would handle real-life flowers. It took me a long while to believe; funny how the things you want most are the things you refuse to hope for.

36

HONG KONG
2015

HOLLY CLARIFIES: "I, the one speaking to you now, am not Holly Zhang."

Susanna says, nonplussed: "I'm afraid I don't follow."

"I am a spirit who took possession of the real Holly Zhang's body many years ago," says Holly. "I was in possession of her when your mama came here, in 1953, and had been for some time already."

"A spirit," says Susanna. "Who took possession."

For a second I think she will ask for proof.

Ryan Li looks ashen, but not especially surprised. I imagine that he has seen and heard much worse things here at Maidenhair.

"Okay. You know what, I'm actually too tired for this," says Susanna abruptly. "I just . . . I can't do this right now. Ma, let's get out of here. Next time, we'll do this right. We'll make plans in advance. We'll be prepared. We'll think of all the possible—"

She stops. Her jaw drops.

She is looking toward the end of the dining table.

My legs lock up.

"Dean?" she says.

The chair at the end of the dining table is empty.

"Dean," she says again, brokenly. "It's not possible. It's not—is it you? Is it him, Ma?"

"No," I say, "it's not."

It's hard to say whether she hears me.

"Dean," she says, tripping over her chair, trying to get to him. "Wait—please! No, don't—*Dean!*"

"Stop screaming," says Holly. "You'll wake the others again."

Susanna turns to look at me.

Tears are running down her face.

Susanna did not cry at Dean's cremation. I wonder if she cried the day he died; cried in the water as she was decompressing; cried because in the water, she couldn't tell that it was happening.

I have never seen my daughter cry. Not since she was a child.

"I'm a ghost too, aren't I?" says Susanna. Every word is a gasp: "That's what's happening right now, isn't it? I drowned too, didn't I? I died down there? Is that why I feel like this, all the time? Is that why the whole world *looks* like this?"

"You're not a ghost," I say. "You feel like one, maybe. But that is grief."

Susanna cries more. She is sobbing so loudly that a whole new urban legend about Maidenhair House might start up. Another Wailing Woman; just like at the Great Wall. My daughter finally stops pretending that she can hold her head up as long as she has, since we arrived here, and she crumples, letting her bag slip off her shoulder, her tablet making a cracking noise as it hits the ground.

"You know what happens next," Holly says to me. Her smile reminds me of sugared water. "You remember what happens after they start seeing things."

37

HONG KONG
SEPTEMBER 1953

MEI SITS UP with the skimmed-over feeling she had when she washed up five years ago on that white Kowloon beach.

She looks around, blinking to make the scene appear faster: She is still in the Puppet Room, surrounded by her own puppets. She does not like to be in this position, looked down upon by her own creations. Like they have just created her.

MISTRESS LAU IS lying there, next to Delia. Blatantly dead, murdered in the same savage stabbing fashion as Delia, as Peng and Cecelia upstairs.

THERE IS A stomping noise down the stairs. It is Jamie Naka-mura and a stranger, a newcomer, in pressed dark clothing. The stranger hisses something to Jamie about being careful but Jamie comes over to Mei anyway, letting her scream silently into his shoulder, and then the stranger is all but shoving them back up the steps. Upstairs, in the kitchen, Jamie cleans her hands and hair with a towel and places a blanket over her and a cup of water in front of her. The stranger rematerializes and asks what she remembers and she tries to answer him over the sound of her own silent screaming: She and Holly and Mistress Lau and Delia's dead body were locked inside the Puppet Room. Jamie had gone off to get help; or so he'd said. Mei was having punishing hallucinations. Holly was saying that there had to be another way out, because all the basement rooms of Maidenhair are joined by tunnels. At some point somebody pinched Mei's cheek, slapping her, shouting, *Stop it, stay awake, stop it, we need you here,* but Mei was already out of reach.

"AND THEN?" SAYS the stranger. He is writing things down on a notepad.

He clearly does not believe in spirit mediums or in séances, and now he will not believe anything else she says.

"And then I woke up," says Mei, the words uneven. "And Mistress Lau was dead too. And you came."

"I'm going to make a few phone calls," he says. "Just down the hall, you said, Mr. Nakamura?"

"In the study," says Jamie, whose hair is dripping with rainwater.

"Right. You two stay put. I'll be right back. Try to stay calm," he says to Mei, but she deduces that comforting people is not his job. He does not deal with survivors.

"Who is he?" she asks.

"Detective. The Peak Station sent him. I don't think they believed me," says Jamie, "but I guess they will now."

Mei wonders at how empty you can feel even when you yourself haven't lost a single drop of blood.

"They're going to find my peony design on the bodies," she

says distantly. "They're going to arrest me. For the murders of four people."

"Yeah," he says. "Likely. But I still don't think you did it."

Mei feels a wet chuckle forming on her lips, but it never takes proper shape.

They wait in silence. There is no clock in the kitchen but Mei knows she is running out of time.

What will she do, in these last few moments of freedom?

She will read.

Jamie may look at her funny. Because it is funny. It's peculiar. To want to do nothing but read, as your whole world implodes.

"I left your novel in my room," she says. "I'd actually like to finish it. If I can. Before they take me away."

"I'll go," Jamie says, without judgment, getting to his feet.

THE DETECTIVE RETURNS before Jamie does. He is a slim man with a flat smile and facial hair like a newly planted field, but his eyes are a stunning shade of gray. He acts as if he's seen plenty of blood-splattered scenes exactly like the one below them, in rooms with more puppets than people, in houses that feel like their own planets. Maybe he has. He speaks in sparse language and his movements are controlled and his use of his notepad is brusquely efficient. He says that they will have more questions for her; that she will need to come to the station. Mei can already tell that he will be even less sympathetic than he is now, once he hears that Mei runs a curio shop, a place steeped in sentimentality and murky origin myths, because if there are only two types of people in the world, those two types are not good and bad, or giving and taking, or intelligent and stupid, or content and restless. Those two types are *story-people* and *non-story-people*.

Mei is one. George Maidenhair was one. And this detective is the other. Whether anyone can change, from one to the other or back again, Mei does not know.

JAMIE BRINGS *THE Peak House*. Time passes and Mei reads and reads. She would love to go back to the very start, but you can never go back to the very start.

When a loud knocking resounds through the house, the detective blinks to attention.

His colleagues have arrived.

Mei has the dullish sense that the second half of her life is about to begin. She already anticipates how uncomfortable the handcuffs will be on her left wrist. The curio shop will have to be closed, of course. Her existence in Hong Kong will soon be forgotten, if not purposefully erased. In a way, she might as well have been swept to sea off the coast of Shenzhen. She might as well have burned in the fires that dotted the countryside of China during the Revolution. She might as well have fallen off the rooftop of the Cathay hotel in Shanghai, for all the difference she has made to the world.

But she has read to the end of *The Peak House*.

Books are my lifeblood, George said to her once. *You know how I know that?*

Because of how I feel afterward.

Like I was meant to read this.

Do you mean, Teacher, that it was fate?

"Jamie," she says, as the detective gets up to answer the door, "where is Holly?"

38

SHANGHAI
AUTUMN 1947

IT IS LATE; past eleven already. I sit on the bed with my legs crossed, trying not to slide off the sheets with sleepiness.

"I've got a letter from my mother's cousin," Max says, sitting next to me. "She had some difficulty finding me. She's back in Munich now. Mei, I want to go back to Europe. I want to find what's left of my family. And I want to study. Would you come with me?"

"Yes," I say, laughing at the way he's asked this, like I might turn him down.

"Yes, just like that?"

"Just like what?"

"You're sure? Leaving your country behind? Your continent? You wouldn't regret it later?"

"Are *you* sure? That you want me there?"

His face turns sweetly serious. "I'm sure."

"You're silly; thinking otherwise."

Max reaches out a hand to the nape of my neck, tugging lightly at the white peony pin, until it gives. My hair cascades past my shoulders. "I've never understood how you can keep all this in place," he says, "with just one pin. And I've never understood how you've never seen the future, yet you can be so sure of things. I envy it. You live without fear."

"The hair is a longtime family secret," I say succinctly. "The other thing is just . . . *yǎn bù jiàn wéi jìng*! What you cannot see does not exist. Ignorance is bliss. You know. Come on, let's go to bed now, before you can think of more questions to ask, that you already know the answer to."

Finally, his face breaks in a smile. "Maybe so, but sometimes I like to hear the answers anyway," he murmurs, closing the distance between us. I don't know where the pin has gone. "If I asked you to marry me when we get there, would you laugh then too?" he says, against my lips. I can feel the shape of his mouth. "Would you call me ridiculous for worrying that you might want something else? A different life than anything I can offer? I have hardly any friends or relations left, and we'll have to build everything up from scratch, in Munich."

"I don't think I could live without you," I say, in honesty. Max is the only thing in the world I could never give up, not without turning myself inside out. I could even give up my art, if I had to.

I have the flushed thought that actually, sometimes, maybe even a lot of the time, I kind of *want* to give up my art.

Maybe in Munich I will start over, too.

We spend the next few hours talking. Making plans. Lying in bed with our faces very close, but without quite kissing, because kissing will put a quick end to the talking. Max was wrong, when he said I live without fear. A lot of the time I am nothing *but* fear, but I fear only one thing. Losing him. Being alone. What if he *did* change his mind, about taking me to Europe? What if he decides he wants to forget his years in Shanghai, turn it into a bad dream? Max has been at my side since I was seven years old. He has been there literally since the day I found out my whole birth family was dead. I don't know what it's like, not to have him. I never want to know. I never want to find out.

This realization isn't tender and delightful; it's terrifying.

Max falls asleep before I do, and when I'm sure he's out, I lean over to get my peony pin back. He is turned away, his breaths deep and invisible. I open his palm and squirrel out the pin and then kiss his cheek, and that is when I see it.

Blood.

Just a few drops, in a thin incandescent line from his mouth. I know instantly what it means.

He has just had a vision of the future.

THE TICKETS ARE bought. The ship will stop in the Philippines and off the coast of India; the journey will take over a month in total. I write to George telling him that I know we're not done with his puppet list, but I am moving abroad and besides, I need a break from making them. My hands feel cramped just composing the letter. I ask if he would like to come visit me and Max in Hong Kew, before our departure, or perhaps I can stop by the House of 100 Rooms?

All this time, all these years, George has refused any visits, but I am beyond politeness now. I need to see him. I need to say goodbye to him.

George writes back to say that he can meet me at the market in Yuyuan.

I ARRIVE AT the appointed time and place, but he is late, so I wander in small circles. The market is a landscape of scrolls and silks and trinkets. One man is selling rocks that he claims were hacked off the Great Wall by his ancestors, and even though they look more like pieces of pavement, I am tempted to buy one. I guess markets like these were made for people like me.

Hunched over one of the tables is the unmistakable form of George Maidenhair.

"Teacher!" I call out, with a frisson of pure joy, but then he turns.

He is so far removed from the man I remember he could be a different species.

Gone is the long, bushy beard that clothed his chin. Gone is the smile that made me feel like I was doing well, even when I was getting everything wrong. Gone is the storybook twinkle in his eyes, which look as though they might even have changed color, to a pale horse's blue. George removes his trilby hat and his hair is a raft of gray and he moves his mouth like he wants to greet me but no sound emerges.

What has *happened* to him?

"Teacher," I say, full of sorrow, and I can't hide it.

"Little Mei," he says, his own voice cracking.

"Teacher!" I throw myself at him, hoping for a hug, but it has been too many years. I am not Little Mei anymore. I am seventeen years old. I am moving to Europe. He cannot hug me as if he knows me the way he did. As if we know each other the way we did. And it seems so unfair; unfair because the war ended two whole years ago, two years in which we could have reunited in person a hundred times, in which we could have read a hundred books together, new wife or not, new life or not. And I know that part of my bitterness is guilt. I left him, after all. I left him to go live with Max. I left him alone and now that I'm back, he's not here, and to have expected him to stay still, to stay exactly the same, all while the world order was upended and whole armies were turning back like tsunamis and I was falling in love, well, that's not fair either, is it?

But it doesn't change the fact that I already miss him, right now, as we're looking at each other.

"Is your wife here?" I say, as if I was hoping he'd bring her, when secretly I was torn. I want to meet her; of course I do. But I also kind of want her not to exist. Because in my mind, this mysterious woman, to whom he has never referred by name, epitomizes, symbolizes, everything that has felt wrong about George since that first letter about the puppets.

"She doesn't like the clamor of the markets," George says. "She used to be an actress, you see. And sometimes people recognize her, and have so many questions for her, and it rather upsets her."

That's odd. I suggested that we meet at his house. He wanted *this*.

"You have . . . children now?" I ask; a stupid question, yes, but I can't think of what to say next.

He looks distinctly ill at ease for a second, and then shakes his head. George always wanted kids; that much I know, that's why I asked, but perhaps I was insensitive to blurt it out like that. I hold out my arm and George takes it and he puts enough weight on me to crush me, but I stay standing.

"So you are leaving Shanghai," he says, as we walk through the marketplace, assaulted at regular intervals by strong smells and pushy people.

"There are other local artists I can recommend," I say, "for your . . ."

What is the collective noun for a group of puppets?

"No," he says, "it has to be you, or no one."

"Alright," I say, trying not to shiver. "Well, I'm sorry, then, Teacher."

"You shouldn't go."

"I beg your pardon?"

"You shouldn't go to Germany."

"Why not? Max says it's safe now. There's absolutely no risk of—"

"You need to finish the puppets. They're of people I used to know, you see."

"What?" I withdraw my arm. George is glassy-eyed, looking down at me. "People you—"

"I made mistakes when I was young," he says. "So many mistakes, that have haunted me ever since. When I saw the puppet theatre in the house, I thought—a puppet show! A story! A chance to play out those bitter moments of my life as if I'd got them right! A chance to redo it all! Those puppets you've been making, they're real people, Little Mei. And when you're done, there will be a performance. In which everything happens the way it should have, in real life."

What?

What mistakes? What moments? What *people*?

This is worse than the letters; people often sound different in letters. People should not sound different in person.

Something has happened to George, since I last saw him in early 1943.

For some reason I'm reminded of Max's warnings about the House of 100 Rooms, but I clamp down on the thought.

"But . . ." I say hopelessly. "But why paper puppets? Why not . . . a real play, for example? Especially if your wife is an actress. She must know people . . ."

He laughs, but not the way he used to laugh. "I don't want real people. With real people, I'd be able to tell that they aren't actually the people I used to know. I want the screen, Little Mei. I want the shadows. I want to be able to watch, without actually seeing."

Silence falls, even though the marketplace is whirling all around us.

War kills most people from the outside in, but it kills other people from the inside out, and that takes a whole lot longer. I have observed it in others by now. Still, the change in George is more harrowing than I've ever seen. Harsher. More clinical. He needs something I cannot give; certainly something that is not endless shadow puppets arriving at his door.

I hope his wife knows what it is.

"Teacher," I say, and my voice is as gentle as his was when he told me that books were magic. "I'm not going to make any more puppets for you."

He doesn't look like he believes me, but we link arms again.

I have the momentary horrible hope that his project is never completed; that he dies before it is done. Oh, it is very tempting to believe in puppets; I have felt this too. It is satisfying to be able to pull and push them around as you wish; it is fun to see their limbs flap and their bodies move. But when the show is over and the lights go off and the puppets go still once again, I worry that George will see that he is, just as he was when it started, all by himself in the midnight dark, left with nothing but a lesson I learned very young.

One single shoddy room full of your loved ones is better than one hundred rooms full of nothing but your own regrets.

"But you have to," says George. "You have to."

GEORGE HAS HIS chauffeur take me home. He says he will scour the marketplace for a few more hours, and waves away my protests. Our parting is abrupt. It feels like our real goodbye was years ago. The chauffeur is a young man with a lidded cap low on his face; his hard-set jaw is nearly all I can see of him. The route he takes hugs the river; going a longer way would have been less stressful, given all the traffic. The lack of conversation in the car is uncomfortable and he must feel it too, because he speaks up.

"He's been going downhill for a few years now," says the chauffeur. "It's not to do with age or illness, what's wrong with him. The docs just don't know."

I don't want to discuss George with a stranger. I also don't want to cry in front of a stranger.

"His wife tries her best, but it's no use."

"Is she good to him?" I say tightly.

"Yeah. She is."

Our eyes meet for less than half a second in his mirror, before he looks away.

"She could have done better than him, if you ask me," says the chauffeur, matter-of-fact.

Who says such a thing about their employers?

I grit my teeth to keep from spitting a reply.

"I've offended you?" says the chauffeur.

"Mr. Maidenhair is a good man."

"If you say so," says the chauffeur. "I don't know him all that well. And given the state he's in nowadays, I don't suppose I ever will." A blank smile, via the mirror, one that I do not return.

I do not like looking in mirrors to begin with.

The George I knew did not employ a chauffeur. He did not like having too many servants, too many people waiting hand and foot, even though he could have afforded legions. He did have his housekeeper; he used to joke that if he married anyone, he'd marry her.

But the George I just met at the market needs a chauffeur. He should not be behind a wheel.

"You're very pretty," says the chauffeur. "His wife should watch out."

"You're very crass."

"I'm realistic. What are you, eighteen? Local girl, judging by your accent? Poor, judging by your clothing, by our destination?

Doesn't take much to put it together. You're taking advantage of a rich man who's no longer in possession of all his faculties. Classic."

What a ghastly human. What a ghastly conversation.

The car skids to a halt as a flood of bicycles turn out in front of us.

"You have identified my motives beautifully," I say, cranking the car handle, one foot already stepping out the door. My eyes are filling with tears, and he must hear it in my voice, because he gives me a brief, startled glance. "I shall stay out of his way, and his wife's. Good day."

MAX COMES INTO the kitchen while I am at the table, cutting red lantern paper. It is the last of my paper and I'm not sure when I'll be able to get my hands on more. Max takes off his eyeglasses and plays with the cutting knife I have left to one side, twirling it round and round. There is something on his mind, that much is obvious: It is early evening and the light is just low enough to make everything look dreamy, but high enough that I can see the many mixed emotions on his face.

Maybe he has anxiety, doubts, about going home at long last. I have no such doubts. I'll have to stuff my pockets full of Shanghainese spices before we board the boat, of course, but at least I'll have a lot of pockets because of how many layers I'll be wearing. Munich gets snow every winter, according to Max, and not just the kind that falls thinly, like pencil shavings.

Or maybe we are going to talk about whatever he saw the other night, of the future.

"Can I have the knife, please?" I ask.

He lets me have it.

"I heard you talking to some people about the A-bomb today," he says.

I nod. "They said that the Americans were trying to end the war, and that it's alright to kill some people to save others."

"You don't think so?"

Is this what he wants to talk about? The A-bomb? The war?

"I don't know what I think," I say with a shrug. "Remember when you told me that you've seen evil in armies, in governments, in people?" I stop for a second, examining my closest cuts. "We both have. You've always made it seem like these two forces are in constant opposition, evil and good. I struggle, sometimes, to see the good."

Max motions that he wants to see my unfinished piece, so I hand it over.

"It's supposed to be a lantern," I say. "But I've cut wrong. I'm not sure how I'll manage to light it later."

He slips on his spectacles, which are cracked and sit funny on his face. He examines the cutting from a few angles.

"I don't think there's anything, anyone, in the world that is completely good," he says. "Because the fight between these two forces, as you put it, is not external, in my opinion. It is internal. That is, *within* every army, within every government, within every people. Within every single person. In all things on earth, both exist, at once, together; opposite but the same. Like yin and yang—"

"In *everyone?*" My skepticism is heavy.

"In everyone."

"In the soldiers who killed my family?"

Another silence, but it is soft.

"I have forgiven the wrongs others have done to me," Max says, lowering the cut. "I have more trouble forgiving the wrongs others have done to others. There are people in this world that I can't, I will not, give my grace. But I also know, I *know*, that in every human on earth, there was once a chance for a different

312

future. A different outcome. That in the beginning, our possible paths are so many, and to have ended up on *that* path, when there were so many others, is a tragic fate. I believe that understanding this—and finding mercy where we cannot find forgiveness—helps us all find the path that is right for us, Mei. It has been that way for me."

"Oh?" I say, with difficulty.

"Yeah," he says simply. "I believe that a life spent obsessed with vengeance, a life spent filled with hatred, would only be another life lost." He places the paper cutting carefully between us. "You know, my grandmother would have really loved you."

"I'm sorry that I won't get to meet her," I say. "I'm sorry you never got to learn all Four Steps."

I'm crying, without making any noise of it, just the tears falling.

"I've just discovered the third step, though," says Max quietly. "Step One: *You see the future and you try to change it.* Step Two: *You see the future, but you no longer try to change it.* Step Three: *You no longer try to see the future.*"

"But if *that's* Step Three," I say, blinking hard, "then how can there be a Step Four?"

"I don't know. I only know that that's what it is. Don't cry," says Max, even though he's crying too, "you'll ruin your own work. Look at this design; how did you even think of it? I've not seen you do this one before."

Before I can reply, the door is flung open.

It is the young daughter of one of our neighbors. She glances at Max and then she whirls on me. Her twin braids fly behind her. "Mei," she says, breathless, "Mei, you have to come with me! *Beeil dich!*"

"What? But—"

"Come on! Right now! Come on!"

I can't imagine what the matter is, but I almost welcome the distraction. I scoot away from the table. "I'll be back in a moment," I say, and Max smiles in understanding, his eyes wet behind his spectacles. I follow the girl and soon we're sprinting down the street, which is still full of air-raid holes and husks of buildings and people hurrying by, hoping to escape the evening humidity. There is a certain absurd thrill in running this hard, until your heart could burst out of your body.

Until we turn the corner.

A huddle of people parts to let us through. There is somebody lying on his back on the roadside. Blood runs from the corners of his mouth. It is the same shade of red as my lantern paper.

The father of the girl who has fetched me is standing over the body.

The girl looks away, but I go closer.

The lenses of his spectacles are broken. They make his wide-open brown eyes look like prisms.

His smile, even through the blood, is still understanding.

All of this is not possible, of course. I just left him at home. He was just sitting across from me. He was just holding my paper cutting to the light.

"He's gone," somebody says, from behind me.

"No, he isn't," I say stoutly, "the blood from his mouth, this is just what happens when he has a . . . I can't explain. But it's normal. He—he's fine! Let's wake him up, let's bring him home—"

"Mei," the father of the girl says, "Max was hit by a car. The driver just— He's gone."

"No. No. I was just with him. He was *just there*—"

No. *No.*

"In his last moments, he asked me to tell you—"

"He didn't say anything to you!" I shriek. The street is quieter than it has ever been. Where are the bombs now when I need them? The airplanes? The gunfire? The tracer bullets? The people shouting to take cover? "Because he's alive! I'm telling you, I just saw him—he's alive! He's alive!" I get to my knees and shake Max by the shoulders and my tears flow until I am finally in the waterfall I have always wanted. People are trying to pull me away from the body now but they don't know, the way I know, that this time, *this time*, I will not be ripped from familiar arms and slung over a stranger's shoulder and shipped to a strange city and left to wonder if my whole life until now was ever real to begin with. This time, *this time*, I will not let go—

I shake him harder and harder and it makes no difference and, like in those moments in which I think about my family, I am overwhelmed not by sadness but by rage.

"Who did this?" I scream at the small crowd that has gathered. Nobody speaks. *"Who did this?"*

I was wrong, that day so many years ago, when I first realized I was in love with Max.

I thought that *that* would be the fire that burned forever. But it wasn't.

This is. This will be.

My anger. My pain. My undoing.

"Mei," says the girl's father. "Max said to me, the very last thing . . . He said, tell Mei that the lantern she's made is beautiful, even if it will never be finished. Even if something will never be finished . . . it is still worth the while."

39

HONG KONG
SEPTEMBER 1953

NOW SEVERAL CHALKY-FACED authority-type men are crowding the Great Hall of Maidenhair House, but their presence is not the surprise.

Mei lurks in the dim light of the hallway, flanked by Jamie, increasingly unsettled.

The surprise is Holly.

Holly appears to be the one who opened the front door to the men, given how she fawns to close it behind them. She welcomes them deeper into the house. She asks: Can she get anybody something to eat? To drink? Did the storm sweep them onto her doorstep?

The original detective steps forward. "Holly Zhang?" he asks, and Holly nods, almost coy. "I am Detective Chief Investigator Ryan Li. There's been an incident here, I'm afraid. We'll have some questions for you. But for now, I'm going to take these men down to the—"

"Oh, goodness. Does this have to do with my stepson?" says Holly, folding her arms over her rumpled nightgown. Her wig, too, is rumpled, casually so. Overall she has the haphazard but well-meaning air of someone who has just been yanked out of bed. "Because you can't believe a thing he says, you know. Darling boy," she says, almost wistfully, "but much too charming for his own good, *lah*." Her Cantonese has turned native again. "Jamie, my dear, what have you gotten yourself into? Troubling all these busy men at this hour of the morning?"

Jamie looks too stumped to answer, and Mei doesn't blame him.

"Go on, then, Detective, sir," says Holly. "What's he done?"

"We're not saying anyone in particular has done anything," says Ryan Li, eyes flicking over the lightly disheveled Holly. "But I'm afraid there have been multiple homicides in your home."

"Multiple homicides!" says Holly, a sharp pant.

"Four in total."

"Who?" says Holly, and Mei feels her stomach seizing up. "Who was it?"

What is Holly doing? Acting like she doesn't know what happened?

Acting like *nothing* happened?

"The victims, ma'am?"

"The killer!"

"As I said, we don't have enough information yet. If you please, you can now go with—"

"Where are these victims located?" asks Holly petulantly. "I'm not budging an inch until you tell me where all these murders happened, in my own house!"

DCI Ryan Li seems to consider this. "Mr. Nakamura indicated that one of the locations is known as the ballroom," he says, as if he wants to test her.

"The ballroom? In the South Wing?" Holly looks affronted. "That can't be. Why, I just ducked in there myself, when I heard people at my door, to check my . . . to look in on my appearance. As you had roused me from my bed. There are no dead bodies in

317

that room. The very idea! Could you have been somehow confused by the mirrors, Detective? The ballroom is walled with mirrors," she says, for the benefit of her larger audience, who are exchanging wary looks.

"I was not," says DCI Ryan Li, "confused by the mirrors."

"Well, there's only one way to find out, isn't there?" says Holly, and she turns, but now she takes a step backward, as if stung by the sight of Mei. "Who are you? Who's *this?* Is this one of your flea-bitten hotel girls, James? Because I told you not to bring them up to the house. I *told* you!"

Mei steps further into the light in case Holly just can't see her well enough, but Holly only protests further. There is a burst of conversation between the men who have just shown up, as Holly continues to bemoan Jamie's bad behavior and the presence of live strangers and dead bodies in her precious home.

"You're saying you've never seen this young woman before?" asks a different policeman.

"Never in my life," says Holly, again.

A rattly intake of breath from Jamie.

"Anyhow, don't take my word for it," says Holly. "Go see the ballroom for yourselves. I'll wait here."

Jamie stays behind with Mei and Holly and officers who have obviously been instructed not to let any of them out of sight. Jamie doesn't even bother to ask what Mei thinks of what has just happened. It is like when birds fly into windows. They are both too stunned.

THERE IS SHOUTING; a slamming sound from afar.

Have they seen the ballroom? The Music Room? The Puppet Room?

The group of men who left reappear eventually. DCI Ryan Li is red up to his hair roots.

"What a morning," says Holly. "I don't usually get this much excitement."

"The bodies weren't there," says Ryan Li. "Nothing's there."

"What?" says Jamie.

"They're not there anymore." Ryan Li's voice is level. "They're *not there anymore.*"

"Then where are they?"

"Yes. You see? He saw them. *She* saw them. The three of us—"

His colleagues look unimpressed.

"Shared hallucination," Holly Zhang says.

There is a moment of deadly quiet.

"It happens in this house," says Holly. "You all know it does. You've all heard the stories. What exactly did you see, Detective? If four people are dead, where have they gone? Ha! Even if someone had moved the actual bodies—and I can't even imagine it! Moving a dead body? Let alone *four*! My knees pop like nuts out of shells just getting out of bed—how could it all have been cleaned up?"

"Sir," interjects the white man on Ryan Li's right, "if I may—"

"There was blood everywhere." The detective turns viciously on Jamie and Mei. "I know what I saw."

"Such visions do tend to strike most, and worst, when there are *groups* of people in the house." Holly's tone is mild but menacing.

Ryan Li seems on the verge of saying more, but something on the stairs behind Holly catches his eye.

For a moment, insofar as she can feel anything, right now, Mei almost feels sorry for him.

"It's them," the detective says, staring up at the double stairs.

Jamie shifts closer to Mei; almost imperceptibly.

"Them?" says Holly, like she is politely interested.

No one else speaks.

"It's them. The two of them. It's the women I saw in the basement—they're coming down the stairs, they're— It's them! *It's those women*! They're—the blood, it's everywhere, it's—"

By the end, Ryan Li is as hysterical as Mei was, when she first woke up in the Puppet Room.

IN THE NOW-EMPTY Great Hall the only sound is of Holly sighing, in that disapproving, motherly, Shanghainese way, like she can't believe the impertinence of the lowly local coppers.

Jamie has sunk onto the bottom step of the stairs.

"Time to get out of my house, James," says Holly staunchly. "And to take your harlot with you, if you please."

"You can drop the act now," he says.

"Act?"

Mei's head may never stop hurting. She reaches up to the back of it, to her pin, checks that it's there.

When she lowers her hand, she sees that her finger is smudged red.

Holly touches around her throat like she's thirsty. "I worry about you, dear James."

"You're seriously trying to tell *us* that we hallucinated this past weekend?" says Jamie. "That none of it happened?"

There is still one death that stands apart from the others.

One victim that cannot be as easily slotted away into the secret vaults of Maidenhair, or wherever it is that Holly has mysteriously, impossibly, hidden the other bodies.

"What happened to George?" asks Mei.

Holly pulls up to her full height. "My husband? Why do you ask?"

Jamie lets out an aggrieved sound.

"He isn't in America, is he?" says Mei. "He's dead. Did you kill him? What happened to him?"

Holly eyes her. "He's alive and well," she says gamely. "Come. We'll call him, shall we? You can hear his voice for yourself. May as well. But you might wish you hadn't spoken to him, afterward."

Mei wishes for so many things, when they find the telephone and Holly puts the receiver coolly to her ear and then suddenly Mei is being handed the handset and she puts it to her own ear, and she hears George's voice, undeniably his voice, sounding muddled, asking for Holly, again and again. Here he is. George Maidenhair. Her Teacher. Her surrogate father. Oh, if only this were yesterday, or last week, or last year; she would have had a long list of things to say, things she had practiced saying to perfection, had gone over and smoothed down as many times as any of the ivory netsukes. And even if those things were all insults and accusations and vows of violence, they still would have been better than this; the silence of an ending.

Mei has not forgiven him. She never will.

But she has forgiven herself.

And so she does not need her vengeance.

He hangs up first, and Mei stands there with the handset still at her ear.

"You see, Miss Chen?" says Holly.

"I thought you didn't know my name," says Mei.

Holly pauses for a second and then she throws her head back and laughs. "Have it your way, my dear," she says. "You lived, Mei. You won."

IT IS A quarter past eleven at night, and the Star Ferry will take one last batch of passengers. Mei is standing on the open deck, facing the cityscape of Hong Kong Island, with Jamie beside her. Mei is watching the swells below, the way the waves shine silver. *Shuǐ guǐ*, the spirits of the drowned, are supposed to inhabit this water; they are the most vengeful of all. People say that you do not see them in the deep until they break the surface. Their white supple hands. Their long stringing hair.

Then they drag you down and drown you.

"See, as I started looking into Holly, after I received that strange letter, I got this crazy idea," says Jamie.

How pretty would his face look when it begins to fray at the bottom of the harbor? How blue would his eyes be with the sea itself inside them?

Mei stares straight ahead.

"I couldn't tell anyone," he says. "No one would believe it. I didn't believe it myself. So I wrote it into a novel. That's how *The Peak House* came to be. I just had to get it out of me. Everything I had to get out of me went into that book."

Mei loosens her grip on the rail. She closes her eyes briefly, but it doesn't block out the lights of Hong Kong. A warm tear sits on her eyelashes.

"You want to know my theory about Holly?" Jamie asks.

"No," she says. "I don't. I'm never going back there. I'm never going to think about this again."

"That's fair. I wish I'd never come up with it."

They have reached the Kowloon side.

The sailors are already shouting for the ropes.

"Mei," he says, and Mei turns toward him now. "When Holly first told me she wanted you to join the competition, I recognized your name, but when you showed up at Maidenhair, I recognized your face. From the day I drove you home. Back in Shanghai. I was awful to you that day; downright despicable. I was so angry back then, not that it's much excuse. I'd just found my dad—my mom had just told me who he was, on her deathbed—but he wasn't all *there*, and had no interest in me at all, and Holly had offered me this job as their driver, and—anyway, it doesn't matter. What I mean is, now we're here, you and me. So many years later. It feels like a second chance. It feels like we were meant to meet again."

The ferry makes a whirring sound beneath their feet. The floor falls out from under Mei for a second, and then the world is flat again.

"It is not enough for fates to be intertwined," says Mei. "There is a saying in Chinese: *Yǒu yuán wú fèn.* Fate without destiny."

"I want to see you again," he says. "If we could . . . somehow . . . ?"

All this time, as a medium, Mei has believed that life and death are equal, just like people say. Yin and yang. But this is wrong. They are *not* equal or even.

Life is a single moment. Death never ends.

The ferry is lurching into position to let everybody off. A hurricane lantern swings off the stern, throwing light.

She knows what he is asking. But Mei has only just started to come back to life. She needs to regain feeling in all of her fingers first. In all of her body. In all of her heart.

"No," she says, "I'm sorry."

"Very well. Goodbye, then," he says, a little hoarse. "Miss Chen."

"Goodbye, Mr. Nakamura."

Mei is Chinese, and in her language, goodbye, *zàijiàn*, means: *I will see you again.*

Jamie is Japanese, and in his language, goodbye, *sayonara*, means: *I will* not *see you again.* It is goodbye for all time. They are disembarking; the ferry is emptying. Mei turns her back on him and no matter how long she feels him looking, watching her go, she doesn't turn. How funny that love is more like death. Eternal. Everlasting. Goodbye for all time.

MRS. VOLKOVA SEEMS to be in her office when Mei lets herself into the curio shop. The light is on and Mei follows it. The finch is already asleep in his cage, his chest-feathers fluffed up, but Mrs. Volkova is at her desk, tirelessly shaving down another of the netsukes. She will give Mei a lecture to end all lectures, in a moment. She will send Mei upstairs and say that Mei had best get back to work first thing tomorrow and not to get any ideas about being served breakfast in bed, just because Mei's been living in a mansion.

"Hello," Mei says unsteadily, standing in the doorway of her office. "I'm home."

"Well, well, look who it is!" Mrs. Volkova says, not looking up. "The lady of the manor, come crawling back!"

Mei approaches, all the way to the desk.

"Dear me," Mrs. Volkova says, startled now. "Are you alright? Did they maltreat you up there? But at least you look to be in one piece still, so there's no sense—Mei?"

Mei falls to her knees and puts her head on Mrs. Volkova's lap and begins to cry. Mrs. Volkova puts down the netsuke and she smooths Mei's hair down instead. Mei's tears are putting out what is left of the fire that has burned inside of her since she was a little girl, and yet right now she feels like she is a little girl again, just wanting her mother to make it all better, and she clings to Mrs. Volkova's sleeves and Mrs. Volkova says something in Russian and Mei understands it perfectly, because when you've spent enough time with somebody, you have your own language with them, and there is no such thing as word-blindness, never, and Mrs. Volkova asks again, over and over, what the matter is. She asks it so many times that Mei stops hearing it.

By the time Mei lifts her head again, Mrs. Volkova has stopped asking.

By the time Mei lifts her head again, Mrs. Volkova is no longer there.

Mei gets to her feet, her whole body trembling, and she looks around her office, and she sits down at her desk, and she picks up the tools that she once put down. She knows that not all the flaws in this netsuke can be rubbed out, not without smashing it to pieces and making it over from the beginning, but maybe it can be put in the window display anyway, maybe it will look better in the light.

40

SHANGHAI
FEBRUARY 1948

PEOPLE ARE FLEEING Shanghai in droves because the Reds are coming. George Maidenhair and his wife are already gone. The House of 100 Rooms has no people in it. I know this because after a few weeks, or months, of lying in bed, living on nothing but crumbs from the cupboards, I finally went there, howling for George, for anybody, and nobody answered, and I went again the next day, and the next, and the next. The rooms are always dark. Sometimes, in the windows, I see faces looking down at me, but I know what they are.

TODAY I GO to George's old house, the one near Amherst Avenue. By comparison, it is large and bright and welcoming. But there is nobody there either. I climb over the gates and I hurry to the door and I scream until I lose my voice. Nobody comes. I turn away and go back to the gates and squeeze the bars. I don't know how long I spend there but suddenly night is falling. I hear a light padding noise around me, but I have been tormented by endless visions and visitors since Max was killed. Ghosts and ghouls are flocking to me. I should be spending my days in linen closets with my eyes closed, but if they get me, they get me; if they want me they can have me.

They probably have more to live for than me.

I SHOULD LEAVE Shanghai, because the Reds might kill anyone who lived through the war just for the crime of living through the war. That is what the gossip says, anyway, if you listen to it, rising up from every street and *lòngtáng* of this city. I will likely not make it until the Reds arrive anyhow, because you cannot subsist on memories as long as you think you can.

The cupboards are bare. I need food.

I go out and wander and I don't know why, but I choose to spend my final few dollars on sea stars. The stars taste better than I expected, perhaps *because* I spent my last dollars on them. They have been boiled with salt and scooped out from the inside. They have a pebbly texture. A bit like eating a tongue.

After a day or so I still have their faint bloody starry flavor in my mouth. The taste keeps me from screaming, long enough that a little of my voice comes back, but it no longer sounds like me.

I DON'T KNOW how the idea pops into my mind to find Big Sister at the Great World, where I last saw her. Big Sister was always so much smarter than me. She knew what to do, right from the beginning. I should have just let her do it.

Max shouldn't have saved me. It doesn't really count as saving, anyway, if you don't do it all the way to the end.

Of course, I have to cross a fair distance to get to the Great World and I end up on all the wrong roads. However empty it is in my home in Hong Kew, it is equally chaotic in the city center, and I am carried along by the crowds to the waterfront. The Whangpoo is stained-looking, like a swamp, and it bubbles with boats, with dockhands and sailors trying to organize the masses, the messes of people, all of them desperate to board, to get away. I am the only one not trying to move forward. Above the bellow of the crowds and the belching of the ships, there's an uncanny, rhythmic noise from somewhere farther down the wharf. Probably gunfire. Red gunners trying to nail any craft that doesn't hit the old Japanese land mines.

I wonder what the Reds will do with a Shanghai that's been scooped out like a fig.

BIG SISTER ISN'T there, or at least she doesn't show herself to me, and the Great World looks different, rebuilt after the bombing a decade ago. Lonely somehow, despite all the signs and boards and advertisements all around. I stand in front of it stupidly for a long time and then I turn away and I stare in the other direction, out at the traffic, and I can't remember how I got here or what I hoped would happen. Maybe that Max would show up again, the way he did last time.

IT'S GETTING DARK once more and I can't face going back in the dark all the way to Hong Kew. I head for Uncle's house. Maybe Aiyi will be there. Or even First Wife. Or even Uncle himself. Anybody will do. But when I turn the corner and I reach the bamboo gate it is swinging open in the brisk winter wind and that tells me there is nobody here. No family, no servants, nobody. They have left Shanghai too. But even though I *know* this I still go through the fence and up the path to the house. The front door is also open.

"Hello?" I say as I enter, in my new, screamed-out voice.

I am living my recurring nightmare, in which everyone I know, everyone I love, everyone who could call me by my name, is *gone*. They're just *gone*.

I OPEN ALL the doors in Uncle's house, starting with the bottom floor, and I shout into all the rooms and I get sick of the sound of myself. I open doors I never opened before, not even when I lived here, because most of these rooms were kept locked, and I hate that they're all unlocked now, I *hate* it, and you never think you'll wish for more locked doors, do you? But now I understand what locked doors mean. They mean you are not alone. Even a jailer is better than nobody at all.

ON THE SECOND floor, at the far end of the hallway, is a door I never really looked at, and I open it too. Just in case. It smells sweet and I go into it because I can't remember the last time anything smelled sweet. It must have been before that morning at the marketplace with George.

This is too opulent of a room to have been spent on servants. Whose room was this? Why was it kept unused? There is a desk facing the window, which looks out at the flower garden. This room must be right on top of the Magnolia; of Uncle's study. I sit down dumbly at the desk. The flower garden below is not in bloom. It is late winter. Everything is dead. But the room still smells sweet.

THE DESK IS covered with a glass pane, through which you can see its contents: Brushes. An inkstone. A scrawl of a picture on a sheet of paper. I press my face to the glass.

Ma painted this picture.

I would know it even if I didn't see her peony signature on it, which I do.

Was this *Ma's* room? Ma, back when she was Fourth Wife?

I lift up the glass pane and pick up the picture. For some reason I am sure that it is yet another painting of the girl-thing that featured in the pictures from the pouch—the attic, George Maidenhair's gates, and the Great World—even though here, the girl-thing looks different.

Here, we can see part of her face.

Here, Ma's peony signature is on the girl-thing's head, floating in her hair.

My own hair is straggly and sticky and falling over my eyes, but somewhere, on the back of my head, is the white peony pin that Max gave me.

THE GIRL-THING IS *me*. Me. Me. Me. These shapeless dark strokes are *me*. In all those pouch-pictures, Ma painted *me*.

I THINK I have stopped breathing and I have to remind myself to start again.

MA WAS HAVING visions of the future. That's what those paintings were. Did she realize that the girl-thing was me? Maybe she did. She left me the pouch, after all. She left me the pictures of my future self. She might have been saying, *Look, Third Daughter, look at what will happen.* She might have been saying, *Careful, or you will turn into this.* It would have been easier if she'd just written it in a letter. But maybe she didn't think I would ever learn to read.

I WAS AT the Great World today.
   I was at George Maidenhair's house today, holding the gates.
   But what about the picture of the wardrobe in the attic?
   I have never been inside that wardrobe. I would never *go inside a wardrobe* where it is dark and scary and depthless. But on the other hand this is what Ma foresaw. This must be my final fate. The day my sisters locked me in that ancestral hall I thought I would die and part of me actually wants to feel that way again. Part of me will welcome it. Yes, I will go in there. It will be the last

door I ever open. I am tired of opening doors. I am losing all sense of time and space but maybe that is what happens after people eat stars.

I LEAVE MA'S room and go up the stairs to the third floor, and then up the steeper ones to the attic, and then I am in the attic, facing that old wardrobe, swaying on my feet. How can any place in the world be so lightless? So hopeless? How can I be so alone? I might even welcome my old friend the half-tongue vengeful spirit, but of course she is no longer around either. Also thanks to me. I reach out to the wardrobe and then I draw back and then I waver but then I reach out again and even the wardrobe no longer bothers to hide its secrets. It opens with an easy clicking sound. But—

But there is something covering the floor of the wardrobe.

There is even something hanging over my head; it feels like another laundry line.

This isn't just a wardrobe.

This is a darkroom.

THIRD WIFE!

I SUPPOSE SHE had to develop her photographs somewhere. Somewhere secret, because she was dreaming in secret.

I PICK UP a few of the pictures and I blow the dust off them and I go over to where the moonlight comes in through the attic windows, to look.

IN CHINESE, THE pronoun *he* sounds the same as *she*. It is a short, simple sound: *tā*. The only difference is in the written character.

Ma was writing to Third Wife through a letter-writer, dictating the words, and he might have got the wrong end of the stick.

The letter-writer wrote *she*.

Ma meant *he*.

He *is following me.*

He *has found me.*

I DON'T KNOW how long I have been in the attic by now. Maybe I have been in the attic this whole time and it's actually just the first night I ever spent in Shanghai and at any moment, First Wife is going to open the door and harrumph loudly and tell me to go downstairs and put meat on my bones. Maybe I will rise from where I am sitting and I will glide down those stairs and I will shake off her attempts to make me right-handed and I will do everything else the opposite of how I ever did it, too.

THESE ARE PHOTOS of Ma and George Maidenhair but they don't know Third Wife is there, with her camera lens trained on them. They don't know they are being watched. They are standing in the courtyard behind George's old house, beneath the golden rain trees. Ma is wearing the same dress she wore at the Dragon Boat Festival, a few days before she disappeared. She is not a young, strange Ma, like in the picture I once found in Third Wife's vanity table. She is *my* Ma, the one I knew and loved and held and hugged.

You can see the low bulge in the belly of her dress, because she bore three babies.

The golden rain trees are just beginning to bloom.

It is the start of summer.

In the first photograph they are talking.

In the second photograph George is angry.

In the final photograph Ma is dead.

I WAS IN love with your mother. . . .

So many mistakes . . .

He has found me. . . .

I STAND UP in the moonlight.

The sweet smell is everywhere; all around me.

It is peony.

The truth is suddenly so obvious, it almost hurts my eyes.

George loved Ma, all the way to that terrible point where love flips around on itself and goes dark.

He loved her and she would not have him and so she left Shanghai, and then she found somebody she *did* love, Ba, but George wouldn't let her go. From Shanghai to Nanking to the village that would one day burn, he followed her. Maybe he would have followed her forever, if she hadn't tried to fight back. Maybe she should have just let him. But you can't live your whole life in a shadow.

George killed her.

I have learned from, I have laughed with, I have *loved*, the man who killed my mother.

THE REAL MONSTERS *live among us* was the last thing she ever said to me.

The real monsters look just like us.

I DO NOT have the strength today, I will not have the strength tomorrow, but one day, *one day*, I will pick up my knives again. One day I will make the cuts I have always made, but not in paper. One day I will take my revenge in the only currency in this country that never runs dry.

You need a reason, after all. A reason to go on.

41

HONG KONG
2015

The Sixth Séance

HOLLY LETS OUT a dribbly cackle; a witch's brew on her lips.

"I'll tell you a secret, Miss Chen," she says. "I control what people see in Maidenhair House. I control it all. You want the truth? Those women killed *themselves*. To make their visions stop. Delia and Peng and Cecelia did it with my kitchen knives. Mistress Lau did it with her own straight razor. I had to pry these weapons out of their hands. Is *that* what you want for your daughter? Oh, look at her," says Holly, with lilting regret. "You should have known better than to bring her here! But I wonder if there is anything you can do, still, to save her."

Holly looks at me from beneath her few lashes.

"Yes," she says, "I believe there is."

SUSANNA IS NOW inexplicably trying to open the antique cabinets. She is scratching her hands bloody on the old wood. Her cheeks are glittering. Her voice is giving out. Ryan Li is gasping something at us; I think he is trying to tell me that he would happily die in Susanna's place, if Holly will take him instead, but Holly doesn't want him.

Holly wants me. Holly wants a spirit medium.

"Let me have *your* body, Mei, instead of this one," Holly says gaily, waving her hands down her dress. "This one is dying."

VERY WELL, I tell her, but I want the truth. I want the truth because I want Ryan Li to walk out of here a free man. I want the truth so that Susanna can share it if she wishes. I want the truth, especially if it's the last story I'm ever going to hear.

"*Bùbile!* As if I have anything more to gain, by lying," says Holly.

Yet Holly hesitates long enough that I think she may try to take refuge in her old story about a collective hallucination.

"The competition was a test," she says at last. "To see which of you five was the strongest. Which of you could stand it. I made all of you see things. Different things. But your mind was the hardest to bend. I tried so hard. I thought the peony design in the skin would do it— But there was some force getting in the way, Miss Chen, almost like a shield; something I couldn't get through. The others bent, one by one, and I planned to take over the winner, whoever it was. I planned to get a new body *then*, at the end of the competition." She looks almost peevish. "I would have taken you over happily. I was so looking forward to it."

"So why didn't you?"

"I was about to. In the Puppet Room. That night. But George stopped me," she says. "In the middle of it. He wouldn't let me. I couldn't control *him*, you see. The visions work through fear and desperation and hope. I couldn't do anything, the way he was."

～

HOLLY SAYS: HER husband was there, living in the walls, the tunnels, the secret stairways of Maidenhair, the whole time. From the start of the competition to the finish. He had long been tortured by memories, she says. He had already been spending more and more time in the basement. They were living in the same house and yet they weren't. Holly didn't mind. She liked George, in fact. She was just happy that he and the *real* Holly Zhang had moved into Maidenhair in the first place.

The real Holly Zhang had had just enough of the Sight to be vulnerable to possession.

"I'm afraid I never did see you in Shanghai, working as a medium," says Holly. "I've never been to Shanghai. I first heard your name in this very house; George would talk about you. Even just to himself. The girl who made his puppets. The girl who saw ghosts. After I possessed Holly, I realized I didn't want to go back to having no physical body. I began thinking: It would be better to have somebody younger. Somebody powerful. That is when I conceived of the competition. I drew up a list of names, including yours, and hired James to find everyone. How lucky that you were already here in Hong Kong! How much luck can feel like fate! I am the Lotus Lady, you see. I am the one who once drowned, who nobody knew where she had come from."

Holly says this lightly, but I know too well what it is like to be lost in water.

"Though I imagine you already suspected as much, since you read James's book, where he puts forth that very idea," Holly continues. "Even if he calls me by a different—"

"Do *you* know where you come from?" I ask her.

"No," she says, surprised. "I don't remember my name. But I think . . . I think I was . . . trying to get away from someone."

Holly pats her cheeks like she hopes to cool them down. "You may recall that phone call between you and George, right before you left Maidenhair? It *was* him, answering, but he was only a few rooms away. In one of the many rooms that nobody can tell is even there. He died some time later; and I decided I didn't want to be as alone as I was, so I retreated down here, to be with the others. I haven't kept them in these cabinets on purpose, I should like to add, Mei. They *choose* to hide there. I think they are afraid. The things you see in the dark are as afraid of you," she says, "as you ever were of them."

Holly wrings her hands briefly; a show of apology.

"That's all," she says. "That's all I have to say."

"Did George recognize me?" I ask. I don't know why it matters; but I will not blame myself for the fact that it does. "Did he call me Little Mei? Is that why he stopped you, when you tried to take me over? Because he realized who I was?"

"I don't think he recognized you," she says, "but I think he knew you."

I TELL HOLLY that I would prefer to proceed with this process upstairs, as I have always found enclosed spaces difficult to stay in, for too long, and she acquiesces immediately. Ryan Li and Susanna stay below. Somehow, at ground level, the world is turning light again: It is summer and the days are longer than the nights. Holly says I can have my pick of rooms. Where do I want to go? Which way do I want to turn?

The ballroom, I tell her.

"Alright. Let's hurry up, then," says Holly, but I think we have time. "I'm sorry it has to be like this," she adds. "It will hurt, at the start. But after it is done, once I fully possess you, you won't feel anything at all."

"You promise you will let my daughter go? And Mr. Li?"

"You have my word. I have no use for them. I am never cruel on purpose," she says.

I feel a glimmer of a smile. "The *Kempeitai*—"

"It was the war, Miss Chen. I did that to help my own people."

"So you were Chinese?"

Her own smile wavers. "I—I don't actually know. I don't know why I said that."

"And the dinner party?"

"Dinner party?" she repeats. "Yes, I—I almost remember— but it was very long ago. Sometimes I remember music . . ." Her hands begin to shake. "Sometimes I remember . . . I am in the garden . . . and looking in, through the glass, at the people . . ."

"Maybe we should begin, Auntie."

"Yes," Holly says, her gaze sharpening again. *"Lái bu jí."*

IN THE MANY mirrors, my reflections are bright and plentiful.

I let my eyes close. My qi is rushing out and I do not try to halt it. I do not build any dams. I let it flow.

I have had six decades of love and life since I left Maidenhair House; I have enough qi to fill every room of it.

I open my eyes, and Holly is not looking at me anymore.

She is looking at my reflection, who has adopted an expression of fright, holding a hand over its mouth.

"Oh, but it's too late now to change your mind now," says Holly, with a light laugh, "you have already given me too much qi. Come, lend me your hand, Mei, and I'll make sure it is over quickly."

There is a shattering sound like I have never heard, not even in war, as Holly launches herself into the mirrors.

A waterfall of glass. A brilliant flash.

When I broke Max's black scrying mirror over the head of the attic ghost so many years ago, I did not know the ghost would become imprisoned in the glass. This time was different. I knew what would happen. In a way I have planned it. But I think the Lotus Lady may enjoy her new fate, stuck in a mirror for eternity, because she will stop disintegrating. She will be eternally admired by people looking into her, seeing themselves. She will never die.

THE YOUNG WOMAN who stands up from the broken glass appears unperturbed. She steps over the shards with her tulip-bulb bound feet, lifting her dress as she does. Her hair is back in a towering bundle on top of her head, the pearl-studded hair stick cleanly in place.

She opens her mouth to say something to me, and then remembers that she has less than half a tongue.

She is free. The Lotus Lady has taken her place, and the ghost from Uncle's attic is finally free. She has been following me through mirrors for so long, I wonder if there will even be times when we miss each other. She looks at me long and hard, and then she walks away, swishing out of the ballroom on those kitten feet, without any indication of where she is headed. Whoever she is, whatever truly happened to her when she was alive, I would tell her to look higher than an attic this time. To go higher. To keep going.

WE STOP BY the Peak Café for breakfast, the three of us, me and Susanna and Ryan. Ryan downs two coffees within minutes and says he can't go down the mountain quite yet, so I suggest that before heading to the Peak Tram, we spend some time at the lookout point, the one with a phenomenal view of the skyscrapers of Central and past that, the harbor and the vastness of Kowloon, and in other directions, the sweet green seas and the buoyant-looking islands. The view does not extend all the way to China, of course. Not all the way back to where I came from.

Susanna soon calls Liana, and they speak in quiet tones by the railing.

Ryan Li and I stand together, drinking in the sight of Hong Kong from what feels like light-years away.

"There must be something wrong with me," he says, "that I still need to know what happened to the bodies."

"I understand," I say. "You've become a story-person."

"What?"

"Holly had the power to make people see things," I say. "She was behind all the visions."

"I know that now, yes."

"She also had the power to make people *not* see things. Actually, it is the same power. Exact and opposite."

Ryan gapes at me.

"You weren't a story-person back then," I say. "It would have taken a story-person to believe in a power like hers. You mustn't blame yourself, Mr. Li. Or your colleagues. *Yǎn bù jiàn wéi jìng.*"

He tries out the phrase, his Mandarin decidedly poor by comparison to his English. "Eye . . . don't see . . . clean. What is unseen is clean? But we did smell it," Ryan says, a whisper. "The blood. I knew I could still smell it. But the bodies were just . . . and there was no evidence that . . . You mean if we had . . . if I had reached out and *touched* . . . ?"

"It's alright," I say. "How many people trust their other senses enough to overrule the eyes?"

SUSANNA IS SURPRISED that I want to stay awhile longer in Hong Kong on my own. She treats me to a bubble tea by the airport MTR station before she has to check in to her new flight, to LA.

She listens to my story.

"That's so sad," she says. "That you never saw your Ma again."

"I did not see her," I say, "but she saw me. She was watching over me."

"You think she was the protective *force* that Holly was talking about?"

"Yes. And she was the spirit who spoke through me, in séances."

Susanna swirls her own tea, awaiting an explanation.

I put down my drink and reach for my purse. I do not carry many things with me anymore, but I carry *this*.

A sketch I made not long after I left Maidenhair House and returned to Kowloon, in 1953.

"A spirit came to me in my first séance ever," I say, "and showed me a vanity table. It came to me again and again when I did the séances at Maidenhair, and I wanted to talk to it one more time."

"But that spirit placed you in great danger," Susanna points out. "Leading you down to the Puppet Room, step by step, like that. Why would your own mother do that?"

"Why did I bring you to Maidenhair House?"

Susanna breathes into her straw, until the tea turns foamy.

"I went into a trance without having asked the spirit a question. Without knowing what it would say." I slide the sheet of paper over to Susanna. "This is the answer it gave."

Susanna squints at the sketch. Susanna is too used to looking at screens.

"That spirit was my mother," I repeat.

"I don't understand," says Susanna. "What is this?"

"This is a drawing of a photograph that I had in my home, when I was a child, in rural China," I say, "of my Ma. It was the only photograph we had of her." Ironically, since there were so many more, gathering webs in a wardrobe.

The photograph showed Ma smiling.

This sketch shows what she is smiling *at*.

It is a little girl with an upside-down rice-bowl haircut, because her hair has just been sold.

It is me.

"She is gone now," I say, "but she was with me for so long."

I was looking for Ma, over so many years, and she was always beside me.

It is true that I will never know exactly who my mother was. But that is the nature of being a daughter.

MY CELL PHONE rings while I am sitting on a bench on the Hong Kong side, looking out across the water to Kowloon. I pick up and the person on the other end sounds a bit out of breath. It's my granddaughter. Liana rarely calls me, but she has called now because I just called her. I think her generation does not do much calling in general. They are always writing and sending small pictures to each other. It is like they miss the era before the telephone was even invented.

"Hey, Po Po," she says, "I'm at the airport waiting for Mom. Her flight arrives in . . . uh, I think, an hour or something. Delayed."

"Liana," I say, "why did you send those letters?"

Another small breath, down the line. "Letters?"

"You sent Dean a letter. Telling him that I was at Maidenhair House in 1953, and that I . . ."

"Oh," she says. "That."

"Yes, that."

"Mom figured out it was me, huh?" she says, resigned.

"Your mother has no idea."

"Then how—"

"You forget that I know the kind of dyslexia you have. And how it shows up in written Chinese."

"Oh," she says again. "I did forget that we had that in common." She inhales. "I started having these nightmares, okay? Nightmares about you, Po Po. I don't even remember when they started. I don't even know how I know it was you, since in the dream, you're my age. But you, in this house, and all these bodies . . . all this blood . . . I went to doctors, psychiatrists, all sorts of . . . you know. But it just got worse and worse. And then I looked up the house. And I *found* it! And found out that there's this whole horrific story and . . . and then I started to wonder if my nightmares were real and everything I was seeing in my head actually happened. I couldn't take it. One day I was just out of ideas, and then I remembered Grandpa's old advice about writing things down and, well, I sat down and I ended up writing those letters."

"In Chinese? You know that much Chinese?"

"It just came out like that. I can't explain it," she says miserably. "It was almost like someone else was using me to write. Then I thought maybe if I delivered them . . ."

"But it didn't help. You're still seeing things?" I ask her.

A pause. "Yes."

"Of what look like ghosts? Are they frightening?"

"Yes."

"Limei," I say, giving my granddaughter the Chinese name she should have been given at birth, "some people can see ghosts. Some people can see the future. Some people, like you, can see the past. Either way, it is called the Sight. This is just something else that we might have in common. Don't worry. I will teach you what you need to know, the way I was taught, and your nightmares will end. One day, perhaps, you may even come here to Hong Kong and visit Maidenhair House, and if you do, you will find that somebody is still there; and if you speak to her and feel that she should be set free, you can set her free."

42

HONG KONG
1958

THE MARKET IS busy to the point of bursting today, and Mei feels like one of the trussed-down chickens hanging in the poultry shops, smelly and squeezed.

She is not here for meat or dried fish or even soft bread buns, but her stomach growls so hotly that she can't ignore it any longer. The prudent thing would be to spend her pocket money on a portion of rice that will last a week. Not to squander it on a snack. She stops by the rice vendors, with their rice laid out in barrels, the cheaper varieties in bags, and she sighs. She wants something that will make her tongue shrivel, it has so much taste. She wants something that will make her feel greedy and gluttonous while she is eating it.

She's not living through a war anymore, is she?

She spins on her heel, and nearly takes off running.

Her favorite is preserved egg. Hundred-year-egg. First they are marinated in tea and then lacquered in salt and spices. Then they are sealed into jars until the whites turn black, until they do not resemble eggs at all, and sometimes Mei thinks that's why she likes them so much. They look like stones, like sculptures, like they should be on display in her shop, not swallowed. She watches as the customer ahead of her rolls his chopsticks in a mix of soy sauce and vinegar, the acid of which is already making her throat prickle. But before she can order, she hears someone say from behind, "Excuse me," and she steps out of the way, her eyes still on the eggs.

"I'm sorry, I think you've dropped this," says the voice, and Mei looks over.

She feels like she has just drunk the vinegar straight; that is how much her mouth suddenly flames.

The man in front of her holds out his hand, palm up. Her peony pin. It has slipped from her hair again. Mei takes it.

She ought to put the pin back in, of course, but she just keeps on holding it.

"Want one?" he says, nodding to the eggs, and she finds her voice.

"Yes," she says. She realizes she is putting the pin away, into her basket. Her hair feels loose and strange and foreign, framing her face. "I mean—that is—you don't need to buy me one—"

But he already has. The eggs are served on plates no bigger than her hand. He gestures that she should join him on the stools. Mei sits with her basket at her feet. For a long moment they eat silently. He is different than she remembers. The same, but different. Mei wonders how *she* must seem, five years after the living nightmare that they endured, five years that she has spent reading books and stocking shelves and finding friends and buying a birth certificate. Five years in which she has not cut paper once, but she has gotten her hair cut several times.

That is why the peony pin no longer stays in, not the way that it used to.

James Nakamura finishes his egg and doffs his hat at her, and then he gets up from his stool, his smile polite, slightly cool, and then he turns away, and he's already being eaten up by the endless crowds of Kowloon. You don't usually find people a second time, not in Hong Kong. There are just too many people. There are just too many streets. There are just too many fates.

"Wait," she says, with her mouth still full.

He looks back.

Mei slides off her own stool, even though she hasn't finished. "You look well," she says.

"So do you."

"Could we take a walk?" she asks, hesitant.

"A walk," he says. "A walk to where?"

"I don't—I don't know," she admits.

Strangers stroll by them and Mei feels a little like she may get knocked over. He goes closer to her, without ever actually agreeing to walk, but they begin to walk anyway, carving a way forward, chastely, side by side, never touching. She asks him if he is still writing and he tells her that he is. He asks her if she's still making art and she says she isn't. The conversation is easy, light, like it could end at any time, but neither of them end it. Mei has often wondered if she will ever feel the way she did long ago, with a young man she once knew and loved, that feeling like there was nothing in the world she wanted or needed, besides him, but in a weird way, it is not even as nice as *this* feeling. The one that she is having right now, just walking, talking, laughing. This feeling that all around her, people are being born and people are dying and wars are raging and ghosts are gathering; that everything is happening, good and bad, that has already happened so many times before, over and over, and always will, for all time.

"You want to get something to eat?" Jamie asks.

"We just ate," she says, smiling.

"Yeah," he says, "but I want more," and she realizes that she wants more too.

In Mei's time, however much she has left, the future rolls out in front of her.

It is a blank scroll of paper, unwritten, unblemished, unbelievable, and she can make it into anything she wishes.

Epilogue

I ASKED YOU to solve a mystery before we left, Susanna: How could I remember an attack from the perspective of my attacker? But to discover this, you do not need your usual tools. You do not need your notes and your file folders and your secondary sources.

All you need is a mirror.

We all have our mirror-selves. The versions of us that look like us, in every possible way, enough that we wonder, sometimes, which is which, except that they live in the past. And most people cannot stand to destroy these other versions of themselves. But the truth is that you have to, to overcome grief. The woman you were, my daughter, she wants you to die. She wants you to drown. She doesn't believe that you can live with this loss. You must fight her as you have never fought anyone, and then you have to wake up, and see her there, lying on the floor, and you will be bleeding too, you will be very badly off, you will hurt everywhere, but the difference is that you, *you*, are still alive.

Then you have to step over her.

You have to leave her behind.

The first few steps are the hardest. *But she is me. And I am her.*

What have I done? How can I walk away? These thoughts will loop and loop around you. But you keep walking. This is what I told you on the way up the mountain, isn't it? On the journey we just made? Your feet, so tired. Your body, so jet-lagged. Your brain, so full of the mountain mist. But you keep walking. You have asked me so many times: Mama, what was it like to be a refugee? I can tell you: It is just like this. You keep walking. You keep walking. You walk without knowing where you are going, or what the path looks like ahead of you.

That, my daughter, is Step Four.

You do not see the future, but you try to change it anyway.

Author's Note

Warning: huge spoilers ahead. Do not read this until after you've finished the novel!

This book is dedicated to my beloved maternal grandparents for several reasons. In the late 1990s, my aunt received a letter from a woman in northern China claiming to be my grandfather's sister, someone he wouldn't have seen, at that point, in over fifty years. That sister turned out to be far from the only family my grandfather left behind when, in his youth, he fled his home village for Shanghai; he would never see any of those people again. He made it to Taiwan during the Revolution, in 1948, and a few decades later to the United States. Parts of this story are based on elements of his early life.

I think I had that letter in mind while crafting both Mei's and Susanna's storylines: the idea that the arrival of a single innocuous sheet of paper can really slice through your current reality.

Following my grandfather's death, my grandmother moved in with my parents, and I moved nearby with my young kids soon after. My grandmother loved to chat, play with her great-grandchildren, and make origami. Toward the end of her life, however, she suffered dementia, eventually to the point that she no longer recognized me. In *The Hong Kong Widow*, Holly Zhang is possessed; the real Holly Zhang, that glamorous movie star, is buried within, and ultimately beyond anyone's grasp . . . but you have to believe that somewhere in there, still, is the person who once took the world by storm. A real-life photograph of my grandmother, as a young woman in Taiwan, was the basis for the drawing of Mei's mother that appears in Chapter 41.

Between 2008 and 2009, I spent a full year in Hong Kong, and somewhere along the line I became obsessed with Hong Kong's rich tradition of ghost stories and urban legends. This book is partly the result of that obsession. Much of the folklore in this novel is based on widely held myths and stories; Maidenhair House itself was loosely inspired by a real-life abandoned colonial mansion on Victoria Peak. Other aspects, I invented to fit the narrative and to shape Mei's world the way I wanted it. Ultimately, however, *The Hong Kong Widow* is a ghost story about the hauntings that are internal rather than external; about the ghosts we choose to carry with us and how to let them go.

The historical events of the time periods covered in this novel were important for me to weave into the narrative, and fascinating, if sometimes difficult, to study. I wanted to stay true to the history, and I've certainly tried, but forgive me for any errors, all of which are my own; at times I sacrificed absolute accuracy for something that I valued more. For example: Ma's painting of the Great World, originally built in 1917, depicts it in a very classic and recognizable way, and not the way it actually looked in 1948, when it was choked with so many billboards you could hardly see the building itself. This was a deliberate choice. I wanted the building, as a symbol of a lasting Shanghai, to shine.

One final note: For anyone wondering who sent the incoherent anonymous letter about Holly to Jamie, as described in Chapter

27, the answer is George; George would have realized, even in the state he was in by then, that something was not right with Holly. I like to think that years later, after settling in Seattle, Jamie would have shown Mei the letter, and Mei would have recognized the handwriting of her former teacher instantly. Maybe Mei could have clarified for Jamie, who misunderstood the contents, that George was not saying that the Holly he married was a different woman from Holly the actress, but rather that the Holly he married was a different woman from the one he now lived with.

Acknowledgments

The person I want to thank first and foremost is my editor, Jen Monroe, for her time, dedication, unwavering belief, fantastic ideas, and game-changing vision for this book. Jen, you are the editor every writer should have! I can't thank you enough.

Thanks go to Sharon Galant and Stéphanie Abou for all the invaluable guidance and support along the way, as well as to Thomasin Chinnery. I am so grateful to the wonderful team at Berkley for making this beautiful book a reality (so much goes on behind the scenes!), and especially to Candice Coote, for your never-ending patience and help.

I was lucky enough to get brilliant feedback on this novel from Matt Kendrick and Michelle Christophorou, both amazing writers and kind, generous people. You two read some of the earliest (eek) drafts of the manuscript and managed to renew my faith in it, and I came away so inspired. Thank you to you both, sincerely.

The incredibly talented Jiksun Cheung created the art for this novel and in doing so transformed it. Seeing Mei's sketches and Ma's paintings brought to life was awe-inspiring (and, frankly, addictive). Thank you for your stunning illustrations and for being so reliable, professional, and great to work with! Readers, go check out more work from Jiksun on Instagram (@jiksuncheung), and it will further blow you away.

To Sue, Felicity, and Charlotte: Your support, honesty, wisdom, and good humor has meant so much to me. I am never voluntarily leaving Critters, ever.

To Samangie: How can I even begin to thank you? There's just no way. Please tell Paige that I hope she enjoys this book!

My family made the writing of this novel possible in so many ways. Thank you, with all my love.

Finally, to my fans and readers, and to the book clubs and booksellers and librarians and online book community, I appreciate you far beyond what can be expressed here. You're the reason.